# PRAISE FOR JOSEPH Fl ... ... ...

"Flynn is an excellent storyteller." — *Booklist*

"Flynn propels his plot with potent but flexible force."
— *Publishers Weekly*

### The President's Henchman
"Marvelously entertaining." — *ForeWord Magazine*

### Digger
"A mystery cloaked as cleverly as (and perhaps better than)
any John Grisham work." — *Denver Post*

"Surefooted, suspenseful and in its breathless final moments
unexpectedly heartbreaking." — *Booklist*

### The Next President
"*The Next President* bears favorable comparison to such
classics as *The Best Man, Advise and Consent* and
*The Manchurian Candidate.*"
— *Booklist*

"A thriller fast enough to read in one sitting."
— *Rocky Mountain News*

# The Good Guy with a Gun

## A JIM McGILL NOVEL

## Joseph Flynn

Stray Dog Press, Inc.
Springfield, IL
2015

# ALSO BY JOSEPH FLYNN

## The Jim McGill Series
The President's Henchman, A Jim McGill Novel [#1]
The Hangman's Companion, A JimMcGill Novel [#2]
The K Street Killer A JimMcGill Novel [#3]
Part 1: The Last Ballot Cast, A JimMcGill Novel [#4 Part 1]
Part 2: The Last Ballot Cast, A JimMcGill Novel [#4 Part 2]
The Devil on the Doorstep, A Jim McGill Novel [#5]
The Good Guy with a Gun, A Jim McGill Novel [#6]
The Echo of the Whip, A Jim McGill Novel [#7]
McGill's Short Cases 1-3

## The Ron Ketchum Mystery Series
Nailed, A Ron Ketchum Mystery [#1]
Defiled, A Ron Ketchum Mystery Featuring John Tall Wolf [#2]
Impaled, A Ron Ketchum Mystery [#3]

## The John Tall Wolf Series
Tall Man in Ray-Bans, A John Tall Wolf Novel [#1]
War Party, A John Tall Wolf Novel [#2]
Super Chief, A John Tall Wolf Novel [#3]

## The Zeke Edison Series
Kill Me Twice, A Zeke Edison Novel [#1]

## Stand Alone Novels
The Concrete Inquisition
Digger
The Next President
Hot Type
Farewell Performance
Gasoline, Texas
Round Robin, A Love Story of Epic Proportions
One False Step
Blood Street Punx
Still Coming
Still Coming Expanded Edition
Hangman — A Western Novella
Pointy Teeth, Twelve Bite-Size Stories

Published by Stray Dog Press, Inc.
Springfield, IL 62704, U.S.A.

First Stray Dog Press, Inc. printing, August, 2013
Copyright © kandrom, inc., 2015

Visit the author's web site: *www.josephflynn.com*

Flynn, Joseph
    The Good Guy with a Gun / Joseph Flynn
    444 p.
    ISBN 978-0-9908412-3-4
    eBook 978-0-9887868-8-2

Printed in the United States of America

PUBLISHER'S NOTE
This is a work of fiction. Names, characters, places, and incidents are either the product of the author's imagination or are used fictitiously; any resemblance to actual persons, living or dead, events, or locales is entirely coincidental.

*Book design by Aha! Designs*
*Cover type effect courtesy of www.obsidiandawn.com*

# DEDICATION

For all the friends of Jim McGill and all his friends.

## ACKNOWLEDGEMENTS

For Catherine, Susan, Anne, Caitie and everyone else who helps me keep my overhead low. Otherwise, I'd have to charge a whole lot more for these books. My thanks to Bernadette Cazobon-Wendricks for greatly improving my use of the French language. A special nod to Catherine, whose cover design for this book really knocks me out.

**AL**
**Reader**
**Discretion**
**Advised**
Contains Adult
Language

# CHARACTER LIST

*[In alphabetical order by last name]*

**Giles Benedict,** artist, forger, fugitive conman
**Richard Bergen,** U.S. Senator [D, IL] Assistant majority leader
**Gawayne Blessing,** White House head butler
**Philip Brock,** Democratic Congressman from Pennsylvania
**Tyler Busby,** American billionaire and art collector
**Edwina Byington,** the president's personal secretary
**Arlo Carsten,** ex-NASA project manager
**Gabriella "Gabbi" Casale,** artist, security officer, U.S. Embassy
**Celsus Crogher,** retired Secret Service SAC
**Byron DeWitt,** Deputy Director of the FBI
**Darren Drucker,** American billionaire, art collector,
**Carolyn [McGill] Enquist,** first wife of Jim McGill
**Lars Enquist,** Carolyn's second husband
**Elvie Fisk,** daughter of militia leader Harlan Fisk
**Harlan Fisk,** commander of The First Michigan Militia
**Laurent Fortier,** French art thief
**Cathryn Gorman,** Chief of the Metropolitan Police Department
**Patricia Darden Grant,** President of the U.S., wife of Jim McGill
**Andrew Hudson Grant** (deceased), the president's first husband
**Jeremiah Haskins,** Director of the FBI
**Sen. Howard Hurlbert,** founder of True South Party
**Bahir Ben Kalil,** personal physician to the Jordanian ambassador
**[SAC] Elspeth Kendry,** head of the Presidential Protection Detail
**Sheryl Kimbrough,** Republican elector from Indiana
**Duvessa Kinsale,** New York art gallery owner
**Donald "Deke" Ky,** Jim McGill's personal bodyguard
**Leo Levy,** Jim McGill's personal driver
**Charles Louvel,** Pruet family employee
**Père Louvel,** French cleric, brother of Charles Louvel
**Craig MacLaren,** Chief Justice of the U.S. Supreme Court
**Louis Marra,** NYPD Detective

**Jim McGill,** president's husband, aka The President's Henchman
**Abbie McGill,** oldest child of Jim McGill and Carolyn Enquist
**Caitie McGill,** youngest child of Jim McGill and Carolyn Enquist
**Kenny McGill,** middle child of Jim McGill and Carolyn Enquist
**Tommy Meeker,** regional security officer U.S. Embassy, Paris
**Bob Merriman,** U.S. Senator [D, OR]
**Roger Michaelson,** former U.S Senator [D-OR]
**Galia Mindel,** White House chief of staff
**Dikran "Dikki" Missirian,** McGill's business landlord
**Jean Morrissey,** Vice President of the U.S.
**George Mulchrone,** retired Catholic priest
**David Nathan,** Director of the Secret Service
**Artemus Nicolaides,** White House physician
**Stephen Norwood,** White House deputy chief of staff
**Merilee Parker,** former press secretary for Senator Hurlbert
**Peter Profitt,** Speaker of the House
**Augustin Pruet,** Yves Pruet's father
**Yves Pruet,** French investigating magistrate
**Joan Renshaw,** director of The AHG Foundation
**Osgood Riddick,** FBI special agent on art crime team
**Odo Sacripant,** Yves Pruet's Corsican bodyguard
**Putnam Shady,** Sweetie's husband
**Maxine Shady,** Putnam's niece
**Margaret "Sweetie" Sweeney,** McGill's business partner
**John Wexford,** Senate majority leader
**Ethan Winger,** art forgery analyst
**Mather Wyman,** former VP of the U.S.
**Kira Fahey Yates,** Welborn Yates' wife
**Captain Welborn Yates,** the president's official investigator

# CHAPTER 1

*The Winstead School —*
*Washington, DC, Saturday, March 8, 2014*

The private high school in Georgetown had been founded a century earlier and was a feeder school to the Ivies and other elite colleges across the nation. Its alumni sat in both chambers of Congress, on the boards of directors of numerous Fortune 500 companies and were found among the top ranks of the military. Never content to rest on their laurels, the administration, faculty and student body of the school always looked for new worlds to conquer.

In two months, on May 8th in New York City, the school had every reason to expect it would collect a new accolade the likes of which few secular private high schools in the country could match. Hal Walker, Winstead class of 2010, Stanford class of 2014, starting quarterback of the Cardinal football team, was expected to become the first player selected in the National Football League draft.

An NFL contract measured in the tens of millions of dollars was sure to follow.

Product endorsement income would dwarf his football compensation.

Barring catastrophic injury, a Hall of Fame career was anticipated.

In the men's locker room that morning, the first day of spring football practice for the Winstead Warriors, Head Coach Don Russell, who'd played three years as an NFL quarterback himself, had shown his players a video Hal Walker had sent to the Winstead team. To say the Warrior players were pumped up would be the understatement of the century. Hearts pounded. Adrenaline rushed. Nobody on the team could sit still as the video began to roll.

"Winning football games is pretty simple," Hal Walker said. "You play smarter and harder than the guys across the line of scrimmage. You play with more focus and discipline. You work just as hard in the classroom as on the practice field because you have to develop good study habits to succeed at football — and everything else in life. You respect everyone who's trying to make your life better: your parents, your teachers, your coaches, your teammates. You never underestimate or belittle your opponents or they'll hand you your ass gift wrapped."

The team laughed at that, until Walker followed with, "And if I ever hear any of you aren't living up to Coach Russell's expectations, doing all the things I just told you, I'll be paying you a visit with some of my new NFL teammates. You won't be happy to see us because we'll be coming to knock heads. Now, get out there on the practice field, work as hard as you can, learn as much as you can, do what your parents, teachers and coaches tell you, and one more thing. Never back down from any challenge you face on a football field or anywhere else."

Coach Russell threw open the locker room doors and forty-two high school boys — Warriors in their minds — roared out onto the gridiron.

Chief Assistant Coach Bill Eccles patted Russell on the back.

He said, "I think this'll be a year nobody here will ever forget."

He was right, but not in a way anyone ever could have imagined.

### McGill Investigations, Inc. — Georgetown

McGill sat in his office alone. He'd worked his way through

the print edition of the *Washington Post* and was now reading the *Chicago Tribune* online. The White Sox and Cubs were at spring training in Arizona. No serious sportswriter gave either team a chance of making the playoffs in the coming season, much less going to or winning the World Series. McGill, who followed the home teams for story content more than exhibitions of sporting prowess these days, thought it was possible the Sox could surprise. The South Siders had good pitching and had acquired some young power hitters who just might pan out. And Boston had gone from worst to first over the previous two years. If the Cubs were to win the World Series, their first in over a century and counting, that just might be the precursor to the Second Coming.

He'd have to check with Sweetie to see if there was any scriptural reference.

McGill had been circumspect about the cases he'd taken so far that year. They were all routine matters easily resolved. Neither the celebrity media nor the president's political opposition had been able to work themselves up about any of them. The work was too mundane; the clients were too obscure.

That didn't mean adversarial motormouths couldn't have embroidered dull facts or lied outright to stir up trouble, but the fact was McGill scared most of Washington's chattering class. They'd all seen the video of him taking on Harlan Fisk as the militia leader stood at the head of his ragtag army. He'd waded in barehanded and left the bully writhing on the ground.

Getting on the wrong side of someone like McGill was not to be chanced lightly.

On the other hand, if the payoff, professionally or politically, was big enough there would always be those willing to take the risk.

Several times during the cold, snowy doldrums of the past several weeks he'd wondered if he shouldn't … he'd be damned if he was going to say the word retire. Maybe go on hiatus. That was what a former movie star like Patti would have said, right? But he wasn't sure he could twiddle his thumbs for the remaining thirty-four months of his wife's presidency, and he didn't know what else he could do besides being some sort of cop.

Sweetie was out of the office much of the time these days. She was embarking on the great challenge and adventure of being a good mother. As McGill knew she would, Sweetie was winning over little Maxi Shady bit by bit. Some name that kid had. Just thinking about it made McGill smile. Almost as much as seeing Sweetie and Maxi walking hand-in-hand down the street.

Sweetie had told him she would have taken over the business, if he'd really intended to stay away for the remainder of Patti's time in the Oval Office. But she would have kept things going by hiring other good coppers and letting them carry most of the load. She'd have done much of the case management from home.

Not that she foresaw such a necessity.

Sweetie had told McGill, "You'll figure it out, how to keep working without embarrassing Patti." McGill had lent a gun to Odo Sacripant when he and Yves Pruet had been in town last year, and wound up spending a weekend in jail as a result. But as Sweetie had also said, "You're not ready to let go or even slow down yet."

Too true, McGill thought.

He'd even started coming into the office for a half-day on Saturdays.

Something he'd never done before.

Something completely unproductive, too, until that morning.

A woman named Zara Gilford had called, saying she needed his help urgently.

But she was already fifteen minutes late for her appointment.

Then Deke, who was manning the outer office, poked his head in. McGill thought it would be to announce Ms. Gilford's arrival. He put the sports section of the *Trib* into his computer's dock.

"Ms. Gilford?" McGill asked.

Deke shook his head. "Roger Michaelson."

McGill heard Michaelson say, "Good manners call for the use of my former title, Special Agent. *Senator* Michaelson."

Deke rolled his eyes.

### Winstead School Football Field — Georgetown

Don Russell, in addition to being the football team's head coach, was also the team's offensive coordinator. Bill Eccles, who'd played middle linebacker at Boston College, was also the defensive coordinator. The Tripartite Athletic Conference (TAC), composed of Winstead and McKinley in DC and four other private high schools in neighboring Maryland and Virginia suburbs, allowed their football teams to have five coaches and a scout.

The additional slots were quarterback and special teams coaches. George Knox handled special teams at Winstead.

As a former NFL quarterback, Russell took on the quarterback coaching job, too. He was paid an additional 50% for doing three jobs. Nobody begrudged him the money. He was the man who developed Hal Walker into a star quarterback — and it looked like the new kid at the position, Jarius Niles, a recruit from a District public school, had even more raw talent.

Truth was, Jarius, though only a sophomore, might be an even better bet for the U.S. men's track and field team at the Rio de Janeiro Olympics. He had speed that was already being compared to that of Usain Bolt. But he also had an arm like a cannon, and he longed to learn the most important position on the football field.

When Russell had talked to Jarius and his mother about coming to Winstead, the precocious athlete told him, "I don't just want to run, Coach. I want to be a leader."

Mrs. Niles said, "I told him leaders have to be smarter than followers. He raised his grades from a C to a B average, but I know he can do better. My son can make A's. But will he get the help he needs at your school or will all you have him think about is football?"

Russell took his phone out of his pocket and called Hal Walker. "Hal, would you mind talking to a mom who has a few questions about sending her son to Winstead."

The coach explained that the young man was a Winstead graduate, quarterback and captain of his high school team and now attended one of the finest universities anywhere.

Mrs. Niles took the phone and introduced herself and spoke of her concerns.

Whatever it was she heard eased her worries, made her smile and then laugh.

Jarius, who knew all about Hal Walker's football career in both high school and college, started bouncing up and down in his chair. His manners were too good to interrupt his mother, but he looked at Russell with imploring eyes. He wanted to talk to his idol, too.

The coach made a gesture, advising patience.

In a quiet voice, he said, "Jarius, I promise you, come to Winstead or not, I'll set up a call with Hal just for you."

Mrs. Niles caught that just as she was saying goodbye.

She handed the phone back to Russell.

"Other than my son, that was the nicest young man I've ever spoken to. He was so polite, but he answered me straight on every question I had."

"What tickled you, Mama? What made you laugh?" Jarius asked.

She smiled again, "He said from what Coach Russell has told him you might be even better than he is … but he didn't think his mama would agree with that."

"God bless mothers everywhere," the coach said.

"The good ones anyway," Mrs. Niles said, turning serious. "You'll make sure Jarius does his best at his schoolwork? I want him to be an important man if he never plays a minute of football again."

That idea almost provoked a remark from Jarius.

But his mother held up a forestalling hand and her son respected it.

Coach Russell said, "Mrs. Niles, I promise you this. Winstead will provide more to Jarius in the classroom than I'll ever be able to give him on the football field. He works hard at his academics, and I know you won't settle for less, he'll go on to study at a top university. No question in my mind."

Elda Niles looked into Coach Russell's eyes a good long time. He didn't blink once.

She extended her hand to him and he took it.

Jarius jumped out of his seat with a cheer and touched his palm to the ten-foot ceiling.

That Saturday morning on the Winstead football field, coaches Russell, Eccles and Knox looked out on their squad for the coming season. To a man, their players were already in game-shape. You couldn't compete on the athletic teams at the school without maintaining a B average. All of their athletes had done that and more and they still had the drive and dedication to hit the gym and show up at the first team practice strong, swift and lean.

The coaches stood on the sideline and watched the offense run ten plays Russell had scripted for them. The defense had to react, just as they would in games.

Knox said to his colleagues, "Would you look at how fast Niles is out there? I haven't said anything to you, Coach," he said to Russell, "but he asked me if he could play special teams."

Russell looked at his assistant. "What? Run back kickoffs and return punts?"

Knox nodded.

The head coach smiled. "I doubt anyone would lay a hand on him. It might almost be unfair to the other teams. I doubt any player in the whole league is within half-a-second of him in the forty-yard dash."

Eccles, the defensive coordinator, said, "I'll bet Ricky Mitchell is."

Mitchell was an unexpected bonus to Jarius Niles' recruitment. He was Jarius' best friend since the time they were little kids and another starter on their public high school team. Mitchell and his mother came to Russell and asked, please, could he come to Winstead, too?

The request was supported not only by Ricky's mother, Nola Mitchell, but also by Jarius and Elda Niles. It wasn't a take-my-friend-or-else situation. Russell could see that. But it was a heartfelt plea. Trouble was, Ricky was only a C-student. Russell talked to the headmaster at Winstead about the situation. He came up with a solution.

Ricky would be allowed to audit a Winstead course — take it without official credit. If he pulled a B or higher grade, on his own merit, he would be admitted. With Jarius and both mothers urging him on, Ricky got his B, was admitted to the school and projected as a starting defensive back on the football team.

"You may be right about that," Russell said to Knox. "If anyone's speed is close to Jarius', it's Ricky's. We're going to have a great team this year."

Eccles was about to agree when he saw a big man walking their way.

The defensive coordinator had a bad feeling and said, "Oh, shit."

Don Russell had a no-profanity rule for his players and his coaches.

No cussing in the locker room or on the field. You never got penalized for what you didn't say. So Eccles' vulgarity took him by surprise. Then he saw the reason for it.

Abel Mays, the head coach of the public school team that both Jarius and Ricky had played for, was coming their way, and he looked anything but happy.

Knox said, "I don't think he stopped by to say, 'Have a good season.'"

Eccles added, "Not after we took his top two players."

Russell took a step forward, saying, "Let me handle this."

Then Mays brushed back the right side of his coat.

And they all saw how much trouble they were in.

### McGill Investigations, Inc. — Georgetown

"I'm sure someone is going to try to kill my husband," Zara Gilford told McGill.

She'd walked into his office a heartbeat after Roger Michaelson had reminded Deke that he was owed a measure of deference. McGill accorded Michaelson all the courtesy he felt the man was due by offering to let him to cool his heels in the outer office instead of tossing him out onto the street.

"Mrs. Gilford has an appointment," he told Patti's longtime nemesis. "If you want to wait, I'll see if I can get to you."

McGill hoped Michaelson would take a hint, but the SOB took a seat instead.

Deke sat behind the reception desk and stared at Michaelson.

McGill said, "Deke, please call Margaret and ask if she might come in."

Then he led Zara Gilford into his office and closed the door. Got her seated and wondered how he might best explain his less than genteel treatment of a former senator. It wasn't necessary. By the time he took his own seat, Mrs. Gilford told him what was foremost in her mind, a mortal threat against her husband.

"What makes you think so, Mrs. Gilford?" McGill asked.

"My husband is Jordan Gilford." When she saw that didn't provide clarity, she asked, "Don't you know the name?"

"Sorry, no."

"Jordan is a whistle-blower."

McGill followed with the logical question. "Against whom did he blow the whistle?"

"The two defense contractors he worked for; he was a senior executive at both companies." Mrs. Gilford provided two corporate names known to McGill. He only glanced through the business section of the newspapers he read. But he recalled above-the-fold stories of each company getting multibillion dollar contracts from the Pentagon.

"Jordan is a highly educated man," his wife told McGill. "He has degrees in engineering, accounting and law. There's very little any business entity could put past him. He turned in the CEOs of two Fortune 500 companies; they were defrauding the taxpayers."

McGill thought about that for a moment.

"Given all you've told me, doesn't your husband have a well-known and formidable reputation in his field?"

"He does and he has for many years."

"Then why would the second CEO who took the fall hire him? He had to know what he was getting when he hired Mr. Gilford, and he had to know he wasn't running a straight outfit. Where's the logic there?" McGill asked.

"I asked the same thing," Zara told him. "Jordan explained to me that CEO number two thought he was far more clever than Jordan, that Jordan would never catch on to him and —"

"By hiring your husband, he'd make himself look good, honest beyond question," McGill said.

"Exactly. Do you know how the federal anti-fraud laws work, Mr. McGill?"

He shook his head. In all his years as a cop the Pentagon had never come to him and said, "We wuz robbed."

"Well, the pertinent part of the law as far as Jordan is concerned," Zara explained, "is that whistle-blowers can receive large sums of money for turning in corrupt company officials."

"What kind of money did Mr. Gilford get?" McGill asked.

"For the two times he took information to the U.S. attorney's office: $53 million."

Damn, McGill thought. With that kind of incentive, he was surprised there was any corruption left in the federal government. Then again, Jordan Gilford, to hear his wife tell it, had an unusual, if not unique, array of skills. How many people could read a combination of engineering specs, balance sheets and law books?

"We don't need the money," Zara said, seeing the look on McGill's face. "For the past ten years, Jordan has never made less than a million dollars a year, and for the last five years his compensation has been well above that."

"So he's not driven by money," McGill said.

Zara shook her head.

"All he thinks about is doing the job right. That means, among other things, being honest. And that makes some people see him as prickly. If he'd learned to be one of the boys, he'd probably be running some company by now. He can't stand it, though, if someone tries to cut even the tiniest corner. Heaven help you if you do something unethical. If you're foolish enough to do something illegal, well, maybe he should wear a whistle around his neck the way those sports officials do."

### *Winstead School Football Field — Georgetown*

Coach Don Russell blew his whistle as he ran at Abel Mays, the man approaching his football team with some goddamn firearm Russell couldn't even identify. It was small enough that he'd been able to hide it under his coat, but the damn thing had a magazine that looked a foot long. Russell hunted ducks, deer and wild pigs. He knew long guns. There was nothing sporting about the compact death machine Mays carried.

It was made to kill people, and with the size of that magazine the body count could be horrific. Russell felt his heart turn to ice as Mays raised the barrel. Even so, he continued his charge and kept blowing his whistle. He had to alert his boys and give them time to run. Save as many of them as he could.

Just when Russell was sure he was about to be shot and killed, Bill Eccles, on his right and ten years younger, sped ahead of him, bellowing like a madman. Mays pointed his weapon at Bill, but then George Knox, on Russell's left and even younger than Bill, took the lead, yelling as he went, "Warriors!"

Mays swung the weapon Knox's way. Then he remembered what he could do with the firearm he possessed. He pulled the trigger and a burst of automatic fire erupted. Swinging the barrel in an arc, he cut down all three coaches, ended their lives in the blink of an eye.

The whistle blowing and the heroism of their coaches had given the entire team the opportunity to flee unscathed. But that wasn't how Jarius Niles and Ricky Mitchell responded. Tears of disbelief filled their eyes and rage consumed their hearts. The men who had given them the kind of opportunities other boys could only dream of had just sacrificed their lives for them.

Jarius and Ricky followed their coaches' example and ran

straight at Mays. Half-a-dozen of their teammates followed close behind Jarius and Ricky. All of them took up Coach Knox's battle cry.

"Warriors!"

The remaining players couldn't find the nerve to join in.

They saved themselves and ran the other way.

Abel Mays saw the players sprinting his way. Jarius and Ricky, the two boys he'd trained last year, the players he had counted on to bring his team a championship this year, the little shits who let themselves be taken from him, were out front, running side by side and coming fast. He'd come to fancy-ass Winstead that morning with them first in mind. Then he intended to get their coaches, the thieving bastards. Doing things the other way around was fine by him, too.

Those other young fools running behind, shit, they'd just made the wrong choice.

Mays dropped the empty magazine and slammed home a full clip.

They were close now, Jarius, Ricky and the others.

Close enough to hope they might reach him before —

He pulled the trigger and the players all went down like bowling pins.

Banging and crashing into each other, falling to the ground.

The soft morning breeze cleared the gun-smoke quickly. Mays could see Jarius and Ricky were dead. So were some of the others. A few were still alive, moaning, one of them crying. He didn't care about them. They lived or died, it was all the same to him.

He started to walk back to his car.

Put a new clip into his weapon.

In case someone else wanted to take a run at him.

### McGill Investigations, Inc. — Georgetown

"Do you think one of your husband's former employers might be looking to hurt him?" McGill asked Zara Gilford.

"Possibly, but I don't think so."

"Why not?"

"Well, the timing isn't right, I think. The first time Jordan went to the U.S. attorney's office was four years ago; the second time was two years ago. I think if someone at either of those companies had wanted vengeance they would have tried something sooner. Isn't vengeance usually an act of passion?"

"Can be," McGill said. "But some people don't want to get caught. They can be patient and calculating."

"Oh, I didn't think of that."

McGill knew that some monsters thought the *perfect* time for getting even was right when the poor sap finally thought he was in the clear. He didn't share that with Zara. He wanted to know who she thought might be a threat.

"Why someone else?" he asked.

"Because Jordan made such a good impression on the U.S. attorney here in Washington, he asked Jordan if he'd like to talk to a friend of his at the Department of Defense. The U.S. attorney joked that he'd find all sorts of opportunity to straighten people out there. So Jordan went for an interview, was offered the job and asked for a couple of weeks to think about it."

"He hasn't even accepted the job?" McGill asked.

"No, he did accept it. He's been at the DOD for six months now. Then last week he got the phone call that scared both of us silly."

"I'm sorry, but you lost me," McGill said.

"Last Wednesday, we were at home getting ready to sit down to dinner and the phone rang. Jordan was closer and he answered the call. He wasn't on the line a minute when he went white as new snow. Then he started to shake, and he's not the kind of man to frighten easily. Just the opposite. But whoever was talking to him got past his guard."

"How did you respond?" McGill asked.

"I asked what was wrong. He hung up the phone without even saying goodbye."

"And?"

"Then I demanded to know what was wrong. Jordan told me an old friend from college had died. I asked who, but he said it was someone I'd never met. With all the schooling Jordan has — all of it before we met — that was plausible."

McGill said, "But you didn't believe him or you wouldn't be here."

"No, I didn't. I have only a B.A. in American History, but I can tell the difference between grief and fear. What I could see clearly, someone had frightened my husband. He hadn't heard a threat that someone was going to take him to court or anything like that."

McGill didn't want Zara Gilford to frighten herself to the point where her answers were the product of emotion rather than reason. He needed to distract her, but to keep things relevant. He asked, "Does your husband know you came to see me?"

"No, he thinks I went shopping."

"Will that cause a problem?"

"Between us. It might, for a little while. I'll pay that price to make sure he's safe."

McGill nodded. He'd do the same, had done the same, in her position.

"So tell me, who do you think threatened your husband?"

"I don't know. The only thing I can think is somebody at the Department of Defense knew of Jordan's reputation and felt he was getting too close to finding out something that person wanted to keep hidden. Something so big he had to scare Jordan off with some awful threat."

"A death threat," McGill said.

"Yes, the next day, Thursday afternoon, Jordan told me we were moving. Not that he wanted to talk about moving; he'd already bought a condo in a high rise. Well, as high as you can find in Washington. It's a new building with all sorts of security features. We have the only space on the top floor. A combination of penthouse and bunker, if you can imagine such a thing."

"What did you say?" McGill said.

"I asked if he'd be attending his friend's funeral."

"Letting him know you weren't buying his story."

"Exactly, but he came up with a new excuse."

"What was that?"

"He said he needed a secure site for the confidential information he needed to start bringing home. I asked if he'd been given any tips on how you furnish a secure site to make it cozy. I also told him we weren't going to sell our home, the place where we've lived quite safely for years, because if I didn't like the new place I wouldn't be staying."

"Have you seen your new digs yet?" McGill asked.

Disappointment clear in her voice, Zara said, "It's actually quite nice, tasteful if not warm and fuzzy. You barely notice the gun turrets."

McGill grinned. The woman was facing a trying situation at the least, but she was doing her best to cope. "Have you moved in?"

"I've spent two nights under that roof. I still think of it as more of a hotel stay, though."

McGill felt it imperative to bring up a delicate subject.

"Mrs. Gilford, has anyone threatened you?"

The question drew a blank look from the woman. "Me? Why would anyone do that? I haven't done anything."

McGill said, "The best way to scare a strong person is to make a plausible threat against someone he or she loves."

Zara Gilford's eyes went wide, her chin began to quiver.

"So your husband does love you?"

She bobbed her head.

When McGill had opened his firm, he'd told his first client he didn't do bodyguard work. Now, though, he knew someone who might fill that bill. "Mrs. Gilford, you have to persuade your husband to tell you everything he knows or suspects about what scared him. Before that, though, I think you should have someone to protect you."

"Is that something you can do for me?"

"No, but I have a man in mind."

"Is he competent?"

"He used to protect the president."

"He'll take the job?"

As far as McGill knew, Celsus Crogher was still looking for a meaningful way to occupy his time. "I think so, and once your husband sees what you've done, maybe he'll feel better about sharing what he knows with you."

"But you'll talk to Jordan, too?"

"If you'll tell me where he is," McGill said, "I'll go see him right now."

# CHAPTER 2

## *Madison Drive NW — Washington, DC*

Jeronimo "Jerry" Nerón sat in a tan Ford parked opposite the National Mall that Saturday morning and waited for his target. He'd been given the range of times during which Jordan Gilford's weekly thirteen-mile run should bring him past the point at which he sat. Jerry had arrived an hour early. When you were being paid to kill someone, the client wouldn't accept tardiness as a reason for not getting the job done.

Exactly where along Gilford's running path the hit was done was up to Jerry. He could shoot the man from his car. He could exit the car and press his weapon against the man's skull if, say, he stopped to tie his shoelace. The client's only concern was that Gilford die; Jerry's focus was on completing the job and getting away clean.

The grandson of Cuban exiles, Jerry had been trained since adolescence by men, now aged, who had been trained by the CIA. Their compatriots' mission had been to reclaim the homeland. Even as a young boy, Jerry had his doubts that would ever be accomplished. He'd heard all the bitter stories about the disaster at the Bay of Pigs from the time he took his first steps.

Did he really want to trust his fate to men who had failed so badly?

His grandfather, Dario Nerón, had comforted him on that point. There were those who had seen the tragedy coming. They'd called in sick, found excuses to stay home, and had been spared being killed by either the Communists' superior forces or their firing squads. It was these farsighted patriots who would train young Jerry.

His mission, of course, would be to kill Fidel Castro.

As soon as Jerry became a man at twenty-one, he was presented with the first plan to accomplish that glorious goal. He took one look at it and called in sick. There was nothing his elders could say about that. They went back to the drawing board.

Over those years of being taught the ins and outs of assassination and spycraft, Jerry had also learned the skills that provided his cover profession: tailoring. His grandmother, Arcelia, the heiress to a sugarcane fortune stolen by the Reds, had learned to sew in Miami. She opened her own shop, designed and created bridal gowns and dresses for *quinceañeras*. She developed a large and devoted following among the women in the exile community.

Jerry took to the needle and thread immediately. His grandmother said it was in his blood just as it was in hers. The boy also liked having the women and girls who visited *abuela's* shop fuss over him and give him candy. As he grew older and ever more handsome, he would steal kisses from the fifteen-year-old beauties who were being introduced to society. He even managed, in later years, to have more than a few midnight trysts with brides-to-be who wanted to be sure they were marrying the right man.

At twenty-one, having passed on his first opportunity to kill Castro, he opened his own shop. Jerry Nerón, Custom Tailoring for Men.

He specialized in fine suits and evening wear.

With grandmother having paved the way in Miami's huge Cuban community, his customer base was present from the start. Jerry had the native intelligence to give special attention and deals to prominent politicians and businessmen in the city. From there, his name spread beyond his ethnic community by word of mouth.

Show biz people, filming in town, started coming to his shop.

They took his suits and tuxes with them across the country and around the world.

The label *Jerry Nerón, Miami* quickly achieved a cult cachet.

If anyone in Washington happened to notice his presence in town that increasingly dreary March day, he had a perfectly legitimate reason to be there. He was doing a fitting for a client, one of several he had among the town's power brokers. Not that he intended to be seen by anyone but that particular lobbyist.

Because while he was never presented with a plan to kill Castro of which he approved, and the exile *viejos* eventually gave up on the idea, he hadn't let the lethal skills he'd been taught go to waste. He made them a part of his business. The private sector had its uses for assassins.

As he sat in his car, waiting patiently, he had a police scanner on at a low volume. It wouldn't do to step out of his car and pop his target if there was a police patrol unit racing to answer a call around the corner. He also had an iPad Mini 3G resting against his steering wheel, streaming a broadcast from CNN.

You never knew. The media might learn of a crime in progress before the cops did.

It paid to be careful, and Jerry took all available precautions.

He thought he'd take Gilford right there on the running path bordering the Mall. The morning had started out sunny and crisp, but rain was predicted and the sky had become overcast and the air had turned chill. The last two pedestrians Jerry had seen passed by ten minutes ago. He'd been assured, though, that Gilford wouldn't skip his run for anything short of a blizzard.

Jerry thought the job should come off just fine. Then a breaking news story came into the CNN newsroom; he dropped the volume on the police scanner to a whisper. The studio personality on the streaming TV feed turned the broadcast over to a field reporter.

"This just in: There's been another school massacre, this time on a Saturday when classes weren't even in session. The football team of the Winstead School, an elite private high school in Georgetown, was having its first spring football practice this morning when a man with an automatic weapon appeared. He killed the team's three coaches, who apparently tried to keep the man away from their players. He also killed five of the team's players and seriously wounded three others when the players apparently ran toward the killer in support of their coaches. The remaining members of the team ran for their lives and are unharmed.

"The killer has been identified by survivors as Abel Mays, the head football coach of a District public high school. The teams of the two schools don't compete on the playing field, and police sources said it would be pointless speculation at this point to say what might have set Coach Mays off on this murderous rampage.

A photo of Mays filled Jerry's iPad screen. Must have been a candid shot. The man looked like he was screaming. Maybe yelling instructions to his players during a game or practice.

As that image lingered, the field reporter said in voice-over: "Once he stopped his attack, Abel Mays left the grounds of the Winstead School and drove off in what witnesses described as a forest green SUV, possibly a Toyota or a Subaru. His whereabouts are unknown. The police, underscoring the obvious, say Mays has to be considered still armed and extremely dangerous. Anyone who sees him should stay as far away as possible and call the police immediately."

The picture switched back to the newsroom personality.

"A horrible tragedy, Jeanine" he told the field reporter. "Once again, we need to remind our viewing audience —"

Not to try their luck against a pissed-off guy with a machine gun.

Jerry lowered the volume on his iPad and boosted the sound on the police scanner.

All sorts of units, patrol, detective and crime scene, were racing to the school where the shooting happened. Ambulances were en route, too. And even an evac helicopter. Must be some fancy school, Jerry thought.

Damn shame, all those kids and coaches getting shot.

His money said it had to be bad blood between the coaches, the cause of it all.

The kids, thinking they were immortal, probably influenced by stupid video games, had thought they could save the day. Paid the price to learn they were wrong.

That pissed Jerry off. He liked kids. Only in his early thirties, he looked at teenagers like they were kid brothers and sisters. Thought he might have children of his own some day.

Some asshole ever killed one of his babies ... he'd teach the bastard taking lives had to be left to the professionals. That last thought reminded him he still had a job to do. He looked at the dashboard clock again.

If Gilford was on the early side of his run, he should be passing by in ten minutes.

Wasn't another passerby in sight. Not even any motorized traffic.

The day kept getting darker as the cloud cover thickened. Felt like temperature was still dropping, too. Just the kind of weather he needed to discourage casual strollers. The cops would be concentrating their people at and around that fancy school for the next little while. Then they'd be out looking for a green SUV not a tan Ford sedan that looked like it might be some kind of government vehicle.

Jerry couldn't have asked for better conditions.

Not that he wanted those kids to die just to make things easier for him.

It really pissed him off, them getting killed. Fucking amateurs and the collateral damage they caused. They were a curse.

His kids or not, if Jerry spotted that Mays guy, he'd show the prick who was armed and dangerous. The thought of going vigilante had no sooner occurred to Jerry than somebody pulled into the parking space behind his car. His first reaction was, "Christ, no end to the empty slots on this block and ..."

He remembered the description of the school killer's vehicle. Green SUV. Maybe a Toyota. Just like the one behind him now. Jerry shifted his attention to the guy behind the wheel.

*Sonofabitch.*

Did he have the time? Yeah, he did. He could pop the guy who'd shot up the high school football team and still get Gilford.

Then he had an even better idea.

### Firepower America — Falls Church, Virginia

A visiting hit man wasn't the only one monitoring police calls and cable news in the Metro DC area. The lobbying and public relations arm of the country's gun manufacturers kept around-the-clock surveillance on mass gunshot killings. The phone rang on the desk of Auric Ludwig, the CEO of FirePower America. A middle-aged man, so tightly wound he looked as if his bulging eyeballs might burst at any minute, Ludwig worked six-and-a-half days per week.

The joke was he needed the other twelve hours to have his bile drained.

So he didn't shoot somebody himself.

Ludwig's office was a study in Spartan simplicity. An American flag and the flag of the Commonwealth of Virginia hung from six-foot poles standing to either side of the office doorway. On the wall behind his desk, resting on brackets, was a replica of a Revolutionary War muzzleloading flintlock musket. From the tip of its barrel to the end of its stock, it measured over four feet long.

In the days when such weapons were used in anger, they were mounted with long triangular bayonets that added another eighteen inches in length. But Ludwig didn't represent bayonet makers and didn't want anyone to confuse the issue. Guns were what mattered to him.

As exemplified by the plaque beneath the musket.

*The Gun That Made America Free.*

He didn't say a word when he picked up his phone.

The voice on the other end offered only two. "Code black."

Another mass murder. Ludwig replaced his phone and turned on his TV, saw that the killing had happened just across the river in DC. Wouldn't have been that big a deal if it had happened in a poor neighborhood. Could have been written off as gang violence. Even if it had happened in an upper reach of the 47% of the population his constituents wrote off, it wouldn't be that big a deal. All the usual suspects could be blamed. Failed family structure, the perverse influence of a deranged popular culture and ... he'd have to see what the latest talking points were.

But this time, goddamnit, the shooting had happened in a preserve of the top one percent.

He knew all about the Winstead School and what it represented.

Hell, most of the families there were the top one tenth of the top one percent.

He was going to feel real pressure this time. The only good thing he'd seen so far was the shooter was African American. People on the other side of the gun-control debate would be careful how far they went in blaming him. Ludwig thought he could make the case that any black head of household, mom or dad, living in a big American city, needed an automatic weapon just to protect hearth and home against the hordes of gang-bangers.

Maybe he'd get lucky and the kids who got killed would all be scholarship students.

Not have the megabucks needed to fight back in any meaningful way.

Ludwig picked up his phone, hit a button and said, "Crank up production."

Code black meant more than the color of death.

It stood for profit, too.

There'd be a run on gun stores across the nation within minutes.

Sales would go through the roof. People who owned more guns than they could ever use would scurry to buy still more. Fearing lawmakers in Congress might finally grow a pair.

To meet the uptick in demand, supplies would also have to rise.

Truth was, in America, bloodshed was good for business.

The gun business anyway.

## Third Street, NW, Washington, DC

Zara Gilford told McGill that her husband, Jordan, was somewhere along the route of his Saturday morning thirteen-mile run, and told him that Jordan ran at an eight-minute-per-mile clip. Consulting her watch, she said he should be finished in a little more than forty minutes. She also asked him to please call her Zara.

After Celsus Crogher arrived, got the details of the situation and agreed to protect Zara, she decided that maybe a small shopping trip was in order after all. One that would give her time to learn how the meeting between McGill and her husband had gone.

Rather than intrude on Jordan Gilford's run and risk putting him in a bad mood, McGill decided to make his approach after Gilford had the satisfaction of completing his exercise. He waited for the man outside the luxury, high-security condo building on Third Street that was his new home.

The structure had no gun turrets that McGill could see, but it did have a narrow sharply curved driveway leading up to the front entrance. The hairpin turn, McGill thought, would make it difficult to do a drive-by attack on the building. God forbid that such a thing would ever come to pass.

McGill had chosen not to clog up the driveway.

He had Leo park at the curb just short of it.

A street sign advised Leo that parking on that side of the street was prohibited, day and night. There was no obvious traffic-flow reason for the restriction. More likely, the security-conscious developers had made a pleading to the District government, perhaps a campaign contribution or two and, voila, the commandment was delivered from on high.

Thou shalt not park here.

Not that a cop writing a ticket was a worry for McGill. Leo would talk to him. If that didn't work, Deke would badge him and send him on his way. Should the cop still proved recalcitrant, McGill would call him over and ask a simple question. "If we each escalate this matter to the tops of our respective chains of command, who's going to win?"

President trumped chief of police, simple as that.

Shouldn't come to that, though.

McGill felt sure there was no city cop so pigheaded as to force the issue that far.

The guy who strode out of the condo building, however, with his buzz cut and square jaw, stretching the seams of his blue blazer and gray slacks with heavy muscle, looked like he was used to getting his way and taking no back-talk at all.

Leo yawned, flipped down the passenger-side visor.

So the hard charger could see the Secret Service star logo thereon.

Deke sized the man up, not pleased that Leo's effort hadn't slowed the guy down. He was reaching for the door release when McGill gently laid a hand on his shoulder. He said, "Let's give it a moment before we go nuclear."

He lowered his window. That diverted the security brute off his path toward Leo and redirected him McGill's way. The guy could move quickly. He had his face in the opening McGill had provided for him in the blink of an eye. Before he could get a word out, though, McGill extended a business card.

"Mrs. Zara Gilford asked me to speak with her husband, Jordan. She said he should be along shortly," McGill told the guy. "If you're unfamiliar with the Gilfords, they just moved in."

The guy took the card and stepped back, crouching so he could keep a eye on McGill.

"I've met the Gilfords." He shifted his gaze from McGill to his card. He did a quick read and looked back at McGill and nodded to himself. "I saw the video of you on the National Mall, taking care of that militia clown. I'm retired USMC."

"Thank you for your service," McGill said.

"You, too. You can wait inside, sir, if you'd like."

"Let's see where Mr. Gilford would like to take our conversation."

"Yes, sir."

"Special Agent Ky will need to check out the lobby if we get that far, if you'd care to let him have a quick look-see."

"Yes, sir. May I keep this card?"

"Sure. You have one?"

The question took the Marine by surprise, but then he smiled and gave McGill his card. Karl Vasek, Security Supervisor. McGill looked at it and extended a hand.

"Good to meet you, Karl."

For just a second, McGill thought he was about to receive a salute.

Then Karl's civilian training overrode the impulse. "You, too, sir."

He led Deke into the building. Leo looked over his shoulder at McGill.

"You're a silver-tongued devil, boss."

"You can never have too many friends, Leo."

The driver nodded. "Got some Alison Krauss ready to play. You want to take a listen while Deke's busy?"

"Sure."

McGill had come to appreciate bluegrass and country music under Leo's tutelage.

But Alison had just started "Paper Airplane" when Deke came sprinting out of the condo lobby. McGill had never seen the man scared before. McGill and Leo both reached for their guns and exited the car from opposite sides, looking for a surprise attack.

They'd found no threat by the time Deke arrived.

"Get back in the car. Leo, get us over to the university."

McGill knew he meant Georgetown University.

Where his eldest child, Abbie, studied. McGill's heart froze. He and the others threw themselves into the armored Chevy. Deke turned to look at McGill as Leo accelerated like the NASCAR driver he once was.

Holding up a hand to forestall questions from McGill, Deke said, "Abbie's okay, but …"

He told McGill and Leo what had happened at the Winstead

School.

The scene of the mass murder was little more than a mile from Abbie McGill's dorm room.

Deke said, "Abbie's detail has her safe in her room and the campus cops have locked down the grounds, but Metro PD says the killer, a guy named Abel Mays, is still free and unaccounted for. I thought we'd all better get over to Georgetown until the cops bring Mays down."

McGill agreed wholeheartedly.

The fear he felt for his own child had to make room for the heartbreak he knew other parents must be feeling right now. Losing someone you loved or even a person you simply knew to some sonofabitch gunning down people wholesale, you wanted to …

Bring the bastard down? Seemed like he should suffer more than that.

McGill realized he was crumpling something in his hand. Karl Vasek's business card. They'd just bailed on his new client. He would make no apology for that. Family came first, always. But if Zara Gilford was right, her husband's life was in danger.

McGill called Karl Vasek, asked him to keep an eye out for Jordan Gilford.

Warned him that Mrs. Gilford thought Jordan's life had been threatened.

### *Madison Drive — Washington, DC*

Jerry Nerón wore black nitrile gloves, the same kind cops used at crime scenes, when he got out of his Ford. He saw the guy in the green Toyota SUV sitting in the driver's seat with his head canted forward now, chin on his chest, like he'd just nodded off. Napping after a hard morning of mass murder. Jerry's contempt for amateurs swelled.

Well, the jerk was about to get his. That and a little extra.

One more name to add to his body count.

Jerry's black Smith & Wesson semi-auto with color coordinated sound suppressor all but disappeared as he held it against his black slacks. Approaching the Toyota SUV, he saw that the safety button on the driver's side was up; the door was unlocked. Maybe the bastard had intended to go for a walk. See if he could jack up his score. With no one out on the Mall, though, he'd decided it was siesta time.

Inattentive prick hadn't even noticed Jerry sitting in the car right in front of him.

Jerry didn't give things any more thought than that. He yanked open the driver's door of the Toyota. The guy never moved. Jerry shot him twice in the head. He grabbed his brass and slammed the door before any gore could leak out onto his shoes.

He went over to the passenger side of the SUV. A compact automatic weapon lay on the seat. An easy grab for the homicidal driver if he'd felt the urge. Well, the guy was all done with that. But Jerry still had his contract to fulfill. And now he had an HK-MP5K.

The MP meant the model was supposed to be limited to military and police personnel.

A former special forces op from a Central American ally had trained Jerry on an assortment of weapons, including the one in front of him. He knew how it functioned.

Damn fool behind the steering wheel had probably bought it online.

Oh, well, Jerry thought. He'd put it to good use.

Five minutes later, after spotting a lone runner in the distance coming his way, Jerry stepped out onto the running path as if he were the only other fool in town out to stretch his legs on a miserable day. He held the automatic weapon against his leg, its length not much greater than the S&W with the suppressor.

Jerry knelt on one knee as if to tie his shoelace, inconspicuously placing the HK behind his lead foot. He looked up and saw the oncoming runner, now staring at Jerry, was his target, Jordan Gilford. The expression on Gilford's face suggested he might suspect something was wrong.

Jerry didn't give himself away. He returned his attention to the shoelace he'd untied moments earlier. Made sure he double-knotted it as he heard the footsteps draw closer. He looked up when he heard the running sounds stop.

Jordan Gilford stood no more than ten feet distant. He wiped sweat from his eyes and squinted. He was looking at the weapon partially hidden by Jerry's foot. It took him only a second or two to complete its outline in his mind. Pretty damn quick for a civilian, Jerry thought.

Jordan Gilford turned to run back the way he'd come. He didn't scream in terror. He didn't plead for mercy. He simply tried to outrun his fate. Jerry admired the man's courage, but he picked up his weapon and cut him down anyway. Shot Gilford across the middle of his back. No question the organ damage, blood loss and shock would be fatal.

Jerry had been taught to shoot automatic weapons in short, controlled bursts.

He'd ignored that lesson and fired the clip dry.

Just as he assumed the fool behind the wheel of the Toyota would have done.

He returned the HK-MP5K to the passenger seat of that vehicle.

His job all but done, he got back in his Ford. He would dispose of the S&W semi-auto and the suppressor where they'd never be found. The car would be abandoned with the key left in the ignition. And then he would be on his way home to Miami.

A master tailor, having outfitted another distinguished customer.

An important man who would further Jerry Nerón's well deserved reputation.


### The Oval Office — The White House

White House Chief of Staff Galia Mindel hurried past the president's personal secretary, Edwina Byington, telling her, "No interruptions … except for Mr. McGill."

She entered the president's office without knocking.

Patricia Grant looked up from the notes she'd been making while reviewing a list of the most urgent infrastructure repair projects the country needed to address. Next to each project were the names of the senators and members of Congress who represented the states and districts in which the repairs were needed. She was trying to work out the grouping of politicians most likely to see that it was in *their* interest as well as the country's to start rebuilding the skeletal structure of the United States. She'd be asking many of them to break party discipline to vote for the construction and repair projects. She thought she could prime the pump, so to speak, by paying presidential visits to the towns and states that would benefit and gin up interest. Tell the local citizens that not only would their roads and bridges be safer, their electrical grids would be smarter, their Internet connectivity would be faster — there would be thousands of well-paying jobs created as well.

In the face of popular support, the president reasoned, demands for austerity budgets would weaken. That or those who held fast to ideological positions would be voted out of office.

Domestic policy was the president's morning focus.

In the afternoon, she'd work on the speech she intended to give saying she would no longer allow China to buy Treasury bills, and the money owed by the United States to China would be repaid on an expedited basis. Patricia Darden Grant had decided she would tolerate no further Chinese cyberattacks on U.S. governmental departments and commercial companies without a vigorous response. If throwing off the shackles of indebtedness to China wasn't enough to jolt Beijing, the next step would be —

Swept from the president's mind the moment Galia rushed into her office, a look just short of panic on her face.

The chief of staff started to speak but her voice caught in her throat.

Tears fell from her eyes.

All of which scared the hell out of the president. It took all her self-control to put on a calm front. "What is it, Galia? What's happened?"

"Madam President, there's been another school massacre. Right here in Washington at the Winstead School. Initial reports say eight dead and three wounded, two of them critically."

"My God ... were there classes today? It's Saturday."

"The shooting occurred at a spring football practice. The dead and wounded were coaches and players."

The president could no longer maintain an impassive facade. She covered her mouth with a hand. For a moment, tears welled in her eyes, too. But she knew immediately that she couldn't afford to indulge an emotional response. It was her job to take command of the situation.

Her face tightening, the president asked, "Was the shooter killed?"

Galia shook her head. "The police are searching for him now."

"He's *not* in custody?" The president's mind made an intuitive leap. "Winstead isn't far from Georgetown University. *Abbie.*"

Jim's eldest child. Her stepdaughter. The world began to spin.

Galia reached her, placed a hand on each of the president's shoulders.

"Abbie McGill is safe. Her security detail has her protected. The campus is locked down. Mr. McGill is on his way there."

Patricia Grant couldn't restrain her tears now. The sense of relief was too great.

"Thank God."

But gratitude was also a luxury she didn't have time for at the moment.

She straightened her posture, cleared her throat and said, "I'm all right now, Galia."

The chief of staff stepped back. "Yes, ma'am."

"Have FBI Director Haskins offer Metro Police any assistance they need. Tell the Secretary of Defense to help with surveillance, if need be. I want the man who did this in custody before nightfall."

Galia had taken both of those steps already, but she said, "Yes, ma'am."

"Please tell Edwina that I'd like to speak with my husband as soon as possible. Abbie, too."

"I will, Madam President, but knowing Mr. McGill —"

Edwina buzzed the president's intercom.

"Mr. McGill and Abigail for you, Madam President."

## CHAPTER 3

### *J. Edgar Hoover Building — Washington, DC*

F BI Deputy Director Byron DeWitt sat at his desk with his
eyes closed and fingers pressed against his temples. He moved
them in circles, forward and back. He felt the blood flow in his
head increase, the tension inside his skull recede and his headache
diminish. Less than an hour earlier, he'd gotten the news about the
shooting at the Winstead School from Director Jeremiah Haskins
and the order, "Give Metro Police Chief Gorman a call and tell her
the Bureau will provide whatever help she might need."

"Yes, sir."

Haskins provided all the details of the shooting that he had.

He finished by saying, "Goddamnit, why can't people settle
things with a fistfight any longer?"

Or even a well-reasoned, clearly articulated discussion, DeWitt
thought.

The director told DeWitt to let him know what Chief Gorman
said.

"I want to update the White House as soon as we know anything
of substance. Mostly, I want to tell the president that the cops have
taken this SOB off the street."

"Yes, sir."

DeWitt had dispatched Special Agent Abra Benjamin to work

with Metro PD. She was the most competent field agent he knew. Excepting himself. Technically, he was a poobah, an administrator of significant rank. But he still thought of himself as an investigator.

Right now, though, he had more investigations to run than he wanted.

He hadn't taken a day off in the past two months. He was doing his damnedest to find out where Tyler Busby was hiding. Busby was the corporate raider and art collector who had supposedly lent the better part of his collection to Washington's new art museum, Inspiration Hall. Only the supposed masterpieces Busby had provided to the museum had turned out to be forgeries.

Several pieces donated by fellow billionaires Darren Drucker and Nathaniel Ransom had also turned out to be fakes. But interviews with both men led DeWitt to conclude they'd been Busby's victims not his coconspirators. Interrogations of crooked art dealer Duvessa Kinsale and her father, the financial swindler and master art forger now known as Giles Benedict, had confirmed the innocence of Drucker and Ransom.

Kinsale and Benedict were talking for all they were worth because they knew the most important matter on DeWitt's plate wasn't forged art. It was finding out who had participated in the plot to blow up Inspiration Hall while the president made an unannounced visit. Presidential assassination conspiracies always got top priority.

Kinsale and Benedict were hoping to avoid the death penalty.

And shorten their inevitable prison terms to something less than life.

Director Haskins had asked for and received sole authority to find, arrest and bring to trial all the culprits involved. He wanted a clean resolution, one that would stand up to the judgment of both the media and history. He told the president he wouldn't stand for an ambiguous or contested conclusion that led to a muddle of conspiracy theories. He'd delegated operational control of the investigation to his most trusted subordinate, Byron DeWitt.

The deputy director had conducted a dozen interrogations of

both Kinsale and Benedict. He'd used every technique he knew from charm to menace. Nothing could get either of his prisoners to admit they knew where Tyler Busby might be hiding. At that point, DeWitt was tempted to use physical coercion.

If he went down that road, though, he'd taint the investigation. Discredit any information he might obtain.

Rather than make a mistake of historical proportions, he turned Kinsale and Benedict over to the U.S. attorneys who would prosecute them. Maybe the lawyers could scare the father and daughter in ways he couldn't conceive. He hoped so.

If they failed, he'd have to accept they really didn't know Busby's whereabouts.

With all the satellites, drones, wiretaps and computer hacks available to the U.S. government, it didn't seem like anyone should be able to disappear these days. Even if you went off the modern communications grid, you'd have to live your life indoors or literally underground not to be spotted eventually. A fugitive couldn't even rely on a new face to conceal his identity anymore. Somatic recognition software had gone far beyond simply comparing facial features to images in a database. These days, subjects could be identified by posture, gait, arm swing and even the shadows they cast.

All those characteristics as they pertained to Tyler Busby were on video files possessed by the FBI. A public figure for decades, an archive of the way Busby looked, moved and even scratched his head lay at DeWitt's fingertips. So where the hell was he?

The answer was simple. Somewhere no photographic lens might snoop.

Not in a cave, a mud hut or even a bunker, DeWitt would bet. He was holed up in posh digs with all the luxuries his billions could buy. Still, someday Busby would get the urge to step outside and feel the sun or a freshening breeze on his face. Maybe a spy camera passing overhead would snap his appearance and forward the location to the Bureau.

A camera or a human asset. There were people looking for Busby, too.

Some of them were on government payrolls, domestic or foreign. Others had been given the word of a bounty on Busby that hadn't been shared with the general public. That had been DeWitt's choice. When monetary rewards were announced publicly, they generated not only multitudes of false leads but also, in cases with geopolitical weight, like an attempt to kill an American president, active disinformation.

Stories that would be disseminated to lead investigators *away* from their target.

Doing everything he could at the office, DeWitt tried other methods in the few hours he got to spend at home, on the days he got to go home. A Buddhist, he meditated on his situation, hoping to open his mind to a consciousness that transcended words and thoughts. So far, enlightenment had eluded him as persistently as Busby had.

When meditation didn't work, he tried distraction, and he had a doozy. Who killed Senator Howard Hurlbert? The successful effort to take the life of a U.S. senator was considered to be almost as important as the foiled attempt to kill a president. More so by some people in the current shrill partisan times. In any event, the murder of Senator Hurlbert was a federal crime, and on whose desk did the investigation land?

His. If he came up roses on both cases, nabbing Busby and Hurlbert's killer, he'd be the most famous G-man since Melvin Purvis, the special agent who tracked down Baby Face Nelson, Pretty Boy Floyd and John Dillinger. Of course, Purvis had run afoul of his boss, J. Edgar Hoover and wound up dying by a self-inflicted gunshot wound, possibly accidental.

If DeWitt swung and missed on both cases, he didn't see becoming suicidal, but his career with the FBI would certainly be kaput.

Not that such an outcome would necessarily be a bad thing.

If the director kept dumping ten-ton cases on him, one after another, he might even —

Answer his ringing phone again.

A United States Park Police officer had been put through to him. She said her name was Tara Lang. She told DeWitt, "We've got a body out here at the C&O Canal National Historical Park you need to look at."

"A homicide in a national park? Wouldn't that be your case?" DeWitt asked.

He silently prayed that it would.

"You'd think so, yeah. But we've also got a lady out here who thinks the … well, they're more like remains than a body. Anyway, she thinks it's her brother, and he had diplomatic status with the Jordanian Embassy."

"Bahir Ben Kalil?"

The name had come immediately to DeWitt's mind. The Jordanians had been greatly upset about the disappearance of their ambassador's personal physician. Absent the attempt on the president's life and the murder of a U.S. senator, the case would have gotten a higher priority.

"Bingo," Lang said. "That's the name the lady gave us."

The park cop was right.

The murder of a foreign diplomat was an FBI case.

One more burden for him to bear, apparently.

### The National Mall — Washington, DC

While the average District resident would have felt that Saturday morning had grown progressively more raw and chill, two other members of the capital's diplomatic community thought it was fine weather for a walk. Rikkard Heikkinen and his wife Ruta represented the commercial and cultural interests of the Republic of Finland at its Washington embassy. They both came from the Sami people who herded reindeer above the Arctic Circle.

Forced to accommodate increasing Western incursion and assimilation, some among the Sami thought it wise to send their children to government schools, the better to learn how to protect the Samis' interests. Many of those children did just that. Others, however, fell prey to a form of seduction with parallels in other places: How you gonna keep 'em up in the Arctic once they've seen Helsinki?

For Rikkard and Ruta, even their nation's capital wasn't enough. They graduated at the top of their university class, got married and joined the Ministry for Foreign Affairs. During their twenty-five-year careers, they'd been posted, always together, in Cairo, New Delhi, Berlin, Buenos Aires and now Washington.

Approaching the time when they'd be able to retire on generous pensions, they decided to go for a walk on the National Mall on what they considered a fine spring morning. Though they'd left the Arctic as teenagers, a thousand generations of Sami blood and genes insulated them against a temperature hovering just above freezing. A sweater and a nylon shell were all each of them needed to keep warm.

The question the two Finns discussed as they walked was where they should spend their retirement years. Ruta wanted a place that was both scenic and peaceful where she might embark on a long-planned writing career. She wanted to do spy novels as told from the point of view of a Finnish diplomat. That was fine with Rikkard. He wanted a quiet and picturesque home, too, where he might begin to paint majestic landscapes. The point of contention was whether their new home should be sited in a temperate or a tropical climate.

They were so caught up in debating the merits of median temperatures and relative humidity that they almost tripped over Jordan Gilford's ballistically riddled, bloodied and ruined body. Ruta, with a keener nose, smelled something wrong, and pulled them aside at the last moment. They stopped and stared at the corpse, both of them struck dumb.

Up to that point, they'd considered the possibility of settling somewhere in the United States. That notion was instantly quashed. As if experiencing a shared epiphany, they resolved the matter by deciding they'd live in Vancouver for half the year and Pape'ete the other half. The Canadians and the French Polynesians were both more peaceful people than Americans.

Then they called 911.

A Metro police patrol unit was the first to arrive in less than a minute.

Two uniformed officers approached the Finns on the run with weapons drawn.

The senior cop called in the dead body found on the Mall.

"The vic's been chewed up. Looks like he caught a burst. Yeah, an automatic weapon, definitely."

In short order, the scene was flooded with cops, their vehicles and tools.

The U.S. Park Police showed up. They had jurisdiction for the body on the Mall.

The Metro cops found Abel Mays' dead body in his green Toyota SUV parked on Madison Drive. They recovered the weapon he'd used to kill his victims.

Rikkard and Ruta Heikkinen presented their diplomatic credentials to assure they would  be treated respectfully, and both the federal and local cops knew the drill. Diplomats got the kid glove routine: please and thank you, yes, sir and yes, ma'am.

Even so, the cops requested the couple wait around for the time being.

Until people above their pay-grade arrived to talk with them.

They agreed, but Rikkard turned away from the body.

He wanted none of his paintings to have an air of Edvard Munch about them.

Ruta, on the other hand, paid close attention to the crime scene activity.

An idea for her first novel was already forming in her mind.

### *McGill Investigations, Inc. — Georgetown*

Roger Michaelson sat alone in McGill's outer office, a cup of coffee in his hand that was every bit as good as any he'd ever had at Starbucks. McGill had hurried out, taking his Secret Service bodyguard with him. He'd barely paused long enough to tell Michaelson he didn't have any time to talk, but someone would be along to speak with him shortly.

A friendly little guy who told him he was the building's owner did appear in a matter of seconds, introduced himself as Dikki Missirian and asked, "May I bring you something either warm or cool to drink, Senator?"

Michaelson said thanks and went with the coffee.

"A pastry perhaps?" Dikki inquired.

Michaelson was tempted but he was trying to get back in shape.

"No, thanks. The coffee will be fine. Black."

That was just what he got and quickly. Now, though, he'd been waiting about five minutes. A thought occurred to him: It might be interesting to look through McGill's files. See what the SOB was up to these days. Only he was sure that McGill would keep his files under lock and key, probably had concealed cameras watching the premises, too.

The guy was no fool; he couldn't let himself forget that.

If he did something stupid like trying to snoop and got caught, McGill would never help him — and it was galling enough to have to ask him for help as it was. Maybe the whole thing was a setup. McGill and his bodyguard were someplace nearby watching to see what he did. Hoping to disappoint them, he just finished his coffee and got up to leave.

Repressing the desire to wave a single-finger salute to the four corners of the room.

Before he could exit, the door opened and a tall blonde entered.

They'd never met but Michaelson had seen photos of Margaret Sweeney.

McGill's former partner with the cops in Chicago and Winnetka.

The current co-owner of McGill's PI firm.

She looked him up and down and extended her hand. "You good on the coffee," she asked, "or would you like more?"

"I'm good."

Sweetie nodded. "Let's go into Jim's office and talk."

"You can speak for McGill?"

Sweetie smiled. "I speak for myself; Jim goes along more often than not."

She went into McGill's office and left it to Michaelson to decide what he wanted to do. He followed. Took one of the guest chairs and looked at the woman sitting behind McGill's desk. She seemed perfectly at ease. That told Michaelson something.

The woman had good reason to be sure of herself.

"You know the problem I'm having, Ms. Sweeney?"

"The FBI is looking at you as a possible party to a plan to kill the president. Is there anything else?"

"That's enough. Just the fact I'm under suspicion makes my wife jump every time she hears a loud noise. The job I got doing commentary for WorldWide News is on hold, though they're being decent enough to pay me. People I used to serve with in Congress won't talk to me, and I can't blame them. Who wants to pal around with someone who might be a traitor? In short, my life has gone to hell."

"So you came to Jim for help?" Sweetie asked.

"Yes. I know you can't prove a negative, that I wasn't involved in the plan to kill the president. But McGill can find out who really did it. For all the trouble I've had with him, and despite the beating he gave me —"

Sweetie said, "You nicked him up pretty good, too."

Michaelson offered a genuine smile. "Kind of you to tell me that. Anyway, I respect the work he's done. He's a hell of an investigator, and he's the one guy I can see who can keep the FBI from pushing him out of an investigation. I want him to find out who set me up to be the patsy and who really was involved in the plot to kill the president."

"He might be able to do all that," Sweetie agreed, "but Jim told me he's not going to work for you. He doesn't have it in him to work for someone who despises his wife."

Michaelson offered a rueful smile and shook his head.

"There was another reason I came to him. I wanted to ask him to tell the president that despite all the bad blood there is between us I'd never do anything to hurt her, especially knowing how she suffered after losing her first husband. I see how my wife is suffering right now; what the president went through had to be far worse."

Sweetie stared at Michaelson. She saw no sign of duplicity. The guy was baring his heart.

"I can call the president for you," she said.

"*You* can do that?"

"Sure, Patti and I are buds. Do you believe in redemption, Senator?"

"I'm hoping for it. That's pretty much all I've got left."

"I'll take your case," Sweetie told him.

"You can do that, too? It won't cause trouble for you to butt up against the FBI?"

"I'll play it straight with the Bureau. Keep them apprised of what I'm doing. And the president really is my friend. The people in power know that." Sweetie picked up the phone. "I'll call her secretary, Edwina Byington, ask when I might have a moment to relay your message."

Michaelson watched, still half-suspecting a practical joke was being played on him.

"Edwina, this is Margaret Sweeney. Do you think the president might spare a minute or two in the next couple of days to speak with me?"

If the woman was pulling a fast one, Michaelson thought, she was one heck of an actress.

Then he saw Margaret Sweeney's face undergo an amazing transformation. It became hard and fierce, but still allowed room for tears to form in her eyes. Nobody was that good an actress. For a dizzying moment, Michaelson wondered if someone had succeeded in killing the president.

"I understand," Sweetie said. "Yes, of course."

As she put the phone down, Michaelson asked, "What's wrong?"

Sweetie told him the news she'd just heard, about the massacre at the Winstead School.

"You'll have to wait a while for me to give the president your message."

But she reconfirmed that she'd take his case.

# CHAPTER 4

## FirePower America — Falls Church, Virginia

A uric Ludwig, the most militant pro-gun advocate in the country, almost swooned.

"You're sure?" he whispered into his phone.

Hearing an affirmative answer, he bunched his free hand into a fist and smiled.

On Ludwig, the expression had all the warmth of a snake about to devour a hatchling.

He listened another moment and nodded, as if the caller could see him. "Yes, of course, you'll get your usual money. For news like this, there will even be a bonus."

Ludwig immediately had second thoughts about his generosity. People should do their work for the agreed upon compensation. Maybe he could make the bonus just a token amount. No, that would make him look cheap and ungrateful. Word would get around and the move would be counterproductive.

"Tell you what," he told the caller, "I'll double your usual amount. How's that?"

The caller thought that was terrific. Ludwig ended the call on that high note.

He decided to look at the bonus as an investment.

The caller had been a Metro PD uniformed officer, calling

from the crime scene on the National Mall. Abel Mays, the shooter at the Winstead School, had been found dead. He'd killed one more person, true, but Mays had been *shot* to death in his car by ... who?

The cops didn't know yet.

At least, his cop didn't.

FirePower America, needing to stay on top of any mass shooting that happened in the country, not only monitored police communications. It recruited cops as confidential informants, men and women below the rank of sergeant, who belonged to hunting clubs or attended gun shows. Any cop who was a card-carrying member of Firepower America was the first choice for recruitment.

Their task was simple: give the organization the first word on any multiple-victim shooting.

For the help they provided, the tipster cops received $500 per month. The payments weren't made in cash, they didn't come in unmarked envelopes, they weren't left inside of newspapers at the cop's favorite diner. Payment was made by check and each cop got an IRS 1099 tax statement at the end of the year.

FirePower America made it clear to their "associate officers" that it was their responsibility to declare all the income they received.

The stated reason for those officers receiving any compensation at all from FirePower America was to provide police-community dialogues about criminal threats in the locales where they served and to update concerned citizens regarding the legal use of their firearms.

The police appearances took place once a month at breakfasts in the banquet rooms of good but not deluxe hotels paid for by FirePower America. Anybody with an FA membership card was welcome. Hot food, warm feelings, gun talk and gales of laughter were the usual menu items.

Good times were had by all.

No mentions were ever made, and nothing was ever written down, about the cops giving Auric Ludwig, and nobody else, the heads-up about the gun crimes that might affect his lobbying efforts.

So Ludwig got advance notice that Abel Mays had been shot to death.

It was news that fulfilled his fondest wish: A good guy with a gun had stopped a bad guy with a gun. The CEO of FirePower America was going to run with that for all it was worth. The only problem was, as he'd later find out, he ran too fast, overplayed his hand. Badly.

People who thought they had the world by the tail never saw their comeuppance coming.

### Connecticut Avenue NW — Washington, DC

That same Saturday morning, Ellie Booker, independent news producer with a first-look deal at WorldWide News, also got a big jump on the competition when Charlotte Mays — Abel Mays' wife — walked into her office suite that morning. Ellie had a five-room layout: her office, one for her freelancers, a reception area, an interview room and an editing bay.

Hugh Collier, the CEO of WWN, picked up Ellie's rent on the suite.

It was a perk stipulated in their latest contract.

The network also covered the fees for Ellie's freelancers.

The soft drinks and snacks consumed at the office, too.

So Ellie felt unconstrained by budgetary concerns when she offered Charlotte Mays something to drink or nosh on while they talked.

"A Diet Pepsi, if that's okay," Charlotte said.

Ellie looked at Ivy, her receptionist. She got a nod.

"We can do that for you, sure."

She waited for Ivy to return and then close the door to Ellie's office behind her.

"We good now?" Ellie asked.

Her guest nodded. Sipped. Put the glass of soda down on a coaster.

Charlotte had spoken to Ellie earlier that morning, the call having been forwarded by an alert staffer at WWN's Washington bureau. The woman had told Ellie she was afraid her husband was going to do something terrible at the Winstead School. She'd been so worried, she'd called the Metro Police, but she'd gotten the feeling the cops hadn't taken her seriously.

Ellie had quickly assessed the story elements: a threat of possible violence, a school for the children of wealth and police indifference. It wasn't a close call. She asked Mrs. Mays to come right over. Ivy had met and paid for Charlotte's taxi at the curb.

Now, sitting with the woman in her office, Ellie asked, "Why do you think your husband might do something violent, Mrs. Mays?"

"Because last night he locked himself in our apartment's bathroom and said he was either going to kill himself or everyone who'd wronged him."

The answer was simple and compelling. Ellie called for a pause right then.

She took the woman into her interview room, had her videographer set up his camera and repeated the question. Got the same answer. "What did you do next, Mrs. Mays?"

"Quiet as I could, I took my daughter, Doreen, to the far end of our place and called the police. I spoke quietly, but I know the 911 lady heard me because I gave her the message twice and she repeated my address back to me. She asked me to wait right where I was. I told her I'd stay as long as I could."

"How long did you stay?" Ellie asked.

"Just short of thirteen minutes."

"Why that length of time?"

"Because I was afraid if I let it get to thirteen minutes, that'd be so unlucky Doreen and I would die."

"And the police didn't respond in that time?"

"No, and Doreen and I waited outside, downstairs in the building's doorway, for another five minutes. They didn't come then either. My sister came in her car and we went to her house."

"Why do you think your husband might act violently against

the Winstead School?"

Charlotte Mays' face tightened with anger. "He's a physical education teacher and the head football coach at Southeast High School here in the District, and he had his two best players, two freshmen, taken from him by Winstead … again."

"What do you mean by taken?" Ellie asked.

The videographer knew to keep the camera on Charlotte then.

"I mean, what they do at Winstead is scout the best players in the public schools, check their grades, too, to make sure they can read and write, and then offer them scholarships to their fancy, rich school."

"Who were the players Winstead took from Coach Mays and Southeast?"

"Jarius Niles and Ricky Mitchell."

"And what did you mean by saying Winstead had taken Coach Mays' best players again?" Ellie asked.

"Just exactly that. Well, the last time it was only one player, but he was the best of them all, Harold Walker. Nowadays, they call him —"

"Hal Walker," Ellie said.

She didn't follow high school athletics, but she paid attention to top-dollar sports stars. They were often grist for her scandal mill, and Hal Walker, she knew, was about to sign his name to a multi-million dollar NFL contract and accompanying megabucks endorsement deals.

"See, you know who Harold is. Winstead took him from my Abel, too."

Ellie knew she'd be pissed having a valuable asset like that filched from her.

Maintaining journalistic objectivity, though, she limited herself to asking, "How do you think your husband might harm himself or anyone else?"

"He bought a —"

A loud knock at the door drew a sharp look from Ellie.

Interviews were never supposed to be interrupted. Ivy stepped into the room anyway. The videographer stilled his camera. The receptionist hurried over to Ellie and whispered directly into her ear. Ellie directed a look at Ivy: *Are you sure?* Ivy nodded, and left.

Ellie looked at the videographer and bobbed her head. The camera rolled.

"I'm sorry, Mrs. Mays. You were saying."

"My husband bought a gun, one of those gangster things like you see in the movies. The ones that can shoot up a storm."

Ellie waited a beat before saying, "I'm sorry to tell you, Mrs. Mays, that your husband followed up on his threat this morning at the Winstead School."

Charlotte Mays' face crumpled. Her eyes filled with tears.

"He killed those two boys and the coaches?"

"The coaches and *more* than two boys, yes."

The distraught woman shook her head. "That's not right." She took a note out of her purse. "I took this when I left home. It says right here who he was mad at. Just the two boys, the coaches. Look, he says right here what he wanted to do."

Ellie knew the moment called for her silence.

Charlotte Mays extended the note in front of her like a plea.

She said, "Didn't the police *ever* come?"

Ellie took the note and shook her head.

"I don't think so. I'm sorry to tell you your husband has also been killed."

Later, as Ellie was about to go on the air at WWN with her interview of Charlotte Mays, word came in that Abel Mays' last victim was Jordan Gilford, the famous whistle-blower. That point was added to Ellie's report.

### Georgetown University — Washington, DC

Abbie McGill had tears in her eyes. She told her father, "This is horrible, Dad. These idiots are shooting up every classroom in the country. Elementary schools, high schools, colleges: Nobody is safe."

His child was safe, McGill thought. For the moment, that was what mattered most to him. There were Secret Service agents outside her dorm room door, on the roof and at the entrances to the building. Anyone making an attempt on his child's life —

"It's embarrassing, too, how safe I am compared to everyone else." A thought occurred to Abbie that brought a look of alarm to her face.

"What is it?" McGill asked, concerned now that he might have overlooked something.

"Kenny and Caitie and Mom, are they safe, too? What about Lars?"

Abbie's siblings, mother and step-dad.

McGill told her, "Kenny and Caitie have added Secret Service protection; the Evanston PD is looking out for your mom and Lars."

For a breath, Abbie looked relieved and then she began to sob.

McGill took her in his arms.

Abbie looked up and told him through her tears, "Too bad those kids and coaches at Winstead didn't have a Secret Service detail, huh? Maybe we should have half the country standing guard over the other half at all times."

It was the blackest joke McGill had ever heard.

He couldn't bring himself to smile, but it didn't matter because Abbie pressed her face back into his chest and resumed weeping. He held her until she exhausted herself. Then they sat side by side on her bed and called his ex, Carolyn, back in Evanston, Illinois and Patti at the White House. Both mother and step-mother were profoundly relieved to hear that Abbie was all right, and to talk with her.

McGill told both women he'd be in touch again soon.

Then he asked his daughter, "You want to spend the night with Patti and me?"

She kissed his cheek and shook her head.

Dried her eyes with the back of a wrist and did her best to look brave.

"Give Patti my love, but I'm staying right here where I belong. I'm going to spend time with my friends and teachers, and I'm going to the chapel and pray ..." Abbie's words stuck in her throat for a moment, but she fought off a return of tears. "Pray for those people who aren't as lucky as me and died today. You're okay with that, aren't you, Dad?"

McGill stood up. Abbie got to her feet next to him. They embraced for a long moment.

"I'm okay with any choice you make."

He knew Abbie would be safe with the Secret Service to protect her.

Even so, he would have been more comfortable if she'd spent the night under the White House roof.

Still, she was a young woman now and he had to respect her choices.

Abbie bussed him again and they said goodbye.

Hearing his daughter tell him of her intent to go the campus chapel, and Georgetown University being a Jesuit institution, made McGill think there was someone he should see.

Father Inigo de Loyola, the renegade priest and sometimes guerrilla, who lived under the staircase in Dikki Missirian's other office building.

### The Oval Office — The White House

After speaking with Abbie McGill, Patricia Grant's heart settled back into her chest from the spot in her throat where it had been lodged. With that switch, her mind shifted gears from stepmother to president. She instructed Edwina Byington to summon the attorney general.

Galia Mindel, sitting opposite the president, watched the transformation.

It never ceased to amaze the chief of staff how many demands could be placed on one person. Or how the president could compartmentalize her thinking. All the while excelling at the variety of tasks demanded of her.

The president was scribbling a note to herself when she stopped to look up.

"What is it, Galia? Why are you staring at me?"

"I was just thinking, Madam President, that you are severely underpaid."

For a moment, the president was nonplussed. The she broke out laughing. Even slapped her desk.

"Thank you, Galia. I needed that. But I don't think Congress is about to vote me a raise."

"No, ma'am."

"Did you call your sons after you heard the news about the Winstead School?"

"I did," Galia said. "Everyone is well. My grandchildren will be spending the remainder of the day at home."

"We can't allow things to continue this way," the president said. "Too much innocent blood has been spilled for too long. It has to stop."

"We might have pressed the issue sooner, ma'am."

The president's expression turned rueful. "You're right, I should have done so."

"You have some ideas in mind, Madam President, ones that won't require Congressional approval?"

"I do." But she made Galia wait to hear them until Attorney General Michael Jaworsky arrived. In the meantime, she went back to writing the note she'd started earlier.

### Q Street NW — Georgetown

Father Inigo de Loyola, namesake of the founder of the Society of Jesus, priest without current assignment, provider of food to the hungry and former man at arms in Central American wars, lived in one of the richest neighborhoods in Washington, DC, albeit quite humbly. His decision to tuck himself in to sleep one night behind the building where McGill had his offices led him to help foil an attempt to smear the good name of the president's henchman.

In this way, he and McGill had become friends.

And Dikki Missirian had offered de Loyola the space under his staircase.

Becoming the first commercial landlord in town to offer his tenants a complimentary confessor. No sin too large to purge. Penance within everyone's reach.

Although not a Catholic, Dikki took great comfort in his conversations with de Loyola.

McGill was happy to find the priest in his tiny room with the steeply slanted roof.

"I haven't come at a bad time, have I, Father?"

De Loyola shook his head.

McGill had never seen the priest wear anything but thrift-shop clothing, never mind a Roman collar. De Loyola had a mane of silver hair and a thick beard of the same color. His brows and eyes were dark brown. His skin struck a warm chromatic compromise between his light and dark features. McGill often saw the priest as a lordly thespian playing the part of a pauper. Only there wasn't an inauthentic whisker on the man.

De Loyola understood at a glance that McGill came to him bearing a burden.

"Your heart is heavy, my son."

"It is, Father."

"You have sinned?"

"Not yet, not that I know of, but the day isn't over."

The priest grinned, but he inquired, "The president is well?"

"I'm sure her heart is heavier than mine."

He told the priest of the school shooting.

"*Madre de Dios.*" De Loyola pressed his palms together and closed his eyes ... but before he began to pray, he opened one eye and looked at McGill. "You have an idea, my son? How you and I might fight this evil? This is why you came to see me?"

"I do and it is, Father."

De Loyola opened his other eye and gave McGill his attention. McGill told the priest his plan.

"The simplicity is breathtaking," de Loyola said, "and completely in line with church teaching. Nonetheless, I will take it to a pastor who will be completely simpatico. We will present the diocese with an *hecho realizado*. A *fait accompli*, should you prefer the French. If the cardinal should quibble, however, I will take the matter to Francesco himself."

That's right, McGill thought, the new pope was also a Jesuit.

If de Loyola needed more clout than that to help him get an audience, maybe Patti could put a word into the ear of the papal nuncio to the United States.

"Is there anything else I might do to help?" the priest asked.

McGill shook his head. "I have to see a client, Father. Tell her I was too late to save her husband's life."

### *The Oval Office — The White House*

Attorney General Jaworsky entered the Oval Office, took one look at the president and her chief of staff and asked, "Are we here today to make history, Madam President?"

Patricia Darden Grant said, "I hope so, Michael. Please have a seat."

Jaworsky sat and asked, "Should I have the solicitor general warming up in the bullpen?"

The solicitor general was the attorney who represented the federal government in cases brought before the Supreme Court; two out of three cases decided on merit by the court each year involved the federal government. Given that ratio, the solicitor general always had to be ready to enter the game. Still, it was useful to advise him what might be coming his way.

The president said, "You may brief him after we conclude our discussion. You've heard about the shooting at the Winstead School?"

"I have. Yet another tragedy." A thought occurred to Jaworsky.

"If I may ask, Madam President, have you heard who the shooter's last victim was?"

Both the president and chief of staff looked puzzled. The president asked, "Are you saying the last person at the school or was there someone else somewhere else?"

Jaworsky said, "The last shooting took place on the National Mall. FBI Director Haskins called me with the news."

The attorney general filled in the details, including the fact that Abel Mays, himself, had been shot by an unknown person. This was clearly news in the Oval Office. More surprising, Jaworsky made a connection between the shooting of Jordan Gilford and James J. McGill.

He said, "Mrs. Zara Gilford told the U.S attorney who worked with Mr. Gilford on his whistle-blowing cases that she feared for her husband's life. She said her suspicions were intuitive and she didn't know whether the FBI would be able to make anything of them, but she was going to plead her case to Mr. McGill."

The president digested that and said, "Jim went into the office this morning. That's a sometimes thing for a Saturday. He didn't say who the client was or what she might want."

"Mr. McGill probably didn't know," Jaworsky said.

"Probably not," the president agreed. "I ordinarily don't ask about his cases, but ..." She kept her own counsel about what might come next between husband and wife. "Michael, you're familiar with Project Exile, I assume."

The attorney general nodded. "It's a federal program started in Richmond, Virginia, back in 1997, I believe. It shifted prosecution of illegal gun possession offenses from state to federal courts so that harsher mandatory minimum sentences might be imposed."

Galia added, "Harsher sentences to be served at federal prisons far from the offenders home town." The chief of staff hadn't been briefed on the president's idea and was curious to know where it might go.

"That's right," the president said. "Harsh sentences and remote confinement. The idea was also tried out in Atlanta and upstate

New York, if I remember right. The first thing I want you to do, Michael, is contact all fifty state attorneys general and tell them the federal government will be taking Project Exile nationwide. We'll want to prosecute all the offenders they can send us, starting with their worst cases."

The attorney general frowned.

The president took a breath before saying, "This is where you can tell me, Michael, all of the problems I'll be creating for you."

"Very well, Madam President. If you want to lock up a lot of criminals, you'll need a lot of money, people and other resources to do it. More judges, prosecutors, marshals, prison space, correctional officers, prison support staff, buses, planes and other means of transport for the prisoners."

The president shrugged. "So we'll make the country safer and create a jobs program. Win-win. I'll do the political lift, and skin the opposition alive, if there is any opposition."

Galia said, "There's always political opposition."

The president raised an eyebrow. "Street gangs, bank robbers and stickup men have their own lobbyists now, do they?"

"No, ma'am," Galia said.

"Do career criminals constitute a major voting bloc, a constituency that might sway Congress?"

Galia shook her head, still looking concerned.

"I know what's bothering you, Galia," the president said. "If the criminals we lock up are disproportionately African-American or Hispanic, some people will cry foul or worse. Well, our answer to that will be it's not black or brown skin that concerns us, it's how much red blood we keep from being spilled that matters. To be fair, of course, we'll be just as tough on white offenders." The president turned to the attorney general. "Your turn, Michael. Any other problems?"

"If you can manage your end, Madam President, I'll manage mine."

"Good, because that was the easy part."

Galia and Jaworsky exchanged a look.

"Michael," the president said, "please refresh me on the legal concept of depraved indifference."

The attorney general sensed where the president was going, but he did as he was asked. "If a defendant's conduct is so wanton, so deficient in a moral sense of concern, so lacking in regard for the lives of others and so blameworthy, it warrants the same criminal liability as that which the law imposes upon a person who intentionally causes a crime. Depraved indifference focuses on the risk created by the defendant's conduct, not the actual resulting injury or death."

Galia's heart sank. She thought the president meant to go after the gun companies. Given the current laws on the books and the makeup of the present Congress, that would be an *impossible* political lift.

But Galia had presumed the wrong target.

The president said, "Michael, I want you to hold a press conference. You'll be just one of the faces of this administration condemning the shooting at the Winstead School, but you'll be among the most important. You're going to announce that any parent, parents or other custodial adult who owns a gun that is used by a child or children to kill anyone else will be charged with … well, when is murder a federal crime?"

The president was taking Jaworsky back to his days as a law professor. "Murder is a federal crime if it takes place on federal property or involves crossing state lines or substantially affects interstate commerce or national security. Acts of terrorism might fall under either of those latter two considerations. A killing that doesn't occur in any state, say on a U.S.-flagged commercial vessel in international waters, would also be a federal offense. Jurisdiction for a homicide that occurs within the borders of a single state and does not involve the crossing of state lines belongs to the courts of the state where the crime occurred."

The president thought about that. "There have been times when a state has either failed to prosecute a homicide or took a case to court and a biased jury returned a dishonest not guilty verdict, and the federal government still prosecuted the offender, right?"

"Not for murder," the attorney general said, "but for a violation of civil rights. In those cases, though, the unlawful act was based on a discriminatory motivation: color, race, ethnicity or religion. Discrimination based sexuality and gender identity is being considered by Congress but has yet to pass."

Both Galia and Jaworsky saw the president was disappointed that she didn't have the latitude she hoped for … but then she had another thought.

She asked the attorney general, "If a person bought a gun manufactured in one state and used it to commit a crime in another state, could that be considered a crossing of state lines?"

Jaworsky nodded. "Yes, it could — if a judge and the Supreme Court says so."

"We'll see what we can get. We'll prosecute adults for depraved indifference whenever we have the jurisdiction. Whenever a weapon should have been locked up but a young person used it to shoot or kill someone."

Galia hated the necessity but felt compelled to play the devil's advocate. "Madam President, you'll be accused of inflicting additional pain on already suffering parents."

The president's response was forged steel. "To hell with their pain. It takes a distant second place to the grief the parents of shooting victims feel. Nobody has a right to behave so recklessly they become responsible for the deaths of other people. That's the essence of depraved indifference, isn't it, Michael?"

"That's it exactly, Madam President."

"All right, then. Mr. Attorney General, please reach out to your counterparts in the states and do so quickly. When you have their replies, let me know. We'll announce to the public that we intend to take every criminal in the country who's carrying a gun illegally off our streets."

Galia was about to comment again, but she decided to wait for the moment.

The president said, "I'll be the one to tell everyone who keeps firearms in their homes that they'd better be kept beyond the reach of angry or disturbed children or spouses. If they don't and there's a shooting using their guns, they'll be going to prison."

The president sighed and slumped in her chair.

"You were about to say something, Galia. What was it?"

"You've made a good start, Madam President. Congress can't interfere with the ideas you've proposed, but some of the state attorneys general might refuse to turn their gun cases over to the federal courts."

The president offered her a bleak smile. "Then we'll just have to accuse them of being soft on crime, won't we? Let them see how their constituencies like that."

Both the chief of staff and attorney general liked that irony.

But Patricia Grant knew Galia Mindel more than well enough to understand she still had something else to say, a political calculation she'd made. She just didn't want to voice it in front of Michael Jaworsky. Fair enough. In Washington, knowledge was as often a liability as an asset.

Hence the notion of plausible deniability.

"Thank you, both," the president said, "I'd like some time to myself now."

Once she was alone, Patricia Grant wept. Abbie McGill was safe, true, but the president had friends who were the parents of Winstead students. She wasn't sure if any of their sons were on the football team. She prayed they weren't. Even that supplication made her wince. Was she asking for tragedy to be visited on someone else? The death of strangers would be less hurtful?

Goddamnit, she hated these killings.

She damned herself, too, for lacking the power to stop them.

Neither a nationalized Project Exile nor prosecutions for depraved indifference would have stopped Abel Mays' rampage that day. There had to be something more she could do.

The obligation to find some answers forced the president to dry her tears.

She picked up her phone. "Edwina, please call Mr. McGill. Tell him I need to see him as soon as possible."

# CHAPTER 5

## *The National Mall — Washington, DC*

M etro Homicide Detectives Marvin Meeker and Big Mike
Walker, aka Beemer, felt as relieved as any DC cop when they
heard Abel Mays had been found dead. That was, until they arrived
at the National Mall and learned that they'd caught a whodunnit.
Namely, who the hell had put two rounds in Mays' head?

Given the magnitude of Mays' crimes, finding his killer would
be worth a bump in both rank and pay. Failing to find the killer,
that wouldn't be so good. They'd be left counting the days until
they retired.

That and fearing how they'd be remembered if the crime was
never solved.

The two chumps who had struck out on their biggest case.

Of course, whodunnits, by their nature, were the cases that
most often went unsolved.

Meeker had once showed Beemer a quote from an NYPD
detective in the *New York Times*. "The big secret of detective work
is you've got to get somebody else to tell you what happened."

"Man's got that right," Beemer had said.

Only it was considered bad form simply to give your phone
number to the media, ask the public for help and sit back and wait
for results. What the public expected from a couple of big-city dicks

like Meeker and Beemer, knocking down 75K each with health benefits and a pension plan, was the stuff they saw on *Law & Order*. Maybe *Sherlock*, if they watched PBS.

The Metro detectives made a pro forma attempt to pass off the case to the FBI, who'd taken over federal responsibility from the Park Police, but the special agent handling the feds' end of things wasn't having it. Special Agent Abra Benjamin told them, "The stiff on the Mall is ours; the stiff in the car is yours."

She pointed out jurisdiction depended on geography. The Mall was federal land, Madison Drive was city property.

Meeker said, "Yeah, but you look at how Mays got shot, the killer had to be standing on the curb not the street. Means he was on federal land when he committed the crime."

"Only we don't have the killer," Benjamin said. "If we did, I'd be happy to arrest him. All we've got — and by we I mean you — is the stiff. On city property."

The two cops stared at the fed. That wasn't a chore. She had shiny dark brown hair, eyes to match, high cheek bones and a nice nose and mouth. Looked like she worked out, all lean and taut. They weren't going to intimidate her or wear her down.

Beemer asked the decisive question. "You're a lawyer, right?"

"A lawyer with a gun, a badge and all sorts of other tricks up my sleeve."

So Meeker and Beemer knew they weren't going to win any arguments.

The detectives walked back to the green Toyota SUV in which Abel Mays had died and still reposed. They did the only thing left to them. They called their boss, Captain Rockelle Bullard, told her she needed to get down to the crime scene. Her superior intelligence and vast experience were required.

Never mentioning the fact that if anyone got stuck with the blame for not solving the case it would be her. If Meeker and Beemer were mentioned at all, it would only be as footnotes. Besides, they did better following orders than figuring out whodunnits for themselves.

Rockelle Bullard knew all that. She showed up anyway.

### Third Street, NW — Washington, DC

McGill and Deke rode the elevator up to Zara Gilford's top-floor condo in the high-rise security building. Leo waited downstairs in McGill's Chevy. The elevator car had four cameras set in its ceiling. Deke looked up at each of them.

"Nowhere to hide in here," he said.

McGill had noticed the cameras, too, not that they were conspicuous.

"Yeah, must be a comfort," he said without feeling. "What about the National Mall? What kind of cameras does it have?"

When Deke was slow to answer, McGill gave him a look.

"You know, don't you?"

"Of course, I know," Deke said.

The elevator doors opened and the two of them stepped out into a vestibule.

"You're debating with yourself whether to tell me?" McGill asked.

Deke said, "The cameras were installed by the Park Police before Holly G's second inauguration. They can be touchy about the release of their security measures."

"But they had to share with the Secret Service."

"Of course."

"Metro PD?" McGill asked.

"I'm not sure about that."

"Probably not, given the way feds look down at local cops."

That kind of snub still stuck in McGill's craw, six years after his retirement from public service. Deke, a fed most of his working life, only shrugged.

Before the conversation could go any further, a tearful, red-faced Zara Gilford opened the door to her condo. She sobbed and fell into McGill's arms. No question she'd already heard the news of her husband's death. Spared McGill the burden of delivering it.

Didn't keep him from second-guessing himself for a minute, the way he'd handled things that morning.

Zara had told him the route her husband ran.

Had given him the man's running pace.

He could have found Gilford with no trouble. Intercepted him on his run. Been on hand with a gun on his hip and had Deke there with his Uzi, too. If Abel Mays or anyone else had tried to shoot Gilford, they could have saved him.

That probably hadn't occurred to Zara yet. She invited McGill and Deke inside.

How had she known they'd come to call?

Karl Vasek in the lobby could have called up.

Just as likely, another security camera spotted them getting off the elevator.

### The Oval Office — The White House

Galia Mindel, on her way out of the Oval Office with the attorney general, had told Edwina Byington, the president's secretary, to hold all calls to the president and allow no visitors for fifteen minutes.

"The president's going to need a little time to herself," Galia said.

"Of course. Will fifteen minutes be enough?"

Twenty-four hours would have been better, Galia thought, but no president had the luxury of that kind of respite anymore. Fifteen minutes of downtime was pushing it. Still, Galia said, "Use your best judgment, Edwina."

The Oval Office was soundproof. Short of the president taking a sledgehammer to the walls, Edwina would be unable to hear what went on inside. She certainly wouldn't be able to tell whether the president was weeping. Still, Galia believed that Edwina was attuned to the president in a way that far surpassed digital technology.

Galia thought of the faculty as dedicated empathy.

Something she felt she also had.

Edwina asked, "And if Mr. McGill should arrive? The president had me place a call to him."

"Mr. McGill is always the exception."

The chief of staff's rivalry with McGill had … mellowed. There were still times they contended for Patricia Grant's time and attention like two kids wanting Mom to hear what they had to say first. But each had come to a better understanding of and respect for the other's needs. Right now, though, it was the president's needs that mattered.

And McGill would be the best one to offer support.

After Galia retreated to her own office, Edwina waited the directed fifteen minutes and more, trying to anticipate what the president's requirements would be when the world and its terrors and torments were permitted to return. Edwina allowed herself a personal moment to feel sorrow for the bloodshed at the Winstead School. Those poor young people, dying so horribly, and their families whose suffering had just begun. It was heartbreaking.

Yet again.

Doing her best to remain silent, Edwina dabbed the tears that fell from her eyes.

Where was the comfort to be found at such a moment?

The answer came quickly to Edwina. Who had comforted the president in the hours after the death of her first husband, Andrew Hudson Grant? Margaret Sweeney had. Margaret had held the president in her arms, prayed with her, soothed her.

Margaret had also called that morning asking for a moment with the president.

That had to be more than coincidence, Edwina thought.

A higher power had to be at work.

At the twenty-minute mark, Edwina was about to buzz the president when she received a call. Putnam Shady, Margaret Sweeney's husband, was on the line. He said he had important news for the president.

Edwina told him she'd see what she could do.

Then she buzzed the president. "Ma'am, Margaret Sweeney

called earlier this morning, asking for a moment. Is there a time you'd like me to schedule her?"

After a brief pause, the president replied, "Please ask her to come in as soon as she's able. If she arrives before Mr. McGill, send her right in."

"Yes, ma'am."

Edwina got back to Mr. Shady. Told him the president was pressed for time, but Margaret Sweeney would be seeing her that day. If he wanted to send word with her …

Putnam Shady said he'd talk with his wife, and thanked Edwina.

The president's secretary hung up her phone.

Feeling she'd done her best for now.

### C &O Canal National Historical Park

As a place for a body dump, Byron DeWitt thought the crevasse in Billy Goat Trail A was no match for Jimmy Hoffa's portal to a parallel universe. Still, if you had little time and few means to dispose of a body, it was a pretty good choice. You had to climb a three-story cliff face and then ignore signs telling you to stay on the posted path to find it. That would buy a killer a fair amount of time before anyone noticed the corpse he had deposited.

Far more than twenty-four hours, from the state of decomposition DeWitt observed.

The old saw that a murder had to be solved within a day of its commission or it never would be was BS. Still, the puzzle got harder to piece together with the passage of time. A body's wrapper of flesh was more disposable than cellophane. Other soft tissue became a party platter for bugs, birds and other scavengers. Mother Nature, using rain, wind and solar radiation, was one heck of a cleaning lady when it came to disposing of physical evidence.

Even so, DeWitt could see from where he stood, maybe twenty feet above the skeletal remnants, poking out of the tatters that had probably been a custom-made suit, that the victim had suffered a blow to the back of his head that had visibly fractured his skull.

The deputy director turned to the two women standing nearby. A ring of cops and assorted crime scene personnel stood behind them.

Tara Lang looked like she might once have been a middle school principal. Fortyish, dark-haired, a little soft around the edges but strong, as demonstrated by her handshake. Her manner with DeWitt was collegial rather than deferential. She was one law enforcement professional dealing with another.

More than just a cop, she was a detective in the Park Police's Major Crimes Unit.

Dr. Hasna Kalil was short and slight, topping out at Lang's shoulder. But there was nothing delicate about her features. Her brow, nose and jaw were all prominent and chiseled. She affected a Western manner of dress, wearing a beret, trench coat, black slacks, rubber soled shoes and leather gloves against the deepening chill of the day. Explaining that she was a surgeon, she hadn't offered her hand to DeWitt.

Some docs were cautious about getting the source of their livelihood squeezed.

"Dr. Kalil," DeWitt said, "what makes you think you've found your brother?"

"He was my twin." She spoke English with a French accent.

"And?"

"And I know him always, even now."

"You're speaking of intuition?"

"Yes, and observation."

"So you've looked at the remains. Can you tell me specifically what you noticed?"

Dr. Kalil took a moment to collect herself. "Bahir and I were fraternal twins, of course, but our physical similarities in height, weight and skeletal structure are ... were remarkable. Looking at him now ..."

Dr. Kalil needed another moment. She turned away from DeWitt and Lang.

They waited in silence for her to look back at them.

She turned back and resumed, speaking in a professional tone. "To my eye, if you were to reposition the skeletal remains to approximate a normal standing position, I would expect them to measure within a centimeter of my own height. If you were to measure the circumference of the skull at the supraorbital ridge, I would expect the result to be no more than a few millimeters different from my own … making an allowance for the fracture."

DeWitt picked up on that. "Would you, as a physician, have any idea what might have caused that fracture?"

Her calm demeanor gave way to cold anger, Dr. Kalil said, "Blunt force trauma."

"Possibly from the fall into the crevasse?"

"No. Ask your specialists in tool marks what might have caused the fracture."

"You're familiar with forensic pathology?" DeWitt asked.

"Only informally. I spent two years with *Médecins Sans Frontières,* Doctors Without Borders, in Africa. I saw much brutality, clubbing and cutting. Also, I know my brother wore Pierre Cardin suits, and the rags left from that garment look familiar."

"I'm sorry for your loss," DeWitt said.

"Thank you. Please let me know when I might take my brother home for burial."

She took out a business card and wrote a phone number on the back.

"I will provide a DNA swab so you may be sure I am not just a foolish woman."

Her tone was almost accusatory, DeWitt thought, as if she thought him to be a sexist.

"No one thinks you're foolish, Doctor, but one last thing, please. How much would you say your brother weighed the last time you saw him?"

"Approximately my own weight, fifty-four kilograms."

DeWitt did the math in his head: just under one hundred and twenty pounds.

"Thank you, Doctor."

The deputy director and the detective watched her depart. One of the Park cops on hand, a woman, offered to help Dr. Kalil down the cliff face. With thanks, she declined assistance, managing the descent nimbly on her own. Both DeWitt and Lang watched closely.

"You think she learned to climb in Africa?" Lang asked.

"Could be," DeWitt said. "I know a little bit about climbing. Did some myself at Yosemite."

"California boy?"

"Yeah. Most climbers, even the ones who aren't hardcore, have strong hands. Looked to me just now like Dr. Kalil has a good grip. But she didn't want to take the chance of shaking my hand."

Lang said, "Maybe it's a cultural thing, a woman not touching a man."

"She refused help from a female officer. Did she shake your hand, Detective?"

"No. Maybe she doesn't like Americans. Is that what you're thinking?"

"It might be something recent, owing to the death of her brother here in the U.S. But, yeah, that's what I was thinking."

"Might be more than that, too," Lang said.

DeWitt gave her a look, got the feeling she was toying with him.

"What do you know, Detective?"

"First thing I have to tell you, I'm politically incorrect as hell."

"In any particular direction?"

"Yeah. I leave the presumption of innocence to juries. If I get a bad vibe from someone, I make a presumption of guilt, and I don't worry if the guy — or the woman — isn't the same color or nationality as me."

"Go on," DeWitt said.

"My family is all about public service. My two brothers served in Iraq, I'm in the Park Police and my sister … we call her the Lang of Langley."

"CIA."

"Yeah. I took one look at Dr. Kalil and the first impression I got wasn't grief, it was a strong yen for revenge. So I excused myself for a minute and called my sister."

"She talked out of school?" DeWitt asked.

"No, she's too smart for that. But after I gave her Dr. Kalil's name and description there was this silence, like she was running the woman through her computer. Then she says there's really nothing she can tell me. Not that she *has* nothing, she just can't tell me."

DeWitt nodded. "She let you read between the lines without spilling any beans."

"Right. So maybe you can talk to Langley. Just in case they forget to call the FBI."

"I will."

"You asked Dr. Kalil about her brother's weight to get a fix on how strong the person who dumped him had to be, right?"

DeWitt nodded. "Lugging a hundred and twenty pounds up a thirty-foot climb takes some doing."

"More than just strong hands," Lang said.

"Yeah," DeWitt agreed, sounding unhappy.

With all the other demands he had on his time, this was the last thing he needed.

A deepening mystery, with CIA involvement.

### Third Street, NW — Washington, DC

Zara Gilford, a prisoner of the manners she'd been taught as a child, offered McGill and Deke coffee. They both declined. After a quick look around the condo, Deke went to stand guard outside the front door. McGill sat on a love-seat next to Zara.

"I'm so sorry, Zara. How did you hear the news?"

"A woman called."

"A reporter?"

"She said she was an independent television producer."

The only person McGill knew who fit that description came

immediately to mind.

"Ellie Booker?"

"Yes, that's her. She said she was sorry to have to tell me the news but —"

Zara began to cry once more. McGill gave her the clean handkerchief he always carried. His father had taught him to do that. Said you never knew when you might need one. Especially if you were a cop. Or even a private investigator.

McGill waited as Zara dried her eyes.

She said, "Ms. Booker told me my phone was about to start ringing off the hook. She suggested I turn it off, and not answer my doorbell either. She told me the media could be relentless. She also said I might consider checking into a hotel under another name, but not my maiden name because that would be too easy to find."

Sorrow weighed heavily on Zara's face. "Jordan is dead and now I have to become a fugitive."

"No, you don't, I'll —"

"I called Karl downstairs. Told him not to let anyone but you come up."

"Good, and your phone is off?"

"Yes."

"But Karl can reach you through an internal line?"

"Yes."

McGill felt compelled to express his personal regret. He told her he should have looked for Jordan along his running path instead of waiting for him. He might well have changed the outcome.

Zara shook her head and gently squeezed his hand.

"No, no. That would have put Jordan into a big grump. He said his run was the one place he could clear his head and just feel the joy of being alive."

McGill persisted. "I might have be able to stop Abel Mays."

Zara released McGill's hand and studied his face.

"You don't think that madman was responsible for Jordan's death, do you?"

McGill frowned. "My Secret Service agent, the fellow who was just here with us, got the details from the police. Jordan was shot with Mays' gun, that's the initial understanding the police have. They'll do tests to make sure, but —"

Zara held up a hand, cutting him off.

She was doing some serious thinking of her own. She reached a conclusion and shook her head. "No, I can't believe that, regardless of what the police think."

"Why not?" McGill asked.

"Even a professional killer couldn't be so callous that he'd kill young boys and their football coaches as a subterfuge for killing Jordan. And he certainly wouldn't allow himself to be killed as part of a cover-up. There has to be some other explanation."

McGill said, "Ellie Booker told you all the details of what happened this morning?"

"She did. She also said she wouldn't bother me with another call. She told me if I wanted to have someone I could trust to tell my story the right way, I could call her. She gave me her number."

Couldn't get much slicker than that, McGill thought. Cut off the source of your story from the competition and then sucker her into calling you.

Zara saw the look of doubt on McGill's face and told him, "She also mentioned your name as a character reference. She said you'd come to her for help once."

McGill had. He couldn't deny that.

"Did you tell Ms. Booker I was working for you?"

"I did, but what do you mean you *were* working for me?"

"You came to me to prevent what happened. Now, it's a police matter."

"But you said the police think this Abel Mays person killed Jordan."

"That's my understanding."

"Do you agree with them?"

McGill replayed Zara's conjecture in his mind. Would a contract killer slaughter several innocent people as a cover for his own crime? No. Not that it was a matter of morality. It was a question of efficiency. Pros kept things simple. Besides that, the initial reports Deke had received described Abel Mays as a high school football coach who had no criminal record before that morning.

If Mays had held a grudge against the boys and coaches he'd killed, that would be a deranged but comprehensible reason for what he'd done. But why would he gun down Jordan Gilford? Because he'd found homicide to be so much fun? McGill couldn't believe that.

Wouldn't have bought the idea if someone else had tried to sell it to him.

Then there was Mays, himself, getting killed.

That was too neat. So what the hell could the answer be?

Zara cut through his reverie with a statement that rang true to his ear.

"Mr. McGill, someone else killed Jordan or had it done."

The woman was right, he thought.

"What I'd like you to do now is find that person or those people."

He was impressed by both Zara's logic and her resolve.

She continued, "Ms. Booker told me if I need help with anything, she'll either do it herself or find someone who can. She also said if you could use her help, she'd be happy to help you."

Zara was telling him she wasn't about to let go.

He had to let her know, now, if he would help.

McGill said, "I'll do everything I can for you, Zara."

### The Oval Office — The White House

Edwina Byington buzzed the president. Despite the chief of staff's instructions to allow only Mr. McGill in to see the president, Edwina had to make a judgment call. After all, through her own scheming, she'd already seen to it that Margaret Sweeney had been given access and would be arriving any moment now. That being the case … in for a penny, in for a pound.

Maybe distracting the president with other business would be good for her.

"Madam President, Majority Leader Bergen is here. He had an appointment, but he says if the time isn't right, he can —"

"No, Edwina, please send Dick in."

"Mr. Majority Leader." Edwina gestured him to the door and he stepped inside.

Dick Bergen, the senior senator from Illinois, had become the acting majority leader when his predecessor John Wexford of Michigan had suffered a stroke, became permanently incapacitated and had to resign his seat. Bergen was elected to the post by his Democratic colleagues in a race with his close friend from New York, Senator David Schumann.

Outside handicappers had thought Schumann would win, but the senator from New York made it a practice of appearing on television at every opportunity. His colleagues feared that electing him leader would make him so ubiquitous a public presence he'd soon wear out his welcome, and by extension that of his party.

Bergen, an eloquent, low-key personality who did most of his work behind the scenes, was judged to be a better bet. The president had remained publicly neutral, but Galia Mindel had dropped hints as to whom she personally preferred. The chief of staff also had led the senators to believe she didn't want another New Yorker to have a position of great influence on the president.

So Schumann was more than a little peeved with Galia but bore the president no ill will.

Bergen shook the hand the president extended to him and took the seat he was offered.

"This is truly a terrible day, Madam President. I won't take more than a few minutes of your time."

Patricia Grant nodded and said, "You've come to tell me about the proposed twenty-eighth amendment to the Constitution. So are we going to elect future presidents by a direct vote of the people? If so, are we going to do so the way I've proposed?"

Having won reelection by a single electoral vote that had been pledged to another candidate, Patricia Grant's return to office so outraged her opponents they were determined that it would never happen again. A new amendment to the Constitution would abolish the Electoral College and provide for direct elections of the president and vice president.

The president didn't object, but she wanted Election Day either to be shifted to a Saturday or if kept on a Tuesday to have the day declared a national holiday. At Galia's urging she also wanted everyone who cast a vote to be given a one hundred dollar credit against any federal income tax payment due. Both measures were conceived to increase voter participation.

Dick Bergen's presence that morning was to inform her how the final vote in both houses of Congress was shaping up. Doing so on a Saturday morning would attract as little media attention as possible. Now, with the media focused on the mass murder at the Winstead School, it was even more likely to go unnoticed.

That was the calculation the president made when she decided to keep her appointment with the majority leader.

"I'll bring the amendment up for a vote in the Senate first thing Monday morning," Bergen said. "It will have language to provide the hundred-dollar tax credit to all voters, but Election Day will remain on a Tuesday to keep that tradition alive."

"Election Day will become a national holiday?"

"Yes, ma'am. In the Senate's rendering of the amendment."

"You think the House Republicans will fight offering the American people an extra paid day off work once every four years?"

Bergen sighed. "I'm afraid the situation in the House is worse than that."

The president momentarily closed her eyes, put a hand over her mouth.

As if she didn't want to voice the thought that came to mind.

Looking at the majority leader, she said, "I had fervently hoped Peter Profitt would never be so foolish."

Peter Profitt, Republican of North Carolina, being the Speaker of the House.

"I thought he would be more cautious as well," Bergen said.

"That's still a possibility. My friends in the House say the amendment would pass if Profitt called for a vote on it. Then we'd have to go to a committee to resolve the differences between the two versions."

"The Republicans won't accept Election Day becoming a national holiday?" the president asked.

"No, ma'am, they won't. Their counterproposal is to enshrine Election Day in the Constitution as the only day a vote for president may be cast, and it must be cast in person."

"That's absurd. They might as well write an amendment saying they're the only party allowed to govern."

"I've heard that notion has also been advanced, if only in jest."

"But with sincere longing," the president added.

"Yes, ma'am. Senate leadership has thought the House Republicans would yield on their Election Day-only voting position if we forgo the idea of making it a national holiday and forget about the tax credits."

The president shook her head both in chagrin and to refute the idea for a political swap.

"All they want to do is minimize voter turnout. I won't have that."

That was when Bergen got to the point of bringing up the subject the president had found unspeakable.

"It might not come to that, at least not soon. My friends tell me it looks like Philip Brock has won the Speaker over to his idea of calling a constitutional convention."

The president cursed. "Goddamnit. I thought Profitt was holding out to have the convention in Raleigh, and was getting no traction on that. That's what Galia told me."

Bergen told her, "That was his position, but Brock persuaded him of two things. First, Pennsylvania would never go along with petitioning Congress to hold the convention, if it were to be held in North Carolina. Second, the convention would be more historically significant if it were held in the same place where the original one was convened."

"Philadelphia," the president said.

"Exactly. What sold Profitt, I'm told, was Brock's political calculation of how to make the convention a reality. All the Southern and Mountain West states are already on board. So Profitt's influence in those region isn't needed. The idea of going to Philadelphia, to walk in the footsteps of the Founders, is what Brock said it will take to bring the one additional swing state that will be needed after Pennsylvania joins the roll call."

The president asked, "Which swing state, Dick?" Before he could reply, she held up a hand and answered her own question. "Ohio."

"Yes, ma'am."

"And the nominal reason to hold a convention at all is to add an amendment to the Constitution that Congress has all but written right now."

"Except for deciding how many people each party would like to see turn out on Election Day," the majority leader said.

The president looked at the senator. She knew he was a Georgetown University scholar, political science as an undergraduate and then law school. He knew, as well as she did, what the true implications of a constitutional convention would be.

"That first convention in Philadelphia," she said, "you remember what its original purpose was, don't you, Dick?"

"Yes, ma'am. The stated purpose was to amend the Articles of Confederation, the body of laws that governed the country up to that point."

"Right. An improvement, an update of existing law. And what happened?"

"The Articles of Confederation were scrapped and a whole new constitution, our constitution, was written."

"And what might happen if a second convention were to be convened?"

The majority leader said, "Anything could happen, Madam President. We might wake up one day and discover we are living in a completely different country."

Exactly what the president feared.

Before she could dwell on the awful possibilities, Edwina

buzzed her.

"Madam President, Mr. McGill and Margaret Sweeney are here to see you."

### The National Mall — Washington, DC

Captain Rockelle Bullard of Metro Homicide watched the crime scene search officer back out of Abel Mays' Toyota SUV holding a small object with a pair of forceps. The officer, Hoshi Takei, was female and Japanese-American. For Rockelle's money, you couldn't beat a woman when it came to cleaning up a mess men had made, and Officer Takei was tops in the department. She dropped the object into a plastic evidence bag and showed it to Rockelle.

The chief medical examiner's people had taken Abel Mays' body to the Consolidated Forensic Laboratory for examination, making Officer Takei's search of the vehicle less revolting, though she had proven at several crime scenes to have an exceptionally strong stomach.

She told Rockelle, "Got a nine millimeter slug, Captain. Not badly deformed. Man must've had a thin skull, I guess. The job would've gotten done even if he'd had a hard head, though."

"The man got shot twice," Detective Meeker said. "Where's the other round?"

Takei said, "Just getting started, Detective. Give me a minute or two, okay?"

Rockelle said, "You take all the time you need."

She gestured Meeker and his partner Beemer away from the SUV.

They stepped across Madison Drive, placing themselves firmly on city property.

Rockelle told her detectives, "I spoke with Special Agent Benjamin. We exchanged business cards."

The detectives had seen that but they didn't comment.

The captain continued, "Turns out the victim on the Mall was one Jordan Gilford, a relatively new but senior employee in the Inspector General's Office at the Department of Defense. The homicide of a federal employee of his standing would be the FBI's case no matter where his body was found."

"Don't see why they wouldn't want to take Mays from us, too, that being the case," Meeker said.

"If Mays hadn't killed all those people at the Winstead School, they probably would. The way things stand now, both sides have distinct responsibilities, and we all have to be good about sharing any information that overlaps from one side to the other."

"You tell the FBI that?" Beemer asked.

A thin smile formed on Rockelle's face. "Special Agent Benjamin and I came to an understanding: If you want to get, you have to give."

The two detectives nodded. They trusted the captain, but not the feds. They'd wait to see how the share-and-share-alike idea would work out.

Rockelle saw Meeker and Beemer's doubt, but didn't call them on it. She was still trying to think of ways to leverage cooperation, if she felt the FBI was holding back on her. Not having any bright ideas at the moment, she moved on to other matters.

She asked her detectives, "In light of Officer Takei finding that nine millimeter slug, what questions should we be asking ourselves?"

Meeker and Beemer didn't object to the captain's use of the Socratic method.

They were used to it. Liked it, in fact. It helped them to grasp things they already knew subconsciously but hadn't yet called to mind.

"The guy who shot Mays used a semi-auto," Meeker said. "So where are the shell casings?"

Beemer followed, "If the guy who shot Mays was a vigilante, someone who knew what he did at the Winstead School, would he have picked up the casings or just beat feet as fast as he could?"

Meeker continued, "If the shooter was a pro who knew enough

to clean up after himself, why would he bother to shoot Mays at all? He's got a kid at Winstead?"

Both Rockelle and Beemer knew Meeker's last question was a joke.

Still, once mentioned, the idea would have to be looked into.

Rockelle posed the next question. "Could Mr. Mays have done something we don't know about that got someone to put a hit on him?"

The three of them thought about that.

Meeker spoke first. "Mays didn't go crazy all at once."

Beemer nodded. "Guys like him, they build up to their blow-ups."

Rockelle summed up. "So it's possible Mays might've gotten on the bad side of somebody who could've killed him or had him killed. Maybe someone who knows a professional killer. If that was the case, it's a real shame the pro didn't get to Mays before he cut loose."

Beemer's phone chirped, indicating the receipt of a text. He saw it came from his wife. The message said: Watch this! A video file was attached.

He showed the text to Rockelle.

The captain said, "Tell me she doesn't send you things just for laughs."

Beemer shook his head.

"Go ahead then, play it."

Meeker and Rockelle huddled on either side of Beemer and watched.

They saw Ellie Booker interview Charlotte Mays. Learned how Mrs. Mays had called the Metro Police Department to warn that her husband might start killing people. Ellie held up a list of the people Mays had targeted.

"Jesus God Almighty," Rockelle said. "Who screwed this thing up?"

The video of Ellie Booker said she was waiting for the police to pick up Mays' note.

"Go get it," she told Meeker and Beemer.

The detectives nodded, but before they left Meeker said, "Something like this happens, you gotta wonder what else could go wrong."

As if in response, Rockelle's ring tone sounded.

She took out her phone and looked at the caller ID.

Saw James J. McGill was calling.

# CHAPTER 6

*The Oval Office — The White House*

M cGill and Sweetie stepped into the Oval Office. Sweetie hugged the president first and then McGill embraced his wife. A moment later, the intercom buzzed and Edwina said, "Madam President, Chief of Staff Mindel would like to know if her presence might be helpful."

All three people in the Oval Office had to smile.

Galia's intelligence network had alerted her not only to McGill's arrival at the White House but also to the fact that Sweetie was with him. Had McGill come to see the president by himself, Galia would have had to stand back and trust that the discussion would be a personal one, and if anything was said that she needed to know, the president would tell her. With Sweetie in the picture, the question of spousal privilege went out the window.

Not that the president couldn't take anyone she chose into her confidence.

But if she did, Galia hoped she'd be advised of that person's status.

The president looked at McGill and Sweetie and got two nods.

She stepped over to her desk and told Edwina, "Please tell Galia to come in."

The chief of staff entered and shook hands with both McGill

and Sweetie. McGill took a seat on one of the room's two facing sofas. Sweetie and Galia sat opposite him. The president stayed on her feet. She said, "Things are going to change. The common wisdom is that nothing can be done about these intolerable shootings because Congress won't allow it. We're going to change all that."

A look of doubt appeared on Galia's face.

The president didn't miss it. "You don't think we can, Galia?"

The chief of staff took and released a deep breath before answering. "I'm at a loss here, Madam President. Are we going to go around Congress? If so, are we going to use private citizens like Mr. McGill and Ms. Sweeney in the effort?"

"Private citizens are going to drive the effort, Galia. Ultimately, Congress will have to decide whether to catch up or look completely irrelevant."

Galia persisted. "If any plan you conceive should threaten Congress's sense of prerogative or frighten members about the hold they have on their seats, they could pass legislation seeking to curtail your efforts. Then what?"

"Then I'll veto that legislation, and you will lead the charge to see that my veto is not overridden," the president said.

Galia saw McGill and Sweetie bob their heads.

Easy for them to agree. She'd be the one who —

In a moment of epiphany, Galia saw exactly what her role would be. Other than being a good mother and grandmother to her family, she couldn't imagine doing anything more noble. Her role might be to act as the person who saved the lives of other people's children.

James J. McGill had been the man who'd saved her life, and he'd shrugged that off.

But Galia had seen the profound gratitude her sons felt for McGill.

If she could do something to prevent the deaths of innocents, she might play the stoic, too.

But she was certain she'd always feel better about herself from that point forward.

"I'd be honored to accept any role you have for me, Madam President."

With that much settled, the president sat next to McGill and took his hand.

It was clear to him Patti had a thought in mind for him, too.

He figured he'd have to step up at least as readily as Galia had.

"Do you remember telling me, Jim, about a paper you wrote while working on your master's degree at DePaul?"

McGill said, "We've talked about a few of my scholarly efforts, but I think the paper you have in mind is 'A Cop's-Eye View of the Second Amendment.'"

"That's the one. I thought you made some excellent points."

Sweetie asked, "Was that the paper where you said cops — but no one else — should have guns?"

"We both felt that way, as I remember," McGill told her.

"Probably wouldn't get much of an argument from any street cop," she agreed.

"How do you feel now, Jim?" the president asked.

"Probably some allowances should be made for private investigators," McGill said.

Sighing, he told the three women in the room about the death of Jordan Gilford and how he was kicking himself for not seeking out Gilford before he was killed.

"My thought was," McGill said, "that if Deke and I had shown up — armed — Jordan Gilford would be alive right now."

The president squeezed his hand, trying to soothe the guilt McGill was feeling.

Still, she asked, "Where do you draw the line, Jim? Who should have a firearm and who shouldn't?"

"I think that's the Supreme Court's job, but if I remember that paper I wrote so long ago, I said the requirements for owning a gun should be that a person is mentally balanced, morally mature and demonstrably law-abiding. The proof for that last part would, at a minimum, be the absence of an arrest record for causing physical harm to an innocent person."

"Do you still stand by those standards?" the president asked.

"I do, but having seen more of life, I'd add an arrest record for psychological intimidation, say stalking or cyber-bullying, to the list of disqualifications for gun ownership. That kind of predatory behavior is a stepping stone to shedding blood."

Sweetie and Galia nodded.

"Those things are terrorism writ small," the chief of staff said.

"I think they're also indicative of mental defects."

"Moral ones, too," Sweetie added.

"What was the summary point of that paper, Jim?" the president asked.

McGill remembered it word for word. "If a situation stinks and you want to change it, you can't let people hold their noses."

Then he told Patti, Galia and Sweetie how he'd acted on his own advice.

When he went to see Father Inigo de Loyola that morning.

He wasn't sure whether he'd get pushback from either Patti or Galia.

From the smile on her face, he knew Sweetie was with him.

Patti showed her approval by bussing him on the cheek. "I think that's brilliant, and I'd be delighted to have the pope weigh in with us. Please tell Father de Loyola to let me know if he needs any help on that front."

McGill nodded. He turned to look at Galia. See what she thought.

"I think it's a good start," the chief of staff said, "but the approach should be more ecumenical. I'll talk to the people I know at the National Conference of Christians and Jews. The Council on American-Islamic Relations, too. Spread the word across the whole spectrum of faiths and denominations in the country."

"Now, I'd like to tell you what I have in mind for you, Jim," the president said. "I know you've been very careful about not publicly involving yourself in either policy and politics. You've made things easier for me — and Galia — by being so discreet."

"Made it easier for myself, too," McGill said.

"Yes, you have, but what I'd like you to do now is go on television and discuss all the points you made in 'Cop's-Eye View" with the American people watching. Will you do that?"

"Sure," McGill said without hesitation, but everyone in the room could see a thought had entered his mind.

"What is it, Jim?" the president asked.

"May I choose the interviewer?"

"You're thinking of a specific person?" the president asked.

McGill told her who and why he thought it was a good idea.

Galia kept a straight face when she heard McGill's idea, but she came to have a new appreciation for the man's growing political shrewdness. She wished she'd thought of the idea. Then she had a spin-off on it, and shared it with the others.

The president and Sweetie beamed in approval.

McGill nodded and came back with an additional move of his own.

Everybody liked that, too.

"All right," the president said, "we're off to a good start. We'll make all these things public as soon as we can."

Sweetie raised her hand like a schoolgirl.

"Yes, Margaret?"

"I have a couple messages on other topics to pass along on, if that's all right."

"Of course," the president said.

"The first is, Senator Roger Michaelson came to see us at McGill Investigations this morning. He's looking for help clearing his name as regards the would-be attempt on your life at Inspiration Hall. Jim said he wouldn't help him; I said I would."

McGill kept his face impassive. Galia frowned.

Sweetie looked directly at the president. "Senator Michaelson also asked me to send along a personal message: Despite all your political and personal differences, he said, he would never do anything to cause you physical harm. He said he could imagine how deeply you must have suffered when you lost Mr. Grant and he wouldn't be a party to anything like that."

The president was silent for a moment before asking, "Do you believe him, Margaret?"

"Yes."

"Very well. What's your other message?"

"Putnam asked me to tell you that a new political party is being formed and will be announced soon. Darren Drucker is funding it, and Putnam is organizing it."

The president and Galia exchanged a look. The chief of staff clearly wanted to ask questions about the new party, but the president forestalled Galia with a raised hand.

Patricia Grant said, "Given Mr. Drucker's political leaning and Putnam's work with him on the ShareAmerica lobby, I take it the new party will be progressive in its outlook."

Sweetie nodded. "'Democrats with backbones.' That's how Putnam put it."

"This is in response to True South?"

"Yes."

"And the new party's name is?"

"Cool Blue."

McGill said, "Wasn't there a cigarette with that name?"

"Putnam mentioned that, too, but this cool is spelled with a 'c' not a 'k.' Putnam checked and there's no copyright infringement issue."

The president gave Galia a nod and she asked, "When does this new party intend to slate its first candidates?"

"This year, 2014. That's all I know." Turning back to the president, Sweetie added, "Putnam said he'll give you a complete heads-up at any time that's convenient."

"Galia, please find a time early next week."

"Yes, ma'am."

"Is there anything else?" the president asked.

There was nothing from Galia or Sweetie.

McGill looked at Patti and said, "Let's set aside some time tonight to talk."

After leaving the Oval Office, McGill put in a call to Captain Rockelle Bullard.

### South China Sea — 4.89°N, 114.94°E

The motor yacht *Shining Dawn* approached its home port of Bandar Seri Begawan, the capital of the Islamic Sultanate of Brunei. The vessel was 180 meters — 590 feet — long, the largest privately owned yacht in the world. It could cross oceans and reach a top speed of thirty knots. For all its blue-water prowess, though, Shining Dawn could also cruise at leisure in translucent shallows. On top of its versatile seaworthiness, the yacht was also one of the most luxurious vessels afloat.

Tyler Busby had traded all three of his lesser but still magnificent yachts for a five-year lease on the *Shining Dawn*. The agreement also provided that Busby's new nautical haven be fully crewed, fueled and provisioned for the term of the lease. Best of all, the deal was verbal, sealed with a handshake.

There was no record of the transaction anywhere, except in the minds of its principals.

The one item not included in the bargain was the matter of companionship. Sailing around the world, no matter how great the creature comforts, would be a lonely business for Busby without someone to share his conversations, meals and bed. Fortunately, the cruise director — the dragon lady, really — of the *Shining Dawn*, Ah-lam, was able to solve the problem.

"If you'd like one lady or many," she told Busby, "all you have to do is ask. I will see that they are provided."

The offer to procure was cost-plus. That didn't bother Busby. He had fortunes stashed away in Singapore and Hong Kong. Asia was the new hiding place for piles of illicit cash.

"Are there any limitations? Ethnically, I mean," Busby said.

"No limitations. Skin color, eye color, hair color: You may choose what you like."

"Does that include you?"

Busby was good at reading people. He knew that Ah-lam had the heart of an assassin. Her main purpose aboard was to keep an eye on him for the yacht's owner. Not let him do anything that might bring embarrassment to or cause inconvenience for that esteemed gentleman. Ah-lam, Busby was sure, would throw him overboard in the middle of the night and the middle of the ocean, if so ordered. And do so without blinking.

Even so, she was a delight to the eye, her every chromosome arranged just so.

He doubted there were a dozen like her in all of China's vast population.

Ah-lam told him, "Just once. And you have to save me for last."

So far, after cruising for more than two months, he been able to heed that advice. Ah-lam had provided him with half-a-dozen courtesans: an Australian, a Kiwi, two Japanese, a Korean and a Chinese. All of them were intelligent, able conversationalists and cover girl beautiful. They all brought focus, energy, technique and even whimsical ingenuity to their couplings with him.

The problem was, no matter how hard they all tried, they couldn't quite hide the fact they were terrified every moment they were aboard. Having given themselves over to a man wealthy enough to own — or lease — such a yacht and a woman so clearly merciless as Ah-lam, they knew their lives continued as a matter of whim. Busby never harbored an ill thought for any of them, had gone to great lengths to be gentle, courtly even. Except when the throes of passion demanded more.

Still, the most sincere kiss he received from each of them was the moment before they boarded the yacht's helicopter to be flown back to the port from which they could make their way home with far more money than they'd ever earned before.

Ah-lam, as astute as she was watchful, understood the problem.

She came to Busby as he idled in the main salon watching what he called a spring training game of American baseball. Ah-lam neither understood the sport nor had any intention of learning it. Busby paused the broadcast when she appeared. He looked at her —

"Now is not the time," she said, knowing exactly what he was thinking. "I'm sorry the Chinese girl disappointed you. I told her she had nothing to fear."

"And yet you frightened her so much she couldn't help but tremble as she slept."

"You were a part of her terror," Ah-lam said.

Busby couldn't deny he'd had that effect on women before. Some of them had thought they'd had their hooks in him. Their only worries were that they'd lose the small fortunes he'd have to settle on them for even the briefest of marriages. As a younger man, he'd done just that three times. Now, he made do, in the fashion of game show hosts, by offering lovely parting gifts.

Other women, though, exhibited true existential angst.

As if his fortune would insulate him even from murder.

Well, truth was, he had tried to help kill a president.

So maybe people, not just women, were right to be scared of him.

He looked at Ah-lam and asked, "Do you have an answer for my problem?"

"I have two answers."

"And they are?"

"My sisters. They know no fear. They resemble me closely. You will like them."

Busby felt better than any time since he'd fled the United States.

"I'll certainly be happy to give them a try. How soon can they be here?"

"They are en route to Bandar Seri Begawan right now. Do you need anything else?"

Busby turned back to the baseball game. Brought the television back to life.

"Yes, I'd like some hot dogs. Nathan's Famous Hot Dogs."

The kind they served at Yankee Stadium.

What was a baseball game without hot dogs? He ordered a Budweiser, too.

You had to find little bits of home wherever you could.

## *The National Mall — Washington DC*

"Nice to see you again, Captain Bullard," McGill said.

"Despite the circumstances."

"Yes, despite that."

Any site that had been bloodied by a mass killing weighed heavily on its community.

A machine-gunning on the National Mall brought the tragedy home to the whole country.

Jordan Gilford's body had been taken away by that time. There were crime scene techs still present and some residual patrol officers to keep away the looky-loos, as they like to say out West. The chill, overcast weather kept that number to a handful. Captain Bullard shivered in the cold, herself.

"Would you like to talk in my car?" McGill asked.

Rockelle looked at McGill's gleaming armored Chevy parked at the curb.

She had a city-issue car with her, not her classic '67 Impala.

"Yeah, your ride has to be a lot nicer than mine. Your friends going to keep us company?"

Meaning Deke and Leo.

"I've got no secrets to keep here, but if you'd like privacy, I'll ask them to step out."

"No, no reason they should be cold on my account."

McGill held the door for Rockelle as she slid into the back seat. That amused her. McGill got in on the other side.

He said to Rockelle, "Might not be the weather for it, but I think we have a few bottles of White House Ice Tea available, if you'd like a drink."

The captain's eyes lit up.

"Captain Yates gave me some of that; my mother and I love it."

"I think we can spare a few bottles. My compliments to you and your mother."

Leo handed Rockelle a bottle. She rolled it between her palms a moment, as if to warm it up. She opened the bottle, took a sip and then looked at McGill with a grin.

"What?" he asked.

"You are one sly man. That or you think you can buy a police captain cheap."

"I used to be a police captain."

"Yeah, and a chief, too. Now, you're married to the president. Some folks keep right on rising in the world."

"You're recently promoted, aren't you?"

Rockelle nodded.

"You keep doing good work," McGill said, "who knows where you might end up?"

Rockelle took another sip, screwed the cap back on.

"Okay," she said, "you want to tell me why we're having this little social?"

"I was hired this morning by Zara Gilford to find out who might be threatening to kill her husband, Jordan."

"Well, hell. Don't that beat all?"

"I'm very disappointed in myself, that I wasn't able to do better for Mrs. Gilford."

Rockelle bobbed her head. "I would be, too."

"Mrs. Gilford would now like me to find out who killed her husband."

"That's an FBI investigation. Why are you talking to me?"

"I'll talk to them shortly. The point is neither Mrs. Gilford nor I believe Abel Mays did it."

"Metro has its own doubts." She told McGill about the Mays' killer taking his shell casings with him. "What's that sound like to you?"

McGill stopped to think. Deke and Leo, who'd been following the conversation, turned to look at him. Clearly, they had their own ideas. Withheld them for the moment.

McGill said, "That's the mark of a pro, just the kind of guy Mrs. Gilford feared might be after her husband. Not some vigilante who happened to spot Mays and decided to grab some glory."

He waited to see if Rockelle saw where he was going.

She said, "If a hired killer was waiting to kill Mr. Gilford —"

"And knew where to find him," McGill said, thinking of another piece of the puzzle.

Rockelle continued the thread, "He'd get to the place he wanted to make the hit early. Set up, check everything out. Make sure he could do his job and get away."

The Metro captain looked at Deke and Leo.

McGill's driver said, "A pro would want the best chance to run and not get stopped. He'd be listening to a police band radio. Taking the whereabouts of local patrol units into account before he took his shot."

"How'd he know who Mays was, what he looked like?" McGill asked.

Deke said, "Mays' picture and info were all over TV. If the killer had a tablet with 4G capability —"

"He could've seen Mays' picture," Rockelle said.

"Decided he'd get tricky," McGill said. "Lay the killing off on a madman who'd already shot up a high school football team."

Everyone thought about that for a moment.

"Maybe we're trying to tie all this up too neat," Rockelle said.

McGill asked her, "Where was Mays' car parked?"

"Right here. This parking space."

Couldn't ask for more than that, McGill thought.

He looked at Deke. "You remember how we were talking about what the Park Police surveillance cameras could do?"

"Yeah," Deke replied.

"You never gave me an answer."

"I'm not supposed to do that."

"So tell Captain Bullard. She has a legitimate interest."

Rockelle leaned forward, seconding McGill's point of view.

Deke grimaced. "Yeah, she does. But I still should probably tell the FBI first."

Rockelle turned to look at McGill.

Her expression saying, "Goddamn feds, what can you do?"

McGill had an idea.

He asked Rockelle, "You get along well with Welborn Yates?"

"Sure do."

"He's a fed, too."

"Nicest one I know."

"Okay, Captain, here's what I'm proposing. I'll bring Welborn into this case. He'll be the official intermediary between Metro PD and the FBI."

"They'll go for that?"

"I have a strong feeling they will," McGill said with a straight face. "He'll keep the lines of communications open. Deke, here, will talk to Welborn about the surveillance cameras."

Deke nodded, grudgingly.

"What are you going to do?" Rockelle asked.

"The best I can for my client," he told her.

### FirePower America — Falls Church, Virginia

Auric Ludwig stood behind the lectern reading his notes in the press relations room of the Firepower America suite. In five minutes, reporters from approved media outlets would enter, sit in plush chairs and nod in approval as Ludwig explained, yet again, that guns weren't to blame for shooting deaths. It was nature's fault, maybe even God was to blame, for providing human beings with trigger fingers.

That was his private joke, of course. Never to be repeated to anyone, not even to his wife or his mistress. He often wondered, though, how far he could venture into the realm of absurdity as he deflected blame from the people who provided him with his seven-figure salary. So far, he perceived no limits.

The talking points arrayed on the lectern were all the usual ones.

Untreated mental illness — no matter that Abel Mays had never been diagnosed with any aberrant condition.

Violent popular culture — not that Mays was known to watch

any film except the ones that featured high school football games, and he was not of the generation to play video games.

Ludwig scribbled a quick note to himself. Maybe football could be blamed as a source of gun violence. That might be risky, as popular as the game was, but what the hell, you worked with the material you were given.

Before he could review the next talking point, his cell phone sounded.

Tchaikovsky's "1812 Overture," the passage with the cannons firing.

The piece usually made his heart swell, but now he was disconcerted. He'd forgotten to turn his phone off. Something he'd normally do before speaking to the press. He took his distraction as a possible warning sign and wondered if the call was bringing bad news.

He almost decided to let the call go to voice mail.

But maybe it was news he needed to know, before he said something he shouldn't.

He clicked the phone on and said, "What?"

The caller was one of his informant cops, the same one who'd given him the news that Abel Mays had been shot to death. Hearing the man's voice, he thought for a moment that he might have more good news. Turned out to be anything but.

"What?" he asked again.

This time, as he heard the reply, a band of cold steel constricted his heart.

"You're sure?"

The caller was.

Ludwig said, "Sonofabitch."

James J. McGill was poking his nose into Mays' final shooting on the Mall.

Like everyone else who lobbied in Washington, Ludwig knew who McGill was and what he did for a living. Ludwig didn't know exactly what that would mean for him, but he felt sure it would be nothing good. Worse, he was uncertain how to play McGill's involvement. How he should spin it? There was no precedent. McGill was the president's husband but he had no official status.

If Ludwig got out in front and condemned McGill before he knew what the man might do or say, he might wind up looking like a horse's ass. Damage to his own cause. He had to find out what McGill was up to fast.

Trouble was, he'd reflexively clicked off the informant's call.

Never thinking about offering compensation to the snitch.

Or what the consequences of such a snub might be.

The doors to the press relations room opened on the dot of the appointed hour. Reporters poured into the room. FirePower America controlled the only video camera in the room. Copies of the event would be edited before they were distributed. Ludwig pulled himself together and gave his usual predictable spiel. Then he got to the good part. The great part, really.

He shared the news that Abel Mays had been killed.

"By the police?" the question was shouted at him.

Ludwig shook his head. "No, not by the police. By a citizen who remains unnamed thus far. Abel Mays, a bad guy with a gun, was killed by a good guy with a gun."

The newsies were astounded by the revelation.

An armed citizen had killed a mass murderer?

When the Metro Police and the FBI heard of Ludwig's declaration, they were caught off guard, too. The circumstances of Abel Mays' death had yet to be officially released.

Auric Ludwig had been too eager. He'd gone too far.

Questions were soon raised.

How had Ludwig learned the authorities hadn't killed Mays?

Who'd given him that information?

Answers were quickly pursued.

### Wisconsin Avenue NW — Washington, DC

Roger Michaelson saw Margaret Sweeney eyeing the condo he was renting. The place cost $7,500 a month, furnished. It was far bigger than he needed, but it was what WWN had found for him when they offered him his job as a commentator, and he decided to keep it. When his wife, Wendy, was in town, about ten days a month, the condo seemed somewhat like a home.

When he was there alone, it was just a place to eat breakfast and sleep. It was comfortable. The furnishings were top end, but he didn't give a damn about brand names in anything except sportswear. When he worked out or played basketball, he liked to have the best gear he could find.

Now, watching Margaret Sweeney check the place out, he examined his Washington home with a newly critical eye. It was definitely over the top for him. Looked like it was intended for a photo shoot in some glossy coffee table magazine.

"What do you think?" he asked Sweetie, not fishing for a compliment.

"Too fancy for me," she said. "When I first got to Washington, I lived in one room in a basement."

Michaelson took that in and asked, "And now?"

"I married my landlord and moved upstairs."

Michaelson laughed. "Well, good for you."

"Good for him, too. We're adopting a young girl named Maxine. She was orphaned when my husband's brother and sister-in-law died."

"That's … I hope that's what I'd do, too, in your situation."

He gestured Sweetie to a chair and sat on the sofa opposite her.

"Was it a hard choice?" Michaelson asked. "Adopting."

Sweetie told him, "It was the only choice for both of us. I was at the White House earlier today. I gave the president your message."

"And?"

"She asked if I believed you. I said I did."

"I was being honest with you; I'll keep doing that."

Sweetie contented herself with a look that said he'd better.

"Accepting your word that you were no part of a plot to kill the president," she said, "that leaves only one alternative. Someone set you up to be a patsy. Who do you think that was?"

Michaelson reflected on the question for a moment.

"I asked myself that same thing a thousand times. Half the Senate and a majority of the House disagreed with me politically. I rubbed plenty of people the wrong way personally. After that beating McGill gave me, some other people thought they could push me around, too."

"Really?"

"Well, it wasn't exactly a prison-yard situation. More just a bump-and-jostle kind of thing, passing in a corridor or getting on and off the Senate subway."

Senators had the use of two private subway lines running between the Capitol and the Russell and Dirksen Senate Office Buildings for their convenience. No metro cards or tokens necessary. The taxpayers picked up the tab.

"Sounds kind of schoolyard," Sweetie said.

"Yeah, well, boys will be boys. But you let them get away with that crap, they'll think they can roll you on legislation, too. After I bumped back a few times, comity was restored."

"So who do you think set you up?" Sweetie said, getting back on point. "Had to be someone you didn't bump back, right?"

"The only answer that makes sense to me is Philip Brock. He's the one who mentioned me on Didi DiMarco's show, and that led to WWN signing me up. Without Brock, I wouldn't have come back to town."

Sweetie thought about that.

"Did you ever have any personal contact with Brock before he brought up your name?"

"No."

"Did you ever take the same side on a piece of legislation?"

"No."

"Were you ever members of the same organization outside of Congress?"

"No. I thought about that. What, if anything, did we have in common? The only thing was we both were elected federal officials who worked on opposite ends of the same building."

Margaret watched Michaelson closely. She didn't see any sign of intention to deceive, neither on the former senator's face nor in his words.

"What do you know about Joan Renshaw, the director of the Andrew Hudson Grant Foundation? She was the one who told the president that she'd informed you when the president would visit Inspiration Hall, the place the assassination attempt would occur."

Michaelson shook his head. "I have no recollection of meeting the woman or speaking to her. But retail politics involves a lot of grips-and-grins."

Shaking hands with strangers and smiling, often in front of a camera.

Again, Sweetie saw only honesty.

Well, that and restrained anger.

She knew she'd feel the same way if she'd been falsely accused.

"You don't believe in coincidences, do you, Senator?"

He shook his head. "Not in general and definitely not in this case."

"So what I'll have to do," Sweetie said, "is look for the connection between the two people who put you into all this trouble. Philip Brock and Joan Renshaw."

"You know the only good thing to come out of all this?" Michaelson asked.

Sweetie shook her head.

"I don't have to worry about becoming a victim of street crime these days, what with all the FBI agents watching me."

Sweetie told him, "You can bet the Secret Service is doing the same."

# CHAPTER 7

## McGill's Hideaway — The White House

Captain Welborn Yates, United States Air Force, Office of Special Investigations, was admitted into James J. McGill's private retreat within the Residence by Blessing, the head butler of the White House. McGill looked over his shoulder from the long leather sofa placed in front of the room's fireplace and waved to Welborn. The captain waved back.

He still had to fight the impulse to salute McGill.

The two of them had worked as mentor and protégé since the early days of the president's first term of office. Welborn had learned as much, and probably more, about being an investigator from McGill and Margaret Sweeney as he had at Glynco — the Federal Law Enforcement Training Center.

The other side of the coin was that Welborn, as a sworn federal agent and a military officer, could provide a legitimate front for the times when McGill, a civilian, needed to poke his nose into governmental affairs.

Beyond the professional dimension of their relationship, the two men had become friends. Welborn had gone to McGill for help after he'd heard a rumor that the president intended to promote him to the rank of major. Welborn and Celsus Crogher had done a bit of good work in helping to foil the recent conspiracy to assassinate the president. He hadn't been looking for McGill's help to lock in the promotion.

He'd told McGill he wanted to remain a captain.

"Something wrong with being rewarded for doing a great job?" McGill had asked.

Welborn hemmed and hawed a bit before confessing, "I don't want to be seen as another Alexander Haig. For one thing, I don't have his combat experience. He has to be respected for that, but —"

McGill held up a hand. He knew the story. "After Al Haig went to work for Richard Nixon in the White House, he rose from being a colonel to a four star general in four years. The only other guy who had ever done that was Dwight Eisenhower."

"Exactly," Welborn said.

"I don't think you need to worry about having stars on your shoulders, Welborn."

"I'd still feel more comfortable continuing to serve at my present rank."

"All right," McGill said. "I'll have a word with the president."

And that was that. Welborn remained a captain.

He got an earful from his wife, Kira, though, after revealing what he'd done.

She thought any chance for advancement was to be seized with both hands.

Welborn had factored that into his decision. Still felt he'd done the right thing.

"May I bring you a drink, sir?" Blessing asked Welborn.

The captain looked at McGill. He held up a bottle with a label that said State Street Pilsner. The fine print, that Welborn was able to discern with his former fighter pilot's eyesight, told him the brew originated in Geneva, Illinois. Close to Mr. McGill's hometown of Chicago, Welborn guessed.

Always good to show solidarity with the people who supported you.

"I'll have one of those, please," he said to Blessing.

"Yes, sir. Right away."

Welborn joined McGill on the sofa, leaving an appropriate distance. Blessing returned with a chilled bottle, a glass and a coaster. "Shall I pour for you, sir?"

Welborn took the bottle and said, "Thanks, but I'll manage."

"Yes, sir."

McGill told Blessing they'd call if they needed anything else.

Once the butler had left, McGill extended his bottle. Welborn tapped it with his and they both drank, not bothering about glasses. Then McGill asked, "Other than your duty weapon, do you own any firearms?"

"I do," Welborn said. "A Remington pump-action shotgun for bird hunting, a Winchester lever-action 30-30 hog-killer and a LeMat 'Grapeshot' revolver."

McGill raised an eyebrow. "Never heard of that last one."

"It's a nine-shot weapon that was the sidearm of Confederate Army officers."

"So it's a collector's piece."

"Yes, it is. Fewer than three thousand were made, and mine is a family heirloom. It's also fully functional. It's in a safe at my country home in Virginia. When Kira, the girls and I are in residence there, I keep it in my nightstand drawer."

"You've heard about the killing at the Winstead School this morning?"

"Yes." Welborn sighed and took a hit of his beer. "Kira has a friend with a son on the football team there."

McGill braced himself for bad news.

It came, but not in the way he expected.

Welborn told him, "Jack was one of the smart ones. He ran and wasn't so much as nicked by the gunfire, but he was grievously wounded all the same."

"Survivor's guilt?" McGill asked.

"More like survivor's agony."

Welborn knew all about that. He'd been the sole survivor when a car thief running a red light in a stolen vehicle killed three of his friends in the car in which they'd all been riding. Welborn had found physical recovery, peace of mind and even an existential measure of justice but the process had taken years.

He told McGill, "When Jack's parents picked him up this morning he was sobbing so hard he was shaking. Kept on at home until he wore himself out and fell asleep. Before that, he told his mother and father that he and all the other guys who had saved themselves were cowards. They'd done a shameful thing. They should have charged Abel Mays, too. He couldn't have killed them all, and the one who'd lived could have torn the guy apart with their bare hands."

McGill could understand that impulse.

But what he said was, "The parents, all of them, have been told to keep a close watch on their boys, right?"

"Kira said the counselors who came to the school advised just that. The administration is reaching out to the student body at large. The faculty and staff, too."

"The families have to secure their own firearms, if they have any," McGill said.

Welborn nodded. "I passed that word along to Kira. She didn't understand the point at first. She thought I meant the boys might try to take vengeance on some innocent third party."

"That's a possibility, too, but it's not what we're talking about."

Suicide was what they had in mind. A teenager who considered himself a coward, someone who should have been willing to risk his life the way his fallen teammates had, might take an alternative way of rejoining them. Raising the body count even higher.

"Kira passed the phone to me and I raised the point to Jack's dad. Then I went to my office and called the Winstead headmaster. Said I was calling from the White House to get through to the man. That was true, though I was acting on my own. I passed the word about gun safety along. As shaken up as the headmaster was, he couldn't honestly remember if that had been mentioned but he said he'd get the word out immediately."

Having covered the preliminaries, McGill told Welborn about

the case Zara Gilford had brought to him and how it had evolved.

"I could use your help acting as an intermediary between the Pentagon and me. Smooth out ruffled feathers, if need be," McGill said.

Welborn took a long pull on his bottle.

"Will there be a role in the actual investigation for me? I'd like to help."

McGill nodded and said, "Sure."

He extended his hand and Welborn shook it, sealing the deal.

McGill was impressed that Welborn hadn't thought to say he'd need the president's approval first. McGill didn't correct that oversight. He'd make sure to get Patti's approval.

### The President's Private Dining Room — The White House

There was precious little the chefs in the White House kitchen couldn't provide to the president and McGill on a moment's notice. Despite having a world of culinary choices, Patti went with a simple smoked trout salad and a glass of California Chardonnay. McGill made do with a corned beef on rye sandwich and a Green Line Pale Ale. It was a day to obey the imperative to sustain oneself not one for feasting.

The First Couple limited themselves to a brief recitation of grace and went without speaking as they nibbled at their spare meals. Then Patti caught McGill's eye. He saw a look there unlike any he'd seen from her. He thought it held an element of rage and perhaps a touch of madness. The combination was disturbing. Patti had always been the most rational —

"Do you want to know a secret?" she asked.

"I'm not sure," McGill said. "Will it keep me up nights?"

"It might."

"Will you be up, too, right alongside me?"

She nodded.

"Okay, then."

"For a long time, presidents have been described as the most powerful men — and now woman — in the world. Truth is, we do have enormous and powerful resources at our disposal: the military, the intelligence agencies, a national police agency in the FBI."

"Yeah?" McGill said.

"If a president were able to direct even a small portion of that combined might against —"

McGill shook his head. "Don't even let the words cross your lips."

"All right, how's this? For all the power a president possesses, she's also tied down like Gulliver by the Lilliputians. In matters of domestic policy, laws, rules and precedents constrain all but your smallest, most inconsequential movements. There are times, as president, you simply want to break free of all those bonds and seize control, do what you know is right. I doubt if there's been a president in this country's history who hasn't felt that way."

McGill pushed his chair back six inches, picked up his glass of ale and took a drink.

"Tell me something," he said. "Would you cast yourself as the first president in American history to attempt a coup? Circle tanks around the White House. Put Congress in leg irons."

The anger and irrationality fell from Patti's eyes.

"Well, if you're going to put it that way," she said.

McGill told her, "The reason neither you nor any other president has gone around the bend and tried to become king is you've all known that even making the attempt would ruin our grand experiment with democracy. How would the people ever be able to trust any candidate for president ever again?"

Patti gave her husband a weak smile. "You're pretty smart for a guy who went to a small religious college in the Midwest."

McGill laughed. "You must be thinking of Notre Dame. De-Paul has the largest enrollment of any Catholic university in the country. We have our share of first-class scholars, too, some of them quite surprising."

"You won't rat me out? Me and my delusions of grandeur."

"What happens between us stays between us."

Patti leaned over, McGill leaned in and she kissed him.

"Derivative but appreciated," she said.

"May I ask for a favor or two?" McGill said.

"Anything within my less than absolute powers."

"I need help from Welborn."

"That I can manage. He's yours as long as you need him. What else?"

"The late Jordan Gilford was known as a champion whistle-blower. He was killed not long after he hired on with the Inspector General's Office at the Pentagon. The detective in me thinks he must have made someone in the DOD or on one of the armed services committees nervous. If my investigation should lead in any of those directions —"

"Talk to Galia. Then, if necessary, come to me. Is that all?"

"For now. I'm sure something else will come up."

Patti stood, extended a hand to McGill. "Will you take me to bed and hold me close until we're sure I'm ready to lead the free world again?"

"My pleasure. You'll let me decide just how long that takes?"

"It might be all night. The idea of Congress in leg irons truly captivates me."

# CHAPTER 8

### *Old Ebbit Grill — Washington, DC, Sunday, March 9, 2014*

Sunday brunch at the restaurant a stone's throw from the White House didn't begin for the public until 8:30 a.m. After receiving a call from the White House, a private party consisting of McGill, Ellie Booker and Deke Ky was admitted at seven o'clock. The manager, the chef and two wait staffers arrived a half-hour earlier to prepare for their VIP guests.

Deke checked out the premises, let the restaurant swipe McGill's business credit card and instructed the staff to do their jobs and then give their guests plenty of room. If the guests required further attention after receiving their meals, Deke would summon a staffer. With McGill's approval, Deke allowed the request for McGill's autograph to be provided to all present. Ellie Booker also yielded her signature.

An entreaty for a photo was denied.

Ellie ordered the Buttermilk Pancakes, bacon side and large orange juice.

McGill, hungry that morning, chose the Steak and Eggs with coffee.

Service was swift, the food hot and tasty. Then McGill got down to business.

He told Ellie, "I'd like to know if you and WWN would care to have first crack at an hour-long interview with me. It would have to be recorded and aired within the next five days."

The producer stared at McGill as she chewed on her pancakes.

She swallowed, sipped some orange juice and replied, "Anything in particular you'd like to discuss? I haven't heard that you've written a book. You have something else you want to push?"

"Take one guess," McGill said.

"Yesterday's shooting."

He nodded.

"Is this something you're fronting for the Grant administration?" she asked.

"It's something the administration knows about and approves, but I got the ball rolling on my own, before I spoke with the president."

All true, McGill thought. He went to see Father de Loyola before he talked with Patti. The idea for him to do the interview was Patti's, but Ellie Booker needn't know that. It was enough that she understood his action had a presidential stamp of approval.

The longer he lived in the White House, the more devious he was becoming.

Still, a glint of skepticism registered in Ellie's eyes.

She wanted to pin down the president for whatever was about to happen.

McGill saw her doubt and said, "You don't want to do this, I'll find someone else. Be a little embarrassing for me since you were my first choice, but I'm sure one of the other networks will be interested."

"How do you know I'll even go to WWN?" she asked. "I'm an independent producer."

"You have a first-look agreement with Hugh Collier. You really think he's going to turn down a chance to air an interview with me? From what I understand, I'm considered a big get for TV people."

"You are," Ellie conceded. The president's henchman often polled higher than his wife in favorability. Of course, that was easy to do when you didn't have to take the lead on political issues. That

Joseph Flynn

and half the male members of Congress found it wise to soft-pedal any criticism of McGill, fearing he might beat the crap out of them if they got on his bad side.

That was a lingering effect of the "basketball game" McGill had played with then-Senator Roger Michaelson. That little sporting event had landed Michaelson in the hospital and had taken on the air of a cautionary myth.

Right now, McGill and Ellie were sparring about who would set the parameters for her interview with him. They both knew neither she nor Hugh Collier would forgo the opportunity McGill was offering them. Having him speak candidly, as he always did, on the shooting at the Winstead School, the ratings would absolutely …

Kill. Unfortunate characterization, but true nonetheless.

The other thing that was indisputable was McGill would get his way on pretty much any conditions he set for the interview. Ellie could try to win a point or two, but she knew she was fighting out of her weight class.

But that didn't mean she couldn't land a jab or two.

She asked "Are you going to raise the points you made in your 'Cop's-Eye View' paper, the one you wrote when you were on the CPD and taking night classes at DePaul?"

That sat McGill back on his seat.

Made him realize how closely his life had been examined.

By Ellie anyway.

She'd caught him off guard. But he rolled with the blow. He'd made an unspoken bargain with the rest of the country when Patti had been elected. Most of his life would become public fodder, the extent to which he was now reminded.

But the idea that someone would take the time to examine his schoolwork?

How far back did the snooping go? To his gold-star papers in parochial school?

He took a sip of coffee and got back to the moment at hand.

"The points I raised in that paper will come up. Are you

interested, Ms. Booker?"

"One more thing. Why me?"

"We've worked together before and it turned out well."

A newly arrived lobbyist in Washington, Earnest Deveraux, had tried to smear McGill's reputation by leaving a bagful of dubious cash out back of his office on P Street. With Ellie's help, McGill had turned that around. Deveraux was the guy who wound up with egg on his face, and Ellie was there with a video camera to see it happen.

That Deveraux was the cousin of the late Bobby Beckley, the former hatchet-man of the late Senator Howard Hurlbert, only made the story more titillating. Ellie got to renegotiate her contract with WWN upward on the strength of it.

Even so, she felt there was something more underlying McGill's request.

But she saw that if she probed further he'd walk away, go somewhere else.

"That was fun," she told him.

Since McGill had the clear upper hand at the moment, Ellie decided to further endear herself to him.

"There's something a little bird told me just last night you might like to know."

"What's that?" McGill asked.

"You know who Auric Ludwig is, right?"

"I do."

"Well, he knows you're working on the shooting death of Jordan Gilford." Ellie held up a hand forestalling any questions from McGill. "I don't know how my source knows that, and don't ask who my source is. I won't tell you, even if it costs me the interview."

McGill saw she wouldn't be budged.

He said, "How about this: Is your source trustworthy with a history of being right?"

"Yes, on both counts. You know what Ludwig wants to do with this story, I'm sure. Abel Mays went crazy, killed all those people at Winstead and then some righteous gunman plugged Mays, not only doing justice but saving everyone the heartbreak and expense of a trial."

"That's the way I see him spinning it, too."

"Then you know how Ludwig will react if you try to rewrite his script."

McGill didn't give a damn about that, but he said, "Predictably. When can we do the interview? The sooner, the better."

"Tomorrow?"

"That's good."

Ellie gave McGill her new address and said, "Let me tell the restaurant to hold the charge on your card. It's my turn to buy breakfast."

### *Chief of Staff's Office — The White House*

Galia Mindel had no idea what people in Alaska ate in the way of breakfast pastries, but she decided to go for a WASPy selection rather than bagels and a schmear. She called the White House Mess and ordered a spread of cinnamon rolls, pecan rolls, croissants and *pains au chocolat*. Okay, so the last two were French baking, but they still appealed to people who liked their bread white. For drinks, she went with with coffee, tea, orange juice and hot spiced cider.

With the goodies on a sideboard, she greeted the entire Congressional delegation, all three of them, of the largest state in the nation, led them to the food and drink, got them seated around the oval table opposite her desk and told them she was glad they could come on a Sunday and short notice.

Senator Dan Carnahan, Democrat, sat to Galia's right. Senator Tom Hale and Congresswoman Lorna Dalton, Republicans, sat to the chief of staff's left. They all went for the chocolate pastry, but Hale had a cinnamon roll on his plate, too.

He neglected both choices to get a jump on the conversation.

"Galia, don't think we didn't notice there's hardly anyone in the building. This almost looks like a covert op."

"Most of the staff have the day off to be with their families, but the president is in the building."

"Will she be joining us?" Carnahan asked.

"No."

"But she knows what we'll be discussing?" Dalton inquired.

"Yes."

Hale said, "But you're still trying to be sneaky here, right? If you're trying to get our support on gun control, even after that terrible event yesterday, Lorna and I won't be helping you. I doubt if even Dan will be on your side."

The Democratic senator shook his head, not disagreeing with his colleague, but indicating he wouldn't support a push for gun control. He was up for reelection in the fall.

"Well, Senator," Galia told Hale, "the event you referred to got a little more terrible this morning. Another of the boys on the Winstead football team who were shot yesterday died. But that's not why I asked all of you here this morning."

The three elected representatives of the people had the decency to look dismayed by the news of another death, but they chose to get back to business without commenting on it.

Hale asked, "What's on your mind, Galia?"

"You remember the federal public works project for which you've been advocating the past few years, Senator?"

"Ten years," Hale said.

Galia knew the number as well as Hale did; she just wanted to draw it out of him. Unlike the other forty-nine states, Alaska had no federal prison to call its own. The Last Frontier shipped its felons south to Washington state for incarceration. Hale had railed against the injustice of the situation. He said Alaskans paid their share of taxes to lock up their bad guys. Why should that money and the jobs that went along with it be exported elsewhere?

He'd argued for a decade that the biggest state should have its own big house.

The other two Alaskans in the room backed that position.

"The president has seen the light," Galia said. "Not only does she think your last request for funding should pass both Houses of Congress, she's decided to withdraw her veto threat if you should attach the expenditure to must-pass legislation."

A favorite legislative trick in Congress was to attach gift packages for the folks back home to legislation considered so vital to the country at large it was deemed must-pass. In this case, the mother-ship was the farm bill that supported both family and corporate agricultural enterprises, aka farms. The typical scare tactic to promote passage of the bill was that the price of milk would go to eight dollars a gallon without it.

Patricia Grant had promised to veto the must-pass legislation anyway, if it was stuffed with pork. Now, Galia was telling her small gathering of federal legislators the bill to fund prison construction in Alaska could go along as a stowaway on the mother-ship. And they'd get even more money than they had requested.

"We'll get two billion dollars?" Hale said. "What's the catch, Galia? If it's not gun control, what does the president want?"

Galia shrugged. "Well, if you get public works money, and it stimulates your state's economy, the president would like the three of you to support infrastructure spending in the rest of the country. There are lots of roads and bridges that need fixing, and lots of people who need jobs. If Alaska's delegation, a bipartisan group, co-sponsors legislation to rebuild America and starts pushing it hard, maybe the spirit will catch on."

Hale was the ranking minority member on the Senate appropriations committee; Dalton was a mid-seniority member on the House appropriations committee. She wanted to grow up to be the next Senator from Alaska when Hale retired. She'd follow his lead.

Galia leaned forward, her eyes turning hard, "But I warn you, if you take the money and then sit on your hands about your half of the deal, I not only will find a way to cut your prison money off, I'll personally manage the campaigns of your next challengers for office."

She sat back and took a sip of tea from the cup in front of her.

The three politicians communicated with each other by rapid

exchanges of looks.

They were like kids who wanted to take a daring leap but fear made them hesitate.

Then Dan Carnahan said, "I'm all for it, I'm in"

A Democrat, he didn't have any philosophical opposition to domestic spending. If he could land the construction of a major prison back home and create jobs in the bargain, better yet. Best of all, if he could steal Tom Hale's idea, and the two Republicans at the table didn't back it, it would be a trifecta win.

That hope was dashed when Hale bellowed, "Wait just a minute now, damnit! This has been my idea from the start." Seeing the put-up-or-shut-up look Galia gave him, he added, "I'm not only in, I'm the lead dog. We'll add our prison money, Galia, and I'll see to it all the other freeloaders on my side of the aisle are kept out. The president and Dan have to keep the Democrats in line."

"I'm good with that," Dalton said.

Hale gave Galia a nod. "Okay, then, Madam Chief of Staff, we'll do our part, but if you cross us, I'll be the one handing out the migraines."

Galia smiled and said, "Have another sweet roll, Senator."

The reason Alaska hadn't been allowed to build its own federal penitentiary years ago was its tiny population, fewer than three-quarters of a million souls, didn't justify the expense. It was more cost-efficient to ship their bad guys down to Seattle.

Senator Hale had always rebutted that reality by saying Alaska could help other states relieve their prison overcrowding by locking up surplus inmates from the lower forty-eight.

If all went well, he'd soon be getting his way.

But never in any way he'd imagined or would welcome.

### Playa Pacifica, Costa Rica

Representative Philip Brock, Democrat of the 9th District of Pennsylvania, looked out over what he'd come to think of as his new kingdom. All 202.343 hectares — 500 acres — of it. In many parts of the United States, that amount of land might be considered a small farm. In Texas, it would be reckoned little more than a vegetable garden. But Brock wasn't using his native country as a measuring stick. The way he looked at things, his property was one acre bigger than the entire principality of Monaco. Like the gilt-edged jewel of the Grimaldi family, his holding featured a balmy climate, coastal mountains and a magnificent beach. Well, technically, he didn't own the beach or even the first hundred meters of land above the mean high-tide line. That belonged to the Costa Rican people in aggregate and for perpetuity.

All that meant, really, was he couldn't put up a hotel, a casino or a shave-ice shack on the beach or the grassland just above the sand. He was fine with that. He didn't want to spoil the panoramic ocean views from his new hacienda anyway.

That rambling building with its central courtyard was his as certainly as any property he might have bought in Bucks County back home in Pennsylvania. Before the Russians, Indians and Mexicans moved in. He couldn't criticize immigrants for wanting to improve their lot, though. He was doing the same thing. He'd bought his property fee simple, paid $9.5 million cash. Roughly an eighth of the money he'd salted away from his days in investment banking.

Costa Rica had a long history of being the most stable and democratic country in Central America, having declared its independence from Spain in 1821. In the intervening years, it remained a model of liberal democracy in a neighborhood rampant with a series of dictators who might have been seen as comic-opera types if they hadn't had so much blood on their hands. The country dissolved its army in 1949, so there was no chance of it having a military coup. Twenty percent of its annual budget was spent on social services, including health care and education. And like the United States, Costa Rica had a female president.

With ironic humor, Brock thought he'd have a much tougher

time plying his trade as an anarchist in Costa Rica than he did as a member of the United States Congress.

The place wasn't quite paradise, though. There were active volcanoes. Earthquakes rumbled through every so often. Hurricanes hit the Caribbean coast — one reason Brock had set himself up on the Pacific side of the country. That was just the mischief Mother Nature might get up to.

Social problems were not unknown. Costa Rica was a transhipment point for South American drugs heading north. Domestic consumption of amphetamines and crack cocaine was on the rise. And there was tension caused by illegal immigration from other Central American countries: people sneaking into the country or overstaying their visas. Just like in the U.S.

Brock saw an opportunity in the immigration issue. He recruited Nicaraguans to work on his land. In almost every case, they were people who were about to be deported. He went to the provincial government, vouched for the people in question, promised that he had stable, long-term jobs to offer them — ones the local people would regard as too menial. His employees would become taxpayers and contribute to the country rather than take from it.

By dint of Brock's advocacy, he found close to two hundred people not only willing to work for him, but to declare their undying loyalty to him. They did the construction of his hacienda, dug wells, tilled his gardens, cooked his meals, tended his home and, most important, defended his little kingdom against anyone with evil designs against him.

For their efforts, they were paid fairly by prevailing standards, and shared in the profits of foodstuffs sold locally and flowers shipped north to America. Brock felt sure that most, if not all, of his people would die for him, should circumstances require.

He also made certain to gather friends in the upper reaches of Costa Rican society and government. He donated to medical charities. He helped fund cultural institutions. He wrote letters recommending students of families rich and poor to U.S. universities. In short, he did everything he could to create the image of an agreeable American.

Someone whose presence in Costa Rica would be stoutly defended.

Perhaps even against the government he purportedly served back home.

What no one could save Brock from, though, were the whims of fate.

When he read the New York Times online that morning he saw a mention that skeletal remains had been found at the C&O Canal National Historical Park and they tentatively had been identified as those of a missing Jordanian diplomat, Dr. Bahir Ben Kalil.

It wasn't the discovery of the bones that puzzled Brock, it was how quickly they had been connected to Ben Kalil. Who could have done that? There was no mention in the short item that Ben Kalil had been a victim of foul play, but the cops had to have seen clear evidence of that. He'd bashed the guy's skull in. So whoever was leading the investigation — and with the death of a diplomat that would have to be the FBI — was being cagey.

Flipping off the conventional wisdom, Brock decided that he would be safer in Washington than Central America. He needed to see what the feebs knew and determine whether he could influence the outcome of their labors. Perhaps point the finger of blame at ... well, whoever best suited his purposes.

Besides that, of course, he still had a government back home to topple.

He was on the afternoon flight north from San José, as planned.

# CHAPTER 9

## *Florida Avenue NW — Washington, DC*

Just to see what would happen, on the third night after Sweetie and Putnam had brought his orphaned niece, Maxine, home, Sweetie had crept out of the bed she shared with Putnam and made her way down to the basement apartment, her original home in the townhouse.

The first thing that happened was Sweetie fell asleep.

Not so deeply that she wasn't awakened by the feeling someone was watching her. She opened her eyes, squinted against the glare of an unexpected light and quickly raised her hands to ward off a possible attack. No assault came. Maxine stood at the side of Sweetie's bed, clutching a stuffed toy lamb against her chest. Sweetie released a deep breath she hadn't known she'd been holding.

Maxine said in a small voice, "Did I scare you? I didn't mean to." Awaiting a reply, she put her right thumb in her mouth.

Sweetie shook her head. "It's all right. I just wasn't expecting a visitor." A thought occurred to her. A former cop, Sweetie always made sure all doors were locked before going to sleep. "How'd you get in here, Maxi?"

The child had told Sweetie and Putnam that was her preferred nickname.

Maxi took her thumb out of her mouth, reached into a pocket

on the lamb's shirt and held up a key.

"Putnam said this is my house now, too. He showed me all the keys and how to use them."

Sweetie smiled. When she and her husband had first met he'd been a collector of bad habits and a firm believer in situational morality. Now, he'd become a champion of the downtrodden and the unhesitating surrogate father to a niece he hadn't known to exist four days ago. More than just a shining example of the power of redemption, he was fast becoming the moral pillar on which his new family depended. One of them, anyway.

Still in cop mode, Sweetie asked, "How'd you know I was down here?"

"I looked everywhere else."

"Did you wake up Putnam?"

Maxi shook her head.

"Why did you want to find me?" Sweetie asked.

"To make sure you were okay." She popped her thumb back into her mouth, but took it right out again. A sheen formed on her eyes. "I miss my mama and daddy. I don't want to …"

A rush of tears left the thought incomplete but obvious.

The poor kid didn't want to lose anyone else.

Sweetie swung her feet off the bed and reached out to Maxi.

After a moment of reluctance, the girl hurried into Sweetie's embrace.

"Honey, Putnam and I aren't going anywhere. We're going to be around a long time."

Please, God, Sweetie thought.

Maxi asked if she could sleep with Sweetie, who thought it would be better to go back upstairs. After making a promise of longevity, she thought it best not to give her husband a heart attack. Waking up and finding the two of them absent from their usual resting places just might turn that awful trick.

Back upstairs, Maxi asked if Sweetie could lie down with her until she got back to sleep.

That was where Putnam had found the two of them, his heart

never feeling better.

On the morning after the shooting at the Winstead School, Putnam saw Sweetie in their kitchen sitting at the breakfast bar with a cup of tea in front of her. Putnam, already shaved and showered, took the adjacent seat. He was wearing the latest in fashion from Under Armour: T-shirt, workout shorts and moisture-wicking socks.

At one time, he'd have hidden his doughy body under baggy sweats.

Now, he was almost sleek. Had just ordered new business suits.

He felt worthy of chiding his mentor in physical fitness.

"Hearty breakfast you've got there, Margaret."

"Being Sunday, and I've already fasted for and returned from early Mass, I added an extra spoon of honey," she told him. "Besides, it's all I have the stomach for."

"Yesterday's shooting?" he asked.

"Yes."

"You've been thinking what if it had happened at Maxi's school," Putnam said.

Sweetie nodded. She and Putnam were in the process of adopting the child they'd been bequeathed, literally. In their will, the late Lawton and LuAnne Shady, requested that Putnam and his wife (if any) take in Maxine to raise to the best of his ability.

To finance that effort, Lawton and LuAnne left Putnam a bit over a million dollars.

A handsome, and fairly suspicious, sum for a non-tenured English professor working under an alias at the University of Maryland Baltimore County and his seafood-cook wife. Putnam felt he'd only recently escaped the shadow of his fugitive con artist parents. At least, he no longer had FBI agents tailing him, as far as he could tell.

He accepted his niece wholeheartedly. He and Sweetie would raise her as their own child. But he wouldn't go anywhere near a penny of Lawton's money. He'd bet a good chunk of his own fortune that million dollars had come from dear old Mom and Dad.

The default legatees were LuAnne's parents, Emory and Sissy Jenkins. Putnam suggested they give the money to charity. They kept it.

Putnam feared they'd live to regret the decision.

At the moment, though, Putnam and Sweetie had a more immediate and heart-pounding fright to deal with: How could they educate their child without taking the risk she'd be killed in her classroom or on the playground? Or, now, even on an athletic field.

"That's just what I was thinking," Sweetie said. "I've been going back and forth between the idea of homeschooling her and sitting in on all her classes until she has her Ph.D."

"Packing your own heat, of course."

"Exactly. Concealed carry is all the rage."

"Do you prefer one alternative?"

Sweetie shook her head. "I hate them both. I hate the whole situation. Things should never have come to this."

"You saw the president. Did she or Jim McGill have any ideas?"

Sweetie outlined the Oval Office discussion to which she'd been privy, and what the First Couple and Galia Mindel had come up with. Putnam agreed with McGill's notion that you can't let people hold their noses, and he loved his idea of how to make the masses pay attention. He approved of the president's and Galia's spin-offs, too.

"They forgot one thing, though," he said.

He almost added that the omission showed their age.

But Margaret was five years older than him. Not that you'd know it to look at her.

"What's that?" Sweetie said.

"McGill's plan has got to go on the Internet. The idea would go viral from the get-go."

Sweetie winced. "I didn't think of that either. Maybe I'm slipping."

"Really?"

Sweetie laughed. "No, but there might come a day."

"I'll knit a shawl for you," Putnam said.

Sweetie gave him a kiss. She told Putnam about taking former Senator Roger Michaelson on as a client. He raised an eyebrow. She told him McGill and the president were okay with it.

She said, "I tried to distract myself last night by looking online for any connections between Joan Renshaw and Representative Philip Brock. Brock brought Roger Michaelson back to Washington and Renshaw fingered him as a conspirator in the plan to kill Patti Grant. But I couldn't find anything to put them together. They grew up in different states, don't have a profession in common or donate to the same charities. They don't share the same church affiliation. Still, the more possibilities I eliminate, the more certain I am there has to be a link."

"Because they're the only two names you've got," Putnam said.

"That and I'm stubborn."

"Persistent."

"Willing to admit when I need help, too. You're a bigshot lobbyist. I bet you know things about the politicians in town that never get posted on the Internet. Is there any dirt you can share on Philip Brock?"

Putnam said, "It hardly qualifies as dirt … well, maybe it does but …"

He drifted off into thought.

"What is it?" Sweetie asked. "Tell me."

"I kept a list of the handful of people who got to see Inspiration Hall after the artwork was hung but before the museum was opened to the public."

"And?"

"Representative Brock was on that list. He was a guest of Tyler Busby. I hadn't thought of that before now. Busby was definitely in on the plan to kill the president. He counted on the destruction of Inspiration Hall to cover up all the forged art he had hung in the museum. Now, I wonder if Brock knew about either the plan to commit insurance fraud or kill Patti Grant."

Sweetie frowned. "The guy's a congressman and a fellow

Democrat."

Putnam took her hand, stroked it gently as if she were a child.

"I've always heard politics in Chicago is a hardball game."

"Yeah, but that's just a bunch of greedy, grubby ... is it really that bad here, too?"

"Worse. Let's not forget that somebody killed Senator Howard Hurlbert."

"Yeah, but —" Sweetie felt the conversation was starting to get off-topic.

"Here's my point," Putnam said. "If I kept a list about the people who got sneak previews at Inspiration Hall, my money says Joan Renshaw did, too. If she knew Brock got an early look with a guy who's now the subject of a global manhunt, she didn't raise a fuss. Why would that be?"

Sweetie saw the possibility there for a connection between Brock and Renshaw.

But she still didn't know what it was or how to prove it.

Putnam noticed her consternation and offered a suggestion.

"Margaret, given your strong moral core, you looked for legitimate points of intersection. Maybe the thing you need to do is look for something more casual, social or even kinky that connects your persons of interest."

Sweetie gave Putnam an imploring look.

"All right," he said, "you take casual and social. If it gets too kinky, I'll pitch in."

That earned Putnam another kiss.

"About Maxi and her schooling?" he said. "I have an idea, but I'm not sure it's great."

"Has to be better than mine," Sweetie told him.

"It's a variation on one of yours, homeschooling. Have you heard of the Khan Academy?"

"I've heard the name."

"It's an organization that provides top-flight classes in a growing number of subjects, online and free. They start with pre-algebra in third grade."

"Maxi's grade," Sweetie said.

"Right. What I was thinking, you could base your curriculum on Khan classes, organize a group of say a dozen kids, boys and girls so you keep the socializing aspect of education, and you're set to go. You select classmates from families you trust. You do one week of classes at each student's house in a rotating fashion. Each mom and/or dad becomes responsible for the safety of all the kids when they're studying under their roof. Maybe you could hire an off-duty cop to sit out front or something."

Sweetie thought the idea wasn't half-bad. "I'd be the one to watch over the kids when they're here."

"Me, too," Putnam said.

Before the idea could be taken any farther, the phone rang. The White House was calling.

### Calle Ocho — Miami, Florida

Jerry Nerón's custom tailoring shop was closed on Sundays, but he was at work upstairs on his latest commission, the legitimate reason for his presence in Washington, DC the past three days. A small television was tuned to a WWN newscast, the volume audible but not a distraction. The Washington client's new measurements had been taken in exacting detail. Fabric samples from Scabal, Zegna and Loro Piana had been examined. Discussions were had to assess the most flattering cuts for the materials. Shirts, ties, socks and shoes to accompany the suits were chosen.

Ordinarily, Jerry would advise the client as to the kind of wristwatch or even ear piercings to wear with each suit. His Washington client, though, had unadorned lobes and wore only an elegant wedding band for jewelry. As to staying aware of the time of day, the client depended on his smartphone which he usually had in hand.

The phone was a slim device, but its dimensions were taken into account when Jerry took his measurements. A master craftsman always did his best not to overlook the smallest detail. Perfection was what concerned Jerry as he sewed the suit for his client.

His getaway from the murder scene in Washington had gone exactly according to plan. The car he'd used was surely stolen within minutes of being abandoned. He'd disposed of the murder weapon quickly and cleanly. The clothes he'd worn to execute Jordan Gilford and Abel Mays had gone into a donation bin that was part of a national charity. They would be laundered, placed in a resale shop and sold to someone who would never be mistaken for one of his clients.

He'd made his plane back to Miami with time to spare. The flight home must've been smooth but he couldn't say for sure. The lead flight attendant in the first-class cabin had gently roused him from his sleep, saying, "We've landed, sir. Welcome to Miami. It's sunny and there's a nice breeze off the ocean. The weather's perfect."

Jerry couldn't have asked for more.

Even so, a nagging thought wouldn't give him any peace.

Had it been a mistake, an unnecessary complication, to kill that madman who had parked behind him at the National Mall? No, he'd needed to do that. He couldn't leave a witness behind, and he couldn't have found a better place to kill either Gilford or the witness.

But using the madman's own weapon to carry out Gilford's execution, laying off his crime on someone else, that had been an unnecessary flourish. It was impulsive, unlike anything he'd ever done. Except for the first time he'd killed a man.

When Jerry was a young man, already well into his training as the potential assassin of Fidel Castro, his grandfather, Dario, had gone to his grandmother, Arcelia, and asked her to start making suits for men as well as dresses for women. Grandfather had feared that sewing dresses in his every free moment might be turning Jerry gay. Arcelia had laughed at the thought, but embraced the idea to broaden her clientele.

Truth was, from the time he was fifteen, Jerry's fittings for the young Cuban-American beauties about to be introduced to society at their *quinceañeras* involved a measuring system that applied Jerry's hands to their breasts and backsides as he nuzzled their necks. By the time he was eighteen, he became even more intimately acquainted with a number of prospective brides who wanted to be sure they were marrying the right man.

At twenty-one, Dario lent Jerry the money to open his own shop. By then, Grandfather had become the one to turn down ever more desperate plans to kill Castro. He wouldn't sacrifice his grandson on the altar of a scheme that would end not only in failure but also in ridicule. It was enough for Dario to watch as Jeronimo — he'd never called the boy Jerry — became ever more proficient in the arts of war: marksmanship, explosives, hand-to-hand combat and especially knife fighting.

Having worked with scissors since he was little more than a toddler, Jeronimo felt immediately at home with an edged weapon. His movements were fluid and so quick even older opponents were both dazzled and dismayed. Not that the boy did anything more than nick any of his *compañeros*. But each of them knew the boy could have killed them, had he wanted.

At the end of his first year in business, Jerry had repaid his grandfather's loan and took his parents and grandparents out to dinner to celebrate. Between his family's business contacts and his friends in the militant exile community, he had all the business he could accept. He often worked sixteen-hour days.

His parents and his grandmother all told him he needed to get more rest. Take things easier. One night, even Dario told him, "Jeronimo, having a passion is fine, but don't let it consume you."

"Advice you've decided to follow, too, Grandfather."

The old man nodded. The fact that his grandson shared his hatred of Castro and would be willing to kill him, if given a reasonable opportunity, had become enough for Dario.

"Even if Castro lives to be a hundred," he told Jeronimo, "surely he will burn in hell for eternity."

"Very well, Grandfather. I will work fewer hours. I will become more discriminating in the clients I accept."

The way Jerry did that was not to accept as a client any man who was more than twenty pounds overweight. He said his tailoring didn't look good on mounds of dough. He was more diplomatic, though, with the men he rejected, referring them to others who would be happy to take their money. In borderline cases, he would make one suit for them, but if they wanted another, it would have to be in a smaller size.

There were those who used that incentive to take better care of themselves.

Others bought the one suit and then went elsewhere.

A third group turned on their heels, angered by the implicit insult.

Jerry could live with that. His new restrictions brought his client list down to a manageable number. Then, one day, Galtero Blanco strode into Jerry's shop.

All 343 pounds of him.

A fellow maybe half Blanco's size darted out from behind him, took a look at Jerry as if he was no threat and darted through the shop and into the back room. Jerry heard the door at the rear of the store open and close. The smaller man returned and nodded to Blanco.

He went out the front door and stood in front of Jerry's shop with his arms crossed over his chest. A sentry guarding against further commerce. Or any other interruption.

Jerry turned to the big man and told him, "I take clients by appointment only."

"I know. I got mine from the guy who's supposed to be here now."

"Mr. Diaz," Jerry said.

"That's right. Poor guy won't be needing any more suits. He fell off my boat. My man, the one outside your door there, threw him a life preserver, but it was too late. A shark got him. Terrible thing to see."

Blanco smiled as he said that.

Jerry said, "I'll send my condolences to his family."

Blanco laughed. He enjoyed a good joke, one directed at

somebody else. Even so, he took a step back as Jerry came out from behind the counter with a pair of scissors in hand. Blanco halted his retreat and pointed a finger at Jerry.

"You know who I am?"

"A reckless boater?"

Blanco didn't see the humor. "I'm the new boss around here. You're in any of the rackets, you give me my share."

Jerry shrugged. "I'm not in any racket; I'm just a tailor."

"Uh-huh. You do real nice work, too. I liked Diaz's suit, asked him where he got it. Before he had his accident. I also buy local. Got a good eye for bargains, and you wouldn't believe how much money the places I buy will make. With you, I figure you can stay and make me some suits."

"I've got no choice?" Jerry asked.

"Sure, you do. You can live or die."

"Guess I better take your measurements then."

"Damn ri —"

Jerry's hand, the one holding the scissors, flashed in front of Blanco's eyes, the blades opened wide. The scalpel-sharp steel didn't touch the fat man. The trailing blade, however, cut through his belt and the waistband of his pants. They puddled around his ankles.

Blanco's mouth fell open, too. "The fuck you think you're doing?"

Jerry thought that was obvious. Grandfather had taught him well: The last thing you could tolerate was some thug stealing what was yours. So Jerry was about to show this gelatinous mound of shit the error of his ways.

Not only trying to steal his business but also costing him a valued customer.

Having been inculcated with fantasies of killing Castro for years, Jerry knew the lesson would have to be permanent. But the young tailor was momentarily stupefied by the sight before him. Blanco was wearing bikini briefs. That was bad enough, a speck of fabric wedged into a mudslide of flab, but some cretin had silkscreened the absurd undergarment.

A woman's head, as seen from behind, was placed opposite Blanco's crotch.

The implication was as obvious as it was disgusting.

Blanco understood the look on Jerry's face and had the shred of decency necessary to be embarrassed. He put his hands down. They were barely able to reach around his belly to his groin. That accomplished, the big man decided to get mad.

"You bastard. You're dead!"

He turned his head to shout to his little partner. "Fidel!"

Castro's namesake? Jerry thought: Perfect.

Jerry turned the inside of his wrist upward and swung his arm in an arc. The trailing blade of the scissors slashed the fat man's carotid artery. Jerry jumped clear as a jet of blood shot out. The crime boss toppled backward like a fallen oak.

Little Fidel, gun in hand, came through the front door just in time to try to catch Blanco. He wasn't up to the job. With a yelp of dismay, Fidel's knees buckled and the mass of the "new boss around here" buried him as both men crashed to the floor.

A muffled shot sounded as they hit.

A new trickle of blood seeped out from under the big man's body.

But whose blood was it, Jerry wondered. Could he really be that lucky? He leaped over Blanco's bulk and closed and locked his front door. Listening closely, he couldn't hear Fidel gasping for breath. He'd surely have to do that, Jerry thought, had he been alive.

He pulled down the shades at the front of the shop.

Then he did hear a wheeze and a rattle. He'd never heard a man expel his last breath before. Blanco, with his throat cut, hadn't made any such sound. But Jerry felt sure that little Fidel was no longer a threat to the Cuban community.

Without touching either body, Jerry called his grandfather and told him what happened. Comrades from the militant exile community arrived swiftly, entering through the back door and leaving the same way with both bodies. Jerry did a superficial mop and wipe of blood and bits of flesh. A crew of Cuban-American cleaning women followed up.

They scrubbed the entire shop as if they were scourging a soul free of sin.

Not a bacterium survived their efforts, much less a trace of evidence.

Grandfather swore to take knowledge of what had happened to the grave.

Somebody talked, though not to the cops.

A week after Galtero Blanco had departed the thug life, Jerry received an envelope in the mail that had been postmarked in Miami but bore no return address. In it was a password to a numbered account at a Singaporean bank. The balance was a million dollars. A friend of his grandfather's later told him a rival had placed a bounty on Blanco's head.

Jerry never tried to retrieve the money.

He focused on dealing with the after-effects of taking Blanco's life. He felt no remorse. Just the opposite. After years of training and imagining what it would feel like to take someone's life, now he knew. At least in the case of Galtero Blanco, it had been wonderful.

As deeply satisfying as completing a perfect suit.

The question that preoccupied him was: Would it feel as good again?

Several weeks later, he got an opportunity to find out. Another envelope arrived at his shop. In it he found an anonymous query asking whether he might be available to kill a Latino jockey who regularly got mounts at Gulfstream Park. Jerry didn't follow horse racing. He didn't know if the man won or lost too many races. Maybe he just ran up a big debt at the casino next door to the track.

The offer of payment was fifty thousand dollars. Even if the jockey weighed only a third of what Galtero Blanco had, the fee wasn't competitive on a per-pound basis. More important, it was possible, he thought, that someone was trying to set a trap for him.

He couldn't call in sick, so he simply burned the message and envelope. Let the jockey work out his own fate. Still, without any personal effort, he was getting a reputation as a killer.

That both frightened and intrigued him.

Someone in the exile community had to be nudging him toward a new profession.

Before he'd bite on any offer, though, he had to be sure he didn't put his foot in a snare. There was a lull of several months, and Jerry tried to content himself with his tailoring. For the most part, he succeeded, maintaining his high standards. When he wasn't working, though, the idea of becoming a paid killer buzzed around his mind like a housefly that refused to be swatted.

Then, a month before Christmas, a sly and very sophisticated plea reached him.

After dining alone, some unseen person attached a note to his credit card receipt. The message asked if he'd be willing to kill a very important young man who enjoyed nothing so much as beating up the beautiful women he dated. If he did, there would be a payment of $250,000 for him. He was given an email address to which he might reply.

Jerry tried to find the young woman, quite lovely herself, who had served his meal. She'd taken the imprint of his credit card and had returned it to him. Along with the note. He couldn't find her, no one at the restaurant even admitted knowing her. She wasn't the kind of woman who would easily slip from memory.

There had to be some sort of conspiracy at work.

But he couldn't smell the involvement of any cops.

He waited a week before sending a one-word answer from an Internet café: More. He left unsaid whether he wanted more money or more information. If the other party was smart, they'd know it was both. Then he pretended for the remainder of the night that he wasn't interested in whether or how he got a response.

The next morning, he found a shoebox in his parking space behind the shop.

Contrary to a multitude of misgivings, Jerry opened it.

He found not only everything he needed to know but more than enough to pique his interest and persuade him to take the job. The target was the playboy son of an agricultural baron, a sugarcane billionaire. A series of before-and-after photos in the attachment showed that he had indeed brutalized a number of young women.

The bastard had avoided a prison cell by either paying off his victims or having his lawyers prevail in court. He'd also been busted for drug possession three times. Two offenses were dropped on technicalities, the third resulted in a stint in rehab. Then he made the mistake of running down a British tourist while intoxicated.

That was the miscreant's downfall.

The victim's family was as rich as his own. Their lawyers were every bit as good as his lawyers, and maybe a bit better. While criminal charges were pending, the opposition lawyers were amassing evidence for a civil suit. They were also feeding every scrap of damning evidence they found to the state attorney to use in the vehicular homicide trial.

The outcomes of both trials should have been a foregone conclusion.

But the fact that an unnamed party had reached out to him told Jerry that someone was worried the *cabrón* might wriggle free yet again. The only way that could happen would be if the fix had been put in. That wasn't hard to imagine. Judges in Florida had been bought before. And when was the last time anyone from a truly wealthy family went to jail?

The fee for making sure existential justice was done had been bumped to $350,000.

Jerry took the job. Did so without the courtesy of replying to his anonymous patron.

To make it look good, he did so after the target's criminal charge had been knocked down to involuntary manslaughter. The British tourist, it had been shown, had also been drinking that unfortunate night. A newly produced witness swore that the tourist stumbled off the curb into the path of the oncoming vehicle. The court's sentence was a hundred hours of community service.

The civil suit was still pending, but it would be contested for years.

The overprivileged prick who caused all the trouble didn't give that a second thought. He threw a party for himself and hundreds of people who didn't mind being seen drinking, dancing and groping with him. It was no problem for the handsome, young, exquisitely tailored Jerry to slip into the affair. He offered his target a drink and toasted his deliverance. *"Salud."*

Health.

Jerry's training and one of the scenarios envisioned for having him kill Castro was to poison the dictator. The glass he handed his target contained a colorless, odorless, tasteless but powerful muscle relaxant. The initial effect would only make him seem drunker but within fifteen minutes his heart would stop beating and he would be judged to have died of a myocardial infarction. That was exactly what happened.

Jerry was already home before his victim died. He never fell under suspicion because the death was ruled to be from natural causes. He kept working at his chosen craft, building a reputation for exquisite tailoring that grew with each passing year.

The client he'd never billed needn't have paid him, and several months passed without any compensation. Then, once again, he received a message attached to a restaurant receipt. Not at the same restaurant. Not from the same waitress. But in similar fashion to the job he'd rejected, Jerry received a password and the number of a bank account.

This time the funds had been deposited in the Cayman Islands, a British possession.

For a five percent commission, an intermediary in the exile community moved the money for him to another account, this one in Venezuela — and Jerry was in a whole new business. From that point forward, he followed the same pattern. The clients remained anonymous. There was no confirmation the job had ever been accepted. Payment was expedited by a third party who never knew how the money had been earned.

Added to that, Jerry decided to do hits only in locations where he could use his tailoring business as a legitimate cover, should he ever need to explain why he'd been in town.

Nothing was ever foolproof, as anyone hoping to kill Fidel Castro could tell you, but Jerry felt his methods provided more than a comfortable margin of safety for him. Without ever having left evidence that he'd ever killed anyone, there was a steady demand for his services. His only problem was the thrill had gone. The housefly in his head had been swatted.

That or boredom bred of repetition had killed the bug.

Money wasn't a motivation. He had more than he'd ever need.

He thought the job he'd done in Washington might well be his last hit.

Until he saw Auric Ludwig appear on his television.

Within minutes, Jerry felt he might have one more job to do.

### WWN News Studio — Washington, DC

Auric Ludwig, CEO of FirePower America, made WWN the first stop on his Sunday morning rounds of news programs to defend the broadest imaginable interpretation of the Second Amendment, one that would keep profits flowing to his employers and earn him an ever increasing year-end bonus.

Even in the face of gruesome, wholesale violence, Ludwig knew he held the high ground. Strategically if not morally. A majority of both houses of Congress was either bought and paid for or intimidated. The most recent Supreme Court ruling had completely discounted a well-regulated militia as being the predicate of a right to bear arms. All fifty states now had concealed carry laws.

There were only two possible hostile blips on Ludwig's radar.

Congress recently had extended for ten years a ban on plastic guns that could go undetected by metal detectors and X-ray machines. None of his employers manufactured such weapons, yet.

The damn things were churned out by 3-D printers in people's homes and offices. But who knew? Within a decade, the big boys might decide they wanted to enter the plastic-gun market. Turn out sophisticated models.

Beyond business considerations, there was a principle at stake. You let Congress get away with passing one gun-control law, it set a dangerous precedent. In the future, the cost of buying off or scaring off Congress could skyrocket. Ludwig had wanted to fight the plastic gun ban, but he'd been told no.

There was an even larger concern to occupy the minds of Ludwig and his bosses: A new chief justice and a new associate justice had taken seats on the Supreme Court. Previous rulings concerning the Second Amendment could be reversed. That would cause a huge uproar, but the high court was the toughest part of government to lobby, the trickiest place to influence votes with blandishments.

But all that was something to worry about another day.

At the moment, Ludwig was telling WWN Reveille Roundup host Jack Landon how yesterday's tragedy at the Winstead School could have been averted.

"The coaching staff of the football team should have had their assailant outgunned."

Landon managed to keep his jaw from dropping, but he allowed his eyebrows to rise.

The host asked, "Are you saying —"

"I'm saying that Abel Mays had a legally purchased weapon. If the three adult males to whom the well-being of that football team had been entrusted had been similarly armed, they would have had a three-to-one advantage and the outcome would have been far different."

Watching from just off-camera, Ellie Booker looked up from the notes she was taking.

She thought Ludwig was either a terrific actor, spouting crap like that with a straight face or he was bedbug crazy. As a betting proposition, the choice was probably a push.

"Is that your answer to any potentially violent situation, Mr. Ludwig?' Landon asked. "Everyone should be armed at all times."

"Well, look at what happened on the National Mall," Ludwig said. "Mays killed one last man."

"A jogger," Landon interjected. "Should people out for a run carry guns, too?"

"Probably would have helped that poor guy, but look what happened next. Someone who was armed took Mays out. That individual was the hero of the day. The good guy with a gun who stopped the bad guy with a gun."

"If that's the case, Mr. Ludwig, why hasn't that noble man or woman come forward to have his or her heroism acknowledged and to receive the acclaim of a grateful nation?"

Ludwig offered a reptilian smile. "Probably because he doesn't need the grief he'd catch from bleeding hearts like you."

Landon returned Ludwig's volley and put a note of personal topspin on it. "So you're saying this — let's call your good guy a man — this man has the courage to face off with and kill an adversary armed with an automatic weapon but he's afraid of being questioned by the press? That characterization is a little inconsistent on your part, wouldn't you say?"

Goddamn liberal, Ludwig thought.

He missed the old days when WWN was dependably right wing.

Ludwig said, "Maybe the good guy just needs a little time to catch his breath."

Landon persisted. "No chance he might be worrying about his legal jeopardy? Of course, if he truly acted in self-defense or was defending an innocent third party, there would be nothing for him to worry about. Maybe your good guy is simply looking out for his own backside."

"You think so?" Ludwig asked. "Well, how about this?" Looking straight into the camera Ludwig knew he was about to take a big risk, but felt he had no choice. Not if he wanted to sustain his good-guy narrative. "If you're the hero I'm talking about, the man who shot Abel Mays, FirePower America will give you one hundred thousand dollars to show up at my office first thing tomorrow morning. We'll give you that money free and clear, and we'll pick up any legal fees you might have. You know, in case somebody like this guy," he hooked his thumb at Landon, "tries to put you in trouble with law enforcement."

The show went to commercial.

Ludwig directed a smirk at Landon.

"Watch what happens now," he said.

"And if no one comes forward, Mr. Ludwig?"

By way of an answer, Ludwig unclipped his microphone and tossed it aside.

He got up and left the set, hoping he hadn't just shot himself in the foot.

If he knew how his call to identify Abel Mays' killer had been received in Miami, he'd have had far greater worries than a foot wound.

### Nebraska Avenue, NW — Washington, DC

Metro Homicide Detectives Meeker and Beemer took Auric Ludwig by his arms the moment he stepped out of WWN's Washington Bureau building. Ludwig might have reached for a concealed weapon to defend himself against a brazen, daylight kidnapping attempt except for a couple of things. He never carried a gun; he had an armed bodyguard. And Meeker and Beemer had their badges on display. Adding to the detectives' advantage, they'd already warned Ludwig's entourage — a personal assistant, driver and makeup artist as well as the bodyguard — not to interfere, and there were four patrol officers present to back up the detectives.

Ludwig's PA used his iPhone to video the cops taking Ludwig away.

Meeker leaned over as he went past and exhaled on the camera's lens, fogging it.

The personal assistant reacted with an outrage at the assault on his phone even greater than the one he felt seeing the boss hauled off to ... well, they didn't know exactly where Ludwig was being taken. The patrol cops wouldn't let them follow the detectives.

Seated in the back of the detectives' car, his blood pressure redlining and his wrists free of handcuffs, Ludwig wondered if he dared to jump out of the vehicle when it stopped for a red light. He looked over a shoulder to see if his people were following to aid in an escape attempt or to document this travesty of justice. Seeing that help was not close at hand, his sense of derring-do waned.

If he tried to escape, all he might do would be to piss off these two cops.

As if reading his mind, Beemer looked over his shoulder and said, "You're not under arrest yet. Do something stupid, that'll change fast."

"Is that a threat?" Ludwig asked.

"It's an explanation," Meeker told him. "You understand it?"

Ludwig sat back and sulked in momentary silence.

"I always thought the FBI would be the ones to come for me," he muttered.

Beemer smiled. "Give 'em a chance. The day ain't over yet."

Meeker laughed. "Maybe we'll call the CIA, give those boys a crack at you, too."

Being the butt of the detectives' humor only darkened Ludwig's mood.

"Where are you taking me?"

"To see a lady who's got some questions for you," Meeker said.

"And if I don't want to answer them?"

"Then we do arrest you and you get to call your lawyer."

Ludwig said, "This isn't going to end well for the two of you and whoever this 'lady' is."

Meeker looked at Ludwig's reflection in his rear view mirror.

"That so?" he asked. "Well, tell me, who is it got put in the back of a police car?"

"And who's ridin' up front?" Beemer added.

Ten minutes later the two detectives and Ludwig arrived at police headquarters.

## CHAPTER 10

*The National Mall — Washington, DC*

MᶜGill thought he was in pretty decent shape, but in recreating Jordan Gilford's last run, along with FBI Deputy Director Byron DeWitt, Special Agent Abra Benjamin and Deke Ky, he was starting to feel gassed by the time they reached the Mall. That was the nine-mile point. None of the others seemed to be bothered a bit by the run. Of course, McGill knew he had at least ten years on DeWitt, and Benjamin and Deke were even younger.

That was small comfort. McGill decided he'd have to up his cardio routine.

Get Patti to run with him whenever possible.

McGill stopped adjacent to the point where Gilford had been shot. Leo had been pacing the runners in an armored black SUV the FBI had provided. He came to a halt on Madison Drive. There was room enough for everyone to scurry inside the vehicle, if they had to run for cover. But the Sunday morning was peaceful, even though there was still blood on the grass from the day before. A lot of it. The crime scene had been released to public use. McGill wondered if the Park Service was going to hose the area down or just wait for the first rain storm.

Trying to keep his breathing from sounding labored, McGill

said to the others, "I don't see any gouges in the grass. When Mr. Gilford was cut down he was facing the direction opposite that of his run. He must have seen the threat to his life and changed directions, presumably by planting a leg hard. He should have left a mark."

Benjamin walked on ahead, looking down. "Here's a divot."

Twenty feet separated her from McGill.

"He didn't get far," DeWitt said. "That could mean a few things."

McGill gestured for the deputy director to continue.

DeWitt said, "One, he was lost in thought, paying only superficial attention to his surroundings. Two, he was distracted at just the wrong moment by a loud noise or an unusual sight. Three, the killer took pains to hide his weapon."

Benjamin walked over to join the three men.

McGill and DeWitt saw her approach.

Deke didn't let himself be distracted. He watched the threat horizon.

Benjamin said, "We know from the ballistics reports that the rounds fired at the Winstead School and here at the Mall came from the same weapon, an HK-MP5K. That's a compact weapon; it would be easy to hide behind a hip."

McGill considered that. "Witness statements from the school say that Mays concealed the weapon under his coat. That makes sense because he wanted to surprise his victims. If the players and the coaches saw him coming with a gun from a long way off, they all could have run. Mays likely wouldn't have gotten all the people he wanted, if he did that. But why would he conceal his weapon to shoot one man at random? From what I've heard so far, no one has established a connection between Abel Mays and Jordan Gilford."

DeWitt said, "The Bureau hasn't found one yet."

McGill positioned his hands in front of his torso as if he were holding a compact assault weapon.

"Do I have the spacing about right for Mays' HK?" he asked.

Both DeWitt and Benjamin nodded.

"So if Mays had been holding the weapon in an open manner,

Gilford must've have been really distracted not to have seen it at a greater distance than he apparently did."

The FBI people had to agree with that, too.

McGill said, "I'll have to ask Zara Gilford if her husband was given to daydreaming as he ran, but I doubt he was." He walked on ahead to the divot Benjamin had found and then added ten more paces. He put his right hand behind his hip as Benjamin had suggested, mimicking a man hiding a weapon, and called out to the others. "If the shooter stood like this, Gilford could've gotten as far as the point where he made his turn, before the weapon was revealed. Gilford was older than I am. He could have had four more miles at a measured pace left in him, but reversing his field and fleeing at an all-out sprint would have been tough. I can see him getting hit right about where he died."

He walked back to the others.

Benjamin said, "Your scenario explains what your client thinks: Some other dude did it."

McGill said, "Not just some dude, a professional."

"Someone who killed Mays first and then used his weapon to mislead the investigation?" DeWitt asked. "How would he even have known who Mays was?"

McGill thought about that. "We'll have to find out when the first images of Mays were broadcast during the manhunt. Compare that time to Gilford's estimated TOD."

Benjamin was about to say something, possibly critical, but caught herself. Had another thought and changed her mind. "I suppose a high-tech killer could have a tablet computer with him to watch streaming news broadcasts."

"Might have a scanner to listen to police calls, too," McGill added.

DeWitt nodded. "Sensible precautions, if there was a professional killer. But what proof of that do we have?"

"You're not buying how close Gilford got to his killer as a sign that maybe Mays wasn't the guy?" McGill asked.

"I'll give you a maybe, but by itself, it's not enough for me."

Oddly enough, the thoughtful expression on Benjamin's face made McGill think she might be starting to lean his way. Or she just played devil's advocate to any position DeWitt took. But McGill wasn't going to get distracted by any dynamic going on between the two feds.

"Okay," McGill said. "How about this? Abel Mays was a big guy, stood 6-4. Jordan Gilford was more than a half-foot shorter, just over 5-9. If Mays killed Gilford, there should be some downward trajectory to his shots, right? The entry points of Gilford's wounds would be higher than the exit points. Anybody checked on that?"

DeWitt and Benjamin gave each other a look.

"Not that I know of," DeWitt admitted. "Have you had another case where this type of calculation mattered?"

McGill nodded. "Once I heard how tall Mays was, it came to mind. Got me thinking that even if the same weapon was used at both crime scenes, maybe the guy on the trigger was different. I've come to trust my client's instincts about her husband's situation."

"It's an interesting idea," DeWitt said, "that shooters can have what amounts to a signature."

Benjamin took that notion a step further. "If that's the case, maybe shooting signatures can be forged like any other kind."

Could be, McGill thought. "How big a clip was used in each crime? Did Mays have to reload after the first shooting?"

DeWitt said, "Thirty rounds were accounted for at each scene. That's capacity for one of the clips the weapon can hold."

"In each instance, the arc of fire was over 130 degrees," Benjamin added.

"Sprayed almost wall to wall," McGill said. He thought about that.

The feds waited politely for McGill to emerge from his reverie. All sorts of people cut him slack. That was one of the perks of being married to the president.

Returning to the moment, he said, "Sorry. I was just thinking: If there was a second shooter, and he was a pro, and he'd heard of Mays' rampage, would he be intuitive enough to mimic an amateur? To forge the other shooter's signature, as Special Agent Benjamin put it so well."

DeWitt said, "If you want to take a look, we have photographs on hand of all the victims, taken where they fell. We could compare the victims at the first crime scene to Mr. Gilford."

McGill winced. "Won't be fun, but I think we'd better."

Deke led the way back to the SUV. He got in front with Leo.

Benjamin sat between McGill and DeWitt in back. Her lap was used as a display table for the gory photos. She professed not to mind, said she had the best seat in the house.

Cop humor, of the darkest kind.

They didn't have to look all that hard to find something probative.

The fatally shot victims at the Winstead School had all been done in — as the photos revealed — by no more than two rounds each, and the distance between wounds was no less than what appeared to be three to four inches. The overall impression was that Abel Mays had wielded his weapon with the speed of the Grim Reaper swinging his scythe.

Jordan Gilford, on the other hand, had three tightly grouped wounds in the middle of his back. The two feds looked at one another and then at McGill. Each nodded to him.

Giving credit where it was due.

DeWitt said, "Mr. Gilford's killer forged Mays' signature, but only up to a point."

"This second guy has had training," Benjamin added. "It took over, and he might not even have noticed it."

"Sonofabitch still got the job done," McGill replied.

### The Oval Office — The White House

Edwina Byington, in her early 70s, still worked a seven-day week when need be. She greeted Putnam Shady when he appeared at her desk outside the Oval Office on Sunday morning. "Thank you for coming in on such short notice, Mr. Shady. The president has instructed me to ask if you'd like something to drink."

"A bottle of Poland Spring would be good."

Edwina pulled one from a desk drawer, still cold, and handed it over to Putnam along with a coaster and a napkin. He smiled at her acumen. Wondered what other preferred goodies she had available to him, if he were to make a request. He decided it would be more fun to speculate than to know.

Even so, he asked, "Ms. Byington, if you don't mind my asking, what did you do before you came to work for the president?"

"Well, I ran a small business. I made a few million dollars selling cosmetics from my pink Cadillac. That and I worked like the dickens to make sure the president won New Hampshire. She appreciated my efforts, and now you really shouldn't keep her waiting."

Putnam stepped into the Oval Office, half-expecting to find Galia Mindel with the president, but only Patricia Grant was there to greet him. She stood in the middle of the room and extended a hand to him. He took it with his free hand, thinking he could see the first signs of aging that the presidency inevitably wrought on anyone who held the office.

"Thank you for coming on a Sunday, Putnam. I woke up this morning and decided I needed to see you without delay."

"Happy to oblige, Madam President." He took one of the two facing chairs to which she gestured him. Put his coaster, napkin and bottle on a side table.

The president sat and asked "Edwina didn't offer you a glass?"

He unscrewed the bottle cap, took a sip and smiled. "She must've heard I like my Poland Spring straight from the bottle. I hope that's all right with you."

Patricia Grant nodded. "How is Maxine?"

"Adjusting well. There are still some difficult nights, but Margaret has a gift for providing comfort, and Maxi says it helps that I resemble my late brother, though I wonder if that isn't a mixed blessing."

The president said, "I hope you won't mind, but I made an

inquiry of the FBI. It's been some time since they last thought you might be in touch with your parents. I instructed Director Haskins that he was to make sure your pending adoption of Maxi was not to be considered a reason to resume surveillance of you or your family."

Putnam wasn't surprised the president knew of his and Margaret's plans to adopt Maxi. Margaret and McGill were partners. Putnam was sure the two of them still held confidences he didn't share, and that was fine. There was no reason Margaret shouldn't have told McGill about the adoption, and if he knew, the president would, too.

He was unprepared to hear the president had intervened with the feebs to make sure he wasn't pestered. He felt more than personal relief. Now, he wouldn't have to explain to Maxi that her paternal grandparents were crooks on the lam. Not for a few years anyway.

"Thank you, Madam President. That's good news."

She nodded and clasped her hands in her lap. "So what can you tell me about Cool Blue?"

"Darren Drucker and I were talking one night. He was complaining about the character defects of most office-holders in Congress. How their primary interest is self-interest. Everything they do is seen through the lens of hanging on to their seats."

"The same might be said of presidents," the president said.

Putnam smiled again. "True enough, but how many of them take leave of their job and risk their skin to save a stepson's life?"

The question caught the president by surprise, took her back to the awful days Kenny McGill's life hung in the balance. Her own as well. "As far as I know, just one."

"I suggested to Darren that maybe a vaccine could be developed to immunize first-time candidates for public office against vain ambition and careerism," Putnam said.

The president smiled.

Putnam did, too. "Yeah, I think that's half the reason Darren keeps me around: I make him laugh. Not many people are willing to take the risk of joking with a billionaire. Anyway, he said my idea would take too long. He told me he wanted to create a new progressive party that would run candidates who were fearless.

"I thought that was more of a reach than my idea, but then I had a thought. Recruit candidates who were charismatic leaders in business, academia and the arts, jobs they could return to after a short stretch in government."

"Term limits?" the president asked.

"Yes, but mandated by the party not the law."

"What do you mean?"

"The Cool Blue party label is good for only three terms of office in House or one in the Senate. Six years in Congress should be enough for any sane person."

"And then what?"

"If you don't leave Washington, your party affiliation gets yanked, and you have to run against a new Cool Blue opponent."

"You're saying you'd discharge a candidate who was a favorite for reelection?"

"Interesting that you'd say discharge, Madam President. The way we're pitching the people we want to join Cool Blue is likening their service to a hitch in the military, one that has a specific discharge date. And, yes, Darren and I would have no problem giving someone the heave-ho."

"You say that now," the president said.

"Yes, we do. That's not to say that former Cool Blue representatives and senators will have to leave matters of governance behind entirely. We expect them to help the party develop our policies regarding domestic and foreign issues. We'll also want them to help recruit their replacements and pinpoint vulnerable opposition seats."

For a long moment, the president just looked at Putnam.

"You're really quite the imaginative thinker," she said.

Putnam shrugged. "I do what I can."

"Are you going to cast your candidates, pick people with pretty faces?"

"Darren and I talked about that. We looked at how you called on your Hollywood friends to help you with your last campaign."

"And your judgment was?"

"We won't specifically exclude high-end beauty or hand-someness, but in general we're looking for people who might be better thought of as character actors. Someone you'd consider your best friend rather than a fantasy figure."

The president laughed. "I'm starting to look like a character actor."

Putnam took a sip of water, put the bottle down and shook his head.

"No way, Madam President. You and Mr. McGill are the most glamorous White House couple since the Kennedys. It's in your interest and the country's to maintain that image."

"If my looks go, so does my political standing?"

"Never let the bastards think they're getting the better of you, right?"

"Never," the president agreed. "I'll have to try to get a little more sleep."

"Whatever it takes."

"How many candidates will Cool Blue run in the mid-term elections?"

"We're starting small. A dozen House candidates, two for the Senate."

"Opposing whom?"

"Evenly divided against Democrats who like to vote against their party and Republicans and True Southers on the extreme right of their parties."

"Do you plan to run a presidential candidate in 2016?"

"Unlikely. If we have success with the Congressional races, we'll start looking at state legislatures next."

Putnam thought that might be the end of his presidential visit, but Patricia Grant turned the conversation back to a personal matter.

"If you don't mind my asking, Putnam, may I ask what effect

the shooting at the Winstead School has had on you and Margaret? Are you considering any changes for Maxi's schooling?"

Putnam told the president of the idea he and Margaret had discussed earlier that day.

Then he said, "I think it'll work out for us, but the downside is it isn't practical on a national scale. I did have another thought on the drive over here … but I was going to save it for Cool Blue."

The president nodded, held Putnam's gaze without further comment.

Not a doubt in his mind the woman's eyes still held star power.

Made you forget all about the few new wrinkles.

"Okay," he said, "you talked me into it."

Putnam told the president his new idea for keeping school-children safe.

Safer anyway. The president liked it, political risks and all.

### Chief of Staff's Office — The White House

While the president was speaking with Putnam Shady, Chief of Staff Galia Mindel was on the phone with White House Counsel Karen Rosemeyer about a question of federal spending. The counsel, also known at the president's official lawyer, was the attorney who helped define the dividing line between official activities and political ones.

Galia said, "Karen, please remind me of the Holy Writ on government spending."

"That's an easy one. 'Thou shalt not spend any funds without the authorization and appropriation of said funds by Congress.'"

"And once the funds are authorized and appropriated?"

"Come on, Galia." The two women had known each other for years. "You know how it goes. Sometimes, most times lately, Congress micro-manages how every penny gets spent. In a diminishing number of other cases, the president has some latitude in directing how funds get distributed."

"Such as the disbursement of FEMA funds in response to

natural disasters."

"Right. What are you getting at here, Galia?"

"Would the public health and social services emergency fund be considered in the same vein?"

"From the Department of Health and Human Services, sure. Are you talking about a public health crisis?"

"Definitely."

"Then there should be no problem. Hey, should I get some kind of inoculation?"

Would that there were such a thing, Galia thought.

"Just be careful out there, Karen."

After saying goodbye to the White House counsel, Galia made a call to Jeffrey Berry, CEO of Eyes Only, the country's largest outdoor advertising company. She introduced herself and apologized for bothering the man at home on a Sunday, but said the federal government wanted to buy specialized billboard space coast to coast and border to border and maintain that purchase for an indefinite period of time. Would that be possible?

Berry replied, "Ms. Mindel, when manna from heaven falls in my lap, I have no problem working on a Sunday, and I'll do everything I can to see you get just what you want."

Galia said, "That's wonderful. I'd like to start with a billboard opposite an office building in Falls Church, Virginia."

She'd checked beforehand to make sure the perfect location was available, and it was.

## CHAPTER 11

### *Bounce City, Wisconsin Avenue NW — Washington, DC*

Sweetie and Roger Michaelson sat next to each other in the parents' viewing area of the indoor amusement center for children. As the name made plain, Bounce City was a series of adjacent spaces where kids could fling, jump and hurl themselves onto inflated surfaces made to represent iconic areas of major American cities and bounce until even young stomachs could tolerate no more. Then they could get their fill of overpriced salty and sweet snacks and soda, and go back to bouncing their way across the country.

At the moment, Maxi and a group of friends who'd come down from Baltimore for the day were laughing and shrieking as they cavorted in a room filled with cartoon replicas of Washington's most famous monuments. The fun at Bounce City for Maxi and all her friends was provided courtesy of Margaret and Putnam Shady. They'd pick up the tab for a late lunch at a proper restaurant, too, before Maxi said goodbye to her friends and everyone went home.

The other moms had given Sweetie and Michaelson their space.

Like Sweetie, though, they kept an eye on their kids by glancing at the closed circuit monitors Bounce City provided for parental peace of mind.

College kids, working for the amusement center, provided polite hands-on restraint in case the younger ones got too rambunctious — and four clean-cut, brawny athletic types made sure no suspicious single adults got inside and walked off with someone else's kid.

For all the good-time fun and security measures, Sweetie still felt on edge.

"Something wrong?" Michaelson asked.

He'd offered no objection when informed where he and Sweetie would have their follow-up discussion of his case. Sweetie held that to be a mark in the man's favor. The fact that he seemed to enjoy seeing children having fun was another.

She'd have to be careful or she might end up liking the guy.

"Did you notice the sign on the entrance door?" Sweetie asked.

Michaelson thought for a moment. "There were at least half-a-dozen."

"The one with the circle around and the slash through a semi-auto handgun."

"Yeah, I saw that. Seems like a good idea to me."

"I left my weapon in a gun-safe in the trunk of my car," Sweetie told him.

"And, what, you feel your little girl and her friends are more at risk? You'd feel better if all the mothers here were packing heat?"

Sweetie turned to look at Michaelson. "You put it that way, no. I'd feel better if I were armed." She went back to scanning the monitors.

Michaelson said, "There were times, not that long ago, when legal rights were for the chosen few. That started a lot of large protest marches, as I recall."

Sweetie's worry about getting too fond of Michaelson receded.

"You like guns?" she asked.

"Me, no. The only thing I like to shoot is a basketball. I've turned down lots of invitations to get up early and go kill Bambi. Not that I object to people who hunt. They help keep wildlife off our highways."

Sweetie nodded. "It was just a couple years ago some Chicago cops had to kill a mountain lion that wandered into my old neighborhood on the North Side. I had to be a lot of things when I was with the CPD, but a big-game hunter wasn't one of them."

Michaelson took the discussion beyond proliferating wildlife. "You're really worried somebody might come in here and start shooting people willy-nilly?"

"That was another thing I didn't have to worry about in the old days. Now, if you think about it, what public space isn't vulnerable to a loon with a military-grade weapon?"

"That's easy," Michaelson said. "Congress and the Supreme Court don't allow guns in their public galleries. You also have to go through metal-detectors to take a tour of the White House. "

A chill smile crossed Sweetie's face. "Yeah, all those birdbrains who cheer on an unbridled concept of the Second Amendment would poop their pants without that bit of hypocrisy."

"Does that include Patti Grant?" Michaelson asked.

Sweetie turned his way and shook her head, emphatically.

Michaelson said, "You know something?"

"How to keep a secret," Sweetie said. "Let's get back to the fix you're in. Tell me what the FBI and Secret Service asked you about. They both interviewed you, right?"

"I didn't think of it as an interview," Michaelson said. "The situation reminded me of my days as a prosecutor with the Cook County State's Attorney's Office. Back then we called it an interrogation."

"But you hadn't been arrested. That's what you told me."

"No, I wasn't arrested. I was a suspect. Still am."

"Why did you talk to the feds at all?"

"To tell them I'm innocent, to get that declaration on the record. I did insist that both agencies question me at the same time."

"How'd you get them to agree to that?"

"I played them off each other. I said if they didn't do it my way,

I'd speak to only one of them and they could decide who it would be."

Sweetie smiled. She liked that. But it also told her how smart and manipulative her new client could be. She'd have to keep that in mind.

She looked up and saw all was still well with Maxi and her friends.

Turning back to Michaelson, she asked, "Did you refuse to answer any questions?"

"No, not that I wouldn't have if I thought they were trying to sucker me into a trap."

"But they played it straight?"

"They did then. Who knows what they might be thinking now? They asked me if I had any contacts with diplomats or business people from Islamic countries. The answer on the business side was a flat no. Regarding diplomats, I've been introduced to a few at social functions, but only people from countries that are supposed to be our allies."

"You think they're continuing to investigate those avenues anyway?"

Michaelson said, "I hope so. They'll see I told them the truth. They also asked me if I knew Andy Grant."

That caught Sweetie by surprise, the idea that Michaelson might have known the president's late, first husband.

"Did you?" Sweetie asked.

"I met him at a candidates' dinner when I ran against Patti Grant for the House seat that she beat me out of. He was a likable guy. Shook my hand and told me it was fine to play hard but keep it clean."

"Did you take that as a threat?"

"More like fair warning. If I had won that seat, though, and Andy Grant hadn't liked the way I did it, I got the feeling he might try to cause some problems for me. I respected him for that."

"But he didn't scare you?"

"No, Galia Mindel did that. The reason I couldn't play dirty against the president was that she would play even dirtier against me. Looking back at things now, I realize my battles were with Galia not Patti Grant."

"What did the feds ask you about Joan Renshaw? She was the one who made the accusation against you, saying she'd told you about the president's planned visit to Inspiration Hall."

Michaelson said, "They wanted to know if I'd ever had a personal relationship with Ms. Renshaw."

"A sexual relationship?"

"They didn't come right out and say so, but that was my inference. I told them there wasn't anything like that. So they showed me a photo of Ms. Renshaw speaking to me at a fundraising party. She was saying something. I was smiling. She had a drink in one hand and her other hand was resting on my dinner jacket. Looked pretty chummy, I must admit, but I'd had no memory of it until I saw it."

"Then the memory came back?" Sweetie asked.

"Yes, Ms. Renshaw and I are fellow alumni of Northwestern. She'd been reminiscing about a Big Ten basketball game. She'd seen me hit the winning basket. She'd had a bet with a friend who went to the University of Illinois. Thanks to me, her friend had to wash Ms. Renshaw's car once a week for the following summer vacation."

The story made Sweetie smile, too.

Nonetheless, she asked for the name of the U of I student. "Joan shared that with you, didn't she?"

"Yeah, she did. The feds asked for it, too. The name Ms. Renshaw gave me was Lisa Stone."

"You don't mind that I asked for the name, do you?"

"I'd have thought less of you, if you hadn't."

"Do you recall meeting Joan Renshaw at any other time?"

"No."

Sweetie nodded and thought a moment. "Do you know where she's being held?"

"You mean where she's incarcerated? No."

Sweetie said, "That's all right. I'm sure I can find out."

Michaelson seemed unfazed by the prospect of her talking to Joan. Sweetie thanked him for his time. She said she'd be in touch if she had any further questions or information for him. They both stood up and shook hands.

Michaelson glanced up at a monitor.

Saw Maxi having a high time with all her friends.

He told Sweetie, "Maxi looks like a great kid. You're very lucky."

Sweetie started to warm to the man again.

### Metro Police Headquarters — Washington, DC

Auric Ludwig, as was his wont, got his grump back on, having been forcibly seated by Meeker and Beemer in front of Captain Rockelle Bullard's desk.

He told Rockelle, "You'll arrest me now with good reason or I'll sue you, your men and the whole police department for false imprisonment."

Rockelle didn't bat an eye. She told Meeker and Beemer. "Accommodate the man. Place him under arrest. Fingerprint him. Get his mug shots. Don't mind if he doesn't smile for the camera. I've seen his smile on TV, and it ain't pretty."

The two detectives hauled Ludwig to his feet.

He was not smiling; his grimace wasn't attractive either.

"I said with good reason," Ludwig protested. "You've given me no reason at all."

"Sit him back down a minute," Rockelle said.

The detectives made him bounce on the chair, a sturdy piece of scarred oak.

"You want to know what you did wrong?" Rockelle asked, her voice hard. "Okay, I'll tell you. You interfered with a homicide investigation my detectives are working. You know what that's called. Don't bother trying to think of the answer. It's called obstruction of justice. That's the legal term for messing with a police investigation, sticking your nose where it definitely does not belong."

Ludwig felt a chill run down his spine, but he did his best not to show any fear.

Being brazen, he'd found long ago, was the best way to go — as long as none of these people smacked him on the back of his head with a phone book or something. He repressed that unbidden image and said, "I've done nothing wrong and when my lawyer —"

He stopped cold when he saw Rockelle shake her head.

"We've got you cold, Mr. Ludwig. You held a press conference yesterday and announced that an unknown person, someone you characterized as 'a good guy with a gun' was responsible for shooting and killing Abel Mays. You made your announcement before any news was released by law enforcement that Mr. Mays had been found dead and who, if anyone other than himself, was responsible for his death. To put it in a way you might appreciate, you jumped the gun."

Try as he might, Ludwig couldn't maintain a façade of bravado.

His face fell and his usual flush of high color went gray.

"You may well have alerted your 'good guy' with your announcement. You might have made it much harder for the police to arrest that person and bring him to trial. By doing that, you have delayed — obstructed — the course of justice."

Ludwig said in a small voice, "This morning, I offered him a hundred thousand dollars to come forward."

Rockelle chuckled and shook her head. "I was watching WWN. What you did was ask a killer to surrender himself to you, not to the police. I'm not a prosecutor, but it sounded to me like you'd just dug yourself a deeper hole."

"What can I do?" Ludwig asked.

Rockelle sat back and crossed her arms over her chest, looked at Ludwig like he was some sort of bug that had scuttled into her office.

"We know that you had to get your information from a cop at the crime scene. You tell us who it was, and how many other cops in town might be leaking confidential information to you and —"

Meeker leaned in and whispered into the captain's ear. She nodded, liking what she'd heard.

"Detective Meeker makes a good point," she told Ludwig. "We'll need to know how many cops you have working for you in DC and around the country as a whole. You give us all their names, the court might take that into consideration."

Ludwig's face hardened visibly. Lose all his informers? Be seen as a traitor to a critically important part of his constituency, gun-happy cops? That was a non-starter.

He shook his head.

Rockelle leaned forward, placed her hands on her desk.

"You know what the punishment for obstruction is in the District of Columbia, Mr. Ludwig? Three to thirty years in prison. Given that your crime involves the corruption of police officers, my money says you'll get the high end of the sentencing range."

Sweat appeared on Ludwig's brow but he remained silent.

Rockelle gave him a silent three-count and then nodded to Meeker and Beemer.

"Arrest Mr. Ludwig, process him, give him his phone call and put him in a cell."

The detectives hoisted Ludwig again, looks of satisfaction on their faces.

They all but had him out of the captain's office, when she said, "Just a minute, Mr. Ludwig. Here's one more thing for you to think about. There was a limited number of police officers who might have called you with the information about Abel Mays' death. We have all their names. It's just a matter of time before we find out who called you. You change your mind about helping us, but you do it too late? That won't help you at all."

As her detectives led the man away, Rockelle could see him shake.

Good, she thought.

### Edgar Hoover Building — Washington, DC

Special Agent Abra Benjamin sat in front of Deputy Director Byron DeWitt's desk at FBI headquarters and said, "I had a hard time keeping it under control with Mr. McGill."

"No, you didn't," DeWitt told her, not looking up from the piece of paper he was reading.

FBI Director Jeremiah Haskins had just delegated yet another task to DeWitt.

The president had issued an order that a lobbyist named Putnam Shady was not to become the subject of renewed surveillance by the Bureau. DeWitt was to see to it that the special agents who had engaged in those duties previously followed the president's order.

The Bureau, as a whole, wasn't given to individual initiative. Special agents didn't work rogue operations the way some local cops misguidedly did. The director simply wanted DeWitt to reinforce discipline. No one was to go off the reservation regarding Mr. Shady.

DeWitt made it part of his job to know who was who in the Washington. Everybody knew James J. McGill, aka the president's henchman, was the president's husband. (That was why Benjamin never would have gotten in his face.) Many people knew Margaret "Sweetie" Sweeney was McGill's longtime friend and business partner. Far fewer people knew that Putnam Shady was Ms. Sweeney's husband.

But DeWitt did. He'd even gone to the trouble of doing a background check on Shady. The man's family name alone practically demanded it. He'd learned about Shady's fugitive parents and how Shady had been watched for years by the Bureau to see if he'd had any contact with Mom and Dad.

More recently, Shady had popped up on DeWitt's radar for his position with Darren Drucker and the role Shady had played in the creation of Inspiration Hall.

Just then, DeWitt felt a moment of inspiration himself.

He made a note to call Margaret Sweeney on Monday morning.

"Byron? Hey, Mr. Deputy Director."

DeWitt looked up, realizing Benjamin must have been talking to him while he was lost in thought. "Sorry. What is it?"

She said, "What do you mean I almost didn't lose it with

McGill?"

"You're a dedicated careerist, Abra. You've told me so; you've proved it beyond any doubt. You'd never try to muscle the president's husband. You know it would be a career-ender."

The special agent frowned, an unusual emotional display in front of a superior.

But then the two of them had been lovers. Benjamin had even given birth to their child, and then promptly put the baby boy up for adoption by Chief of Police Ron Ketchum and his new wife, Keely Powell, in Goldstrike, California. Benjamin hadn't asked DeWitt if he'd like to raise the child as a bachelor father.

DeWitt, briefly, had been tempted to do just that, had thought to sue for custody of his son. He didn't care if a legal battle would end both his career and Benjamin's. But that kind of legal slugfest wouldn't be resolved quickly. That raised the question: Who would care for the child while the suit was grinding through the judicial system?

Benjamin had made it painfully clear motherhood wasn't for her.

DeWitt's workload was crushing. He could always quit his job, but that would mean walking away from the investigations of a presidential assassination attempt, the murder of a U.S. senator, the murder of a foreign diplomat and the manhunt for a fugitive billionaire involved in the assassination conspiracy.

Tallying up his burdens, DeWitt thought he should have quit his job.

Only his sense of responsibility wouldn't allow that.

So maybe his karmic punishment for a misbegotten fatherhood was that his workload would multiply until it crushed him. Looking outside his own feelings, he came to the conclusion that his son would be better off being raised by loving, adoptive parents. He also liked the idea of the California Sierra as a place to raise a child. He'd decided not to object to the adoption.

He didn't transfer Benjamin to some remote FBI outpost because she was valuable to him as an investigator — and he knew she'd sue him for being punished without professional cause.

The most important reason he kept her close, though, was to remind him not to make the same mistake twice.

"There are worse things to be than a careerist," Benjamin said.

She thought DeWitt might have come to share her sense of ambition when he declined to fight for child custody. But when he also passed up the chance to renew their sexual relationship, despite clear overtures from her, she understood things had changed. The deputy director was a smart and even decent guy. He'd treat her fairly, but now she was just another subordinate.

No, not really, she thought. Byron knew enough not to try to punish her for a personal decision, but if she ever made a serious professional mistake, one that would hold up before a board of review or in court, she wouldn't get a second chance. Her career at the FBI would be at a dead end. She'd have to do the thing she'd least want to do: quit.

Realizing that now, she saw her implicit criticism of McGill was a mistake.

So she changed her tune and said, "You're right. I was just griping about an outsider poking his nose into an FBI case. Sorry."

"An outsider with considerable police experience who gave us a whole new take on our investigation of Jordan Gilford's murder," DeWitt said. How had he forgotten to account for that on his to-do list?

"You know," Benjamin said, working on recovering lost ground, "Mr. McGill's catch on the second killer using Abel Mays' gun to kill Jordan Gilford gives me an idea."

"What's that?"

"Well, if the second killer was a pro, a hired hitman, he wouldn't have left any of his fingerprints on Mays' weapon, right?"

"Most likely right, but one can always hope," DeWitt said.

Benjamin continued, "But at least a few of his gloved fingers must have overlapped points where Mays also held the weapon. So it stands to reason that the second killer must've smudged some of

Mays' prints, also right?"

DeWitt had to smile. If some of Mays' prints were smudged, that would confirm McGill's idea of a second killer. Redounding to Benjamin's credit. If there were no smudged prints, that would mean the wound pattern on Jordan's back was an anomaly, there was no second killer and McGill was a small-time jerk who should leave major investigations to the FBI.

Either way, Benjamin would get something out of it.

She might well be running the whole damn Bureau someday.

"Also right," DeWitt conceded. "Check it out."

"There's more to think about."

"Such as."

"If Jordan Gilford was killed because someone was worried what he'd find as part of the DOD's Inspector General Office, then the person who hired the assassin is probably some muckety-muck in the defense industry or the Pentagon. Maybe even Congress."

DeWitt felt sure he'd known that but had repressed the thought. Was there no end to his tribulations?

Benjamin, on the other hand, looked like she couldn't wait to jump on the case with both feet. The instinct for self-preservation, as much as any intellectual calculation, led DeWitt to the answer. "Special Agent Benjamin, you now have operational control of the murder investigation of Jordan Gilford … if you feel you can play well with James J. McGill and any of the friends he may call upon."

For the blink of an eye, DeWitt saw conflicting emotions race across Benjamin's face.

Then she said, "Thank you, sir. I'll do whatever's necessary to make sure this comes out right for everyone."

Her intention to please included calling him sir again. Letting him know she understood the new lay of the land. DeWitt both appreciated that and felt something once precious had just died.

Benjamin wasn't quite done and said, "There's one more thing."

"What's that?"

"As my investigation — and Mr. McGill's — proceed, the pressure on the guilty parties is likely to grow. The bad guys might get desperate. If they hired a hitman once …"

DeWitt knew just where she was going.

"They might make James J. McGill their next target."

# CHAPTER 12

*McGill's Hideaway — The White House*

McGill had made a personal call on Zara Gilford before going back to the White House. Celsus Crogher was at Zara's condo when he arrived. He spoke to Celsus, giving Zara the moment she said she needed to put on her face.

"Everything's all right?" McGill asked.

"Security in the building is top notch, for a civilian structure."

"You're getting along okay with Karl Vasek?" The building's security director and retired Marine.

"Yeah, I like the guy. Might ask him to go to work for me."

"For you?" McGill asked.

"You're the one who suggested I do private security, remember?"

"You didn't sound too enthused."

"I wasn't. I've got a good pension. Don't really need more money."

"But you do need something to do," McGill said.

"Just like you when you came to Washington." Celsus sighed. "I hate to admit it, but I'm coming to understand you better. A little anyway. My reluctance to start a private firm was I thought I'd have to work for a bunch of dicks. Guys I'd sooner throw into a line of fire, not catch a bullet for. Mrs. Gilford, she's a sweet lady. Opened my eyes to other possibilities."

McGill said, "You're in business for yourself, you get to choose your clients."

"Yeah, that's a whole new idea after a career in government."

Zara Gilford appeared, looking apprehensive. McGill had told her he had news for her.

They sat next to each other on the living room sofa. McGill held both her hands in his and told her he'd found persuasive evidence that her husband had been killed by someone other than Abel Mays. He was taken by surprise when she asked what the evidence was, but he told her.

Celsus, standing nearby, overheard and nodded in agreement with McGill's assessment.

Zara's tears came, as McGill had felt sure they would, but she caught him off guard again when she smiled. She took the handkerchief McGill offered her and dried her tears. That done, she smiled.

"My heart is still broken," she said. "I'll always miss Jordan, but I'm so happy his death won't just be wrapped up in another tragedy for the sake of convenience. If you can find out who really killed my husband, Mr. McGill, and see that justice is done, it would help me so much."

Before McGill might feel obliged to make a foolish promise, Zara kissed his cheek and said she needed to be alone. She returned to her bedroom.

McGill asked Celsus, "You've got someone to relieve you?"

"I'm good for the night, and I've got an ex-Secret Service colleague coming in the morning."

"Good."

"You think you can catch the SOB who killed Mr. Gilford?"

McGill said, "I'm going to do everything I can."

"From what I've seen, that usually works out. A couple of things, though."

"What?"

"Tell Deke Ky to really be on his toes."

Celsus had the same thought Abra Benjamin did. Somebody

might be coming for McGill next. Then he added his second point of information.

"Mrs. Gilford says she's going home tomorrow. Back to her real house."

When McGill got back to the White House, he called his ex-wife, Carolyn, and spoke to her and their two children who still lived in Evanston. "Everybody's okay?" he asked his ex.

"We're good. Security, federal and local, is thick on the ground. Jim, how long will that be necessary?"

"You decide what you and Lars need." Lars Enquist was Carolyn's husband, the kids' stepdad. "Why don't we give Kenny and Caitie an extra school week?"

Normally, Carolyn wanted the children to have as close to normal a childhood as possible.

What with having the president of the United States for a stepmother.

Now, however, she said, "I think that would be wise."

As with most parents in the country, both McGill and Carolyn increasingly felt the simple act of sending your children off to school in the morning had become an exercise in faith and courage that they would return unharmed. That or an act of denial that there was any danger.

Kenny came on the phone and told McGill, "That was bad, Dad, what happened to those football players and their coaches. Danny Murtaugh said we should put posters up in every school: If you're thinking about murder-suicide, skip step one, go directly to step two."

"Danny's father is a doctor, isn't he?"

Kenny had gone to school with Danny since first grade.

"His mom, too."

McGill had forgotten about that. "Okay. You think Danny's parents would advocate suicide as a good public health policy? And how do you feel about what Danny said?"

Kenny was also planning a career in medicine.

"I don't know how Danny's parents might feel. I wouldn't ever want to tell someone to kill himself, but Danny's idea would cut down on the body count."

"You're angry," McGill said.

"Yeah."

"Because you don't know what to do. You don't want to meet violence with violence because then you'd just add to the problem."

"Yeah." Kenny's voice broke. "I almost died, Dad. I pretty much know what dying is like. Why can't people see how horrible it is to shoot someone?"

McGill didn't have an answer for that. "Patti and I are going to do our best to make things better. Why don't you see if you can think of something to help that doesn't involve any body counts at all?"

Kenny said he'd try, but he didn't sound optimistic.

Caitie came on. She'd obviously overheard a good deal of her brother's conversation.

"I'm the one who's really mad, Dad."

"And your answer to the problem, my dear?"

"I'm going to become a cop."

McGill was struck dumb.

"Dad, you still there?"

"I am, but I think either my hearing or my mind is slipping."

"I'm not kidding, Dad. Somebody's got to protect people."

Caitie had only recently completed a speaking role in her first movie.

The premiere was set for the coming summer.

A stepping-stone, she'd said, to following in her step-mother's footsteps to the presidency.

"I know what you're thinking, Dad. I'm just a kid and I don't know what I want."

"I'm beginning to wonder," McGill conceded.

"Well, Dennis Farina was a Chicago cop who also was an actor."

"After he retired from the police department."

"So maybe I'll do some more acting, become a cop, then go back to Hollywood."

Anything must seem possible when you were thirteen, McGill supposed, but to the best of his recollection his plans at that age were far more modest.

"What about politics and a run for the White House?" he asked.

"Patti told me the presidency is not all it's cracked up to be."

McGill was glad to hear that plan might be crossed off Caitie's list. "Have you told your mother any of this? She used to worry when I was a cop."

"I thought I'd better tell you first. I wouldn't want to scare Mom but …"

"What?"

"She can't divorce me."

There were other forms of alienation, but McGill didn't want to get into that.

"Do me a favor," he said, "don't tell your mother about this until we have a chance to talk in person, okay?"

"Okay, but if everybody in this country is going to have a gun, I want a badge, too."

Now, that sounded like Caitie. It was also one of the saddest prospects for the future he'd ever heard. He told his youngest child he loved her and always to be careful.

"You, too, Dad."

Ten minutes after saying goodbye to Caitie and staring at his still-active wood-burning fireplace — perfect for a day bleak in every sense of the word — McGill was joined by Patti. She sat next to McGill on the room's large leather sofa. Took his hand in hers and sat in silence for a minute.

Staring at the fire along with McGill, she asked, "Would you care for a drink?"

"No, I'm depressed enough as it is."

He told Patti of his phone call home and what Carolyn, Kenny and Caitie had to say.

"A cop, really?" Patti asked.

"She has no idea of what it means."

"No, she has some idea. She understands there's a legal advantage to being a police officer. You can carry a weapon openly in public. You have more latitude in the use of that weapon. And if you wear body armor you're less vulnerable than most people."

McGill looked at Patti. "You really think she knows about body armor? The last time I wore a Kevlar vest, she wasn't even —"

Patti held up a hand. "What about the Evanston PD officers who provide security for Carolyn and Lars? She's seen them for five years now."

McGill hadn't thought about that. "Sure, they wear armor. The idea of a drink is sounding better."

"Let's give it a minute. I'll tell you about my meeting with Jean Morrissey."

Patti had brought the vice president up to speed on where things stood with a response to the slaughter at the Winstead School, and she told McGill something new.

"I'll be speaking to a school assembly at Winstead tomorrow. There will be no media presence. This is just for the school community and me. I'll express the grief I share with them, give them an outline of what I plan to do and solicit ideas from the students, parents, faculty and administration."

"You want me to be there?" McGill asked.

"I'd love to have your company, but you have your investigation to work, and I'd like you to confirm your interview with Ellie Booker and make it ASAP. I'll speak to the country shortly after you do."

McGill nodded. "I'll get up early and hit the ground running. Did Jean have any suggestions for you?"

"She did. She's a hunter. She's going to see if she can recruit hunting clubs and organizations to support basic reforms of gun laws. And then she told me something else that broke my heart."

"What?"

"Jean has a friend in Minneapolis who's the head of an ad agency that's won every award for creativity the ad business has to offer. She said the agency has a TV spot for gun control in the can.

It's been ready to air for three years, but the people who sponsored it decided not to run it. They aren't afraid of push-back; they just don't know if they can take the heartbreak all over again."

"What does it say," McGill asked, "what does it show?"

Patti told him.

"Jesus," McGill whispered.

"Jean is going to talk to the sponsors, see if she can persuade them to let us use it."

Better her than me, McGill thought.

He and Patti had one drink each and went to bed.

### Connecticut Avenue NW — Washington, DC

Representative Philip Brock, Democrat of Pennsylvania, double murderer and anarchist to the bone, got home late. Two flight delays, one for a late-arriving flight crew, the other for mechanical problems, had made the trip from Costa Rica to Washington seem interminable. Brock had bought a copy of the New York Times during his layover in Miami and read about the nation's latest shooting atrocity, the one at the Winstead School. Yet another sign, he thought, that the existing order had to be overthrown. No civilized country would permit the recurrent slaughter of its children and other innocents.

He hadn't thought specifically about what might happen to the Second Amendment, should another Constitutional Convention be convened. Logically, it would be as up for grabs as any other part of the country's foundational laws. He didn't see, though, how the right to bear arms could be any more broadly interpreted. Allow John Q. Public to buy surplus from defense contractors? Every man could have his own armored fighting vehicle, attack helicopter and killer drones.

That'd make the neighbors think twice about their loud, late-night parties.

Unless they had superior firepower, in which case thing could get really loud.

The prices of large-scale weapons, however, would be beyond the reach of anyone but the country's billionaires. Still, if a private market were allowed to develop, canny capitalists would likely find a way to meet consumer demand. If things came to that, though, Brock thought that moving to Central America might not be a sufficiently distant retreat.

Tasmania might look better.

On the other hand, do-gooders, and they were still a majority, would seize the opportunity to rewrite the anything-goes license currently afforded by the Second Amendment. Tighten it up considerably. Not that the other side would ever give up. It would be the abortion debate all over again, only with a lot more bang-bang.

Oh, well. The country needed to end its schizophrenic nature.

Decide who it truly was.

Brock's taxi dropped him off at a high-security condo building, not far from the one to which Jordan Gilford had relocated himself and his wife. Unlike the Widow Gilford, Brock had no intention of leaving his secure nest until he departed the country. He settled down in his living room with two fingers of Pappy Van Winkle bourbon, the 23-year old reserve stuff, and returned his attention to the now ruffled copy of the Times he'd brought home.

The updated story of Bahir Ben Kalil's death had made the paper, too. The Jordanian diplomat — no mention of his terrorist affiliations — had been tentatively identified by his sister, Dr. Hasna Kalil. The FBI was investigating the death as a homicide. Of course, they were. Accidental death and natural causes were out of the question.

Brock strained to think if there was any trace of physical evidence that could connect him with Bahir's murder. He couldn't think of one. Even if he'd made some unnoticed slip-up on Billy Goat Trail A the night he'd killed Bahir, shed a follicle of hair if not a tear, it would have been washed away by months of Washington winter weather.

He honestly didn't think he had anything to worry about.

Not from the FBI or any other law enforcement agency. But who was this sister, Hasna Kalil? Jihadis were hardly advocates of women's rights, but they weren't above using females to commit acts of violence, even to the point of letting their veiled ladies blow themselves up for the cause.

Was it possible Hasna would try to kill him, if she decided he'd killed her brother?

Brock decided it would be foolish to think otherwise.

He revised his threat assessment on the homefront upward.

From there, he took the jump to another possible worry overseas.

Tyler Busby was still on the run, no doubt in great style, but hiding out was not really the man's style. He loved the limelight. If Busby were to decide his role as a fugitive was getting old, he might see what consideration he could get for himself, in the way of reduced punishment, by giving the feds a treacherous member of Congress. Him.

Oh, well. He'd known all along he was playing a dangerous game.

He'd just have to speed things up. Stay a hop, skip and a jump ahead of the hangman.

He picked up his phone and made a call, not caring that he'd wake up the other party.

In Harrisburg, Pennsylvania, a groggy speaker of the state House of Representatives answered, after looking at his caller ID. "You couldn't have called earlier?"

"Sorry. Travel problems," Brock said.

"Well, you'll be happy. We've got the votes. The roll call's ... I was going to say tomorrow. But it's really later this morning."

"Sonofabitch," Brock said, "We're going to do it."

"If we get Ohio, we will."

"We'll get Ohio."

"Then, Congressman, the United States will have its second Constitutional Convention."

It couldn't come fast enough to suit Philip Brock.

# CHAPTER 13

*White House Gymnasium — Monday, March 10, 2014*

McGill lived up to his promise to the president, almost. He woke up early, five-thirty, and hit the treadmill running. He was still a little leg-weary from his run yesterday and that annoyed him. No one who had led an athletic life ever liked to admit that his strength, endurance or flexibility was slipping. He'd never been an elite athlete in most regards, but he'd been a damn good recreational jock.

The one physical gift he had that could go up against the very best anywhere was quickness. He'd always had an abundance of fast-twitch muscles, a simple genetic legacy. If he needed a burst of speed, he had a first step few could match. That was important if you wanted to get off a clean basketball shot or slip a punch. Throw a punch, too.

Any muscle, though, depended on having great tone for peak performance.

McGill felt maybe he'd been taking things for granted lately, had gotten just a bit lazy. That was exactly the wrong approach to take as time continued to pass at its relentless pace and gray hair was lurking around the next corner. He didn't care that much about cosmetic changes; it was maintaining the ability to function at a high level that mattered to him.

A mile into his run on the treadmill, he warmed up. He felt a spring return to his stride. His hips, knees and ankles swung through their ranges of motion without complaint. His heart and lungs expanded and contracted in rhythm. Sweat flowed steadily and breathing came easily. He stepped up the pace and did two more miles, the latter of which was completed with someone watching him.

A glance at the mirror in front of the treadmill showed Elspeth Kendry, the Secret Service special agent in charge of the presidential security detail had stopped by. She looked at him run without giving any sign she had come to speak with him. That was reassuring. If she'd had any dire news concerning the president, she'd have been at his side in a heartbeat, telling him to cut his workout short.

McGill finished his run, toweled off and took a measured gulp from his Poland Spring bottle. He gestured to Elspeth to join him. She stepped his way but stopped outside his sweat radius, as measured by the puddle forming around his feet.

"Something we need to talk about, Elspeth?"

"Today is one of Special Agent Ky's rare days off. If you don't mind, I'll be replacing him."

McGill had had his ups and downs with Elspeth. That was pretty much a given for him. The Secret Service, as an institution, was still adjusting to not having a polite, compliant First Lady to usher around. He knew he was a pain in the ass to them in many ways, but their job wasn't an easy one in any case. The bullet-catchers would have to evolve. He wouldn't be the last man to be married to a female president — and the way society was changing it was conceivable a man might one day be the spouse of a male president.

That might be a ways off, but once something could be imagined …

"Fine with me, Elspeth." Despite their occasional contretemps, she was far more congenial company than Celsus Crogher had ever been. Before the guy had retired. As a civilian, Celsus was starting to show signs of becoming human. "You haven't been up all night, have you?"

The time now was only six o'clock.

"No, sir. I was given a heads-up that you'd awoken early."

"Sorry about that. Have you had breakfast?"

"No."

"That'll be on me then. We'll eat in the Mess." McGill had a thought. Elspeth's presence, dressed in a dark suit cut for a woman and sensible rubber-soled shoes, presented him with an opportunity to keep his reflexes sharp. "Would mind doing a little light sparring with me, Elspeth?"

He'd seen real-world examples of just how quick she was.

Elspeth nodded. "As long as it's not full speed. The president might chastise me if I broke your nose."

McGill grinned. "I'll write you a note if that happens, but I'll do my best to avoid it."

Elspeth hung her coat on a wall-hook that held a twenty-five pound resistance band. She stood, hands at her sides, facing McGill and asked, "How do you want to do this?"

"Not like we're boxing. More like street fighting. I'll stand like this, with my palms out, as if I'm trying to appease you. 'Hey, lady, I don't want any trouble.' You try to land a punch to my head, almost. You want to measure your reach, so you don't get in trouble with the boss?"

"No, I'm good. I know where to stop a punch."

"Okay, then. Use both hands and start whenev —"

Elspeth threw a straight left, trying to catch McGill by surprise.

He swung his right arm in an arc, the back of his wrist pushing her arm aside.

Elspeth fired a right. McGill's right hand reversed the arc, diverting the punch with his palm. Elspeth, emotion showing in her eyes now at the ease with which McGill had parried her blows, threw two lefts in succession and followed those with a kick from her right foot. They hadn't discussed kicking, but McGill had said it was a street fight.

He blocked the first of the successive lefts as he had before, with the back of his wrist. He stepped forward inside the second left, letting it go by. Elspeth felt the fingers of McGill's right hand slide across her cheek, soft as a lover's caress. Only his thumb was coming straight for her eye. Elspeth felt it touch her eyelashes as she reflexively closed her eyes. By instinct — she'd done her own share of street fighting — she tried to kick McGill with her right foot.

The attempt was blocked inches from the ground by McGill's left foot hitting her shin. He wore sneakers, and Elspeth could tell he hadn't put much force into the counter-kick. So she was able to step back, get her hands up in front of her face and open her eyes.

She saw McGill had also retreated slightly, but the SOB was smiling.

"That was great," he said. "I don't suppose you have a metal baton we could work with."

Elspeth did, in fact, have one in her suit coat.

But she said, "I don't want to hurt you any worse than I already have."

That being the case, McGill said he'd shower and meet her for breakfast in twenty minutes.

### The Winstead School — Washington, DC

Patricia Grant stepped onstage in the school auditorium in front of an audience of high school students and adults, each of whom was clean, well-dressed and a display of raw grief. Galia watched from the wings. The headmaster, Geoffrey Cooper, had given an introduction that was as simple as it got, "Ladies and gentlemen, please welcome Patricia Grant, the president of the United States." The assembly got to its feet and offered a round of applause.

The president saw more than a few familiar faces, including Kira Fahey Yates and her uncle, Mather Wyman, the former vice president of the United States. It wasn't a morning for a prolonged ovation. The president quickly said thank you and asked everyone to be seated.

"I came here today to tell all of you how sorry I am that you've lost so many friends, classmates, teachers and colleagues who meant so much to everyone here. I'm sorry for the loss of Coaches Russell, Eccles and Knox. I'm sorry for the loss of Jarius Niles, Ricky Mitchell, Paul Dirksen, Christopher Malloy, Gianni Tomaselli, Melvin Kendricks and Evan Wellstone.

"I pray the Lord has greeted them all as the heroes they are. I pray that all the young men who have been wounded in body and in soul recover fully and speedily. I pray that no one here ever again experiences such a terrible day.

"If that is to happen, if we are to put an end to such murderous rampages, then I have to do a better job for you. I've taken the oath of office to be your president two times. I've sworn to preserve, protect and defend the Constitution of the United States. That's not good enough. Concepts of government are important, but the day-to-day reality of how we govern ourselves matters more. Reality trumps theory.

"Any government that allow schoolchildren to be murdered even once has to be thought of as flawed, but a government that repeatedly lets its children, and other innocents, be killed has to be considered a failure. As the head of such a government, responsibility for that failure begins, but doesn't end, with me.

"It's often been said, that the presidency is an impossible job to do at all, much less to do well. There are simply too many tasks to perform and too many competing interests to reach a consensus for the common good. Nonetheless, we share a widely accepted bit of wisdom that tells us your right to swing your fist ends short of where my nose begins.

"Both this aphorism and the law tell us that there is no right to assault another person. There is no right in civil society to be an aggressor. The only context in which aggression is justifiable is warfare, as was the case when Japan attacked Pearl Harbor and Germany declared war on the United States. We were morally correct in taking the fight to them, not simply sitting back and arraying ourselves in a defensive posture.

"But civil society is not — or shouldn't be — a state of war. We must not allow our streets and parks, our classrooms and our shopping centers to become war zones. But that's just what is happening because the companies who manufacture firearms in our country and the companies who import firearms into our country, have decided to sell military-style weapons to civilians, to the American public.

"These companies made a judgment that there would be a market for such weapons and to our sorrow they were right. Included in that market was Abel Mays. Included in that market were the young men incapable of rational thought and unpossessed of a moral compass who have killed students in other schools, moviegoers in theaters and voters meeting with their elected representatives.

"The weapons all these killers used were weapons of war. They brought the wars within their twisted minds and tortured hearts home to all of us, and the results are horrifying. Just as the right to swing a fist is limited, the right to possess weapons of war must be limited. It must belong solely to those we send to war to protect us against the aggression of others.

"I'm sorry that I have failed you all so terribly. I promise I will do everything I can think of to end the kind of tragedy and sorrow you are enduring right now, but I have to tell you, I won't be able to succeed alone. I'll need help from each and every one of you.

"Please add my name to the list of those for whom you pray.

"Pray that together we'll all succeed."

Every word the president addressed to the Winstead School community was heartfelt. So were the ones she delivered to a smaller gathering of twenty Winstead parents in Headmaster Cooper's conference room. Only the tone was different. It was hard as granite and carried a weight measured in metric tons.

Galia Mindel stood in front of the only door to the room. Her expression said nobody was getting by her to enter or exit. Not until the president had said her piece.

The president began, "Almost forty percent of the firearms manufactured in this country fall under the ownership of one privately held investment banking firm: Liberty, Unlimited. Their arms companies make hunting rifles, shotguns and semi-automatic military-style assault rifles. They are also moving into the handgun market.

"Their business model, like so many others, calls for them to sell ever increasing numbers of their products. Only their products, with increasing frequency, wind up killing innocent people doing nothing more than going about their daily lives. The gun lobby's answer to mass murders is to put even more guns into circulation, never mentioning that would only fatten their clients' profits and cause more deaths.

"If I were able, I would nationalize every gun manufacturer in the nation. Only President Kennedy tried that with the steel companies and the Supreme Court told him he lacked that authority. There is, however, no obstacle to the people in this room pooling their resources and joining with like-minded friends and business partners to either buy out Liberty, Unlimited or do your best to drive them out of business."

Contrary to Auric Ludwig's fondest wish, not all of the dead football players were scholarship students. Five of them came from some of the richest families in the country. Their suffering was equal to any parent's, but their means to do something about it was far greater.

The president continued, "From the latest financial filings I've seen, Liberty, Unlimited is a half-billion dollars in debt and reported a net loss of six million dollars for 2013. It seems to me with the right combination of carrots and sticks a sale of the company to new ownership should be possible."

One of the fathers in the room raised a hand.

"Yes?"

"A sale of the company to what end, Madam President?"

"The newly owned and, I presume, renamed company would stop selling military-style weapons to civilians."

Another man raised his hand, and the president nodded to him.

"I know something about that company, ma'am. Assault weapons are their hottest sales models. How are we to approach investors to buy an indebted, money-losing company, if we tell them the company will no longer be able to sell its most popular product? Also ..." The man had to take a deep breath; he'd lost his son. "The weapon that killed my son, Christopher, was made overseas and imported. How would the purchase of Liberty, Unlimited affect that for the better?"

The president wanted to respond harshly, but she reminded herself of the pain the man had to be feeling. So she tempered her answer. While not avoiding its core truth.

"What you have to do, sir, and it won't be easy, is to let the people you approach see just how badly broken your heart is. Allow them to see that and tell them if nothing changes what happened to you can happen to them, too. If we don't change things soon, there will be no safe public places left in this country. No one's children will be safe."

More than a few of the mothers in the room began to cry.

Under other circumstances, the president would have wept with them.

She had more to say, though, and had to lead the others where she wanted them to go.

"There's another point you can make to investors. Once the new company initiates its no-assault-weapons policy, I will rally the American people to join me into pushing Congress to buy weapons for our military only from companies that refuse to sell such weapons to civilians."

What the president didn't say, to avoid any charge of insider trading, was that she intended to use her power as commander in chief to cancel any federal contracts with arms manufacturers that refused to go along with her program.

If Congress wanted to fight her on that, she'd welcome it.

"As regards the importation of military style weapons from

foreign countries, I will ask my fellow heads of state to ban the export of such weapons to the United States. If they refuse to do so wholeheartedly and without delay, I will make plain to them their overall relationships with our country will suffer greatly, and again I will rally the American people to our cause."

The men in the room looked reassured the president had given them something to work with. The women looked absolutely determined to support her efforts. More than a few people among each gender clenched a fist in a show of solidarity.

The president said, "If any of you should have a suggestion of how we can carry our mission forward, I will review it as soon as I possibly can." As a final note, she added, "I am so, so sorry for all of you."

And then Patricia Grant allowed herself to cry.

### White House Mess

The Navy culinary specialists at the Mess would have whipped up any breakfast McGill desired, but to maintain his persona as a man of the people he ordered off the menu: a fruit cup, hot cakes and coffee. Elspeth had the French Toast and orange juice. While their food choices were standard fare, the kitchen did open early for McGill. Breakfast service, for most people, began at nine a.m.

They had the place to themselves.

McGill's first cup of coffee and Elspeth's OJ had just been served when McGill's phone sounded. Sweetie was outside and wanted to talk with McGill. He spoke to a uniformed Secret Service officer and a visitor's pass for Sweetie was issued. McGill asked if Sweetie would like some breakfast. He put in an order for Raisin Bran and skim milk for her.

"You and Ms. Sweeney have been close for a long time," Elspeth said.

McGill nodded. "You've heard about the time she took a bullet for me?"

"Yes. That meant a lot to everyone in the Secret Service."

"To me, my kids and my ex, too."

"Ms. Sweeney also comforted Holly G. when she lost Mr. Grant."

"Yes, she did. Some people transcend friendship; they become family."

"So you have no problem with Ms. Sweeney working for Roger Michaelson?"

For a moment, McGill wondered how Elspeth knew that. Then he realized the Secret Service was keeping a close eye on Michaelson. That was just as it should be. He'd been implicated as a possible participant in a conspiracy to assassinate the president.

The fact that there was no evidence beyond Joan Renshaw's word — that and the man was a former U.S. senator — were the only reasons Michaelson wasn't locked up right now.

McGill sighed and shook his head. "I heard you were raised Catholic, Elspeth. Is that right?"

"My dad's Catholic; my mother's Bahá'í. I was raised in Beirut and attended Catholic schools. Christians were tolerated to a degree because of the old French colonial influence. But Bahá'ís? Unh-uh. They've been persecuted in Iran for a long time, and the Iranians have big-time influence in Lebanon. Mom kept a really low profile there."

"So you have more than one religious influence. Do you believe in redemption?"

Elspeth grinned. "Selectively."

"Yeah, that's my problem, too. I've always seen Michaelson as an enemy because of his hostility to the president. Beyond that, it's almost as if I need a certain number of bad guys in my life to affirm that I'm one of the good guys. If the bad guys start redeeming themselves, then my position becomes less clear."

"Moral relativism, I can understand that. So how do you feel about Ms. Sweeney working for Michaelson?"

"I have to give her the benefit of the doubt. She's much closer to godliness than I am."

"Closer than me, too. But do you think Michaelson was involved in the plan to kill the president?"

"As much as I hate to admit it, no," McGill said.

Elspeth thought about that a moment, then said, "Here comes Ms. Sweeney now."

Both McGill and Elspeth rose to greet her.

Sweetie looked around and said, "Place doesn't do much business, does it?"

"Not before it officially opens," McGill said. "Have a seat."

He and Sweetie sat. Elspeth remained on her feet.

"I can take another table, if you like," she said.

McGill asked, "Margaret?"

"No need on my account." Sweetie gestured to a chair and Elspeth sat.

"How's your case going?" McGill asked.

"I'm looking for connections between Joan Renshaw and Philip Brock. I haven't come up with any obvious ones yet. Putnam's helping me look for one off the beaten path. Later this morning, I'm going to try to talk with a woman named Lisa Stone."

Sweetie explained that she was a schooldays friend of Renshaw and might provide an innocent explanation of the photograph of Michaelson with Renshaw. Her interest piqued, Elspeth leaned forward and said, "I'd be interested in hearing about that."

The arrival of two Navy mess specialists with the breakfast orders delayed a reply. McGill took a topping-off of his coffee and a bite of his hot cakes. He told the specialists, "Everything's great. My compliments to the guys in the kitchen. We'll let you know if we need anything else."

The specialists knew how to take a hint and departed. Sweetie shared Michaelson's explanation of how he came to be in a picture with Renshaw.

Sweetie said, "I'll ask Ms. Stone if she remembers her bet with Joan Renshaw and if she paid off by washing Renshaw's car. That and ask if she knows who took the picture of Renshaw with Michaelson."

Both McGill and Elspeth liked that. Elspeth asked, "Would you mind if I followed up on your call, Ms. Sweeney? Talk to Ms. Stone for myself."

Sweetie shrugged. "Fine by me, but give me first crack."

"Of course."

"You have any other angles to work?" McGill asked.

"There is one, but I need to check with Galia Mindel about it. You know if she's in yet, Jim?"

"No idea, but she usually gets to work early."

"I can check," Elspeth said. She spoke into a microphone at her wrist, frowned, but apparently got a response. She told McGill, "Static in my communications rig. I think you might have damaged it when we were sparring."

Sweetie gave McGill a look. He shrugged.

Elspeth continued, "Anyway, the chief of staff is in her office, Ms. Sweeney. I can have an officer escort you after you finish your breakfast."

"Thanks."

The three of them set to work on their food. Halfway through his hot cakes, McGill asked Sweetie, "You still feeling good about your client?"

"Good enough to keep going. Keeping my eyes and mind open. We'll see what happens."

Sweetie didn't need the Secret Service officer for an escort. McGill took her to Galia's office, saying he needed to pick up Welborn Yates who worked nearby. Elspeth trailed a step behind, wondering what business Margaret Sweeney might have with Galia Mindel.

She'd have to see if she could find out, discreetly.

Knowing everything that went on in the White House was part of her job.

The chief of staff met Sweeney in the doorway to her office, nodded to McGill and closed the door behind herself and her guest. McGill saw the curiosity in Elspeth's eyes. It mirrored his own.

"Don't ask me," he told Elspeth. "I don't know what's going on."

The two of them headed for Welborn's office. They'd only just arrived when McGill's phone sounded again. He answered and heard Celsus Crogher's voice.

"You should get over to Zara Gilford's condo fast. There are two guys here from the Department of Defense. They have an order to seize Jordan Gilford's laptop computer and any hard copy files related to the work he was doing for the DOD. I checked and they're legit, but ..."

"But what?" McGill asked.

"I don't like these guys. Authorized or not, they're wrong."

"I'm on my way," McGill said.

He told Welborn and Elspeth, who'd been listening in to his half of the conversation, "Let's go, I'm going to need my own feds on this case."

### Florida Avenue NW — Washington, DC

Putnam Shady knew he was wily enough to go up against the slickest operators in town and do no worse than a draw. Win more often than not. But the decision facing him, one over which he was agonizing, had him stumped.

Should he send Maxi to school that morning?

As far as she was concerned, the question didn't exist. She was going. Having lost her parents and having been snatched from Baltimore and the only group of friends she'd know in her short life, she'd reached out to the kids at her new school, and for the most part had the good fortune of having her overtures for companionship reciprocated.

She was determined not to be isolated again.

Putnam was equally insistent that she not die before she reached an age counted in double digits, maybe closing in on triple digits. He wanted to explain his feelings to Maxi, but he couldn't think of a way to do so that wouldn't terrify her. How did good parents handle such situations, he asked himself.

That was a big part of the problem. He had no point of reference for being a father. His own had decamped for parts unknown when Putnam was young, and for good measure had taken Mom and little Lawton with him. Emory Jenkins, the adult male to whom his upbringing had been entrusted, was a good man, but he'd taken pains to tell Putnam that he wasn't his father.

Emory, along with his wife, Sissy, had made sure Putnam was sheltered, fed, clothed and educated, but Emory had always told Putnam that one day his Mama and Daddy would come back for him. That was exactly what Putnam wanted to hear, of course. By the time, Putnam reached his teens, though, credulity faded. For a brief period, he began to think maybe the Jenkinses would bail out on him, too. By the time he was a junior in high school and had started looking at colleges he might want to attend, he decided he no longer gave a damn. He could take care of himself.

What he'd never learned, though, was how to take care of someone else.

Margaret certainly could take care of herself and more.

She seemed to be finding her footing as a mom, too. Not rushing it. Positioning herself close to Maxi so the kid could take comfort from Margaret's large, looming presence, but letting Maxi close the final few feet between them if she needed a hug or a word of reassurance.

Before Margaret had left that morning to work her case, she'd told Putnam to have faith in himself. He'd make the right choice. Ha! If faith were calisthenics, he wouldn't be able to do the first push-up.

He tried to tell himself that Maxi went to a good school; that was undeniable. It was private, expensive and ... it fed into high schools just like Winstead. Not that elementary schools were so safe these days. No target was too young for lunatics.

With no decision in sight, Putnam sought refuge in distraction.

Margaret had asked him to see if he could find a point of connection between Joan Renshaw and Philip Brock. Looking at the two people generically, from a jaded lobbyist's point of view, Renshaw was a checkbook and Brock was a pol who always needed campaign checks. There were clubs where such people met, oh so many in Washington.

Putnam knew every last one in town, was able to summon phone numbers from memory. He settled into the task, hoping Maxi might take ten years to get dressed and brush her teeth. He started calling in alphabetical order.

Still early, he got the morning maitre d's and bartenders who were setting up their wares for the day. Well, some of the bartenders were also serving eye-openers to early drinkers. Washington had more than its share of high-functioning alcoholics. Ones who kept enough breath mints on hand to get them through the day.

The letters A and B in Putnam's mental address book returned no results worthy of consideration, but when he called The Constellation Club, he got the senior bartender, Henry Tillman, who was filling in for the morning man.

Putnam, from his first day as a lobbyist in Washington, had treated every person he met in a service job with respect, good humor and big tips. By now, he'd banked a surplus of good will equal in size to the national debt. Henry Tillman was no exception.

"What can I do for you Mr. Shady?"

"I was just wondering, Henry, whether you've ever seen Representative Philip Brock in your bar with a woman named Joan Renshaw." Putnam described Renshaw's appearance.

Henry said, "No, sir, I can't say that I have. Congressman Brock, he must meet his lady friends somewhere else. The last several times I recall seeing him here he was with …"

Putnam heard the pause and jumped on it, embellishing his reason for the call. "With whom, Henry? I ask because I'm helping James J. McGill with an inquiry."

Sort of true, Putnam rationalized. He was really helping Margaret, but if she succeeded, some of the credit would reflect on McGill Investigations, Inc. Margaret had rehabbed Putnam's character over the years, but at the heart of him there was still a rascal alive and well.

"Well, sir, Representative Brock was with poor Senator

Howard Hurlbert. The two of them had a number of long, quiet conversations right before the senator got himself shot dead. After that happened, I don't believe the congressman has ever been back to our club."

Putnam thought about what that might mean. There was the obvious implication, of course. Brock knew something about Hurlbert's death that he wasn't sharing with anyone.

Henry seemed to have a similar idea. "I thought the police were supposed to talk with people who were the last to see someone alive."

"Generally, they do," Putnam said, "but they have to know who those people are. Have you said anything to the cops?"

"No, sir. It's not my place."

But Henry had shared the information with him. Putnam didn't know if Henry thought that was simply innocent conversation with a valued friend or if he'd made the calculation to let Putnam go to the police first and see how things worked out. He didn't press the bartender on the matter.

"Thanks for your time, Henry."

He'd no sooner hung up than Maxi appeared: skin glowing, eyes sparkling, smile gleaming, dressed for school and ready to go. How could he ever take the chance of losing her?

"I'm ready," she said.

Before Putnam could reply his home phone rang. The caller ID read FBI. What the hell?

The president had said she'd told those bastards to butt out.

Putnam answered by saying, "Whatever the hell you want, I don't have time. I'm taking my girl to school."

Maxi gave him her best smile and they walked out the door hand in hand.

With Putnam's heart beating so hard and fast he was sure it would explode.

### Third Street, NW — Washington, DC

The two guys from the DOD were gone by the time McGill,

Elspeth and Welborn arrived at Zara Gilford's high-tech security building. Before going up to Zara's condo, McGill stopped to talk with Karl Vasek, the building's security director. He was not in the best of moods.

He took the measure of Elspeth and Welborn before he decided he could be blunt enough to tell McGill, "These two dicks wanted me to let them up to Ms. Gilford's unit before I called to let her know they'd be coming. They wanted me to let them ambush her."

"And you told them?" McGill asked.

"I said no with emphasis."

"Loudly?" Elspeth asked.

"The one I shoved let out a good yelp."

McGill said, "They didn't try to overwhelm you?"

"The idea occurred to them, I could see that, but they thought better of it. They said if I didn't let them up, they'd call in reinforcements, including lawyers and military officers with federal agent status and have me arrested."

"You did the right thing," McGill said, "allowing them to enter."

"I called first and made sure I spoke to SAC Crogher. He said let them in, too. I still wasn't happy, but I felt better when they came back down. They told me I'd better erase any video I had of them being in the building."

Welborn said, "And you replied?"

"Bite me." Vasek laughed. "Then I did just what they said."

"Because?" McGill asked.

"I'll let SAC Crogher or Ms. Gilford tell you that."

Zara Gilford was sitting at the apartment's wet-bar when McGill, Elspeth and Welborn entered. She didn't look upset. She had a drink in her hand and was smiling. Even Celsus seemed in a good humor.

"Okay, what's the joke?" McGill asked.

"The two nimrods who were here?" Celsus said. "They think they got away clean because Karl deleted his video of them in the lobby."

Zara picked up the thread. "What they don't know is every

unit in the building has its own video cameras. Normally, people leave them on when they go out for the day or away on vacation. If they have children, they might use their system to watch their nannies, I suppose. But once Karl called to let us know what was happening, I turned the system on."

"And I copied the video to a Secret Service server," Celsus said. He looked at Elspeth, "After getting permission, of course."

McGill said, "That's good, but I was hoping I might get to look at Mr. Gilford's computer and files."

"Oh, you couldn't do that," Zara said.

"Why not?"

"Well, Jordan's work was classified, of course. Top secret. I never got to see any of it."

"You don't have that clearance, do you?" Celsus asked McGill with a touch of glee.

"No, I don't."

"I do," Welborn said. He stepped forward and asked Zara. "I'm sorry for your loss, ma'am. Would you know if Mr. Gilford was in the habit of backing up his work?"

"Oh, my, yes. Jordan worked very hard and was very careful not to lose what he'd done. I know he put it somewhere, but I didn't ask where."

Elspeth took a thumb drive out of a pocket. "Did you ever see one of these around, Ms. Gilford?"

She brightened. "Yes … but not for some time, now that I think of it."

"Maybe at your house," McGill suggested.

"Yes, that's it, of course."

Celsus leaned in and whispered to McGill, "Those two bastards might be ransacking her home right now."

McGill agreed. "Take Welborn. If they're there and they don't have a search warrant, kick them out. If they won't take no for an answer, if they threaten to bring in their top people, hold your ground, call Galia Mindel and tell her I said we need the president's involvement."

Celsus smiled.

"What?" McGill asked.

"I'm glad I'm on your side this time."

"Yeah," McGill said, still finding the irony a bit unsettling.

Celsus told Zara another former Secret Service agent would arrive shortly to look after her. Then he and Welborn left. Zara finished her drink and stepped over to McGill.

"I don't usually tipple this early, but I think those two brutes who came here are proof Jordan had upset someone very powerful."

"So it seems. Zara, did Jordan have any colleagues or protégés he might have taken into his confidence?"

She shook her head. "I don't know of any. He was very tight-lipped about his work, and I knew better than to pry."

"Do you know who hired Jordan at the Department of Defense?" McGill asked.

"Yes, of course, that was Hume Drummond. We all had a lovely dinner together when Jordan signed on."

"Do you know Mr. Drummond's title?"

She shook her head. "It wasn't offered, and I didn't ask." With a note of sorrow in her voice, she added, "It never bothered me when Jordan was here, how little I knew about what he did. Now that he's gone, though, I wish he'd let me in on a secret or two."

McGill thought it was safer for her that she didn't know. He waited until Celsus Crogher's stand-in arrived, before he and Elspeth left.

They were about to join Welborn and Celsus at Zara's house when McGill got a call from Ellie Booker. "You wanted to do your interview soon. How about now? It'll air tonight."

McGill told her, "Give me an hour."

### Carl Moultrie Courthouse — Washington, DC

The judge said, "Bail for the defendant is set at one hundred thousand dollars."

Auric Ludwig started to open his mouth in protest. He was an important public figure in any jurisdiction in the country, the way he saw things. He never should have been arrested in the first place. After just one night in jail, he felt as if he'd have to be sandblasted to get clean. Any right-minded judge should have dismissed the case against him outright. At the very least, he should have been released on his own recognizance.

How could he be a flight risk? There was no other country in the world that would let him do the job he did in the U.S. He had nowhere else to go.

Before he could get out a peep, though, his lawyer, Ellis Travers, discreetly stepped on Ludwig's toe to shut him up and said in his courtly Virginia accent, "Thank you, Your Honor. Mr. Ludwig will post bail in cash."

The method of payment drew a snort from the judge.

He banged his gavel and they were done except for the formalities.

Ludwig got into the back of his Cadillac limousine with Travers forty-five minutes later. The vehicle was made to resemble a presidential limo as far as possible. The exact defensive and retaliatory capabilities of Patricia Grant's Thing One and Thing Two were top secret. But the personal ride of the CEO of Firepower America would withstand the assault of anything short of a Hellfire missile.

He wasn't about to get gunned down by some jerk with a grudge.

At the moment, Ludwig was the one feeling high resentment.

"That black-robed bastard should have let me go with a rebuke to the cops."

"He could have set bail at a million dollars, Auric."

That possibility raised Ludwig's ire further, but he put his feelings aside to ask, "Did you bring that much money?"

"Yes."

Ludwig slumped back on the seat, relieved that there had been no chance he might have spent another night locked up. It had been a miserable experience. He'd been given a cell to himself.

There had been no chance he'd be physically brutalized. But word of who he was and his presence in lockup had been made known. Those two damn detectives must have spread the word. The cat-calls and jokes at his expense had gone on until the wee hours. He'd become a source of vast amusement to the cretins all around him.

"Yo, Ludwig. You there, man? Bastard cops locked me up for armed robbery. They gonna give me an extra ten years on my sentence just for bringin' my gun to work. That has to be against the Constitution, don't it?"

The laughter from that and a multitude of other jailbird jokes still rang in Ludwig's ears.

One con wanted to know where he could get silver bullets.

His girlfriend being such a bloodsucking vampire.

That nitwit was told by another inmate that you needed a wooden stake for vampires; silver bullets were for werewolves.

Ludwig was asked to arbitrate the dispute. He declined. Got called a pussy.

He never want to go back to —

Travers interrupted his dark reminiscences. "You have to realize, Auric, you're in big trouble here. Obstruction of justice is a serious offense. You really stepped in it, getting out front of a police investigation with your announcement of a 'good guy' shooting Abel Mays."

Ludwig's temper, never far from the surface, boiled over.

"But there is a good guy, goddamnit. How else would you describe someone who shoots a mass murderer? He's a hero."

"Washington isn't the wild west. You're not playing a role in a movie. How you or I characterize whoever shot Abel Mays is irrelevant. It's how the law sees him that matters."

"What are you saying?"

"Detective Meeker told me you were informed that helping the police find out who gave you your information might mitigate the sentence you receive."

"Sentence?" Ludwig asked. "If you're giving up on me already —"

Travers held up a hand. "They've got you. Cold. Right now, my job is to make the best of a bad situation. If your choice is to spend a short time in a minimum security facility with a few actual amenities or a very long time in a place that will make the city lockup feel like the Ritz, I know what I'd do. It's what I'd advise you to do, too. Be a snitch."

"Never. I'll make this a political trial. The government is out to get me and —"

"You've got the government, the legislative branch at least, in your pocket. You'll never get the public to believe they're coming after you."

"I'll get my people to believe. They'll all believe me." A thought popped into Ludwig's head. "Do you know James J. McGill is snooping around Mays' death. Word is he thinks Mays didn't kill the last victim."

Hearing that, Travers instructed the limo driver to pull to the curb.

He looked at Ludwig and told him, "Making this a personal duel with Mr. McGill would be a very bad idea. You want the president to remain neutral, if possible. But if you go after her husband, she's going to come back hard at you. She never has to face another election, and she might see bringing you down as the capstone of her presidency."

Ludwig didn't say a word, but Travers could see he hadn't persuaded the man.

He opened the limo door and stepped out onto the sidewalk.

Looking back at Ludwig, he said, "I will notify the court I've resigned as your attorney."

"Pussy." Funny how fast prison habits could be picked up, Ludwig thought.

"I'll send you my bill," Travers said in an even tone. "Pay it promptly. The only way you could be more foolish than taking on James J. McGill would be to raise my ire, too."

# CHAPTER 14

*Chief of Staff's Office — The White House*

Galia Mindel listened to Sweetie's proposal without interruption. She'd never heard anything like it in all her years in politics. Not that she could find anything legally wrong with it. Even so, Galia couldn't immediately sort out the politics of it. Would it turn out looking like a clever move that produced a desired outcome or would it leave the administration with egg on its face? The answer to that, of course, would depend on the results the idea produced.

"I honestly don't know what to say," Galia told Sweetie.

"How about you'll give it a try?"

"I'm hesitant."

"Because you think it might make Patti look bad?"

Sweetie's casual use of the familiar form of the president's first name reminded Galia that the person sitting in front of her was no mere supplicant. It was meant to; the chief of staff understood that. She also knew that Margaret Sweeney could have gone around her. Taken the idea to McGill and had him ask the president. Instead, Ms. Sweeney came to her.

Manners mattered to Galia. So did clout. "How my decisions might reflect upon the president is always a consideration."

"Sure, that's natural. Do your feelings about Roger Michaelson make you reluctant? Jim couldn't take the case because of the way he feels about the man. That's why I'm doing it."

"You don't resent him?" Galia asked. She certainly did.

Sweetie took a moment to respond. "I didn't care for him when he came to the office. Patti is a friend. I hold her close to my heart. She's in my prayers every day. Despite all that, I saw Michaelson as a man in trouble. I believe I'll be judged not for getting the easy things right but how I handle the hard moral challenges."

From everything Galia had learned about Margaret Sweeney, she knew the woman wasn't just another phony putting on a holier-than-thou front. She was acting out of conscience. That was also something Galia didn't see often.

It was hard not to be persuaded by such a person.

Sweetie wanted Galia to arrange the transfer of Joan Renshaw to the same prison currently holding Erna Godfrey, the woman who'd killed Andy Grant, the president's first husband. Erna, as a reward for aiding the effort to take her husband, the late Reverend Burke Godfrey, into custody, had been allowed to start a prison ministry.

That had proved to be a good choice. Erna's efforts had led to a reduction of inmate violence and an increase of inmate education. The woman was doing good work. A convicted killer had found repentance and was working toward redemption.

"You're hoping that through Erna Godfrey's benign influence Joan Renshaw will recant her accusation against Roger Michaelson," Galia said.

"That and reveal who was really involved in the plot to kill Patti. Confession is good for the soul. And Erna has already demonstrated she can get people to talk."

Galia nodded. Erna Godfrey had been written up in Time magazine for getting inmates to admit to crimes they'd previously denied as a part of getting right with God. There was at least a chance she could do the same with Joan Renshaw.

"What I worry about is this," Galia said. "Doing this might make the president look like she's condoning the use of a jailhouse snitch. It might also hurt the good work Erna Godfrey has been doing if other inmates see her as acting as a tool of the president."

Sweetie considered that. "Two things. I think Erna has earned the reputation for being sincere in her ministry. If her only reward for getting Renshaw to tell the truth is the satisfaction of saving another inmate's soul, how could anyone spin that the wrong way? As far as Patti is directly concerned, how could anyone accuse her of misusing her power when she'd be helping a longtime political adversary?"

Galia sat back and stared at Sweetie.

"You have quite the political mind, Ms. Sweeney."

"Comes from having been a Chicago cop," Sweetie said with a smile.

"All right. I'll take your idea to the FBI for an opinion. Pitch it to them just the way you did to me. We'll see what happens."

"That'll do," Sweetie said.

She had faith things would work out.

### The Greenwood School — Washington, DC

FBI Deputy Director Byron DeWitt drove his private ride, a new BMW 535, to the private school on 16th Street NW. He'd taken his tie off and even ruffled his longer than regulation surfer blonde hair. None of that mattered.

When Putnam Shady exited the school, having dropped off Maxi, he made DeWitt immediately.

"Fed," he said to DeWitt, the word a slur in his mouth.

The deputy director shrugged. "Guilty."

"What's the problem? You didn't get the memo from the president?"

Putnam stepped up to DeWitt, his manner combative in a way he never would have been before Margaret had inspired him to become physically fit. He knew striking a federal officer would be a heavy-duty felony, but he didn't give a damn. The SOB had the nerve to follow him to Maxi's school? That kind of shit was going to stop immediately.

DeWitt saw the situation for what it was. Potentially regrettable. He moved to defuse it.

"I got the president's memo this morning. It came to me directly from Director Haskins. I routed it down the chain of command. Everybody who needs to see it has seen it by now."

"And yet here you are," Putnam said.

His tide of emotion began to recede. He looked for whatever game this fed might be playing. He had to want something.

"I tried to call your wife to ask if she might act as a go-between. Mr. McGill knows me; we've worked together. Ms. Sweeney wasn't available. She'd gone to the White House, I was told. By the way, there is no surveillance on you. Just me, and all I want to do is talk to you for a minute or two."

Putnam said, "If nobody's watching me, how'd you know where to find me?"

"You told me you were taking your girl to school."

He had, Putnam thought, but that was all he'd told the guy.

"I didn't say which school."

"Darren Drucker gave me the name, but only after I told him why I wanted to talk with you."

That rocked Putnam back on his heels. He turned his back on DeWitt, walked several paces down the street and made a phone call. It wasn't a long one. Putnam retraced his footsteps, a thoughtful look on his face.

"If this is your car," he said nodding at the BMW, "let's go for a ride."

As soon as they were out of sight of the school and Putnam didn't have to worry about Maxi looking out a window and see him talking to a stranger, he said, "What do you want?"

"I'm trying to catch Tyler Busby. A thought occurred to me this morning. The memo from the director about you prompted it. You had early access to Inspiration Hall and so did Busby." DeWitt held up a hand to forestall any objection. "I'm not saying you had any connection with what he tried to pull. I'm just looking for any insight you might have about the man. Some clue as to how I might find him."

Putnam leaned to his right, tried to get a good angle on DeWitt's profile.

"You didn't give your name," he said.

"Byron DeWitt, deputy director."

Putnam had heard the name and a story or two.

"You're the guy with the picture of Chairman Mao in his office?"

"That's me."

"How do you get away with that?"

"By making myself useful. I'm the go-to guy on China. I speak the Beijing dialect of Mandarin and a little Cantonese. Have some understanding of the culture. Make a decent mu gu gai pan. I'm pretty much one of a kind at the Bureau. They tell me to get rid of my Warhol serigraph, I go with it."

For the first time, Putnam felt a spark of kinship.

"You have them over a barrel?"

"Up to a point. If I tried to redecorate my office in Politburo Moderne, they'd probably call me on it."

Putnam laughed. So, okay, the guy was human and had a plausible story. Better still, Putnam had a deep desire to see Tyler Busby spend his remaining years rotting in prison … and that made him think of something, the way DeWitt said he'd been inspired.

Before he got to that, he asked DeWitt what the FBI had done so far to find Busby.

The deputy director was surprisingly forthcoming: contact with all allied police agencies and organizations around the world; distribution of Busby's photo to all U.S. diplomatic missions and military bases with a call-us-if-spotted directive; a request-to-apprehend notice if seen by any U.S. intelligence agency, select private snoops and satellite surveillance.

DeWitt stopped for a red light, looked at Putnam and answered an unasked question, "No, we don't have satellites watching you nor are we using any other methods."

"You're sure?"

DeWitt thought about that. "Fair question. I'll make sure."

"Good."

"So what can you tell me?"

Putnam gave the question a moment's thought. "I think the best thing I can tell you is Busby will have an easier time hiding himself than his ego."

"Meaning what?"

"Have you found any of the art he's stolen?"

"No."

"Have you found any of his yachts?"

"All three. They've been sold twice already. The current owners seem legitimate and uninvolved with Busby in the past."

"What about the intermediate owner?" Putnam asked.

"A yacht broker in Singapore, a legitimate business."

Putnam said, "Check the broker out. See who his connections are."

DeWitt nodded. "Okay. Getting back to Busby's ego ..."

Putnam said, "Busby's sold his yachts, the art he stole is available to sell, he probably has overseas bank accounts you don't know about, so he has big money to spend. Given his sense of grandiosity, he's going to buy or lease a big place as his hideaway. You'll never find him in a furnished studio apartment in some innocuous building."

"All right, I can see that."

"He's on the run, so he can't wait to have something built to order. What I'd do is look for are recent purchases or lease agreements on very top-end mansions. He'd use a cutout, of course, so you'd have look behind whoever the front man is."

"You're talking about palaces?"

"Yeah, exactly. Anything that doesn't already have a royal family living in it."

"Okay. Any idea of where?"

"Your yacht broker is in Singapore, and you speak Chinese, start in that general area and ..." Putnam took a beat to consider other possibilities. "Take a look at a globe. See what's on the far side of the world from Singapore. If there are any palaces there, check that out, too."

DeWitt nodded. He liked the way Putnam thought. "Any other suggestions?"

An idea came to Putnam, as if he'd just been waiting for the fed's prompt.

"Part of Busby's scam at Inspiration Hall was to have all his forged paintings destroyed and then collect the insurance money on them as if they were masterpieces. Skinning an honest insurance company would be one way to go, but colluding with a crooked company, one where a top executive or two would get a hefty kickback of the payout, that would be more of a sure thing. Crooks wouldn't look hard to find Busby because they'd be putting themselves at risk."

DeWitt liked that a lot. He drove Putnam back to the Greenwood School to pick up his car.

"Thank you for your cooperation, Mr. Shady. You've been a big help."

"Yeah, well, I like the idea of a subversive working at the FBI."

DeWitt laughed.

"Here's one more thing for you to think about," Putnam said. "I'm not sure where it might lead but I found out this morning that Representative Philip Brock had some quiet conversations at The Constellation Club with Senator Howard Hurlbert shortly before the senator was killed."

DeWitt didn't say a word, but his mind began to race.

Putnam noticed the uptick of energy in the fed's eyes.

He said, "Brock was also Busby's pre-opening guest at Inspiration Hall. I saw the list of everyone who got that special privilege. Could be just a coincidence, but who knows? I'm going to pass this information along to my wife. So James J. McGill will get it, too. Maybe all you fine law enforcement minds should get together and sort out what it might mean."

"That's a fine idea, Mr. Shady. Thanks again."

"Right, just don't tell anyone other than my wife and Mr. McGill I cooperated with the FBI."

DeWitt promised he wouldn't.

A minute later, driving back to his office, DeWitt got a call from Galia Mindel.

### The Residence — The White House

The president told McGill which of his half-dozen suits he should wear to do the WWN interview with Ellie Booker. "You look best in the Pierre Cardin." Textured black wool, two button coat. The suit's slim cut was yet another reason for McGill to stay in shape. One donut too many and he'd start popping seams.

He'd bought the suit almost four years earlier when he and Patti had spent a week's holiday in Paris. The look was classic enough, he'd been assured, that it would never appear dated. Whenever McGill got dressed up, he thought he'd come a long way since his days of shopping at Sears men's store.

He relied on Patti's advice for a choice of shirt, tie and shoes, too.

"And get a trim," his wife told him.

The White House used to have its own barber shop, but the Department of Homeland Security had taken over the space. Somehow, McGill hadn't been consulted on the decision. He accepted the new reality with grace. The young pixie who'd cut his hair during his time in Paris had given him a referral in Washington.

"Would you like to do my makeup?" he asked Patti.

"If I had the time, I would. But WWN has good people. They're big on pretty faces over there."

McGill batted his eyes at her.

"You will remember to be serious, Jim?"

He stopped kidding. "I will. I'll put my game-face on. The hard part will be not to call out certain people for being the bastards they are. But I'll watch out for that, too. I'll do you proud, Madam President."

"Thank you. Now I have to get back to the grind."

She gave McGill a kiss and departed for the Oval Office. The hair stylist came, snipped and left in a flash. McGill put on his meet-the-American-people clothes and was ready to do his star turn when the White House photographer popped in.

"President's request, sir," he told McGill.

He took six shots, and McGill was almost out the door when his cell phone sounded.

Father Inigo de Loyola was calling. "It's is done, *amigo*. Your shocking idea has been brought to reality at the parish of Saint Martin de Porres. You know where this is?"

"Roughly. It's in South East, right?"

"*Sí.*" The priest gave McGill the street address.

"Was this done with the hierarchy's approval?"

"They are still discussing the matter. Father Dennehy, the pastor at Saint Martin's, grew impatient with their dithering. He went ahead on his own."

"Has the sign attracted any attention?"

"It is functional, but we have draped it. Father Dennehy and I thought you should have the honor of revealing your idea to the world."

"So there's no media present yet?"

"No. But some curious parishioners have gathered. Will you be joining us soon?"

"I'll be there shortly."

McGill placed a call to Ellie Booker.

"I can expect you any minute, right?" she asked.

"Would you like to delay our interview for, say, sixty minutes to get some video you can add to it?"

"Pictures are always good, if they're relevant and have some punch."

McGill told her what was planned at Saint Martin de Porres.

Ellie asked, "Anybody else know about this?" Meaning other media.

"Not yet. You want me to pick you up?"

"Meet me at the church," Ellie said, "I'll get there before you do."

She sounded like a firefighter rushing off to fight a blaze.

McGill smiled and got out of the White House without further delay.

### McGill Investigations, Inc. — Georgetown

Sweetie knew she had influenced Putnam in any number of ways, all to the good as far as she was concerned. To a somewhat lesser degree, he had influenced her, too. She had been a late adapter to cell phones, and still preferred the dumb models to smart phones. She particularly disliked the idea she could be tracked just by having her phone on.

McGill had told her, "I know it's unlikely, but what if someone overpowered you and —"

"The guy was as dumb as he was strong?" Sweetie asked. "He might forget to check if I had a phone on me?"

"Okay, what if I am in a bad spot and need help?" McGill asked. "I have just enough time to call you before the spit hits the fan and yell for help."

Sweetie was averse to vulgarities; McGill accommodated her whenever possible.

"Yeah, you're a noted hysteric," Sweetie said, "always flying to pieces."

McGill never was able to give her a good reason to get a smart phone. She did it just to humor him. But she absolutely refused to be trendy and get an iPhone. Until Putnam had told her just recently, "Maxi asked me for one."

"Give me one good reason she should have an expensive phone like that."

"I've got one. She has phone envy, and then there's FaceTime."

Putnam explained that video calls were easy on the iPhone, and when either of them wanted to call Maxi, they'd be able to see her as well as hear her. That did have appeal, Sweetie had to admit. Still, she asked, "Aren't there other brands that can do that?"

"They can't do it with iPhones, and if Maxi and I have them ..."

Grumbling, Sweetie said she would let herself be coerced.

"Cajoled," Putnam said.

They settled on persuaded as the description, and that day at the office Sweetie was glad of it. She looked up the year Joan Renshaw had graduated from Northwestern and then called the University of Illinois alumni office in Champaign and asked if they had a grad named Lisa Stone in the same year's class.

Sweetie explained that she was a former Chicago cop now working as a private investigator. She dropped McGill's name and asked if the alumni office would call Ms. Stone and have her call Sweetie. They were happy to oblige.

So was Ms. Stone, and the first thing she asked after saying hello was, "Do you have an iPhone?"

"Of course," Sweetie said.

"Let's do FaceTime then."

They established a video link, and Sweetie saw the first professional benefit of owning the phone. If you were a cop or a PI, you could see if the person you were talking to was telling you the truth. Facial expressions were a dead giveaway to a trained observer.

Unless you were dealing with a sociopath.

Ms. Stone seemed anything but. She was bright, cheerful and somewhat starstruck.

"You really work with James J. McGill?"

"I do, and have for a long time."

"Have you ever met the president?"

"I saw her just the other day at the White House."

"Really?" Lisa Stone looked like she was the one studying Sweetie's face for any sign of deception. Finding none, she laughed and said, "That must be so cool."

The woman had to be forty years old, but in some ways, at least, remained young at heart.

"Would you mind if I asked you a few questions?" Sweetie said.

"About what? I can't imagine why a private investigator would want to talk with me."

"I'd like to confirm some information I was given about Joan

Renshaw."

"Oh." Ms. Stone turned glum. "Poor Joanie. I don't know what could have come over her, and now she's in jail."

Sweetie saw the regret was real, but something else caused Lisa Stone to look away from the camera for just a moment. She knew something that she didn't want to reveal. Sweetie chose to go after easier information first.

"Did you once lose a bet with Joan that involved your washing her car."

Lisa Stone's good humor was back and she rolled her eyes.

"I sure did. It was a school pride bet. Illinois versus Northwestern. Both our basketball teams were pretty good our senior years. She won; I lost; I paid off."

"You washed her car four times in a month?"

"No, just three."

"She let the last one slide?"

Ms. Stone shook her head. "Oh, no. Joanie never let anything slide, not even when we were kids growing up. She told me she'd defer the last car wash for another favor, and she called me on it fifteen years later. You know what she asked me?"

Sweetie felt sure she did. "You took a picture of her with Roger Michaelson."

"How did you know?"

"I heard about that picture. Michaelson won that basketball game for Northwestern."

"He sure did, the sonofagun. Anyway, I grew up to be a professional photographer. I shoot layouts of high-end homes for glossy coffee-table magazines, but I know how to take a portrait, too. The shot I took for Joanie would have cost anybody else a few thousand dollars. You could buy a lot of car washes for that kind of money."

Sweetie saw the memory had brought back some feelings of resentment.

She soft-pedaled her next question.

"Anything else you'd care to tell me about Ms. Renshaw or Mr. Michaelson?"

Sweetie saw Lisa Stone nod. The secret she'd withheld earlier was going to emerge.

"Right after I took that picture of the two of them, I took Joanie aside, asked her if she was going to make a move on Roger. She laughed and told me maybe if he'd gone on to play in the NBA instead of becoming a state's attorney. From the time we were kids, she told me she was going to marry some rich man, and then she got that job working with Andrew Hudson Grant and, darn, if it didn't look like she wasn't going to make her wish come true."

Joy departed Lisa Stone's face once more.

"But I guess we both know that didn't happen, for a couple of reasons."

Mr. Grant meeting Patti Darden, and then getting killed.

"Thanks for your help, Ms. Stone."

"Hey, can you do me a small favor or two?"

"If I can, sure."

"Please tell the president I voted for her and say hi to Mr. McGill for me."

"Will do," Sweetie said.

It was a small price to pay to learn Roger Michaelson had told her the truth.

And that Joan Renshaw had been a gold-digger.

# CHAPTER 15

### *St. Martin de Porres Church — Washington, DC*

The church was a rather grand structure for a fairly modest neighborhood in the southeastern corner of the city. Constructed of pale gray limestone at the beginning of the twentieth century, admission to the church might be gained through any of five tall archways. Above the central arch a circular stained glass window measuring twelve feet in diameter admitted the light of an ascending sun and flooded the church with hand-crafted rainbows during morning Mass.

On the support column to the left of the central archway a glassed-in display board enumerated the daily and Sunday schedules of services. On the support column to the right of the central archway a cloth draped a new display case. Whatever it was, it would be impossible to miss for anyone entering the main doors of the church.

Fathers Inigo de Loyola and Alphonsus Dennehy stood in front of the cloaked fixture.

"We are certain to hear from the archbishop about this, Al," de Loyola said.

Dennehy shrugged. "What can he say? We got ahead of ourselves? We should have waited for the nobility to give us the nod? I'll do an extra fifteen minutes of penance the next time I confess my sins."

"You might become a pariah like me, a man with a calling but no fixed occupation."

"Fine. I'll go back to Boston, resume smoking, have two drinks with dinner instead of one and become an Episcopalian. I hear they're hurting for clergy."

De Loyola laughed. "A fine plan. Save a place at your table for me. Oh, look, a television truck has arrived. There'll be no hiding our disobedience now."

"Indeed. Our celebrity will be established beyond doubt. Maybe we can get our own TV show with, who is it? Oh, yes, WWN."

The two priests saw an intense young woman and a man with a video camera bolt from the van and head their way. The dozen or so neighborhood residents who'd been lingering on the small plaza in front of the church saw their numbers swell with the arrival of the television truck. The chance to do a man-on-the-street interview was not to be missed.

Watching the TV people scurry toward them, de Loyola said, "Mr. McGill will be here momentarily. He is a man of his word."

"Good to know someone is. You know the one thing I regret about this, Inigo?"

"What's that, Al?"

"That I didn't think of this idea first."


### U.S. Senate Committee on Appropriations — U.S. Capitol

The chairwoman of the committee, Senator Darla Kozinski, Democrat of Maryland, nodded to her colleague Senator Tom Hale, Republican of Alaska: The fix was in. Two billion dollars of construction money for a federal prison in Alaska had been attached to the Farm Bill. Now, all Hale had to do was keep the other members of the GOP on the committee in line, get them to vote unanimously for the bill now, and oppose any filibuster attempts when the bill came to the floor of the Senate for a full vote, and the funding would be his.

Assuming the House went along with it.

And a reconciliation committee of the two bodies of Congress didn't scotch it.

Still, with the president backing the effort from the Democratic side, and Hale urging all his long-time Republican colleagues to vote for his project, things looked good.

Madam Chairwoman even went so far as to shake Hale's hand.

She was another Senate veteran who understood what it meant to take a decade to finally get big money for your state. He appreciated the sentiment. He wasn't so sure about the optics, though, the two of them shaking hands publicly before a vote. Putting the fix in was one thing; letting the public see it happen was another.

Hale never noticed that the moment of comity had been photographed.

He still had the uneasy feeling Galia Mindel and the Democrats were pulling a fast one on him somehow. True, he was getting every thing he wanted and more, but hoary words of warning still rang in his mind: Be careful what you wish for, you might get it.

Even if everything was kosher, Hale was troubled by his own conscience. That wasn't something that happened often, but even if the whole plan worked exactly the way he wanted, he was already looking for ways to wriggle out of the commitment he'd made to Galia to support infrastructure projects in other people's states. Let those suckers put their noses to the grindstone for ten years. Then, maybe, he'd support them.

As for Galia Mindel and the president, they'd be gone before long, but he'd hold his seat until he breathed his last.

Madam Chairwoman called for a committee vote. The ayes had it. Thirty to zero.

The unanimous vote both thrilled Hale and made him even more uneasy.

Senator Kozinski leaned over and whispered into Hale's ear, "Now get your friend, Representative Dalton, to do her part in the House."

Senator Hale left the committee room to do just that.

### FirePower America — Falls Church, Virginia

Auric Ludwig took two showers in his office's private bathroom, one to lave himself clean of the stench of jail, the other to scour the stink of the betrayal perpetrated by his former attorney, Ellis Travers. He dressed in the spare suit he kept in the office closet, all the while assuring himself that there had to be a criminal defense lawyer in Washington or New York who could keep him from ever spending another night in lockup.

Problem was, every time he persuaded himself that people like him didn't go to prison, he heard Rockelle Bullard's voice telling him he was going to get the high end of the sentencing range for obstruction of justice: thirty years. He couldn't begin to imagine the horrors of that reality. For one thing, with his blood pressure, he doubted he had that much time left.

Even if he were able to survive physically, his mind would never stand up to such a vile existence. He knew, of course, that a gun in a home was far more often used for suicide than to defend against an intruder … and he was beginning to think that might be a reasonable thing.

No, no, no. He would not give in, not even to his own demons.

He would triumph, as always. He would —

Respond to his secretary's buzz on the intercom.

"You asked to be alerted to any news regarding James J. McGill, sir. He's going to appear on WWN momentarily."

"To say what?"

"There was no word on that, but there's a video setup in front of a DC church."

A church? What the hell could that be about?

Ludwig turned on his television.

### St. Martin de Porres Church — Washington, DC

"Here he comes now," Ellie Booker said, inclining her head toward McGill getting out of his black Chevy sedan at the curb in front of the church.

Her videographer pointed his camera that way and started recording McGill's every move and word. So far, though, he hadn't done much more than shake some hands and say hello to people who had gathered in front of the church. McGill seemed at ease. The woman with him, his Secret Service protection, looked anything but relaxed.

"Want me to get up close, boss?" the videographer asked.

"Better not. You might get shot."

Ellie saw how nervous the Secret Service agent was. She even knew who the woman was, Elspeth Kendry. The head of the White House Security detail. A thrill ran up Ellie's spine. This could be really good. Something big. As McGill climbed the steps to where a priest and a guy with a beard and scruffy clothes were waiting, she waved to him.

McGill waved back and called out, "Get a good vantage point for your camera guy."

Talk like that almost made Ellie swoon. She urged her companion forward, only to see that the approximation of a front row center spot had already been staked out — by her boss, WWN Chairman Hugh Collier. The brawny gay Aussie stepped aside to let the videographer have a direct line on McGill and the two other men standing four steps above them.

The press of the growing crowd nudged Ellie up against Collier.

"What are you doing here?" she asked.

"Galia Mindel called me yesterday. Said I might want to keep a close eye on Mr. McGill."

Ellie frowned. "Damnit, the White House is playing us."

Collier laughed. "Yes, but isn't it great fun they've chosen us as their playmates?"

Ellie had to admit it was pretty cool.

## Calle Ocho — Miami, Florida

In the cutting room of his shop, Jerry Nerón worked on the first suit for the client he'd seen in Washington. To the hum of the air conditioner and the murmur of a television set to a low volume, he'd done the cutting blueprint on strong white paper a meter wide and two meters long. The completed blueprint was called a draft. That was followed by the production pattern, a duplicate of the draft made with a pricker wheel on brown card stock called oaktag. The first two steps proceeded with a Zen flow, every millimeter perfect.

It had been years since Jerry had to think about his tailoring.

The oaktag pattern was cut with shears. Jerry always kept his honed to exquisite edges. The one distraction he allowed himself was to recall how deftly he had put an end to that fat *cabrón* Galtero Blanco, employing the same tool he used to ply his trade. A flick of the wrist. Zip. Three hundred and forty-three pounds of *mierda* hit the floor.

Several years earlier, Jerry had a girlfriend who read Stephen King novels in bed after the two of them had made love. He didn't mind. He just fell asleep as his girlfriend read the stories to him. He'd absorbed enough to realize King thought just about anything could be haunted. Including a 1958 Plymouth Fury, for Christ's sake.

That made Jerry wonder if Galtero Blanco might haunt the shears that had been used to kill him. He could see the way it would play out. His shears wouldn't attack him, oh no. The way it would go, one night all the men who wore the suits Jerry had tailored for them with a murder weapon would come for him. The best-dressed zombies anybody had ever seen.

They'd all have their own shears. Slice his ass to pieces.

He was pretty sure he could sell that story to Hollywood.

Once he decided he was tired of living and wanted the state to pick up his funeral expenses.

Until then, he'd go about his chosen professions. One of them anyway. Doing people in was getting tiresome. And he didn't like the way his last job had gone. Improvising at the last minute had been foolish. If he'd gone ahead and killed his target the way he'd planned, that would have been the smart thing to do.

Coming in the wake of the slaughter at the school — those poor kids — his homicide would have gotten much less attention than it would have normally.

But, no, he couldn't leave well enough alone.

Maybe that was the curse that would get him.

He'd become as stupid as Galtero Blanco.

Jerry moved on to the next step in his work. He placed the production pattern on the cloth he and the client had chosen for the suit. Wool as smooth and soft as a young girl's cheek. He used a piece of sharpened chalk to draw thin, clear lines.

He wondered if he could use the chalk to the same effect as the shears.

Zip. Someone's throat got slashed.

Before he could arrive at an answer, a story on the television caught his attention.

He used the remote to boost the volume.

James J. McGill was standing in front of a church in Washington. He pulled at a piece of cloth and revealed an electronic display board with flashing numbers on it. A title above the numbers defined the board's purpose.

Holy shit. Someone had gone to the trouble of tallying his work.

Well, his and a lot of other people.

### FirePower America — Falls Church, Virginia

Auric Ludwig watched the same WWN broadcast Jerry Nerón saw in Florida, and his eyes all but popped from his head. "Goddamnit, goddamnitall to hell."

McGill had just revealed the nation's dirtiest secret.

He was showing America how many people guns killed in the country.

That was the legend across the top of the display board: National Gun Death Counter.

And, goddamnit, the thing was actually counting. The number had gone up twice in the few seconds Ludwig had been watching. The total was measured in the thousands, and it was only March. Just wait until summer and the weather got hot. That damn thing would be spinning like a slot machine.

Maybe it wouldn't even take that long. The counter would take a big spike the next time there was another mass shooting. Christ Almighty, that would be just the kind of visual TV news would eat up. Worse, there would be no way he could stop them.

For a brief moment, Ludwig thought he heard the sizzle of his brain frying.

That'd take care of any worries about his going to prison.

McGill began to explain the sign's purpose: "Every day in our country, an average of thirty people are murdered with firearms. Another fifty-three people kill themselves with guns every day. Those are just the deaths; that's all that we're counting on this display. But another one hundred and sixty-three Americans are wounded by firearms daily.

"These figures come from the FBI and the Centers for Disease Control.

"You add up all three numbers and you get two hundred and forty-six people who are gunshot victims in the United States every day. These are the kinds of casualty numbers we might not expect to see anywhere but in a major war. In the United States, however, we just shrug them off as being a part of everyday life in what we like to call the greatest country in the world.

"We can't do that any longer. The killing must stop. There must be a ceasefire. When I was both a police officer and a grad school student in Chicago, I wrote a paper in which I said, 'If a situation stinks and you want to change it, you can't let people hold their noses.' That's the purpose of this National Gun Death Counter, to keep people from holding their noses, to make them revolted by the stink and to get all of us to make our country a safer place.

Thank you for your attention. Father Alphonsus Dennehy, the pastor of Saint Martin de Porres parish, would also like to offer a few words."

Father Dennehy stepped forward. "The Catholic Church has consistently and ardently advocated a pro-life doctrine. I've always been proud of that. After hearing the figures Mr. McGill shared with us, that doctrine must include an all-out effort to end the scourge of gun-death killings and maimings in our country. I challenge every Catholic parish in the country to prominently display a gun-death counter as we at St. Martin de Porres have done. To my friends of other denominations and faiths, we ask that you look to your souls, talk with your congregations and decide what is right for you. Thank you."

Ludwig snapped off his television.

Holy God, he thought. If all he had to deal with was one poor church in Washington, he could handle that. But if Catholics and Protestants across the country started equating gun deaths with abortions, he'd be in real trouble.

That fucking McGill. Maybe attacking him would be the way to fight back. McGill was the bastard trying to prove that a good guy with a gun hadn't killed Abel Mays, but Ludwig needed that good guy to exist now more that ever.

Ludwig went to his office window, hoping the view might inspire him as to how to mount his counterattack. Instead it staggered him. There was a billboard opposite the FirePower offices. The ads that appeared on it were invariably innocuous commercial appeals, but no longer.

A second National Gun Death Counter was going up.

Ludwig knew it was no coincidence. He was being challenged directly.

### Saint Martin de Porres Church — Washington, DC

McGill told Ellie Booker he'd meet with her to shoot his interview in thirty minutes. Then he stepped through the crowd, shaking hands as he went, Elspeth watching for unfriendly faces, and came to Captain Rockelle Bullard and Detectives Meeker and Beemer. They'd parked their city car behind McGill's Chevy.

McGill had called them en route to the church.

Rockelle told McGill, "I knew things were bad, but I didn't know they were that bad. And I'm a homicide cop. I hope that priest lights a fire under a lot of people."

"Me, too," McGill said. He told Rockelle and her men about the two guys from the DOD seizing Jordan Gilford's laptop computer and his hard-copy files.

"I know everything's all about national security these days, but I sure would have liked to know if any information Mr. Gilford might have possessed could lead to his murder," Rockelle said.

"Any good cop would," McGill agreed. "Captain Welborn Yates has top-secret clearance. He's going to be talking to some prominent people at the Pentagon in the very near future. If he sees anything he thinks you or I should know, he'll tell us."

Both Meeker and Beemer looked unpersuaded.

Rockelle reassured them. "Captain Yates is as straight as it gets. I'll trust Mr. McGill to be the same way. Let me have that envelope we brought with us, Detective Meeker."

She took a manila envelope from Meeker and handed it to McGill.

"The Park Police delivered some pictures to my office this morning and were very polite about it. It was almost like someone way up the federal ladder told them to play nice. So we made copies for you."

McGill took three eight-by-ten color prints out of the envelope and examined them.

Rockelle told him, "Nothing showing Mr. Gilford's actual murder, but the car in the pictures shows it was parked right in front of Abel Mays' SUV. Man at the wheel drove off just about the time the medical examiner established as the time of Mr. Gilford's death."

"He's wearing a baseball cap and sunglasses," McGill said.

"On a morning that was cloudy," Beemer said.

"Doesn't look like was styling either," Meeker added.

McGill agreed. "No it doesn't. The plates on the car are visible, but they've got to be stolen."

"They were," Rockelle said. "My detectives and I think that car is so plain it might as well be invisible. Then Detective Beemer had a thought on how it might be made even more so."

McGill guessed, "You're thinking a compactor? At a scrapyard?"

The two detectives looked at each other properly impressed.

Rockelle said, "You got it. The detectives will be making the rounds, and contacting their counterparts with the state police in Maryland and Virginia."

McGill said, "Good. Maybe another camera at a scrapyard has a better shot of the driver."

"That or a junkyard dog took a good bite out of him," Beemer added.

"Either way," Rockelle said, "we're all keepin' our fingers crossed. One more thing."

"What?" McGill asked.

"I like Captain Yates. He's a fine young man. If Mr. Gilford was a threat to some big shot's action, Captain Yates will be, too. Don't forget that."

"I won't," McGill said. "One more thing for you, Captain."

"What's that?"

"I'd suggest Metro PD assign additional patrol units and maybe some plain-clothes officers to keep an eye on the church's new sign for a few weeks."

"You think somebody's gonna come by and vandalize that sign?" Meeker asked.

"Maybe even shoot it up," Beemer said.

"Could be either," McGill told them.

### Connecticut Avenue NW — Washington, DC

Ellie Booker got straight to the point with her first interview question. "Mr. McGill, are you crusading for, and do you support, stricter gun-control laws?"

The two of them sat in facing chairs, offset by a few degrees so they didn't bump feet or knees, but closer than two people engaged in conversation would normally sit. Per Ellie's suggestion, McGill had left his hair a bit wind-tousled. She'd said it would make for better continuity with the video shot outside the church.

McGill was wearing makeup; he'd learned the wisdom of doing that long ago.

The videographer and Hugh Collier, sitting out of camera range, were the only other people in Ellie's interview room.

McGill said, "No, to both halves of your question."

Ellie blinked, taken by surprise, but she was a pro, ready with an alternative question to an unexpected answer.

"So you're fine with things as they stand? You just happened to support a provocative measure like the unveiling of the National Gun Death Counter at Saint Martin de Porres Church today?"

"I'm not fine with the status quo. I deplore the gun-deaths of innocents at the Winstead School and anywhere else in the country. I not only support the National Gun Death Counter at Saint Martin de Porres, it was my idea. I can tell you now that other such counters will soon be put in place in cities and towns throughout our country."

Hugh Collier leaned forward, smiling.

WWN had just been given a major scoop.

Looking thoughtful, and feeling a measure of actual respect for McGill's cunning, Ellie said, "You're acting on what you said earlier today. You're looking on a situation you think stinks —"

McGill interrupted. "There's no thinking necessary about this situation. The murders and suicides of dozens of people every day, tens of thousands of people every year, isn't a situation anyone has to ponder. It's a vast national tragedy and it has to stop."

"If you don't support stricter gun laws, how do you propose to do that?"

McGill said, "By changing the way the American people think

about guns."

With incredulity in her voice, Ellie asked, "You think that will be more effective?"

"I think it's an imperative first step. At one time we had a Constitutional amendment against the sale, distribution and possession of alcoholic beverages, commonly known as Prohibition. It didn't keep anyone from drinking, and it gave rise to modern organized crime.

"If you had a Congress that wasn't bought and paid for by special interests, including the gun lobby, it could pass a gun-control amendment to the Constitution, but that wouldn't matter any more than Prohibition did. Except that a lot of cops would get killed trying to enforce it. Gun ownership in the United States is more than a right, it's a fact of life. Banning it would be like trying to ban wine in France or beer in Germany. Never happen."

"So you want to change people's thinking. But a lot of people think the Second Amendment is absolute, in effect an anything-goes-for-guns amendment."

McGill was ready for that argument. He'd reread his grad school paper.

"Well, let's take a look at the history of that amendment. It was written, along with the rest of the Constitution, in 1787. At that time the United States Army had a standing force of 800 soldiers and officers. The Navy and the Marine Corps had been disbanded after our victory in the Revolutionary War and the Air Force, of course, remained undreamt of.

"There were no police departments at the time; it would be another fifty-one years before the first department with daytime patrols would be established in Boston. Given those circumstances, and the fact that the country was largely a wilderness and there were ongoing hostilities with Native American tribes, you'd think that would be enough to inspire the Framers to include a right to bear arms, but many historians think there was another root motivation for the writing of the Second Amendment."

Ellie had taken the time to read a copy of McGill's paper, too.

But she took her cue anyway. "What would that be?"

"The year prior to the writing of the Constitution, in 1786, there was an act of insurrection in Massachusetts known as Shays' Rebellion. A group of war veterans who'd never received full pay or promised bonuses for their service and a number of ordinary citizens who felt oppressed by a tax increase decided to rebel against the state government. The governor raised militias to put down the rebels before they could raid the state's Springfield Armory and arm themselves. The militias barely succeeded. The rebellion was fresh in the minds of the men who gathered in nearby Pennsylvania the following summer for the Constitutional Convention."

"So your point here is …" Ellie asked.

"That you can't forget the predicate clause of the Second Amendment: 'A well-regulated militia being necessary to the security of a free state …' The militias raised by Massachusetts were the forces that put down the insurrection. The militias were all any state had to provide for their security when the Constitution was written. They not only had to be well-regulated, they had to be armed. So the right to bear arms was provided to any potential militiaman, and by extension everyone else."

"And what's your takeaway from all this?" Ellie asked.

"That the inspiration and the very nature of the Second Amendment is defensive. It's meant to protect our security collectively and individually. I've never heard of any Constitutional scholar who claimed that the right to bear arms is a license to make war against the government. The Founders had only recently fought for the freedom to establish their new government. It's just plain crazy to think they'd institute a right to bring down their own creation. Likewise, it's madness to think the Constitution gives anyone the right to make war against his coworkers, against schoolchildren or against people sitting in a movie theater or shopping at a mall."

"You're talking about assault weapons now," Ellie said.

"Assault weapons or weapons of war: They're the same thing. Our country has two hundred years of history without civilians owning weapons of war. During that time nobody ever complained that their rights under the Second Amendment were in jeopardy. Then, in the late 1970s, a gun manufacturer thought it would be cool to make weapons of war for people he characterized as 'military wannabes.'"

"People who could pretend they were going to war without facing the life-or-death risks of the real thing?" Ellie asked.

"I'll leave the psychological profiling to the professionals," McGill said.

"So do you think you or anyone else can change the way people think about guns?"

"We have to. Allowing the wholesale bloodshed to continue is intolerable. We have to change people's thinking first and then their mood. We have to make Congress irrelevant until it has no choice but to be responsive. If the overwhelming majority of Americans reach certain conclusions about the places, uses, and types of firearms we'll permit in our society and inscribe those judgments in legislation, then those laws will be respected and obeyed."

"And do you think your gun death counters will be a good first step?"

"I do. People will see the terrible toll of the current madness rise every day; they won't be allowed to hold their noses. There's one more idea that I'd like to mention."

"What's that?" Ellie asked.

"You know that old celebrity game, Six Degrees of Kevin Bacon? It says that any actor in Hollywood can be linked through his or her film roles to a Kevin Bacon movie within six steps. I'd like every adult American to think of how many steps it would take to link him or her to a murder, a suicide or a wounding caused by gunshots." McGill paused, a look of regret on his face. "My bet, for most of us, it wouldn't take more than four."

Ellie knew that would be a good place to end and signaled the videographer.

She shook McGill's hand and Hugh Collier stepped forward to do the same.

"We'll run your interview with Ms. Booker at nine p.m. Eastern Time, sir," Collier told McGill. "That will give it the widest exposure across the country."

Though she already knew the answer, Ellie asked McGill, "You were shot in the line of duty as a Chicago cop, weren't you?"

"Just barely, but yeah."

"Still, you must have thoughts of what might have been."

"You mean dying, not seeing my children grow up, never meeting the president or marrying her?"

"All of that," Ellie said.

McGill told her, "Not a day goes by that I don't think of those things."

Ellie walked McGill to the elevator bank. Elspeth summoned a car and made sure it was unoccupied by assassins. McGill asked her to hold it for a minute. He led Ellie a few feet away and spoke in a quiet voice.

"The interview was good material for you?"

"You know it was." The producer knew McGill was going to ask her for something. She almost felt he'd set a trap for her. Probably for Hugh Collier, too. She reminded herself that she could never underestimate this guy. "What is it you want, Mr. McGill."

"I have one more idea. You can decide if it will fly."

"What's your idea?"

"You know how TV networks report war casualties? Why is it you don't report the number of gunshot deaths that happen every day in the United States? That's the war we're fighting at home."

"You'd like us to do a daily report?"

"Yes, the number of fatalities that day and the cumulative number for the year. Doesn't have to be more than that."

"But we could run pictures of some victims, note their ages, give capsule bios."

"You could do that, too," McGill said.

"Don't let people hold their noses?"

"Exactly."

When McGill followed Elspeth out of Ellie Booker's building

he saw Welborn Yates and Abra Benjamin leaning against a government-issue sedan parked at the curb. Each of them had their arms crossed over their chests, a defensive posture for sure, but McGill had seen them exchanging what he'd guessed was light banter. So they weren't yet chums but at least they were keeping things cordial.

They brought themselves to full upright when they saw him, not exactly coming to attention but showing a measure of respect. Still, McGill was glad that Welborn no longer reflexively started to salute upon seeing him. Simple courtesy was good enough for him.

Welborn and Benjamin looked at each other as if to decide who should speak first. Welborn deferred and Benjamin proceeded. "Mr. McGill, I've been given the lead on the FBI's part of the investigation into the death of Jordan Gilford."

McGill asked, "Who delegated that authority to you?"

"Deputy Director DeWitt."

"Good." He got along with DeWitt better than the gloomy FBI director, Jeremiah Haskins. He asked Benjamin, "Have you come to confer or ask questions?"

"Both. I've just spoken with Captain Bullard of Metro PD. She gave me copies of the photos the Park Police passed on to her. She brought me up to date on your recent conversation with her. I've assigned special agents in Maryland and Virginia to look into the idea that the vehicle that was parked in front of Abel Mays' SUV might have been compacted."

"Always nice to have plenty of manpower working an investigation," McGill said.

Benjamin wasn't sure if he was twitting her, but decided there was no advantage in making an unfavorable inference. "We'll have all the people we need, I assure you."

McGill told her, "I've been thinking about that situation, scrapping that car that was in front of Mays' vehicle."

"Yes?" Benjamin asked.

"If the man who killed Jordan Gilford had as his first concern leaving no electronic trail, he probably had another car close to wherever he scrapped the first one. He gets in the second car and drives ..." McGill looked at Welborn, passing the conjectural baton to him.

Welborn picked up his cue without missing a beat. "Maybe he drives all the way home or maybe he scraps the second car, too, and uses a third vehicle, say a truck, to get home. In any case, we look for security cameras near any scrapyard where a car was crushed on Saturday afternoon and see if we can find someone who resembles the driver in the Park Police photos."

McGill nodded. "That or the guy lives far away, maybe even outside the country, and wanted to get away as fast as possible. So we look at security footage from all the airports from, say, Philadelphia to Richmond to see if we can find a match for our guy in the car."

Benjamin asked, "And by we you mean?"

"You, the FBI, of course," McGill said. "Is there anything else, Special Agent Benjamin?"

"I believe Captain Yates has something to tell you, Mr. McGill. I'd like to hear what that is."

"Welborn?"

"No problem for me." He looked at Benjamin and offered a polite smile. "Celsus and I went to Mrs. Gilford's home and found everything locked up tight. There were no signs that anyone had broken in, but we're not specialists in that area and if someone who was good at sneaking into people's houses had been there, we might have missed it. Celsus stayed on the premises to await Mrs. Gilford's return home." He checked his watch. "That should be any minute now. Maybe she'll notice something out of place."

"And maybe some FBI techs should give the house a once over. Something might have been taken or listening devices might have been installed," Benjamin said.

"Good point," McGill said. "I don't think Ms. Gilford would object, if your people are polite." He told Benjamin about the two hard-chargers from DOD seizing Jordan Gilford's computer and files.

"My people will mind their manners," Benjamin said.

McGill said, "Good." He asked Welborn. "Is Celsus going to stay with Zara?"

Welborn nodded.

Without crediting Rockelle Bullard, or speaking exclusively of Welborn's safety, McGill mentioned that the people responsible for having Jordan Gilford killed might be desperate enough to target other federal employees, namely an FBI special agent and an Air Force captain. Both Welborn and Benjamin looked mildly surprised by the idea of personal jeopardy, but they adjusted their thinking quickly.

People caught in bad situations weren't known for impulse control.

Welborn and Benjamin could be shot and killed as easily as anyone else.

McGill told Benjamin, "I was going to ask Captain Yates to visit the Pentagon to speak with Hume Drummond, the man in the Inspector General's office at the Pentagon who hired Mr. Gilford. I'd like to hear what Mr. Drummond had in mind when he hired Gilford. Captain Yates has the security clearance to hear anything Drummond might have to say. How high is your clearance, Special Agent Benjamin."

"I'm not supposed to say," she told McGill.

He grinned. "Well, that sounds like it might qualify. Why don't the two of you go to see Mr. Drummond? You can watch each other's backs."

Benjamin looked at Welborn. "How's your marksmanship?"

"As good as it gets."

The special agent looked like she wanted Welborn to prove it. But she saw McGill watching her.

"Can't ask for more than that," she said.

McGill nodded. "Good. Welborn, if any of the brass hats at the Pentagon give you or Special Agent Benjamin a hard time, call Galia Mindel. She'll speak to the president and cooperation will be forthcoming."

This time, Benjamin gave McGill a doubtful look.
He saw it and told her, "Take it as gospel, Special Agent."

Joseph Flynn

# CHAPTER 16

## *J. Edgar Hoover Building — Washington, DC*

Besides having an Andy Warhol serigraph of Chairman Mao on his office wall, Byron DeWitt exhibited certain other Sinophile tendencies. He had Chinese take-out delivered to his office for lunch. He ate the food using chopsticks. To prove his true-blue loyalty to the good old US of A, however, he would often listen to intercepts of meetings of the Politburo Standing Committee of the Communist Party of China provided by the NSA.

The director of national intelligence thought DeWitt might pick up nuances that other translators, even the native speakers, might miss. The DNI confided to FBI Director Haskins that he thought DeWitt was more than bilingual; he was bicerebral. He could think like both an American and a Chinese.

Had DeWitt been informed of this evaluation, he would have shaken his head.

At most, in his opinion, there was only a partial duality.

Of course, even that facility might provide a critical advantage.

That day, however, DeWitt was listening to Jerry Garcia not President Xi Jinping. He used the earbuds of his iPod Nano. Playing Grateful Dead albums through bookshelf speakers at FBI headquarters probably would have been taking one liberty too many. Nonetheless, the lyrics and music he'd listened to during his college days acted like a Zen koan for DeWitt. They demonstrated the inadequacy of logical reasoning to lead to enlightenment.

And when "Uncle John's Band" played and Jerry sang the question to him, "Have you seen the light?" DeWitt did. At least, he thought he did. A cascade of facts rippled through his mind.

Senator Howard Hurlbert had been shot on the night of Saturday, January 12, 2013.

And when was Bahir Ben Kalil reported missing? DeWitt pulled that information up on his computer. Ben Kalil had been scheduled to arrive home in Amman, Jordan on Sunday, January 13, 2013. He never made it. The FBI was contacted by the Jordanian embassy on Monday, January 14, 2013.

Sonofagun. Looked like Hurlbert and Ben Kalil might have died within hours of one another. What else might they have had in common? The tide of revelation continued to swell. An anonymously sourced audio recording of Howard Hurlbert discussing the planned assassination of the president had been delivered to FBI headquarters and …

Tyler Busby was involved in the attempt to kill the president at Inspiration Hall and …

Busby had invited Representative Philip Brock to a pre-opening visit to Inspiration Hall and …

Henry Tillman, the bartender at The Constellation Club, had seen Brock having a series of quiet conversations with Hurlbert in the bar and …

Shit. The FBI had watched Brock for months without finding anything to link him to the assassination attempt. But …

Had the Bureau been watching Brock on the night Hurlbert had been killed?

Did Brock have any known connection to Bahir Ben Kalil?

Did Ben Kalil have any reason to want the president dead?

DeWitt had work to do. But now, at least, he stood a chance of finding answers to specific questions. He got up from his desk to do just that.

As he left his office, the Dead hit the opening notes of "Truckin.'"

### *The Pentagon — Arlington, Virginia*

More than a dozen years after the 9/11 terrorists had crashed an airplane into the Pentagon, the Department of Defense felt secure enough to allow civilian tours of the building. More than 100,000 visitors a year took the opportunity to see the hub of the nation's military might. They strolled almost a mile and a half through the buildings corridors, taking in displays illustrating the missions and accomplishments of the country's five armed services.

Despite all that openness, Captain Welborn Yates, United States Air Force, Office of Special Investigations, and FBI Special Agent Abra Benjamin were denied admission at the first security checkpoint they approached. They'd asked to see Mr. Hume Drummond in the Inspector General's office.

When queried if they had an appointment, they replied honestly that they did not.

"Think of it as a snap inspection," Welborn told the officer in charge of the checkpoint.

Being a Marine, he'd didn't see the humor.

Benjamin, however, seized the moment to ask Welborn, "Time to send up the Bat Signal?"

Welborn appreciated the jibe and grinned, but he didn't miss the point.

He had to prove his clout to the special agent. The security guys, too. He took out his phone and called Galia Mindel and explained the situation in a voice loud enough for everyone within a twenty-foot radius to hear. He concluded the conversation with, "Yes, ma'am. Thank you, ma'am."

He put his phone back in his pocket and still speaking loudly told Benjamin, "The chief of staff is speaking to the president right now. She assures me that within the next few minutes the secretary of defense or the highest civilian official currently on the premises will be here with an all-access VIP pass for us."

Welborn saw the Marine officer pick up a phone.

He said, "You really don't want to do that. You might not like your next posting."

The Marine thought about that for a moment and put the phone down.

Five minutes later Welborn and Benjamin cleared the checkpoint in the company of the deputy secretary of defense and an Air Force major general. Benjamin was suitably impressed. In fact, as handsome as Welborn was and as closely connected to the Oval Office as he'd proven to be, she had a hard time not falling in love. Two things stopped her from doing that: He wore a wedding ring and he seemed like the kind of guy who'd take his vows seriously.

Neither of which precluded her from becoming a really good friend.

One who'd be happy to engage in mutual backscratching.

Strictly in a professional sense, of course.

The deputy secretary said nothing to his unexpected guests except, "Please follow me."

The Air Force general asked Welborn, "Aren't you the OSI officer who cleared Colonel Carina Linberg of the adultery charge brought against her?"

"That was my first case, sir. It was resolved only when the accusation made against the colonel could no longer be sustained, after Captain Dexter Cowan, United States Navy, died."

"I heard about that. He crashed his Viper, trying to ram the car in which you were riding."

"Yes, sir. Mr. McGill's driver, Leo Levy, deserves the credit for saving our lives."

"You're a modest man, Captain."

"With much to be modest about, sir."

The general laughed. "And yet you can call the White House, get the ear of the president and waltz right into the Pentagon when need be." The general held up a hand. "No need to explain yourself. I just want to say I'm an old friend of Colonel Linberg's. I appreciate what you did for her. If you need to stop in here again at a moment's notice, just call me. We'll keep things within our branch of the service."

He handed Welborn a card with his name and phone number on it.

Major General Thomas Lunn.

"Thank you, sir, I'll do that. If you see Ms. Linberg before I do, please give her my regards."

With that exchange of military courtesy done, Welborn and Benjamin were left at Hume Drummond's office. It was a large, well-appointed space. Turned out Drummond was the inspector general. Despite his eminent position and lavish surroundings, Drummond seemed anything but comfortable to see Welborn and Benjamin.

His discomfiture grew visibly when Welborn told him, "Special Agent Benjamin and I are here to talk about the death of Jordan Gilford, sir."

The man looked as if he'd rather speak about his prostate troubles.

Having been reminded of Carina Linberg, Welborn recalled that when somebody was in trouble at the Pentagon he'd do well to take that person out of the building. He suggested as much to Mr. Drummond.

Benjamin added, "Many people find my office a good place to speak freely."

With that, the three of them were off to FBI headquarters.

### The Oval Office — The White House

Mather Wyman kissed Edwina Byington on the cheek after she told him, "It's so good to see you again, Mr. Vice President."

The best part of the greeting was Wyman knew the president's secretary was sincere in her show of affection. "You, too, Edwina. Do I need to cool my heels for a few minutes? I know I'm a bit early."

"No, sir. Madam President said you're welcome to join her as soon as you arrive."

"Well, that's nice."

Wyman felt Patricia Grant was also truly glad to renew acquaintances. Unlike Edwina, though, he was sure the president would also want something from him. He even had a good idea of what it was.

He entered the Oval Office and the president got to her feet the moment she saw him. She graced him with a smile that would have caused a straight man's pulse to race. Absent the sexual note, it made him a bit happier to be alive. She came around her desk and took both his hands in hers. Her face assumed a look of sympathy.

"I saw you at the Winstead School yesterday."

Mather Wyman saved her the necessity of asking the question.

"Kira and I know the family of one of the boys who was wounded not killed: Peter Greenlea." Wyman shook his head. "Quite the dismal day, isn't it, when we have to take comfort in an act of violence being less than mortal. At least for Peter."

The president squeezed his hands and told him, "We're going to move on a number of fronts to stop the bloodshed. Please have a seat."

Wyman sat only after the president returned to the chair behind her desk.

He'd been right. They were there to do business. If the meeting had been purely social, it would have taken place in a less formal setting.

"Do your plans include anything you can get through Congress?" Wyman asked.

"We're not bothering about Congress."

Wyman raised his eyebrows. "The revolution has begun? You'd like me to head a tribunal? Send all the bourgeoisie to the firing squads?" The former vice president's own words made him frown. "Sorry, this is definitely not the time for firing squad jokes."

"No, we'll table those for a later date. Would you like me to tell you what we intend to do about preventing gun violence? Or should we get down to the business at hand?"

"First things first," Wyman said. "If you'll allow me to show off just a bit, I'll say you're worried about the Ohio legislature."

The president nodded. "It looks like Pennsylvania is going to —"

"Petition the federal government to call a constitutional convention. In fact, the decision has already been made. I've heard from the speaker of Ohio's house. He said his counterpart in Pennsylvania had called him. It's a done deal in Harrisburg."

The president sighed. "How do you feel about it, Mather, our country having another constitutional convention?"

He laughed. "I'd have my doubts about doing it again with the original cast. Thinking about using a bunch of today's stand-ins makes me shudder, but ..."

"It's damn tempting, too," the president said, "to think you could rewrite the constitution as you would like it to be."

"Yes, it is. The seduction lies in thinking you can go the giants of American history one better. It's Walter Mitty with a political slant, but who doesn't indulge in those sorts of fantasies?"

The president shook her head. "I fantasize about a simpler life and quiet times."

"Well, sure, you've done it all. The rest of us are still striving."

"Hah. I hear from my spies that your greatest pleasure comes from visiting your granddaughters."

Mather Wyman had neither biological children nor grandchildren, but his niece Kira had anointed him as a surrogate grandfather to her twin daughters, and immediately had dropped surrogate from the description.

He beamed at the president. "Aria and Callista are the lights of my life."

"Then we'd best leave them a constitution written by true giants."

"I suppose we should. If I were still governor of Ohio or even if I hadn't come out as a gay man, I'm pretty sure I could win the day for us, Madam President. But now? All I can say is I'll do my best."

"That's all I can ask. Now, would you —"

Edwina buzzed and said, "Madam President, Vice President

Morrissey is here."

Mather Wyman gave the president a look. "Should I go? Two vice presidents is one too many, no?"

"Please stay, Mather. Edwina, please send Jean in."

Vice President Morrissey entered the Oval Office, took in Mather Wyman's presence without batting an eye and had the grace to extend her hand and say, "Mr. Vice President, a pleasure to see you again."

"And you as well, Ms. Vice President."

Jean held up an iPad and said to the president, "Here's the TV spot my friends in Minneapolis did, the one arguing against the sale of assault weapons. It's been updated to use the victims at the Winstead School."

Wyman raised his eyebrows, questioning just what was going on.

Morrissey told him, "The original spot was filmed using the victims of another shooting, but the format is modular. It can be updated whenever there's another shooting. This version will never be aired without the permission of the families involved."

Edwina buzzed again. "Madam President, Chief of Staff Mindel needs a word."

"Send her in, Edwina."

Galia entered the room, acknowledged the president and shook hands with Wyman and Morrissey. "I have some news, Madam President."

"Can it wait just a moment, Galia?"

"Yes, ma'am."

"Good. Let's all take a look at the TV commercial Jean has brought us."

The vice president handed her iPad to the president. She and the others clustered behind the president to watch. The president tapped the tablet's screen to start the video.

The sun rises over a Minnesota pond and a flock of geese takes flight.

On the shoreline three hunters are ready. Two raise shotguns.

One raises an assault rifle. Both his friends push the barrel down.

"Geez, give 'em a chance, why don't ya?" one friend says in disgust.

A buck with ten-point antlers steps into a forest glade.

Two camouflaged hunters are waiting. One raises a deer rifle.

The other raises an assault weapon. His friend shakes his head.

"Damn sporting of you."

A husband-and-wife team stalks a wild turkey in the woods.

Spotting it, the wife raises her rifle; her husband raises an assault weapon.

She sneers at him. "What kind of man are you?"

A voiceover announcer asks: So what kind of game can you hunt with an assault weapon?

The sound of an automatic weapon firing starts as ...

School photos of the six dead football players and three dead coaches from the Winstead School appear sequentially. The gunfire continues throughout.

When it finally stops a message appears on the screen.

Hunting season lasts all year long ...

Until you stop it.

The president stopped the video. She and the others were silent for a moment. Then she said, "I'd run this ad in a heartbeat, but it's the parents' call."

"That's what we said in Minnesota, too. The parents in our shooting couldn't bear to do it," Jean Morrissey said. "As governor, I was the one to ask them the question. If you like, Madam President, I can do the same at the Winstead School."

"No, let me do it, please," Mather Wyman said. "I know the people there. They're my friends."

The former vice president's eyes were moist.

"Would that be all right with you, Jean?" the president asked.

"Yes, of course, Madam President."

"You'll talk with the parents soon, Mather?" the president asked.

"Them, the administration and the student body. I think it would be best to get everyone on board. I'll go as soon as I can get a copy of the video."

"Thank you, Mather. You're a good friend."

"A pleasure to serve, as always, Madam President."

"What do you have for us, Galia?"

The chief of staff turned to the vice president. "May I borrow your iPad a moment, Ms. Vice President?"

Jean Morrissey nodded and the president handed the tablet computer to Galia. She pulled up the Twitter home page and pointed to the Trending in the U.S. column. Number one was #FourStepsToMurder.

Galia said, "This is a point Mr. McGill made in his interview with WWN. That anyone in this country is only four steps away from knowing someone who has been killed, has committed suicide or has been wounded by gunfire."

"But the interview hasn't aired yet, has it?" the president asked.

"No, ma'am. But somebody leaked at least this part of it, and it's already the hottest topic of discussion on Twitter domestically. We're getting people's attention."

"Word of mouth," the president said. "There's nothing more powerful."

# CHAPTER 17

## *WWN Washington Bureau*

Hugh Collier wanted to edit Ellie Booker's interview with Mc-Gill at the network's offices. Ellie agreed with the provision that the final word on any cut was hers. Perfectly aware that Mc-Gill had made his approach to Ellie not WWN, Collier agreed. He said he only wanted to have the final product in hand as soon as possible.

That and to keep any clips out of competitors' reach before WWN started airing them.

Ellie had made the executive decision to leak the #FourSteps-ToMurder meme on social media. Both she and Collier were over-joyed how quickly the ghastly parlor game had gone viral. People were sharing the word coast to coast.

The ratings for the McGill interview would be over the moon.

Amidst the mutual good feelings, Ellie raised the idea McGill had shared with her off camera, "So is WWN going to start airing daily and cumulative gun death totals on the evening news?"

"I don't think so," Collier said.

"Why not?"

"Don't you think it'd be too damn, pardon the phrasing, deadening?"

"If it was just numbers, sure. But if you show the human

element, just who gets killed on any given day, and do a brief but poignant sketch, it'd be a legitimate horror show. Look who we lost today. It's more than a shame; it's goddamn outrage. It'd be compelling."

Collier saw Ellie was genuinely working herself up.

But she was always one spark away from becoming an inferno.

"I have to disagree with you on this one," Collier said.

"Fine, I'll do it myself. Put it online. Do any follow-up interviews with McGill that way, too."

"Only after I get my first look," Collier said.

"Yeah, don't hold your breath. You don't like what I do, sue me."

Ellie stormed out of Collier's office.

He considered the surly departure a considerable improvement from the time she'd waved a knife under his nose on a New York street. The truth was, he and Ellie needed one another. Short of one of them killing the other, they'd remain codependent for a long time.

He'd give Ellie's take on McGill's idea a bit more thought.

Right now, though, it just didn't grab him.

### The Playground — Washington, DC

The sports bar on a quiet street in the Brookland neighborhood of Northeast Washington was called Kinzie's, but the clientele nicknamed it The Playground. The place was a byproduct of the long overdue decision to have the nation's intelligence agencies share information. In the discussion of how to achieve that goal, one sharp thinker who preferred to remain anonymous came up with a bright idea.

"What we need," this genius said, "is the equivalent of a good cop bar. A place where all our people can meet, gripe and gossip. You know, a place to buttonhole one another and say, 'Hey, did you hear about …'"

Some stuffed shirts thought this was a far too informal way to exchange vital information and in some cases, with the really big stuff, they were right. But for everyday chatter that might turn into something big, it proved wonderfully effective. Gave competing operatives the opportunity to get to know and trust each other as people.

Bridge building with drinks, munchies and war stories.

Half-a-dozen federal agencies chipped in relative nickels and dimes from their budgets to open the place. Within six months, the bar revenue made it self-sustaining. Like any good cop bar, it gave off a vibe that it was really a private club. Non-members took one look around and turned around, frequently apologizing for making the mistake of stepping inside.

Sports events from around the world were shown on a dozen large TVs but that was just window dressing. Few of the customers paid any attention. They were more interested in the global varieties of spirits and beers.

Just north and south of the Playground, the city's crime rates were substantially higher. Occasionally, there was some bleed-over into Brookland. Bad guys showed up where they shouldn't have. One Tuesday night, when the place was crowded, a member of an armed robbery gang burst into The Playground.

Not to rob the place but hoping to elude the police.

When two Metro cops charged in minutes later, they all but skidded to a stop. They recognized the atmosphere immediately. And they knew it wasn't one of their cop bars. Having a job to do, the senior cop still asked, "An African-American guy with a gun just come running in here? Looked to us like he might have."

In fact, that was exactly what the cops saw.

The lead bartender, however, shook his head. Nobody else so much as blinked.

The level of cooperation didn't please either cop. Before they could object, a blonde-haired guy who looked like he was half a hippie stepped forward and showed his FBI identification. Sonofagun was a deputy director.

He told the cops, "This is a quiet place where federal officers come to relax. If we turn up any information on your guy, we'll be sure to let you know."

The deputy director's tone was sweet reason. His subtext was: Don't bother us.

Both Metro cops knew there was no point to fighting the feds. Their own brass would shut them down.

So that was it. The cops were positive they saw Dontell "Don't Tell" Marsh, an armed felon with a rap sheet as long as his leg, run into Kinzie's. Only no one there was going to tell them dick. And — poof! — just like that a fucking armed robber was gone, never to be seen again.

That last part was okay with the cops. Guys like Don't Tell deserved to disappear.

The next part was even better. An anonymous snitch called in a tip giving the Metro cops the location of Don't Tell's stick-up gang right after they pulled their next job. The bust netted six repeat offenders with the proceeds of their latest heist. The messages were clear to both the cops and the creeps.

Cops: Work with us, we'll work with you.

Creeps: Steer clear of The Playground.

The second message was supplemented by the rumor that Don't Tell had been cleaned up, dressed up and passed off as a radical American imam whose release had been demanded by Somali pirates in exchange for a couple from Newport Beach, California whose boat had sailed into the wrong waters.

The rumor was true. The guy who came up with the improvisation was the same dude who'd talked to the Metro cops that night.

Now, Byron DeWitt took one of the booths in The Playground and ordered two bottles of South Pacific Export Lager, the pride of Port Moresby, New Guinea. He filled his glass and by the time a fine, foaming head had built Oscar Rogers slid into the booth opposite him. Rogers grabbed his bottle, ignored the glass and said, "Cheers."

He drained the top half of his beer at a swallow.

"Takes the gloom off a gray day, a good beer does," Rogers said.

"Who could argue with that?"

"Some effete, wine-sipping —"

"Don't say Californian," DeWitt warned.

Rogers grinned. "Okay, do they drink wine in Oregon?"

"Only screwtop."

"We'll drop the subject then." Rogers finished his beer and called for two more.

DeWitt had never learned Rogers' exact title at the CIA, but the man had told him he'd once been a field operative who had worked Southeast Asia from Bangkok to Port Moresby. Rogers' cover was that he had been an African-American radical on the run from the law.

He'd loved it when he heard the stunt DeWitt had pulled with Don't Tell.

He'd introduced himself, bought DeWitt a South Pacific and they became friends.

Going more slowly with his second beer, Rogers paused to ask, "So what can I do for you, Byron?"

DeWitt said, "Tell me everything the Agency knows about the Kalils, the late Bahir Ben and his sister, Hasna."

## McGill Investigations, Inc. — Georgetown

The turns in their separate investigations brought McGill and Sweetie back to the office at the same time. Sweetie had stopped at a convenience store along the way to pick up some liquid refreshment. Two tall slim plastic bottles of a dark red liquid.

McGill asked, "What's that?"

"Something Putnam introduced to me. Blamed me for, actually. Said it was my fault he's started looking for non-alcoholic, sugar-free things to drink."

"Fruit juice?" McGill asked.

"Maybe. There's a reference to fruit on the bottle. It has green tea extract, too. I tried it and liked it. I'm trying to decide if we should let Maxi drink it. It tastes good, doesn't seem to have anything bad in it and it's carbonated for fun."

She handed a bottle to McGill. They went into his office and sat down.

"Black raspberry?" McGill said, reading from the bottle. "Never heard of that."

He unscrewed the top and gave it a try. "Hey, that's good. Maybe you and I should drink a case first, before you let Maxi risk her health."

The two old friends laughed.

Sweetie said, "I've always seen how much your kids mean to you, Jim, and I love them with all my heart, too, but —"

"You've got a whole new fix on things with Maxi in your life."

"Exactly. The feeling is so intense sometimes it almost takes my breath away."

McGill glanced at the wall clock. "Isn't it about time to pick Maxi up from school?"

"Putnam's doing that. He dropped her off this morning. He's feeling pretty wound up about letting her go to school. Afraid of copycat shooters."

"Can't blame him," McGill said. "How do you feel?"

"I'm saying my rosary twice a day now. But Putnam and I found some time to talk and we came up with an idea for school safety maybe you can pass along to Patti."

"Sure. What is it?"

"Well, it'd have to be implemented on a individual school-district basis, but if Patti liked it and pushed it, that would help. What we're thinking is when any student registers for classes, the parents or guardians would have to disclose whether they keep any guns in their home."

McGill thought he saw at least part of what Sweetie had in mind.

"If they do," he said, "somebody from the school district goes to the home to make sure all weapons are properly secured. Can't fall into the kids' hands."

"Close. We thought it would carry more weight if the local PD sent out a cop to check things out."

"Yeah, that'd be better. I like that. What if Mom or Dad has a gun and keeps it on the night stand?"

"That falls into the same category as what if the parents or guardians refuse to say whether they own any firearms at all?"

"Okay," McGill said, "what then?"

"You send the kids whose parents play ball or don't own any guns to one set of schools and the other kids get sent to a second set of schools."

"Wow," McGill said.

"I know. It's almost like the idea punishes the kids who live with irresponsible adults. The response to that is our plan endangers fewer kids."

Both Sweetie and McGill took hits from their soft drinks.

"What about the teachers at the second set of schools?" McGill asked. "You couldn't just put newbies or the dregs in them. You'd get charged with discrimination."

"Right. Putnam said teachers should be offered a hazardous-duty pay premium, and the schools with non-compliant parents should have extra security people to cut down on everyone's risk."

"That would make it more doable," McGill said.

"It would also put pressure on all but the true hard cases to get with the program."

"That or home school their kids."

Sweetie said, "Home schooling is what Putnam and I were originally thinking of for Maxi. But she loves her school and we don't think she should be isolated or punished for other people's recklessness."

"I'll talk to Patti about the idea. I'm sure she'd have to get a legal opinion on it. I'll let you know if ..." McGill looked at Sweetie and read her mind. "Even if Patti were to say no, you and Putnam are going to make the idea public, aren't you? Try to start a movement."

"Yeah. We feel we have no other choice."

"Good, you should do that. I'll tell Patti that, too."

"I don't want to cause any hurt feelings, Jim."

"Not a chance, not with me, not with Patti."

"Good."

That matter taken care of, Sweetie told McGill of her conversation with Lisa Stone, and her proposal to Galia to get Erna Godfrey to work as a jailhouse snitch.

For a moment, McGill was at a loss for words.

Then he said, "Use Erna Godfrey to accomplish something good? That being to clear the name of Roger Michaelson? Hard to believe."

"You know what they say about God moving in mysterious ways."

"More so now than ever, apparently," McGill said. "And Joan Renshaw's friend said she was looking for a rich husband? Having Patti take that away from her must have hurt."

"Enough to fester for years, it seems."

McGill said, "If Galia hasn't spoken to Patti about the idea of Erna helping you yet, I'll talk to her about that, too."

"Good," Sweetie said.

# CHAPTER 18

## *Rayburn House Office Building — Washington, DC*

The lobbyists in Washington lingered in the hallways of the House and Senate office buildings waiting for an office holder or a senior staff member to appear in the same way vultures circled a dying animal waiting for it to expire. In anticipation of feeding.

Constituents from back home would amble down the corridors checking the numbers and names on the office suites they passed. Finding the one they wanted, they'd beam and tell the spouse and kids, "Here he/she is honey. Let's go in and say hello."

Sometimes the constituent visits were scheduled, in which case chances were good they'd actually get a minute or two of time from the person for whom they'd voted. If the drop-in was a matter of impulse, they might get a brief tour of the office and have to make do with that.

Discerning the status of the visitors to the Congressional office buildings was easy. Constituents, far more often than not, were the picture of casual attire. Lobbyists wore business suits. They were often custom made. Many of them cost more than a constituent's entire trip to Washington — even if they came from Alaska or Hawaii.

Though she was only eight years old, Maxi Shady was immediately able to distinguish between the two classes of people in the

Rayburn Building. She had gone there straight from school with Putnam, whom she was starting to think of as Daddy. She also had no trouble discerning to which class Putnam belonged.

"You're a fancy man, Putnam." She was still reluctant to call him Daddy.

Fancy man was an archaic term for pimp, but Putnam felt sure that wasn't what Maxi meant. The irony was, he felt it was entirely apt for many of the lobbyists they passed. It might even have applied to him before he met Margaret and left the dark side. Hell, of course it had.

"I like to dress well," he said.

He took more pride than ever in his attire as his fitness increased.

"You look pretty spiffy, too," he added.

Maxi beamed. Then her face fell. "You and Margaret buy me nicer clothes than Mama and Daddy did."

Putnam stopped and dropped to one knee. He put his hands on Maxi's shoulders.

"Tell me the truth. Did your mom and dad love you with all their hearts?"

Maxi nodded, a tear rolling down her cheek.

Some of the tourists noticed; none of the lobbyists paid any attention.

"Honey," Putnam said, "as long as someone is doing their best for you, that's all you can ask. You understand that, don't you?"

Maxi wiped away the tear and nodded again. "I'm okay now."

Putnam stood and said, "That's my girl."

Maxi took his hand and held it tight. A moment later they entered the office of Representative Philip Brock, Democrat of Pennsylvania. Putnam got Maxi seated and doing her homework on her iPad. Then he presented himself to the receptionist.

She gave him a questioning look. Not about Maxi. She'd smiled in her direction. But the receptionist had made Putnam for a lobbyist, too. It was considered bad form to drop in on a representative or a senator without an appointment, usually made for an hour when the building was quiet and there were few if any TV crews lurking.

Putnam hadn't let protocol deter him.

He gave his name to the receptionist and said, "I'm not here to ask for a single thing. I'll only be a few minutes, and I have something to tell Representative Brock he'd really like to hear."

Part of the receptionist's job was to know when people were blowing smoke.

Putnam sounded good to her, and she'd never seen a suit bring a little kid with him.

She picked up her phone and said, "Let me see what I can do."

What she did was summon the congressman's chief of staff, who came out of the great man's personal office. Putnam repeated his spiel. Unlike the receptionist, the chief of staff knew who Putnam was, by appearance and affiliation, if not personally.

"You work for Darren Drucker, don't you, Mr. Shady?"

"With Mr. Drucker, yes." Parts of speech mattered.

It also didn't hurt to let the other person bring up a billionaire's name.

By this time, Philip Brock had come to stand in the doorway to his office. He cleared his throat to get his chief of staff's attention. Then the congressman pointed at Putnam and made a beckoning gesture.

Surprisingly, Brock told his senior staffer that he'd see Putnam privately.

The two men shook hands and took seats on opposite sides of Brock's desk.

"ShareAmerica," Brock said, "that was your idea, wasn't it, Mr. Shady?"

"It was."

"A mutual fund lobbying group working for the public interest. Ingenious. How's it going?"

"We're starting to make some headway."

"Have you gotten any legislation passed yet?"

"Not yet, but we've stopped some legislation we didn't like."

"Made a few enemies?"

"That's inevitable, all a part of the game."

Brock didn't question Putnam's characterization of government as a game. He felt the same way. He also knew to whom Putnam Shady was married, Margaret Sweeney. James J. McGill's partner in his private investigations agency. The man had connections any other lobbyist would kill for.

"What can I do for you, Mr. Shady?"

"As I told your staffers, I came to do something for you."

"What's that?"

Putnam told Brock of the new political party he and Darren Drucker were forming.

"Cool Blue?" Brock smiled. "Love the name."

"Thank you, sir. I thought I'd extend you the courtesy of telling you that Cool Blue will be running a candidate against you in the upcoming election."

Brock laughed. "Well, that's everyone's right, including a brand new party."

"Yes, sir. We're innovative in a number of ways. All our candidates come fully pre-funded so they don't have to spend a lot of time grubbing about for campaign contributions. We also let our opponents know how we'll run against them. In your case we're hoping that, since you call yourself a Democrat, you'll start voting like one."

"My voting record is highly popular in my district."

"In that case, the honest thing to do would be to change your party registration to Republican or True South."

Brock's smile remained in place, but he was quiet for a moment as he studied Putnam's face. Putnam looked back without blinking.

"Are you trying to make me angry, Mr. Shady?"

"No, sir. What Cool Blue is trying to do is improve the chances that someone with progressive views will represent your district whether that's our candidate or you with an increased allegiance to the Democratic Party."

Brock nodded. "I see. Well, thank you for stopping by. I'll take what you've told me into consideration when I campaign for reelection."

The congressman stood. Putnam got to his feet and they shook hands and said goodbye. Putnam picked up Maxi on his way out and they headed home. Maxi asked, "Was your meeting fun?"

"Great fun," Putnam said.

He hadn't gone to see Brock to give him a political heads-up. He was sure Brock was smart enough to know that. So now the congressman would wonder what Putnam had really wanted. Meaning that Putnam had sown confusion in Brock's mind: a benefit in itself.

What he'd really visited the man's offices for was to get a close look at his walls. See what photos, plaques and awards resided there. Find some possible point of connection between him and Joan Renshaw for Margaret.

The most interesting thing to attract Putnam's notice, though, hadn't been inanimate. It had been Brock's face. The man had the start of a nice tan. The sweet blush of the sun, not the rotisserie roast of a tanning bed. Natural high color wasn't something he had acquired locally.

So where had Brock gone recently? Had to be someplace sunny and warm.

Didn't matter if he'd traveled on the public purse or his own dime.

Either way, his tan suggested he had found the leisure time to darken his complexion.

That made Putnam wonder: Had Brock and Joan Renshaw ever taken a vacation together?

### J. Edgar Hoover Building — Washington, DC

For a special agent, Abra Benjamin had a pretty big office, Welborn thought. Nicely furnished, too, with a good view of Pennsylvania Avenue. For just a second, he wondered if he would have been given a new office at the White House, if he'd accepted the promotion to major. Maybe Kira had been right and he should've —

No. He pushed thoughts of self-aggrandizement aside.

Benjamin had just asked Hume Drummond, inspector general of the department of defense, if he'd like a cup of coffee or tea, and he'd declined both.

The amenities observed, Welborn jumped in with the first question, while Benjamin was still fiddling with her audio recorder.

"Mr. Drummond," he said, "is Zara Gilford in any danger?"

Appearing startled, Drummond asked, "What kind of danger?"

The look Benjamin shot Welborn told him he was the one in trouble. She must have thought that just because she'd seated Welborn next to Drummond, on the visitors' side of her desk, that he'd sit silently by and observe. Welborn had no such intention, and no worries about any reprisal from Special Agent Benjamin.

His boss, the president, could beat up any other boss in town.

"The kind of danger Mr. Gilford experienced," Welborn said.

"You think someone might kill Zara?" Drummond looked even more incredulous.

"It's your opinion that concerns me, sir. Is Zara Gilford in danger?"

Welborn saw that Benjamin wanted to seize control of the questioning, but she was interested in Drummond's response, too. She bided her time. The man was clearly examining the idea that Welborn had presented to him.

"I ... don't think so. Jordan told me he never talked shop with Zara."

"Do you think the people who had Mr. Gilford killed know that?" Welborn had beaten Benjamin to the punch again. She might have complained, but once more she wanted to hear the answer.

"I can't say; I don't know who they are, and there's no way to say what they might have in mind."

"So, it would be a good idea to err on the side of caution?"

"Yes, of course."

"And the DOD will be happy to pick up the tab?"

"Yes."

Welborn nodded to Benjamin. Whenever possible, it was

a good idea to allow more than one interrogator have a go at a subject. Not just good cop, bad cop. Subtle differences worked well, too. They forced the respondent to relocate his balance each time the verbal baton was passed.

The easiest way to deal with such circumstances was to speak honestly.

Lies or even pauses for equivocation became glaringly obvious.

Benjamin, recovering her bearing nicely, set up the next major question.

"Mr. Drummond, was anyone other than you involved in making the decision to hire Mr. Gilford?"

"No, it was strictly my call."

"Why did you hire Mr. Gilford?"

"He has … had an all but unique array of skills and a track record of exposing wrongdoing at major corporations. That calls for strength of character as well as a high intellect."

Welborn was curious to see if Benjamin let Drummond's evasion go unchallenged.

She didn't. "That tells us you thought Mr. Gilford was well qualified. It doesn't say a thing about the reason, the purpose for which you hired him. Please don't try to tell Captain Yates and me that it was an ordinary recruitment and you had nothing more in mind than hiring the best man available. Unless, of course, you can cite examples of other routine hires being gunned down on the National Mall."

Drummond looked stymied.

He'd wanted to say Gilford was nothing more than a good personnel move.

But Benjamin's challenge to name someone else who'd come to grief simply by signing on with the inspector general's office left him no room to maneuver. Welborn liked that. He saw there was a measure of satisfaction in Benjamin's eyes, too.

With nothing left to do, nowhere else to go, Drummond told them, "I can't tell you."

"Why not?" Welborn asked.

"I'm not even sure I can tell you that."

"Very convenient for you, but I'm not sure that's a lawful position."

Benjamin told Welborn, "It's not unlawful, but it is a risky strategy. You know why, Captain Yates?"

"Oh, yeah," Welborn said. "The right to remain silent applies only to people who have been arrested. Since we haven't placed Mr. Drummond under arrest, well then, any pre-arrest silence can be introduced into evidence at trial."

"From which a jury might reasonably infer guilt, since an innocent person would feel free to talk."

It was a nice pincer movement, but now Drummond was getting testy. Welborn and Benjamin, being young, had underestimated him. He had a lot on his mind, was even fearful to a degree, but with a Juris Doctor degree from Duke Law School and decades of real-world experience, he wasn't about to buckle under their threat like some mope off the street.

"Oh, balls," he said, "I'll never go to court or face a jury."

"Why not?" Welborn asked.

"Two words: national security."

Welborn and Benjamin looked at each other. Those were the two best words anyone in government could use to cover his heinie. There was no getting around them. Not if the claim was legitimate. Or even plausible.

Drummond sighed. "But you two are right, I'm going to have to talk with someone, and the only person I can think of is the woman who appointed me to my job."

"The president?" Benjamin asked.

"Yes. You don't have the number to her private line, do you?"

Welborn said, "I do."

"Really?" Both Benjamin and Drummond had asked the question.

"Really, but one thing before I call," Welborn said. "Do you think you're in danger, too, Mr. Drummond?"

He said, "I may well be."

## FirePower America — Falls Church, Virginia

Auric Ludwig felt threatened, as he never had been before. He'd found a new lawyer after making hours of phone calls. He finally succeeded in hiring Spencer Dryden, the flamboyant Montana lawyer who affected a cowboy appearance and was known for carrying a concealed weapon up to the courthouse doors — where he yielded it to the authorities for safekeeping until he won his case at which time he would reclaim his weapon in front of the building with the television cameras rolling.

Dryden had demanded a million dollars up front.

He'd told Ludwig, "You really stepped in it this time, son. We're not talking a Second Amendment issue this time. We're looking at an obstruction of justice charge. That police captain told it to you true. You could be looking at a very long spell in prison."

"How are you going to fight it?" Ludwig asked.

"Only one way to do it that I can see. The cop who gave you the news about this Abel Mays fella is gonna have to carry the weight. He took the initiative to call you all on his own."

Reading between the lines, Ludwig assumed the cop would have to be paid off.

Reading Ludwig's mind, Dryden disabused him of that notion.

"There can't be any quid pro quo here. I'm not going to enter into any conspiracy to obstruct justice. What you do is give me the man's name and phone number. I'll tell him things have gotten real serious and advise him to hire a lawyer. I won't give him a referral because that might be considered an element of a conspiracy, too."

"So what will you do for your million dollars?" Ludwig demanded.

"I'll appeal to the man's understanding of the greater good."

Ludwig didn't question that idea. He understood it implicitly. As someone who professed a reverence for the unconditional right to bear arms, the cop would be guided to the understanding that without Ludwig's leadership that sacred right might be diminished. The cooperative cop would become a martyr to the cause.

Not that he'd have to outright die for it. His lawyer would naturally fight to get him the lightest sentence possible, and when he was released from prison he would be regarded as a hero and would enjoy tangible appreciation for his status.

That was how Ludwig imagined Dryden's approach anyway.

Praying that the scenario he'd painted was more than just wishful thinking.

He told Dryden. "All right, we'll do it your way."

"Just as soon as my fee is deposited in my account," the lawyer replied.

The money had been wired hours ago.

Ludwig hadn't left his office in the hours since. He felt trapped by his circumstances. Worse than that, he had that goddamn billboard outside his window taunting him. National Gun Death Counter. Shit. He couldn't imagine anything worse. Or anything more likely to give guns a bad name. To actually move the usually indifferent mass of the American public to make his life harder. To cut into the profits of the companies that paid him. Maybe even to scare the invertebrates in Congress into passing effective gun control laws.

He had drawn his curtains so he wouldn't have to look at the damn billboard, but he couldn't help himself. Every ten minutes or so he had to get up from his desk and take a peek, hoping like hell the number had held steady. In a moment of fantasy, he'd even imagined the number rolling backward, as if to correct a mistake. Every time he looked, though, the damn number had gone up once more.

It was enough to impress even him, how regularly the number of gun deaths increased.

He hated the billboard all the more for that.

He went to the window again, praying, though he didn't really believe in God, that a power shortage or something would interrupt the counter's electricity. No, a thunderstorm would be even better. A bolt of lightning turning the damn thing into smoking rubble would be just the thing. A sign from on high that his side had been right all along.

To his amazement, he did see flashes of light in the darkness.

Only they were coming from the ground in a steady stream, not from the sky in a jagged bolt. Then Ludwig heard the sounds that accompanied the light show. The steady mechanical tattoo of an automatic weapon firing. No, there were two weapons.

Ludwig watched as the billboard shattered in front of his eyes.

The goddamn number that illuminated the death count disintegrated.

A surge of pure joy flooded through Ludwig. Of course, that was the way to handle the damn sign and any other like it that might be erected. It was all so simple. He didn't know why he hadn't thought of it.

And then he was reminded why it wasn't such a good idea after all.

Sirens blared. More lights flashed. Not from gunshots, but from cop cars.

He looked down at the street. Two men were proned out on the pavement. Cops were running toward them like ants over-running a picnic blanket. The police hadn't appeared by magic; they'd been waiting for something just like what had happened.

A tremor of fear ran through Ludwig. It was quickly replaced by rage. If he was going to go down, he would go down fighting. He decided he had to open another front in his war to stay out of prison.

He had to make the whole situation political, and get the three million members of FirePower America behind him. He had to do everything he could to find his good guy with a gun, the one who'd killed Abel Mays. His effort would start now.

Just let James J. McGill or anyone else get in his way.

See what happened to them.

### McGill's Hideaway — The White House

McGill and Patti decided not to spoil their dinner so they

waited until afterward to partake of a digestif and conversation in McGill's White House lair. The weather outside was chill and damp. McGill put some logs in the fireplace and set them ablaze. He joined Patti on the long leather sofa and accepted the glass of Laubade VSOP Bas Armagnac.

On most occasions, McGill was a beer drinker, and contentedly so. As his marriage to Patti continued to mature, though, he let her coax him into trying something new every so often. She'd persuaded him to try the Laubade by telling him the brandy had the fragrances of vanilla, chocolate and nougat.

McGill hadn't been able to resist making a comparison. "Sort of like a Milky Way bar."

Patti had said, "If you like. Give it a try."

He did and found it pleasing in moderation.

After watching the flames in silence for the length of time it took to sip their glasses empty, Patti said, "Are you ready to talk?"

McGill put his glass down. "Sure."

"I think you did a wonderful job with Ellie Booker. Galia told me your interview won its time-slot ratings by a large margin."

"I have a future in television?"

"Well, you are handsome and well spoken."

"Thing is, I don't like reading other people's scripts."

"A prima donna. Perfect. You'll fit right in."

McGill paused to look Patti in the eye and ask a serious question. "Will you want me to give up the private eye biz when we leave the White House?"

"Maybe move into management anyway. I'll teach theater arts. We'll do some good works, and we'll have time to take more romantic vacations like the one in Paris."

McGill leaned over and kissed his wife. "You could make a weekend in Dubuque romantic."

Patti laughed and returned the kiss. "Let's do some more of that after we talk."

"Do we have to?" McGill asked. "Talk, I mean."

"I feel better when we do. You're the one person I know who

has absolutely no hidden agendas. The one person who's not afraid of getting on my bad side."

"As if there were one."

"Really, Jim. Please."

"Okay. How was your day, dear?"

"Pennsylvania's legislature voted to petition Congress to call a constitutional convention."

McGill recalled where that left things standing. "One more state and the carnival comes to town?"

"The talk is the convention would be held in Philadelphia, just like the first one."

"The better to provide self-delusion for all the fools in the room," McGill said. "Which state is on the bull's-eye, the one to clinch the matter?"

"Ohio. Mather Wyman's going to work the legislature in Columbus to vote no, but he's not sure he can pull it off, having come out as a gay man."

"I don't understand how one thing would affect the other, but if it does and things go the wrong way, there's only one thing for you to do."

"What's that?"

"Pack the convention with loyalists and allies so you get most, if not all, of the things you want."

"And how would I do that?" Patti asked.

"Well ... I think you use a combination of threats, favors, deceit and nepotism."

"In other words, politics as usual."

"Pretty much. I'll have to check out my copy of the Richard J. Daley handbook to see if I'm forgetting anything. Like dire threats."

Patti moved on to her next subject. She told McGill about the TV commercial Jean Morrissey had brought in.

McGill winced. "That had to be tough to watch."

"That's the whole point. Mather's going to handle that job, too, talking to the Winstead families to get permission to use their photos. I was thinking of buying the time slot immediately after I speak to the nation tomorrow. Run the commercial then."

"That'd be the place to do it. If you put it up front, you might lose a big chunk of your audience, even some people who share your views."

McGill waited to listen to whatever was next, but Patti told him it was his turn.

"Sweetie and Putnam have an idea for school reform," he said.

He told Patti what it was. She thought about it for a moment.

"If I were simply Mrs. James J. McGill and we were living in, say, Evanston, Illinois, and my stepchildren, Kenny and Caitie, were attending public schools like most other kids … I'd want a plan like that in place."

"You'll bring it up when you speak?"

"I will."

"I've thought of a couple of other things since I talked with Sweetie."

"What?"

"You've got eighteen-year-olds in a lot of high schools. They're old enough to buy their own weapons in a lot of states. Mom and Dad might never know. What's to keep them from bringing a new purchase to school?"

"Please tell me you have some idea of what to do about that?"

McGill said, "Schools need to have intelligence officers. My suggestion would be tech-savvy college students. They could be hired part time. Their jobs would to monitor all the social media outlets for every student in a school. We know most kids can't stop themselves from blabbing to each other on social media. Chances are if some student has bought his own weapon, it will be the subject of an online discussion. You bring the gun-buyer in and explain if he keeps his weapon, he'll be attending a special school, too."

"That sounds like it could be a very dangerous school," Patti said.

"That brings me to my other thought. Every school has got to have some sort of perimeter defense. Stop any would-be shooter outside the school. Never let them make it into the building. Raise property taxes to pay for the security. Let people know that's the price they have to pay for having the gun laws the way they are. Maybe they'll get mad enough to change things."

Patti nodded. "I think you're right, but I don't want to hit people with too much all at once. I'll go with Sweetie and Putnam's idea when I make my speech; I'll raise your points at a press conference the following day."

"Can we call it quits with business for the day?" McGill asked.

"I think so."

A ringing phone said otherwise. McGill answered. It was his hideaway.

"Really? Yeah, that's good. I'll tell her." He put the phone down.

"What's good?"

"That was Captain Rockelle Bullard of the Metro Police. There have been two shootings of gun death counter billboards. One outside FirePower America; one outside St. Martin de Porres Church here in DC. The FBI arrested two guys in Virginia; the metro cops grabbed a single shooter here in town. So we know where those three will be going, don't we?"

"We do, indeed," Patti said.

McGill stood and extended his hand to Patti. They took their first steps toward the door when the phone rang again. Both of them grimaced. They longed for the day when a ringing phone might be ignored, but it hadn't arrived yet.

McGill answered once more. He listened and then told Patti, "It's Welborn. He and Special Agent Benjamin of the FBI would like to know if they can bring the inspector general of the DOD to come see you."

The president made an executive decision.

"Tomorrow morning, ten a.m. in the Oval Office."

McGill relayed the message. Patti took his hand and they went to their bedroom.

What little remained of the night was theirs to do with as they wished.

# CHAPTER 19

## President's Private Dining Room — Tuesday, March 11, 2014

McGill was having breakfast alone, reading chicagotribune.com on his iPad. The paper's baseball columnist was evaluating the Chicago White Sox's off-season acquisitions and how they might fare in the upcoming season. Blessing, the head butler at the White House, interrupted McGill's reading when he entered the room bearing a message.

Handing it to McGill, he said, "From the switchboard, sir."

The White House, in the spirit of democracy, had a phone number the public might call: 202-456-1414. Once reached, though, you had to leave a message — in a quaint 20th century fashion — with an operator. You couldn't just say, "I want the president." Or "Get me McGill."

The staffers on the switchboard were trained to assess the importance of each message. In a world of endless hierarchies, some rose to the top of the stack, others sank to the bottom. The one McGill received that morning rated immediate delivery.

It came from Ellie Booker who pointed out to McGill that his cell phone was off.

He knew that. The choice had earned him thirty minutes of peace and quiet with his morning eggs, toast and baseball news. But the world would not long be kept at bay.

Ellie informed him that Auric Ludwig, in ten minutes' time, would be giving a live interview on SNAM, Satellite News America, the new purveyor of anti-administration vitriol now that WWN had taken its distemper shots. McGill was going to be a featured name in Ludwig's commentary. He might like to watch. If he had remarks to make in response, Ellie would be happy to share them with the masses.

Just how Ellie had come by this tidbit, McGill didn't know. But he assumed she had an intelligence network at least equal to the one he'd proposed for the country's schools. He knew that Patti had the Farm Bill signing this morning and would be using that as the televised springboard for sharing her views on what should be done to rein in gun violence.

So he wasn't going to bother her with Ellie's news.

He called Galia, and found out she already knew about Ludwig's TV appearance.

It seemed everyone had their spies, except for him.

So he had a decision to make: Watch Patti or Ludwig.

Not a tough choice. He'd watch Patti. Catch Ludwig later on YouTube.

Get back to Ellie Booker if he had something that needed saying.

## The Oval Office — The White House

Thirty seconds before the president would speak live to the nation, Mather Wyman slipped into the room, careful to stay out of frame of the camera focused on the president. He caught the president's eye and gave her a thumbs-up. Then he whispered ever so softly, "Warriors." The name of the Winfield School's athletic teams.

The president read his lips and nodded.

The parents and wives of those who'd lost their lives at the school had given permission to use the photos of their loved ones in the commercial Jean Morrissey had dug up. Warriors, indeed, the president thought. She gave her own thumbs-up to Galia, who would see to it that the commercial ran.

Also present, off-camera, was Senator Richard Bergen, the Senate majority leader. Just before the president had taken her seat behind her desk, she'd given Bergen a message. "Dick, I'm about to make your life more difficult."

Bergen blinked. "For any particular reason, Madam President?"

"It's nothing personal."

"It never is."

"I'm going to blast Congress. Not everyone, just the senators and representatives who kowtow reflexively to the gun lobby."

"That's still quite a large number."

"I know, but they've earned it. I should have done it long ago. I'm ashamed I didn't."

"Looking forward, not back," Bergen said, "it will be harder for me to get my members, much less the other side, to pass any legislation you want to see enacted."

"I know, but with the House in the hands of the Republicans and True South, there's little chance of getting much accomplished anyway."

For the first time, the president thought a constitutional convention might be a good thing. The country could move to a parliamentary system. If the people elected a party to a majority position in the legislature, they got to run the show until the electorate kicked them out. There would be no gridlock.

She asked the majority leader. "Have you heard about Cool Blue, Dick?"

He blinked twice this time. Clearly, he hadn't heard.

"It's a new progressive party being formed by Putnam Shady and Darren Drucker. I'll tell you all about it after I'm done speaking to the country."

Leaving the poor man on tenterhooks, she took her place behind her desk.

The president was given her cue and she reacted not by speaking but by signing the Farm Bill into law. She used just one pen to do it. She intended to donate the Mont Blanc to the Smithsonian. With any luck, it would become an object of historical significance.

That task accomplished, she looked at the camera and said, "My fellow Americans, I've just signed into law what is commonly known as the Farm Bill. Over the next five years, this legislation commits our country to spend nearly $1 trillion on crop insurance subsidies, price supports and other benefits to support the agricultural sector of our economy.

"There's a good deal of debate as to whether this is a prudent measure to guarantee abundant, moderately priced food supplies or a vast giveaway to large corporations. I'm not going to get into any of that right now. Instead, I'm going to talk about a $2 billion spending provision in the bill that has nothing to do with farming or food. This money is intended, instead, to build a federal prison in Alaska.

"You might ask what prison construction has to do with agricultural legislation. The answer is, nothing at all, but sometimes that's just the way things get done in Congress. You have to graft somebody's pet project onto a completely unrelated piece of legislation if you ever hope to have a chance of getting the money for your own pet project.

"For more than ten years now, the senior senator from Alaska, Thomas Hale, has sought the funding to build a federal prison in his home state. Up until now, Alaska has sent people convicted in federal courts to prisons in Washington state. The reason was, this was a more cost effective way of dealing with these prisoners. Alaska's population is as small as its size is great.

"Nonetheless, Senator Hale wanted a federal prison for his state. He argued that his constituents' tax dollars should be spent at home where they would create high-paying jobs with benefits. He said that even if his state didn't provide enough local convicts to fill a new prison, Alaska could house surplus inmates from other states, relieving their prisons of overcrowding. It would be a win-win situation. Getting a federal prison became Senator Hale's pet project.

"Just recently, in the wake of the tragedy at the Winstead School, it has also become my pet project, too. I worked behind the scenes to make the new federal prison in Alaska a reality. And as you've just seen, with a stroke of my pen, I created that reality.

"At this point, you might well ask what does a school shooting in Washington, DC have to do with building a new prison in Alaska? It might seem as irrelevant as putting the money for prison construction into the Farm Bill. Well, here's the thing. Not all that long ago, there was a program called Project Exile. It was a program started in Richmond, Virginia that shifted prosecution of illegal gun possession by convicted criminals from local courts to federal courts.

"The reason for doing that is federal court sentences tend to be longer than those handed down in state courts and criminals can be incarcerated far from home, far from their families, friends and comfort zones. Working with Attorney General Michael Jaworsky, I intend to nationalize the concept behind Project Exile.

"The federal government will ask all fifty states to shift the prosecution of any felon found to be illegally in possession of a gun or any person falsifying information to obtain a gun or any person furnishing a gun to a felon to a federal court. If a person is convicted in a federal court of any of those crimes, he or she will be sentenced to a minimum of five years imprisonment, and that sentence will be served in the new prison that will be built in Alaska.

"When the experts look at the effectiveness of how we punish criminals, their two main areas of concern are incapacitation and deterrence. Incapacitation is simply the length of time a criminal is incarcerated instead of being out on the streets committing his or her crimes. Deterrence is harder to measure. It begs the question of how many would-be criminals are dissuaded from starting lives of crime. The exact number, of course, can never be known.

"But my considered opinion is that the prospect of serving time in a remote area of Alaska will prove daunting to more than a few young people tempted to take a wrong turn in their lives. And the fact that a federal sentence would take them so very far from home for a longer time than they presently have reason to expect will, I think, also make them think long and hard before turning to a life of crime.

"I know that there will be critics of my plan, and they will condemn it in the harshest terms. That, of course, will be the height of irony because it is usually Democrats who are mocked as being soft on crime. What I intend to do is to use our laws and our resources to launch the greatest assault on drug dealers, street gangs and any other predators who either use guns or furnish them to criminals that our country has ever known.

"I'll be blunt about this. Anyone who criticizes my plan had better have a clearly reasoned response and a better alternative or I'll be the one calling them out for being soft on crime. I intend to make the streets of the United States, from our biggest cities to our smallest towns, safer than they've ever been in our history.

"Achieving that goal will be a great victory on its own, but it will also be a stepping stone to adding a measure of reason to another ongoing debate. Once the chance of accidentally being killed in a drive-by shooting, becoming the victim of street gang vengeance or having your home invaded by thugs with guns is made remote, our fear will diminish and we can have an intelligent debate about another subject of critical importance.

"That being, just what kind of firearms should be available to the American people? After all, Abel Mays wasn't a drug dealer or a street criminal. He was a physical education teacher and a football coach. By all accounts, he was accomplished at both of those demanding jobs. But when an element of competition was introduced to recruiting the best high school football players and he came out on the short end of the contest, Abel Mays snapped.

"Worse than that, he had easily available to him what until recently was considered a weapon of war. And so Abel Mays made war on the players who'd spurned him and the coaches who had recruited those young athletes away from his team. Abel Mays brought such horrifying firepower with him to the Winstead School that he killed four other young men whose only mistake was to stand with their teammates and coaches in confronting the shooter who had come to their school.

"For all we know, Abel Mays had no intention of killing the young men whom he had never met. Maybe they just got in his way. To him, they were nothing more than collateral damage. But to the mothers and fathers and wives of all the boys and men who were killed last Saturday morning on the football field at the Winstead School, they were among the most important people in their families' lives."

The president had tears in her eyes now.

But the set of her jaw showed an iron determination.

She said, "These abominations must stop."

She took a moment to compose herself before resuming.

"Neither the Second Amendment nor any other articulation of our rights as American citizens is absolute. Nothing in the Second Amendment provides for the right to manufacture, sell or import firearms. Nothing in the Second Amendment construes the bearing of arms as the equivalent of a right to amass a personal arsenal. Nothing in the Second Amendment says you have the right to bear arms without creating a public record of the firearms you own. Nothing in the Second Amendment provides for the right to make war against the government of the United States. Nothing in the Second Amendment provides for the right of one American to make war against his fellow Americans in school buildings, shopping malls, movie theaters or any public place at all.

"If I thought it would do the least bit of good, I would submit legislation to Congress that would allow firearms manufacturers to operate only under the license of the federal government; that would allow firearms to be bought and sold only through retail outlets that were licensed and closely monitored by the federal government; that would end the importation of any firearm that ought to be limited to the military.

"The prospect of these actions would terrify some Americans. They fear their government, in part, because they've been taught to fear their government by those who would manipulate them for cynical political purposes. The truth is, our government is not some distant, alien force; it is the tangible expression of who we are as a people.

"The preamble to our constitution starts with the words, 'We the people,' not we the government. Our Declaration of Independence says 'Governments are instituted among Men, deriving their just powers from the consent of the governed.' The United States is the world's oldest constitutional democracy. From the local level to the federal level we hold our elections with clockwork regularity. If you want to make a change, you cast your ballot, having worked to persuade as many others as possible to cast their ballots the same way.

"So if you fear your government, you really fear your friends and neighbors. You also fear the soldiers, sailors and marines who fought to give us our independence and who, along with their brothers and sisters in our air force, have kept us a free nation for more than two centuries. If you really think the armed forces of the United States would turn on their fellow Americans and oppress us, shame on you.

"For all our strengths, we are far from perfect. I spoke conditionally of the kind of legislation I would like to see passed because I know such legislation currently stands no chance whatsoever of being passed by Congress. The sad fact is, there are too many cowards, careerists and ideologues in Congress to pass any meaningful gun law reforms.

"Some polls show ninety percent of the American public favors criminal background checks on all gun purchases. Other polls show lesser but still overwhelming numbers of Americans favor background checks. I would sign such legislation in a heartbeat. But Congress has yet to act. The very branch of government that is supposed to write laws to protect us refuses to do so.

"That is a disgrace. The members of Congress who cower before the gun lobby and the ideologues who think the sacrifice of human life on the altar of their extremism is an acceptable price to pay are disgraces to the offices they hold."

The president paused momentarily to let the sting of her condemnation be felt.

"The only thing left for me to do is to follow the advice my husband, James J. McGill, offered to us all yesterday. We have to make Congress irrelevant until it has no choice but to be responsive. I will be traveling to every part of our country in the coming days, weeks and months to tell you of my ideas and the ideas I've heard from valued advisors, such as a suggestion I recently heard as to how we can quickly make our schools safer.

"I'll also listen to your ideas. Together we'll build a consensus as to just what we want done. Then we'll present Congress with a package of legislation that a strong majority of the American people not only favors but demands. Congress will either respond affirmatively or the voters will replace its intransigent members come the next election.

"Thank you for your time. May God comfort all of us who have lost loved ones to violence and bless us all without exception."

After the president finished speaking, the TV commercial featuring the gun-death victims at the Winstead School aired. It also was put on YouTube and went viral in minutes.

### SNAM Washington Bureau

Monty Kipp was the former Washington bureau chief for WWN who ran afoul of McGill when, in a drunken moment, he let slip to White House Press Secretary Aggie Wu that he harbored the ambition to get a topless shot of Patti Grant to sell for £1 million to a London tabloid. McGill, in response, had invited Kipp to see a demonstration of his shooting prowess at a government firing range in Virginia.

McGill's hands had been a blur, drawing his weapon and firing it. Blighter was a crack shot, too. Then he'd taken Kipp to a gun-cleaning room where he'd fieldstripped and cleaned his weapon, never needing to look at the work he was doing.

He'd stared at Kipp the whole time.

Telling him he'd heard what Kipp wanted to do: photograph the president in dishabille, publish the picture and cause his wife great humiliation. All for Kipp's base amusement and financial gain.

As McGill had reassembled his Beretta, Kipp had stood there paralyzed, all but unable to breathe. When McGill had slapped a full magazine back into the weapon Kipp had squeezed his eyes shut, waiting for the end.

"Mr. Kipp," McGill had said.

He'd opened one eye.

"My wife is never going to appear on page three of any tabloid anywhere in the world, is she?"

"No, never."

"Because I'd hate to think what might happen if ..."

McGill hadn't needed to complete the threat. Kipp, though a naturalized American citizen, had beat a quick retreat to his native London. He'd even left WWN to take a job with Satellite News UK. After six years, he felt — hoped — he was safe and returned to America as the Washington bureau chief for Satellite News America, SNAM.

Now, he was sitting in front of a camera with Auric Ludwig.

The two of them had agreed to postpone Ludwig's live interview until after the president had finished speaking. They wanted to speak to at least a part of her audience as well as SNAM's usual viewers. Ratings, after all, were king.

Watching Patricia Grant speak, Kipp thought she looked as smashing as ever. A bit older certainly. The presidency had that effect on everyone, but through some personal magic the brush of passing years had only painted more depth into her beauty. She still made Kipp's pulse race.

He continued to wish he could see her ... no, he'd best not go there.

McGill undoubtedly was still up to making short work of the likes of him.

For that matter, how would McGill react to a political assault on the president?

Surely, that would be in bounds. Wouldn't it? Kipp felt a chill run down his spine.

Had he just made another terrible mistake?

Before he could give the question a moment's thought, the red light on the camera came on and he and Ludwig were ready to speak live to the American people. A self-professed atheist, Kipp nonetheless said a silent prayer that McGill wasn't watching. Would never see his interview with Ludwig.

The producer's voice in Kipp's earbud said, "Haven't suffered a stroke, have we, Monty?"

Kipp bestirred himself, forced the facsimile of a smile onto his face.

"Good morning, America. Monty Kipp here. Like many of you, Mr. Auric Ludwig, CEO of FirePower America, and I have just finished watching the president speak of many things: the legislative process, prison construction, scouring the country's streets of criminals and how she intends to preside over a national discussion to change the country's gun culture."

Without waiting for his cue, Ludwig jumped in.

A move that irked Kipp.

"Listen, Monty," Ludwig said. "There is and will always be only one gun culture in our country: complete and total freedom. The American people will never stand for anything less."

Ludwig had his chin thrust forward and his complexion was edging from its normal red to purple. Kipp knew he had a script to follow, but Ludwig's deviation from it brought out the trouble-maker in him, a trait once pricked was all but irrepressible. If he did go off-script, though, he'd have to do it in a way that produced bigger than expected ratings.

He'd either get the big numbers or he'd get the sack.

Ah, well. He'd always loved to gamble, too.

Kipp took the plunge and picked up on Ludwig's assertion. "So you're saying, Mr. Ludwig, that you disagree with the president's statement that no right, even those provided in the Constitution, including the Second Amendment, is absolute. Is that right?"

"The Second Amendment is absolute."

Kipp strived to look reflective, rested his chin on his right hand.

While posing that way, he actually came up with some thoughtful questions.

Provocative ones, too, naturally.

He said, "At the end of her remarks, the president asked for God to comfort all those who had lost loved ones to violence. That, of course, would include her. She lost her first husband, Andrew Hudson Grant, to violence. He was killed by a rocket-propelled grenade. Under your absolutist view of the Second Amendment, should anyone in America be able to buy a rocket launcher? Are rocket-propelled grenades included under the Second Amendment's right to bear arms? If not, how can that right be, in your words, complete and total?"

Ludwig stared at Kipp. Those questions hadn't been ones they'd rehearsed.

Nonetheless, the producer's voice coming through his earbud told him, "Say something, Mr. Ludwig."

The problem for Ludwig was, none of the companies for which he fronted manufactured rocket-propelled grenades. He wasn't at all sure they'd wanted to be associated with such weapons. Of course, if they wanted to branch out that way in the future ...

"Come on, Mr. Ludwig," the producer said.

Ludwig said, "I was speaking in terms of more common firearms, for the time being."

Kipp did his best to keep the glee he felt off his face. "I see. So, at the moment, you wouldn't advocate that the wealthier folk among us use tanks and attack helicopters to protect their estates?"

"You're being ridiculous now," Ludwig said, his voice turning surly.

"Not at all," Kipp said. "I'm simply trying to understand whether the Second Amendment is indeed absolute or if it has limits. If, say, a Texas billionaire chose to protect his ranch, which is the size of some small countries, with as much military hardware as he could afford to buy, should he be allowed to do so?"

Ludwig chose to go hard core. "In principle, yes. Texas is a border state. He should be allowed to defend himself against any threat coming out of Mexico."

"I see. The Mexican threat. There are real dangers, of course, from the smugglers of drugs and immigrants — people who show no respect for the United States border."

"Exactly."

"So let's say our superbly armed billionaire rancher does real damage to these foreign criminals, but for some reason the Mexican government takes offense and decides to show him what real military power is all about. Should he have to fight a foreign country on his own?"

"Of course not. That's absurd. You're talking about an act of war against the United States. No individual, no matter how rich he is, can go up against an entire country. The U.S. Army and Air Force would have to respond."

Kipp nodded. "You're right, they would. But now let's examine another scenario involving that same billionaire rancher. Let's say he's a swindler. Most, if not all, of his fortune is ill-gotten. A warrant for his arrest has been issued. Only when the police arrive to take him into custody, they find themselves hopelessly out-gunned. It would be suicidal to try to bring the man in. Would the authorities be justified if they called on the U.S. Army and Air Force to balance the scales?"

Kipp thought he could hear Ludwig's molars grinding.

He pushed the man a step farther. "The president said the Second Amendment doesn't give anyone the right to declare war on the government. You say the right to bear arms is complete and total. So in a conflict pitting those two propositions against each other, which is right?"

Ludwig said, amidst a spray of saliva visible to the camera, "This is bullshit, all this make-believe crap. This isn't what we're supposed to talk about. This isn't what we agreed —"

Ludwig cut himself off, too late.

He wasn't the first victim of a Monty Kipp live-television

ambush to put his foot in his mouth. God, the little Brit thought, it always felt so good. Tabloid journalism was the next best thing to sex.

Rising to number one after your willie lost its starch.

In a calm voice, Kipp asked, "What would you like to talk about, Mr. Ludwig?"

"I'd like to talk about my being persecuted by the police. I've been charged with obstruction of justice simply for asking the hero who killed Abel Mays to step forward and identify himself. A Metro PD police captain had me arrested for obstruction of justice and told me if I were found guilty I could be locked up for as long as thirty years."

Kipp adopted a grave expression, all the while laughing to himself.

"I assume you've taken on able legal representation."

"Yes, I have, and now I'm taking my case to the court of public opinion. I ask all my freedom-loving friends to let your elected representatives know I should neither be prosecuted nor persecuted. Call them, email them, and if you live anywhere close to Washington, go to their offices on Capitol Hill."

Having long experience with self-righteous wankers hiding their dirty little secrets, Kipp asked, "Surely, the police must have some reason for charging you with such a serious crime, no? If all you wanted to do was to help them find a criminal —"

"A hero," Ludwig said. "The man who shot Abel Mays is a hero."

"As you like. You're still saying all you tried to do was help identify a person the police certainly want to find. There's a gap between your doing that and their charging you with a crime. Would you care to fill in that gap, sir?"

Ludwig looked at Kipp like he wanted to strangle him. "I can't talk about that; my lawyer told me not to."

"Ah, well, always best to follow expert legal advice."

"What I can and will say," Ludwig told Kipp, leaning forward, "is that James J. McGill is investigating the death of Jordan Gilford, the last man Abel Mays killed, and you can bet he's looking to pin that murder on someone else."

Oh, dear, Kipp thought. McGill was entering his life once more. He'd have to be careful.

"Why would Mr. McGill do that?" he asked.

Ludwig rolled his eyes. "McGill is married to the president. He's her tool. He also makes a living as a private investigator. If he admits the obvious, that Mays killed Gilford, his case is closed and he loses money. But if he joins in a conspiracy saying somebody else killed Gilford then …"

The CEO of FirePower America seemed to lose track of his own reasoning.

Kipp instinctively helped him. "If someone else killed Mr. Gilford, then maybe that person also killed Abel Mays."

Ludwig smiled. The little foreign jerk was finally playing ball with him.

"Yeah, exactly. That's the line of BS they're trying to sell, McGill and the president."

"I see," Kipp said. "Well, given what you've told us, we can assume that Mr. McGill is pursuing the investigation as he sees it. What are you doing to prove your contention?"

Ludwig looked directly at the camera. "I've already offered $100,000 plus a promise of paying the legal fees of the good guy with a gun who killed Abel Mays to come forward. So far, I've had no credible response. So what I'm going to do now is offer $1 million to anyone who can legitimately tell me the identity of the shooter who killed Abel Mays."

The camera lingered on Ludwig for a beat and then went to Kipp.

He said, "A million dollars. I'm sure Mr. Ludwig's phone is ringing already."

## CHAPTER 20

*Calle Ocho — Miami, Florida*

Jerry Nerón, having learned that Auric Ludwig had offered him a hundred grand to step forward and claim credit for the death of Abel Mays, had put Ludwig's name on a Google alert. He'd checked it first thing that day and found the lobbyist would be interviewed on Monty Kipp's morning show on SNAM.

The show would also be live-streamed on SNAM.com. Jerry could have watched it on his tablet, his laptop or his smart TV. But doing that would have left a record in a device's memory. What he did was watch the interview on a small, old, brainless TV that still had a sharp picture and would never tell any cop anything useful.

Jerry watched Kipp make a monkey of Ludwig. He enjoyed that, but then Kipp let Ludwig spout his line of bullshit at the end. Then that sonofabitch Ludwig put what amounted to a million-dollar bounty on Jerry's head. *Cabrón*!

Thinking about the situation for a minute, Jerry realized he was in deep trouble. The client who'd hired Jerry to kill Jordan Gilford didn't know his hitman's name. The client didn't know where Jerry lived. A series of technological and other cutouts prevented that — up to a point.

Jerry had studied Jordan Gilford, as he did every target. He'd learned Gilford's life story, knew the man had recently gone to work at the Pentagon. The Department of Defense was more than just the place where generals and admirals had their brass polished. The Pentagon was the home of the biggest, best-funded spook shop in the country, the Defense Intelligence Agency.

It wasn't hard to imagine someone somewhere in the military didn't want Jordan Gilford poking his nose into whatever it was they did with their money. Some budgets were supposed to be totally off-book. The better to fund covert operations. But secrecy was also the perfect cover for any number of scams.

Jerry knew from his discussions with the Cuban exile *viejos* that a lot of their money came from the CIA, a name the old ones said also stood for cash in advance. Not that there was ever as much money as the exiles wanted. The government people said that was because the funds for the exiles were off-book. They could only squeeze so much secret money from Congress.

That was back in the old days, though, before the jihadis hit the country.

After 9/11 defense spending jumped over the moon.

Better than half-a-trillion dollars a year was what Jerry had read.

So, with all that money pouring in, what if someone at the Pentagon decided to stick a hand in the till? Corrupt politicians in Iraq and Afghanistan had certainly been doing it. It would have been only natural for some people on the American side to think: Hey, what about us?

But all it would take to screw up somebody's gravy train would be one honest man.

Enter Jordan Gilford. He certainly couldn't be allowed to work his whistleblower magic.

So Jerry had been brought in, a private contractor, to get rid of Gilford. Hiring someone from the private sector to do the hit would give the insiders at DOD distance and deniability. There might be some blowback about Gilford getting killed, but any investigation would go nowhere. After a year or two, the case would be effectively as dead as Gilford.

Only now that moron Ludwig was publicly trying to hunt Jerry down. That had to be making Jerry's client nervous. And if the client had the resources of the Defense Intelligence Agency behind him he'd have ways of overcoming Jerry's safety precautions.

Hell, Jerry thought, his client might be searching for him already.

If the client got rid of him, a loose end would turn into a dead end.

Jerry realized he was going to have to take a vacation, maybe a long one.

First, though, he had to put an end to that prick Ludwig. The bastard's reward offer would die with him. Jerry had no choice, really. The way things stood, with a million-dollar incentive and the way technology could track people these days, maybe even some teenager with a computer might find him. Shit, just thinking like that scared him.

But with Ludwig gone the pressure should lessen.

That good guy with a gun Ludwig liked to talk about was coming for him. Put an end to Ludwig's worries about going to prison and everything else. Jerry couldn't get sloppy, though. He had to be more careful than ever.

He wouldn't fly commercial this time. More than one friend from the exile community had his own wings. Most of them didn't use their private jets anymore. Kept them only in case a miracle happened and they got to fly back to a free Havana in triumph. That being a pipe-dream, he wouldn't have a hard time finding a plane to borrow.

Jerry looked over at the first suit he'd finished for his client in Washington. It was a thing of beauty, as all his tailoring was. He'd deliver it personally. Say he wanted to have the pleasure of seeing it worn for the first time. Make sure the rest of the client's order was equally superb.

That would be his cover story. He'd shutter his shop and put a sign on the door.

Taking a well deserved rest.

With a bit of luck and Ludwig dead, his client would stop worrying. He'd be back in his shop before the end of the year. Having given up his sideline of killing people.

If his luck turned bad, though, he'd have to become an exile just like his grandfather. Truly, his situation would be worse. He would have to both run and hide. Maybe for the rest of his life. Goddamn Ludwig.

Jerry picked up his phone and called his client in Washington. He said, "Putnam Shady, please."

### *The Oval Office — The White House*

Hume Drummond sat alone on the sofa opposite the president and her chief of staff. He'd hoped and argued to speak privately with the president. As a concession, the president had asked Welborn and Special Agent Benjamin to wait outside. Welborn was his usual gracious self; Benjamin was savvy enough to nod politely. Galia Mindel sat next to the president and would be present for the duration.

"Mr. Drummond," the president said, "you have our full attention. Don't hold back anything."

The inspector general of the Department of Defense bit his lower lip, as if to get off to a proper start for what would be an exercise in pain. "Madam President, I think we're looking at a rogue operation in the DOD and possibly the worst government scandal since the Iran-Contra debacle in the 1980s."

Drummond referred to the political upheaval that beset Ronald Reagan. Members of his administration secretly sold arms to Iran, violating an embargo on such sales and then used the proceeds to fund the Nicaraguan Contras, contravening a bill passed by Congress and signed into law by Reagan himself.

Investigators concluded that Reagan didn't have knowledge of the illegal activities, but fourteen government officials, including Secretary of Defense Caspar Weinberger, were indicted. Eleven of the men were convicted. Only one served time, sixteen months.

Presidential pardons, aka the fix, spared others from far longer terms of incarceration.

All that had happened during a time of far greater political comity than existed during Patricia Grant's presidency, the second term of which was regarded as illegitimate by a quarter of the electorate. A new scandal on the scale of Iran-Contra could result in open political warfare.

Galia grew visibly tense.

The president remained impassive and asked, "What's the nature of this scandal, and how did it happen?"

"I'm neither trying to shift nor assign blame, Madam President, but as far as I've been able to discern the problem began in the final year of your predecessor's second term. That was when a group called the Tabulation Team came into being. Just who its architect is, I've yet to discover.

"The stated purpose of the Tabulation Team is, upon request, to do preliminary audits for each of the five armed services to make sure that funds provided by Congress are being spent appropriately. If any irregularities are found, they are supposed to be reported to my office for further review."

Galia asked, "Have you spoken with your predecessor about this Tabulation Team?"

"Not yet, Madam Chief of Staff."

"Why not?"

"I think this matter should be closely held until we can document its scope."

The president said, "Documentation can be elusive in a digital age, can't it?"

"It can be difficult, Madam President, but every keystroke leaves a trail."

"Continue, Mr. Drummond."

"As you and your chief of staff know, Madam President, the Pentagon has a well-earned reputation for both misspending and overspending enormous sums of money. Part of the blame for the DOD being known as a spendthrift, though, really rests with

Congress. As one example, last year Congress appropriated $950 million more than the Navy requested for an attack submarine program."

"And I signed the defense appropriation bill," the president said.

"It was must-pass," Galia reminded her.

"That only compounds the problem," the president replied.

"On a far larger scale," Drummond said, "during the Iraq war, your predecessor sent between six and eighteen billion dollars in cash to be used in that country's reconstruction effort, but the money disappeared. In blunt terms, that staggering amount of currency was stolen, the most lucrative robbery I've ever heard of.

"The point is, even with oversight, there's so much money flowing through the DOD, it's easy for large sums to go astray or in this case be misdirected."

"Are you saying there is now a gang of thieves working inside the Pentagon?" Galia asked. "This Tabulation Team you've mentioned?"

"That is my strong suspicion, yes," Drummond said.

"DOD functionaries can't be pulling this off on their own," the president said.

"No, ma'am, but I think they are both the masterminds and the middle-men, the clearing house, if you will. In my opinion, there have to be crooked defense contractors on one side of the Tabulation Team and corrupt members of Congress on the other."

Galia said, "So you brought in Jordan Gilford to uncover the details and organize the evidence in such a way as to be useful to federal prosecutors?"

"That or have Jordan Gilford's reputation scare someone into coming forward and provide us with the evidence we need."

"Instead, someone had him killed," Galia said.

Drummond's face sagged and he said, "Yes."

"You've considered that Mr. Gilford's death might also be a message to you?" Galia asked.

"I have, but I'm a widower. I have no children. I'll do my job as long as Madam President sees fit."

Thinking aloud, the president said, "These people must have a second line of defense. Something that they are counting on to protect them in case of discovery. What's their hole card?"

"Jordan asked himself that very question, Madam President. Then he played a hunch. He said there had to be a foreign bank involved, a place where all the stolen cash could be deposited and later transferred elsewhere. He felt the bank had to be in a country where a bribe to the host government would guarantee that the transactions were never reported to U.S. authorities. He found a bank in Uganda that fit the bill perfectly. He flew into and out of Kampala within a forty-eight hour period.

"While Jordan was there, he found a bank official who promised to tell him the whole story for $10 million. Jordan said he could get the man more money than that legitimately under the whistle-blower law, and he could relocate the man to the U.S.

"The guy liked the idea of hitting a bigger jackpot than he'd hoped for, but he didn't want to come to the U.S. because he said the money in question was used to pay assassins to kill jihadis — people Washington wanted dead without anyone being able to prove who did it. The bank official said he needed time to think of another country where he'd like to live."

Galia said, "So this inside man either let something slip or his cooperation was just a ruse. Either way, well, I've already mentioned what happened to Mr. Gilford."

Drummond nodded, his face now a mask of regret.

The president kept her focus on the main problem. "The Ugandan bank official, whatever else his role, detailed the Tabulation Team's hole card. They diverted Pentagon funds to bankroll a covert operation to kill sworn enemies of our country. People who would commit acts of horrific terror against us unless we stopped them. If we were to claim the Tabulation Team's true goal is to enrich its members, we would be denounced as unpatriotic."

"Politically, that would be a strong accusation," Galia said. "With one-in-four people."

The president picked up a phone. "Edwina, please tell the secretary of defense, the attorney general, the director of the FBI and the secretary of state that I need to see them in the Oval Office immediately."

Galia intuited what was about to happen.

She wanted to warn the president against taking precipitous action.

But the look in the president's eyes made Galia hold her tongue.

"Mr. Drummond," the president said, "do you have copies of everything you and Jordan Gilford found out about this Tabulation Team?"

The inspector general took a thumb drive out of a coat pocket.

"Right here, Madam President."

"Galia, please take that device."

The chief of staff took possession of the drive.

"Mr. Drummond, you should have come to me earlier with your information."

"Yes, ma'am."

"Attorney General Jaworsky will place you in protective custody. For the moment, you are relieved of your official responsibilities."

"But Madam President, if I'm suddenly absent from my post, the people we want to investigate will know something is wrong. They'll either destroy evidence or flee."

"They already know there's trouble, Mr. Drummond. Jordan Gilford's death is proof of that. Within hours, the FBI is going to arrest the Tabulation Team and anyone else you suspect of being involved with this rogue operation and the death of Mr. Gilford."

Patricia Grant could almost feel the apprehension radiating from her chief of staff.

It wouldn't be long before the news of the scandal went public.

The political ramifications would be impossible to predict.

But they certainly wouldn't be good.

The president picked up her phone again, "Edwina, please call Mr. McGill. I need to speak with him as soon as possible."

## McGill Investigations, Inc. — Georgetown

"No comment on Auric Ludwig's tirade?" That was how Ellie Booker said hello when she called McGill at his office.

He got right down to business, too. "The man's words speak for themselves."

"Can I use that?" Ellie asked.

"Yeah, if you preface it with your question. Be sure to use 'tirade,' too."

"Context, huh?"

"Helps people to understand. You up for doing me another favor maybe?"

"What's the favor and what's the maybe?"

"If you know any car thieves, that's the maybe, I'd like to put word out on their grapevine, that's the favor. An assist would be worth five hundred dollars to the winning tipster, and payment can be made anonymously."

"What do I get out of it?" Ellie asked.

"Increased good will."

"Oh, boy. Does that mean the next time I need an investigator you're gonna help me?"

McGill had turned Ellie down the first time she'd asked for his help.

He asked, "Is Sir Edbert coming back from the grave?"

Sir Edbert Bickford had owned WWN before he fell off his yacht and drowned in the Potomac. He'd been one of Patti's most venomous critics. Ellie had been his minion when she'd needed McGill's help.

"God, I hope not."

"No luck getting Hugh Collier to announce the day's gun deaths on his national news?"

"Not yet. I'll work on him some more."

"Okay, you need my help again, and you aren't busy slamming the president, I'll be there."

"And I'll do your favor, never admitting I know any criminals."

"Of course not."

McGill emailed the photo of the car that had been parked in front of Abel Mays' SUV to Ellie. So far no one with a badge had come up with any leads on it by checking junkyards. That led McGill to wonder if the car hadn't just been left somewhere in the District to be stolen. Maybe, as bait, a wallet had been left on the dashboard, and to make things really easy the key was in the ignition, too.

Someone with a suspicious turn of mind and a three-digit IQ might be wary of such easy pickings and back off fast, but criminals, by and large, weren't critical thinkers.

McGill's phone rang again. Captain Rockelle Bullard, Metro PD, was calling.

"You free to go for a ride?" she asked.

"As long as it's in my car, yes. What's up?"

"Detectives Meeker and Beemer came up with something interesting."

"What's that?"

"They found the car we were looking for, and the thief who stole it."

McGill laughed. "I was just thinking of that."

"Sure you were."

"Really."

"Well, my guys found it."

"That's great. But tell me one thing."

"What's that?"

"Did someone leave a wallet on the dashboard?"

McGill heard Rockelle curse under her breath.

He took that as a yes.

She told McGill where she, her men and the car were.

He'd just gotten into the back of his Chevy with Deke and Leo up front when his cell phone chimed. Edwina Byington this time. With a message the president wanted to see him immediately. Not to worry about anyone's health, though.

McGill's heart unclenched. "Edwina, do you know if Welborn

is in the building?"

"Captain Yates is sitting not ten feet from me."

McGill sent Welborn to meet with Rockelle and her men.

Special Agent Benjamin took it upon herself to tag along.

# CHAPTER 21

## *The Oval Office — The White House*

With Leo driving like he was going for the checkered flag at Daytona, McGill beat all four of the poobahs Patti had summoned to join her. She was alone in her office and he saw immediately that something big was up. It wasn't really the time to crack wise, but he had to make the effort. Otherwise the woman he loved might not have a laugh all day.

"Sorry I took so long, but I had Leo stop for flowers."

Patti didn't laugh, but she did smile. "You did not."

McGill brought his right hand out from behind his back.

He held a dozen red roses in a vase. On impulse, he'd bought them off Aggie Wu, the White House press secretary, who'd received the bouquet for her birthday. He'd paid double what it would cost to replace the flowers and promised to tell her a great story she could share with generations of Wus to come.

He didn't tell Patti any of that; it never hurt to let your wife think you could do magic.

Patti buzzed Edwina and told her, "No visitors for five minutes."

McGill asked, "You really think we can do it that fast?"

Now, Patti laughed. She took the flowers from McGill and placed them on her desk. Then she embraced her husband. "We have time for this."

She gave him a kiss he'd remember for the rest of his life.

He told her, "My knees will wobble for a week."

"That's all?" Patti said. Then she led McGill to a sofa and the two of them sat close to each other. "Okay, time to get serious. Right?"

McGill nodded. "Right."

Patti told him of her meeting with Hume Drummond, and the one coming up with the heavyweights from her cabinet.

McGill sighed. "I don't envy you, Madam President, but at least now we know the motive for someone wanting Jordan Gilford dead."

"You can't tell Zara Gilford yet, Jim."

"Eventually?"

"Maybe. Probably."

"May I have a copy of the information on the thumb drive Galia took from Drummond?"

"Galia's working on that right now, reading it and seeing what she thinks might apply to your investigation and what we'd better keep from someone who doesn't have any security clearance."

McGill frowned. "I'm not questioning your decision. I certainly don't want a security clearance. But I'm not sure Galia would know what I'd find valuable to an investigation."

"I know. I thought of that, but this is best we can do for now. If you can't find the man who shot Jordan Gilford soon, I might have to leave some top-secret material on my nightstand while I go to the loo."

"You've done that before and I've never peeked."

"This time, I won't mind."

"So you want me to work my case? You and Zara Gilford are on the same page with that?"

"Yes. It will be fine with me if the Metro Police or the FBI find the killer, but I put my faith in you first."

That earned Patti a kiss from McGill. Not in the same league as hers but close.

"I'll do my best," he said.

"Two more things, Jim. Nothing matters more to me than your

staying alive and well, and if at all possible, I want the man who killed Jordan Gilford brought in alive. His testimony might well be the key to getting to the bottom of this mess at the DOD."

"Bring him back alive it is, Madam President."

That being the case, McGill thought, he might well have to find the bastard before anyone else did.

## Ritz Carlton Hotel — Washington, DC

Darren Drucker stood at the podium in the conference room, a large portion of the capital's political media seated in front of him. They waited politely as he arranged his notes and took a sip of water from a green bottle. With any figure of lesser standing than the president, the newsies might have been chattering among themselves or working stories on their phones. Not so with Drucker getting ready to speak.

The reporters all harbored the fantasy of becoming a confidante of the down-to-earth multi-billionaire. Maybe even striking up a personal friendship. If being written into the great man's will was too much to hope for, maybe getting a quiet stock tip would be possible. That could set you up for life, too.

Standing several feet to Drucker's right, in a corner of the room, was his closest political advisor, Putnam Shady. Putnam had won Drucker's complete trust by giving him the most accurate readings he'd ever had about the day-to-day workings of Congress and the White House. That and never asking for a nickel more than the fees and perks they'd agreed upon when forming their partnership.

While Drucker put his script in order, Putnam was having a quiet conversation with Sweetie, who'd charmed Drucker upon making his acquaintance that morning.

"Your husband keeps telling me he's a scoundrel with a law license, Ms. Sweeney, but all I've seen is one of the most bluntly honest men I've ever met. He claims any shred of virtue he might possess is all your fault."

Sweetie had replied, "Putnam likes to think of himself as Cary Grant in that movie where he plays the jewel thief who went straight."

Putnam said, "*To Catch a Thief,* and the only reason I might see myself as Cary Grant is because Margaret reminds me so much of Grace Kelly – with better muscular definition."

Once they were alone, Sweetie had asked Putnam, "Are you feeling any better about Maxi being at school today?"

"No. How about you?"

"It requires a vigorous exercise of faith."

"I found out something for you, about Representative Phil Brock."

He told her about seeing the man's tanned face. "I found out through some people I know on Capitol Hill that Brock has land and a house in Costa Rica."

"And that's significant because?" Sweetie asked.

"I thought you might find out where Joan Renshaw likes to sun herself, when she's not turning ghostly white in prison."

Sweetie beamed at Putnam. "I'll make a detective out of you yet."

Putnam smirked. "Being a lifelong snoop is a pretty good headstart."

Standing in a room filled with newsies, Mr. and Mrs. Shady limited their public display of affection to squeezing each other's hand. Then Sweetie leaned in close and whispered to Putnam, "I'm going to call Jacqueline Dodd, the new director of the Andrew Hudson Grant Foundation. She worked for Joan Renshaw. She might know how Joan used to spend her leisure time."

"Or where she traveled on business," Putnam said. "Fun in the sun feels so much better when it comes with a legitimate tax deduction."

Sweetie grinned. Putnam was still a bit of a scoundrel.

She quietly left the room as Darren Drucker began to speak.

As Margaret left, Putnam's phone vibrated; he'd received a text. His answering service was letting him know he'd received a call from his tailor, Jerry Nerón. He'd return the call later.

Right now, Darren was starting his speech.

"As some of you might know, I do a bit of investing."

The audience laughed.

"For most of my career, I've put my money into the private sector, looking for promising new companies and undervalued established enterprises that were ready to make big comebacks. A few years back, after the Supreme Court ruled that money is speech and corporations are people, quite a few other people nearly as rich as me decided to buy their way into politics.

"I've observed that they might have found more winners if they'd taken their money to the track and played the ponies."

The newsies chortled again. Everyone loved to see the wealthy make fools of themselves.

Drucker continued, "I think part of their problem is that our two major political parties have proven to be far more interested in their own success than in having our country succeed. That's unfortunate but also understandable. Both parties have been around for a very long time and it's the inevitable nature of any institution to become self-serving.

"Quite recently, a third party emerged: True South. Its core principles, though, are even more conservative than those of the Republicans. Part of my success as an investor comes from taking chances on companies that look to the future. It's more comfortable, of course, to cling to what's familiar and even long for the past. But the world keeps turning toward the future and countries around the world, with which the United States competes, keep racing forward.

"The countries that are our competitors or even our adversaries would like nothing better than to see the United States simply run in place or better yet fall far behind them.

"So, I feel it's imperative for our country to have a vital progressive political party oriented strongly toward the future. With that in mind, Putnam Shady and I have put together a group of twelve candidates to run for the House of Representatives and

and two candidates to run for the Senate in 2014 under the party banner of what we call Cool Blue.

"The blue in our name stands for the end of the political spectrum in which our principles are based; the cool means our approach to politics will be based on reason and expressed in a friendly, temperate manner. Our candidates will not be or ever become professional politicians. They will be educators, business people, working artists and retired military. Each of them will limit himself or herself to no more than six years in Congress. Should they be tempted to stay longer, Cool Blue will withdraw its party affiliation.

"In future election cycles, we will work to increase the number of our candidates running for Congress. We'll run people for state legislatures, too, if the talent pool proves deep enough. At present, we have no intention of running any candidates for the presidency. If we prove to be successful as a party at the legislative level for, say, twenty years, we'll reconsider having a presidential candidate.

"We hope to raise funds from a large number of progressive donors in amounts both large and small, but to get us out of the starting gate, I have a few dollars I can spare."

The newsies liked that one, too.

"You'll receive handouts listing our core principles and profiling our candidates. This information will also be available online." Drucker gave them the URL. "Before I take any questions, I'd like to tell you of one issue on which all our candidates have unanimously agreed. Random acts of gun violence, especially those causing the deaths of large numbers of innocent people, must end. They must end as soon as possible.

"Any future presidential candidate who does not include this goal as one of his or her top two priorities, along with defending the nation against foreign attacks, is at best not up to the job and at worst a coward.

"President Grant has not solicited Cool Blue's support, but we stand behind her efforts to keep guns out of the hands of felons and to change both the discussion and the reality of the place of firearms in American society."

Drucker asked if there were any questions.

They flew at him like a hailstorm.

### *The Oval Office — The White House*

Galia Mindel was well set financially and the idea of marrying for money had never occurred to her even in the days when she needed to work for a living. But upon hearing Darren Drucker speak she almost fell in love.

She turned to Patricia Grant and said, "Wasn't he wonderful, Madam President?"

"He was certainly helpful. But I think Putnam Shady was the architect behind the questions that will be asked a thousand times during the 2016 presidential election campaign: 'Mr. or Ms. Candidate, what will you do to end the glut of gun-death tragedies in our country? If you have no specific and effective plan you will push with all your might, are you an incompetent or merely spineless?'"

Galia nodded. "It was a brilliant stroke, equating the prevention of domestic massacres with the defense against foreign attacks, and defining both as primary presidential responsibilities."

The president sighed. "We should have thought of it a long time ago. Meanwhile, we have to push as hard as we can in the time we have left in the White House."

"Yes, Ma'am."

"On another matter that won't wait, have you made plans to speak with Erna Godfrey?"

Galia nodded. "I have."

The woman who had killed the president's first husband, Andrew Hudson Grant, was confined at the Federal Correctional Institution at Danbury, Connecticut, a medium-security prison for women. After Erna had given the names of former friends in the radical anti-abortion underground who had committed crimes up to and including murder to the attorney general, she had been provided with a special protective detail of correctional officers for her personal safety.

Even at a place like Danbury, far from the worst federal lockup, some of the inmates had no use for snitches. The possibility that a prisoner there might try to kill Erna for her betrayal was real. Under the possible threat of death, Erna had been studying under the guidance of volunteer faculty from Northwestern Theological Seminary to earn her doctorate of divinity.

If she achieved that goal, she would be allowed to preach to women throughout the federal prison system by means of streaming video and podcasts.

"I'll leave for Danbury in the next half-hour," Galia told the president.

"Has Joan Renshaw been transferred from Hazelton yet?"

The United States Penitentiary in Hazelton, West Virginia was the only maximum security federal prison for women in the country. Erna Godfrey had been incarcerated there before her cooperation with the government had earned her a step-down to less harsh confinement.

Galia nodded. "She should be arriving later today."

"She'll be sharing a cell with Erna?"

"Yes, ma'am. Both women have been told their housing is a matter of cost efficiency."

"How is Erna doing with her scholastic efforts?"

"Very well. The report I read calls her an extraordinary student, not only dedicated to her studies but able to challenge her professors in their thinking, as well as learning from them."

"Well, good for her."

"Two questions have crossed my mind about this visit, Madam President."

"Yes?"

"Erna Godfrey has already snitched for us once, what if she doesn't want to do it again? And what if she wants to speak with you?"

The president said, "If either situation arises, Erna and I will have a chat."

# CHAPTER 22

*30,000 feet above South Carolina*

The G150 was a relatively modest private jet compared to its Gulfstream siblings. It carried only six passengers in its executive layout. But it could haul ass. Normal cruising speed was 610 miles per hour, and it could jack that number up a bit if you were in a real hurry. The plane's ceiling was 45,000 feet but the flight north from Miami to Washington, DC was smooth as glass right where the pilot, Arturo Gonzales, had it.

Gonzales was on the sunset side of sixty, but he was lean and fit, had stopped smoking decades ago upon fleeing Cuba, drank only moderately and by his own assertion had sex only with *señoritas* who gave him a good aerobic workout.

He'd been trained to fly the F-4 Phantom fighter-bomber by the U.S. Navy, in cooperation with the CIA. For one giddy month or so the Calle Ocho exiles thought they'd have their own squadron of F-4s to take out any defenses Castro might have to stop an invasion from Miami. Then the Cuban missile crisis and the escalation of the war in Vietnam put an end to that plan.

A product of the 1960s, the F-4 had a cruising speed a bit slower that the modern G150, but the fighter-bomber's top end had been 1,473 miles per hour or what Gonzales called "fast enough to get away from your mistress's husband and your wife's divorce lawyer, both." For him, the Gulfstream's cruising speed was like idling your car looking for a parking space.

"You good back there, Jerry?" Gonzales called through the intercom.

Jerry Nerón said, "The ride's so smooth I could be making you a new suit."

Gonzales laughed. "I don't doubt it."

Jerry had made the tuxedo the pilot had worn at his daughter's wedding. He'd confided to Jerry that he'd told his new son-in-law that he still had access to an armed F-4, and he'd be happy to drop napalm on the young man if he ever made Arturo's daughter cry.

Making marital fidelity a concern for some men more than others.

While Jerry had never thought of using napalm to make a hit, he could have brought any kind of gun he wanted aboard the private aircraft. He decided not to do that. He'd used two firearms last time: his own and that goddamn thing he'd taken from the SOB who'd used it to shoot all those poor kids. He should have know that using Abel Mays' weapon would bring bad luck. Stephen King would have figured that shit out right away.

In any case, he chose to go with edged weapons this time.

Throw a little confusion the cops' way.

Hide his killing tools in plain sight.

Not one person in a million would guess what he had in mind.

Well, maybe one, but no more than that.

"Be on the ground in less than an hour, Jerry," Gonzales called. "Weather isn't as warm as Miami. Remember to button up."

"Roger that," Jerry said.

He and Gonzales both laughed.

Jerry had never been a pilot.

But Gonzales had been one of the men who'd carried off the remains of Galtero Blanco.

He knew Jerry had what it took to engage in mortal combat.

### C&O Canal National Historical Park

Dr. Hasna Kalil had agreed to meet with Byron DeWitt, but she wanted to go back to Billy Goat Trail A. She was wearing the same beret, trench coat, black slacks and rubber soled shoes as before. Her face, if anything, looked harder than ever.

Detective Tara Lang of the Park Police kept the random passersby at a distance.

"You've heard the DNA results?" she asked. She and DeWitt were standing next to the crevasse where the remains of Hasna Kalil's brother had been found. "There is no question this is where Bahir's body was dumped."

"I heard. I'm sorry for your loss."

"Are you?"

"Well, assuming you and your brother were on good terms, I am. In any case, I regret it when anyone is murdered."

She stared at DeWitt. He accepted the pressure from her eyes without pushing back. He'd learned long ago that was the way to win a visual challenge. You let the other person do all the work. They'd get tired before you did, as happened right now.

Dr. Kalil turned her gaze back to the gash in the earth.

"I was close to Bahir. For most of our adult lives we lived far apart. But whenever the calendar brought us to a day with special meaning, we always talked to one another. I'll never know that happiness again."

Having already expressed his feelings, DeWitt remained silent.

Dr. Kalil looked back at him, without confrontation this time.

"Have you learned what sort of object shattered my brother's skull?"

"We know the size, shape and approximate weight."

"You also measured the bone density of the areas adjacent to the fracture?"

"Yes."

"And your conclusion?"

"Your brother was most likely killed with a lug wrench. From the angle and the dimensions of the fracture, we concluded he was bent forward at the waist and the blow was struck from behind."

"He was taken by surprise," Dr. Kalil said, "but was it a matter of theft or betrayal?"

"There's no way to determine motive from the physical evidence. The state of decomposition of your brother's remains indicates that he'd been left out here for a long time. Too long for any traces of blood or soft tissue to survive. We found no fragments of bone, but they might have been washed away by the rain or swept away by the wind. So we don't know if he was killed nearby or somewhere else."

"Not here."

"No? Why not?" DeWitt asked.

"Bahir was not an outdoorsman. He was a city person. Besides, he was about to come home. He might have stopped for a meal before going to the airport. He would not have come out to a wilderness area."

DeWitt nodded. "If he did dine out on his last night in Washington, do you have any idea of who might have joined him? Or did he keep to himself?"

"Have you asked the Jordanian embassy if they might help you?"

"I did. So did the Park Police. Your embassy expressed their regrets. They were unable to be of help. I had to conclude that they were trying to preserve your brother's privacy as well as that of their king's government. I'm sure you also must have asked the embassy for help. Did you do any better?"

Dr. Kalil cranked up her stare again, but only for a moment.

She was a quick learner. She stuck a hand in a pocket of her trench coat and pulled out a piece of folded paper. She gave it to DeWitt.

He unfolded it, saw it was a photocopy of a list of names.

Some of them he knew; others he didn't. One jumped out. He kept a straight face, refolded the sheet of paper and put it in a pocket.

"If we find the person who killed your brother," DeWitt asked, "what would you like to see happen to him?"

The veil of polish, education and even civilization fell from Hasna Kalil's face.

The visage that remained was primal and vengeful.

"I don't know exactly what I would do, but it would be something truly awful … gruesome down to the smallest detail."

That fit exactly with what the CIA suspected of Dr. Kalil, according to Oscar Rogers. He'd told DeWitt that she did wonderful humanitarian work for an internationally respected organization of concerned physicians. In her free time, though, she'd disappear from public view and use her surgical skills to inflict dimensions of pain on her victims that brutes wielding crude instruments could only envy.

All in the name of establishing the global caliphate.

So far, though, Hasna Kalil's dark side was a matter of legend not proof.

But Rogers had said if it were up to him, she'd be on the Agency's date-with-a-drone list.

And her reply to DeWitt made him think his CIA friend's judgment was on the mark.

She hadn't said what she'd like to do; she'd implied what she would do.

"Are you shocked, Mr. DeWitt?" Dr. Kalil asked.

"Sure. Preserving the ability to be shocked is essential to being able to understand both yourself and the world around you. It's when you get emotionally callused you can go off the deep end."

That seemed to disturb Hasna Kalil.

The very idea that she might be mistaken about anything.

"You will let me know if you make an arrest?" she asked.

"Of course."

Once we have the bastard safely locked up, he thought.

Although threatening the killer with being delivered to Dr. Kalil might be a card to play, too, should there be an advantage to that. He hadn't said so, but there were times when DeWitt could shock himself.

## *Winstead School Football Field — Washington, DC*

"Damn, that was fast," Ellie Booker said to her videocam operator.

The cameraman nodded.

McGill had called her immediately after his meeting with the president. Told her not to bother looking for a car thief; the Metro cops had already pinched the guy who'd boosted the car that interested him. Ellie's response had been predictable.

"Does that mean you don't owe me the favor we talked about?"

"It means I don't want you to waste your time, and I have another favor I'm going to do for you."

Ellie couldn't keep the suspicion out of her voice.

She felt McGill was playing her like a fiddle.

"What're you going to do for me?"

He told her to get over to the Winstead School with a camera. They were going to make some news over there. She'd get the exclusive. Go to the football field.

Call him when she was done covering the story.

So there they were and she had to admit it, there was a story here.

Not fifty yards from where the school's football players and coaches had died, opposite the scoreboard that tallied the school's fortunes on the playing field was a new structure. At the moment, it was still draped, but the school's headmaster, Geoffrey Cooper, had greeted them, told them Mr. McGill had called ahead to say they were coming.

He told them what would be unveiled shortly.

Ellie's expression said she didn't believe him.

Cooper had nodded: Believe it.

Then he'd gone to talk with a group of parents and one guy who looked nervous.

Ellie hadn't been invited to join that little discussion group so she did the next best thing. She discreetly took a photo of them with her phone. She'd identify their faces later and see if there was a story she should pursue, what those people might be saying.

Then she and her video guy set up to get a straight-on shot of the unveiling.

The bleachers around them filled in with students, parents, faculty. All of the faculty and some of the parents and students looked like everyday middle-class people to Ellie. A majority of the parents and students, though, looked as if they'd never missed a ski season in Aspen much less a meal. More interesting than that were the expressions on their faces.

These people were spoiling for a fight.

And with their money, if not their knuckles, they could do some damage.

The young man who stepped to the microphone on the field looked like he could do both. Ellie recognized Hal Walker, former quarterback from Winstead and Stanford, the expected number one choice overall in the upcoming NFL draft.

Headmaster Cooper joined him, shook his hand and spoke first. "I'd like to thank everyone for coming out to join us today. This is as solemn an occasion as any I've known in my twenty-eight years in education, but it is also a time for everyone here to be strong and to share our strength with everyone we meet. I now have the privilege of introducing Hal Walker, Winstead class of 2010. Hal."

Walker embraced Cooper before stepping to the microphone.

Before the young athlete said a word, tears rolled down his face. He made no move to wipe them away.

"To the families, friends and colleagues of the players and coaches who died here at Winstead last Saturday, I can only say that my heart has been broken, too. When I first heard the news, I didn't believe it. I didn't want to believe it. Something that bad couldn't happen at a place like Winstead. Only it did.

"And if it can happen here, it can happen anywhere. We can't forget that. Even more important, we can't let anyone else forget it either. If someone like the man who killed our sons, husbands, and brothers — my brothers — can do what he did here, it can happen an-y-where.

"That's why we decided this is the appropriate place to put up a memorial to all the wonderful boys and men who died here at Winstead."

Walker keyed a remote control and the draping fell from the new structure.

It was a National Gun Death Counter. It was up and running. The number on the board went up by one the second it was visible.

Hal Walker said, "I hate that thing. I hate that it's necessary, but if it's up to me, that's right where it will stay. Until we don't need it anymore. That's when the people we lost will rest in peace. Then I'll be the first one to take a sledgehammer to it, and we can put up something new and beautiful."

Walker sobbed and Cooper hugged him again.

Then the headmaster stepped to the mike again.

"I think everyone here should know that all six schools in the Tripartite Athletic Conference, of which Winstead is a member, have decided to put up their own counters, not necessarily on their playing fields, but in prominent public locations. Winstead has also contacted independent and public schools throughout the country asking them to join the effort.

"Families here are raising funds to help schools that can't afford to put up their own counters. We'll also be spearheading other projects to help other schools avoid the type of tragedy that has so deeply afflicted the souls of everyone here. Thank you all for coming."

Ellie looked at the people around her. Just about everyone was crying. She couldn't keep herself from feeling their pain and tears welled up in her eyes. The one thing that made her feel a little better was she could see that everyone was pissed off, too. These people, with all their resources, were going to kick some ass.

Then the news pro in her reasserted itself. Jeez, this was going to be a big story. For a long, long time, too.

With that realization came a question.

What was she going to owe McGill now?

# CHAPTER 23

## *Federal Correctional Institution — Danbury, Connecticut*

The warden's office looked to Galia like the typical space of someone two-thirds of the way up the federal bureaucratic ladder. The furnishings and lighting were comfortable and adequate respectively. But there were no homey touches at all. No family photographs, no plaques or awards from community organizations.

There were the American and Connecticut flags flanking the warden's desk.

A photograph of the warden taken in dress uniform during her days as a colonel in the Connecticut State Police hung on the wall directly behind her desk chair. It was meant to convey a don't-fuck-with-me attitude and it did. Even so, Jeanette Timkins had been nothing but gracious to Galia since her arrival, had met her at the main gate and walked her past all the security checkpoints where other visitors would have to prove they weren't trying to smuggle weapons or contraband into the prison.

Galia had decided the moment she set foot on the prison grounds that she would rather die than be incarcerated. Entering Danbury had also forced her to do a quick mental review of all the questionable campaign moves she'd made during her long career in politics. Some had skirted the edge of the law; a few might have tiptoed over the line ever so slightly.

Thank God those indiscretions had happened when she was much younger. The statute of limitations had long since expired on them. Now, in her advancing years, one visit to a federal prison had scared her straight. There'd be no more cutting corners for her. Probably.

Warden Timkins brought Galia a cup of coffee and sat with her at the office's conference table. "This place makes you nervous, doesn't it, Ms. Mindel?"

Galia nodded. "It shows, I suppose."

The warden laughed. "Just a little. My guess is you had two good parents and a nice home, growing up."

"Yes, I did."

"For quite a few inmates here, this is a step up in living conditions."

"You're pointing out the correlation between poverty and criminality?"

"Well, that's just one intersection between the general public and law enforcement. There are folks from middle-class backgrounds who are criminally stupid, and a few rich people who are just plain evil. Generally speaking, though, graduating from high school and getting a regular paycheck reduces the likelihood someone will rob a convenience store."

Galia smiled. "I might have guessed that."

"I've been trying to make up my mind about Erna Godfrey since I got this job. From what I've read about her former life, she wasn't exactly rich but she was certainly well off. She had a college degree and her husband was a famous preacher. So what was it that set her off to commit a murder?"

"Zealotry."

"Yeah, I got that, but what I wonder is how can some folks be so sure God is talking directly to them? Without parting the sea for them or dropping manna on them, you know?"

"I can't say," Galia replied. Then she asked, "Have you heard about Erna's vision?"

The warden shook her head. "Something she believes she saw?"

"Something she's shared with the president."

Galia told the warden about Erna seeing Jesus and Andrew Hudson Grant when she tried to commit suicide and was on death's door. "Jesus wasn't pleased with her but Mr. Grant had clearly made the cut, and that's when she turned herself around. She also gave us several people who hadn't seen the light yet and are currently serving their own sentences."

"So as long as she doesn't have another revelation that sets her off down another path, she should continue to be a model inmate?"

"Well, I imagine you keep a close eye on all your inmates."

The warden nodded.

"I don't think Erna should be an exception, and what I have to ask her today she might find troubling."

There was a knock at the door, and a correctional officer led Erna in.

Manacled, shackled and wearing a smile once she saw Galia.

"Why, Ms. Mindel, it's so nice to see you again." Needing just a heartbeat to determine the reason for Galia's presence, Erna's smile faded and she asked, "You want me to do something for you again, don't you?"

Galia said, "The president sent me to ask for a favor."

### Marshall Heights — Washington, DC

Antawn Duke was Detectives Meeker and Beemer's pinch so Captain Rockelle Bullard let them tell their story again, this time to McGill. Leo had made quick work of getting to the neighborhood in North East Washington, hard against the Maryland state line. Meeker and Beemer were happy to repeat their story; it still had plenty of emotional juice.

First, though, Meeker had a question for McGill, who was peering into the back of the Metro patrol unit holding Antawn Duke. The car thief, with a shaved head and a sullen expression, looked back at McGill and hocked something up from his throat. But some instinct told him not to commit even a symbolic assault.

Maybe he guessed the dude checking him out was someone not to be dissed.

Or he knew cops got pissed if you made a mess in their cars.

Whatever, he swallowed his spit and turned away from McGill.

Meeker asked, "You really figured out it could be a car thief?"

McGill looked at the detective. "God's truth. I used to be a cop, too."

Beemer smiled. "Still got some moves, huh?"

"I do what I can." McGill said.

Meeker said, "Beemer and I were just driving around parts of the city where certain types of activities are known to happen. We saw the car we wanted and figured we might be in for a chase, Maryland being so close by. We radioed ahead for support from their state cops."

Beemer laughed. "Only no sooner do we see old Antawn than, boom, he pops a tire. He ain't goin' nowhere fast."

Meeker said, "But he does keep goin', at least until we force him to the curb. Ask him why he's drivin' on a flat tire."

"He says he doesn't have a jack in the car," Beemer said, laughing.

"We make him open the trunk. There's the jack. Antawn says, 'I meant my other jack.'"

The two detectives were rocking with laughter.

Beemer told McGill, "I say, 'Antawn, you got a special jack for each day a the week?'"

Meeker said, "He says, 'Yeah, man, that's it exactly.'"

Rockelle, with Welborn and Benjamin standing beside her, shook her head.

"These two are going to audition for Arsenio's show, soon as they retire."

McGill said, "They did good work. What do we know about Mr. Duke?"

Meeker started to answer but his boss held up a hand.

"We don't have time for another routine," she said. "Antawn

Duke's been down twice for grand theft auto; this makes strike three. Cars'll be flying by the time he gets out. He swears he didn't see anyone park the car he stole or walk away from it. He claims ..." Rockelle sighed. "He saw a wallet on the dashboard. He thought it would be the right thing to do to try to return it, and since the keys were in the car he could cover more ground driving than walking."

Meeker and Beemer, unable to restrain themselves, started to laugh.

"I don't suppose there were any picture IDs in the wallet," McGill said.

Rockelle shook her head. "Our shooter's smarter than our car thief. A little cash but no credit cards in the wallet. But Captain Yates with those fine eyes of his spotted a hair on the floor behind the driver's seat that's too long and straight to belong to any African American, but probably too short to be a woman's. Special Agent Benjamin just happened to have an evidence bag and a pair of tweezers on her. She volunteered the FBI lab to see what they might tell us."

"Sharing the results with everyone in a timely fashion?" McGill asked.

"Of course," Benjamin said with a straight face.

As if the FBI was known for its willingness to share.

"Good," McGill said. "The White House will be happy to hear the results, too."

Letting Benjamin know there'd be no going back on her word.

McGill told the others, "Good work everyone. One more thing, Captain Bullard."

"What's that?" she asked.

"When you and your detectives question Mr. Duke again, if you get any feeling at all that he might have seen the driver and is holding back to see what kind of trade he might make ..."

"Yeah?"

"Tell him if he has information that pans out, there might be a presidential pardon in it for him. If he thinks that's BS, remind him he saw me. Then show him a picture of me with the president."

Meeker asked, "You're talkin' about playin' him, right?"

McGill said, "If he helps us grab the guy who killed Jordan Gilford, maybe not."

Rockelle asked, "You hear about the guy we nabbed for shooting the sign at Saint Martin's?'

"No," McGill said.

"Man was a convicted felon. Wasn't supposed to have a gun much less shoot one."

"Same with one of the two guys caught in Virginia for shooting the death counter opposite FirePower America," Benjamin said.

"Just one felon?" McGill asked.

Benjamin nodded. "The other one was the shooter's son. Fifteen years old, driving daddy's getaway car on a learner's permit."

"Damn," McGill said.

The boy was younger than his son, Kenny, and his life was already going to hell.

Benjamin added, "Both Virginia and DC are going to kick the cases to federal courts. So it looks like the president has her first two mopes to send to Alaska."

"Won't be any pardons for them," McGill said.

## McGill Investigations, Inc. — Georgetown

Sweetie sat in McGill's chair, behind his desk and used his phone. He didn't mind her use of his space and office equipment. Putnam had suggested to Sweetie that she and McGill should find a new suite of offices, one with a space for her befitting her status as a partner in the firm. She'd kissed her husband but said she was the kind of girl who had never wanted to be put on any kind of pedestal.

When she'd been a Chicago copper she was content to stop her climb through the ranks as a sergeant, a position of respect and authority but still a working cop. She had no doubt she could have passed the lieutenant's exam, but she never really saw herself in that role. Same thing happened when Jim had brought her with him to the Winnetka PD. As the new chief of the posh suburb's department, he'd offered to make her deputy chief.

She'd declined, forgoing a substantially larger salary.

When she'd first moved into Putnam's townhouse, she'd occupied a one-room basement apartment. She'd been entirely content with it. She had only gradually adjusted to moving upstairs with Putnam. She had come to appreciate the greater comforts available to her, but she never attached any importance to the status of living in eight rooms rather than one.

There was a great deal to be said for living a modest life, Sweetie thought.

If you placed no importance on material wealth, such things as fancy houses, cars and clothes held no temptation for you. There were far fewer opportunities for anyone to lead you astray. Making the moral choice became far easier.

There were still times when Putnam was traveling that she liked to revisit her basement digs. She found a sense of quiet and peace there that was unavailable anywhere else. In a similar way, she felt at home sitting at her desk in the outer office of McGill Investigations, Inc.

It made her feel like a front desk sergeant again.

As to leaving Dikki Missirian's building for another location, that was not going to happen. Sweetie knew that McGill's Secret Service code name was Holmes. His leaving their P Street offices would be like Sherlock moving away from Baker Street. It would just be wrong.

Sweetie used McGill's personal office when it was available and she thought it might be advantageous to help her with an investigation — in a metaphysical sense. Just as she could and did pray anywhere, she went to church when she felt the need to be closer to God. In a similar way, she sat behind McGill's desk when she wanted to feel closer to understanding a riddle of police work.

Not that McGill was anywhere close to being the Almighty, but he was the sharpest cop she ever knew. With that comforting thought in mind, Sweetie called Jacqueline Dodd — Joan Renshaw's successor at the Andrew Hudson Grant Foundation in Chicago — and asked if she might answer a couple of questions.

Jacqueline listened to what Sweetie wanted and told her, "I don't know if I can find out where Joan went on vacation. She never really shared that information with me. But I certainly have records of where she traveled on foundation business. Those expenditures have to be listed as part of our filings with the IRS, and Mr. Grant, from the beginning, made them part of the public record so the foundation would be seen as being beyond reproach."

"Of course," Sweetie said, "but it's reasonable to think that travel and lodging accommodations weren't done on the cheap, right?"

Jacqueline laughed. "We work hard around here to make other people's lives better, but nobody wears sackcloth. Per Mr. Grant's guidelines, anyone working on a foundation project flies business class at a minimum. Four star hotels are the norm. I fly first class and stay at five star hotels; so did Joan when she was here."

That fit nicely with Lisa Stone's description of Joan Renshaw as a social climber.

Joan had to be furious with Patti Darden when the movie star had snagged Andrew Hudson Grant. Even so, she'd stayed on at her job to keep her salary and perks. That went to show what could happen when someone got hung up on goodies. It became harder to move on when that was the right thing to do.

And now look at where Joan was.

"Would you like me to email you the list of business trips Joan took while she was with the foundation?" Jacqueline asked.

"Yes, please."

"Will this …" There was a beat of silence.

"What?" Sweetie asked.

"I'm not going to put Joan in any more trouble, helping you, am I? I know whatever she did had to be horrible to lose her job and get arrested, but she was always nice to me."

"You can't hurt Joan any worse than she's hurt herself. What you might do is help someone else avoid being punished for something he didn't do."

"Oh, okay. I can do that, sure. I'll send the list to you within the hour."

Sweetie gave her the email address and said, "Thank you."

She hung up, wondering how she might search for records of Joan Renshaw's private travels, asking herself how McGill might do it. Turned out that wouldn't be necessary. Jacqueline Dodd's email came in only twenty minutes after she'd spoken with Sweetie.

During Joan Renshaw's time with the Grant Foundation, she had traveled dozens of times domestically to cities large and small. Internationally, she'd visited London, Paris, Geneva, Tokyo, Nairobi, Johannesburg, Manila, Sydney, São Paulo …

And San José, Costa Rica. Twice.

The last time just a year and a half ago, August, 2012.

Sweetie's immediate impulse was to fly down there and see if she could find someone who could put Joan Renshaw together with Congressman Philip Brock. Only Putnam was up to his eyeballs in work getting Cool Blue off the ground. And the two of them now had someone besides themselves to think about: Maxi. Sweetie couldn't just leave her alone.

So what could she … No, who could she ask to do the job?

The answer came to her immediately as if it had been channeled through …

McGill or an even higher power.

Father Inigo de Loyola. Who'd been born, raised, ordained and fought in Central America. He'd do better down there than she would. He knew the territory and the language. He was a man so selfless in terms of the material world he lived under a staircase in Dikki Missirian's other office building. There'd be no temptations to distract him from completing his quest.

Sweetie would have called him, only the priest had no phone.

She left the office to look for him.

## Kalorama Circle — Washington, DC

Celsus Crogher opened the door to Zara Gilford's home for McGill and let him step inside. Deke stood guard outside the large red brick house. Leo had McGill's Chevy parked out front at the curb. On the drive from the other side of town, McGill had thought briefly that maybe he should bring the widow flowers, as he had to Patti.

The gesture would be made to convey condolences rather than affection. He'd never expressed such a sentiment to a client before, but the regret of not having sought out Jordan Gilford before he'd been killed still gnawed at McGill. He had no doubt it would continue to do so for a long time.

So what would it hurt to bring the lady some flowers?

He would have followed through on the notion if it hadn't inspired another idea. From everything Zara had told him, she and Jordan had had a close relationship, not unlike the one he and Patti did. Jordan had realized he and Zara were in some danger from his work, so he'd moved them into their high-security condo.

Part of that move, though, might have been a head-fake, McGill thought, a feint to get the opposition to lean one way when they should have gone the other way. If you moved into a secure location, most people would think you'd take your most valuable secrets with you. It would be foolhardy to leave anything valuable behind in a house where they might be far more easily seized.

But where would you hide any prized information? It had to be a place that your wife would look, but no one else would pay it any special attention.

You'd hide it in a bouquet of flowers, McGill thought.

Not literal blossoms, of course, but somewhere a grieving widow would find emotional healing. Some object that held sentimental value. A memento that she might take into her hands and regard closely to bring back memories of a happier time. Only to notice something new and different that would point her in another direction.

That or he was all wet and imagining things, McGill thought.

Celsus closed the door behind McGill and told him, "An FBI team came by and with Ms. Gilford's help they went through every room in the house. Ms. Gilford didn't notice anything out of place. Neither did the FBI people and they didn't find any bugging devices."

"That's good." McGill took a close look at Celsus.

"What?"

He'd never seen bags under the man's eyes before. "How long have you been awake?"

"Who keeps track? You're the guy who said I just plug myself in when I need to recharge."

McGill was able to laugh at his own expense. "Yeah, but now you're an older model."

Celsus snorted. "I'm still good for at least another night."

"Good. Where's Zara? Is she up for a little chat?"

"In the kitchen, and I think so. You making any progress?"

McGill told Celsus that the cops caught the guy who stole the murder suspect's car, and Welborn had found a suspicious hair.

"That's a start."

McGill followed Celsus' directions and found Zara sitting at a breakfast island, picking at a green salad. Seeing him, her face took on a hopeful expression, as if he'd bagged the bad guy and could soothe at least a little of her heartache.

"You have news?" she asked.

McGill gave her the same rundown he'd shared with Celsus.

Being careful not to share the information Patti had told him to withhold.

About the Tabulation Team ripping off the DOD of God only knew how much money.

"I decided to come by mostly to see how you're holding up but on the way over here I had an idea. First, though, I have to ask: Were you and Jordan very close? It seems that way from what you've told me."

Tears welled up in Zara's eyes. She nodded. "Yes, we were."

She dabbed her eyes with a napkin.

"That being the case," McGill said, "do you think it's possible Jordan might have looked ahead and left a message for you? In case he couldn't speak to you himself."

Just the idea galvanized Zara. She sat up straighter and nodded.

"Of course, he would have. Why didn't I think of that?"

They both knew grief was the reason why, but McGill didn't want to get bogged down.

"All right. Where do you think he might have left his message? My thinking is it would have to be —"

Zara got off her breakfast stool and opened a deep cabinet drawer in the island.

"Bread box," she said, "but we're out of bread and today I'm using it for this."

She pulled out a photo album and put it on the counter.

She placed a hand on the album and looked at McGill. "We have twenty or so photo collections like this. We both love photography and anytime we went somewhere special we both took our cameras. This is our best-of collection, the absolute favorites. Jordan would have been sure I'd look at it."

"And you have been?" McGill asked.

"Yes."

"Did you notice anything different?"

"No ... but I might have missed something trying to see through my tears."

McGill understood. "Are you up to giving it another try with me looking, too?"

Zara Gilford firmed her jaw. She pulled out a stool for McGill. "Yes."

By McGill's count they closely examined thirty pages of photographs, each neatly arranged under a transparent plastic overleaf. They were pictures the Gilfords had taken over the years, starting when they were decades younger: portraits, candids, landscapes, city scenes, all of them well composed and sharply focused.

With Zara's permission, McGill removed each print, looked at the back of it and the area on the page it had covered. He found no messages anywhere and put each one back in place. By the time they reached the final page, McGill was thinking his idea had been wrong.

Then Zara frowned as she looked at the final three prints.

McGill saw nothing unusual about them.

But Zara said, "These shouldn't be here."

"Why not?"

"Well, they're not on their proper pages; they're out of sequence. I mustn't have noticed before. I wasn't looking for any special meaning. But each of these photos should be on other pages. See, look at this top one of me. I was much younger when it was taken." She took the photo off the back page. "It should be way up here."

She flipped back to the third page of the album. She was right. The photo from the back of the book fit in much better as the third print in the vertical column on the page. Removing the shot that was currently there, she replaced it with the one from the back of the album.

McGill took out his notepad and wrote down the placement of the repositioned photo: 3-3.

Working in the same fashion, Zara moved the next print from the back of the album to the very front page at the top of the column. McGill wrote: 1-1. The final misplaced print was moved to page nine and the second slot. It fit with a series of three exposures each of which showed Zara comically mugging an expression of being startled. McGill wrote: 9-2.

"I don't get the sequence," he said. "It's six digits long. One too many for a zip code; one too few for a phone number. Could be a date, if 3-3-1192 means anything."

He looked over at Zara and saw her face change as she came up with the answer.

Or maybe just a possible answer, McGill thought.

"It is a date," she said, "but not the one you said. Three times three."

"Nine followed by … one, one. Nine-eleven. But what do the nine and —"

"Nine times two: eighteen. As in 18 State Street, Boston. You remember where you were on 9/11, don't you, Mr. McGill?"

"Of course. I was at work in my office at the Chicago Police Department."

"Jordan and I were living in Boston. We were in a bank there to rent a safe-deposit box. The bank clerk helping us asked if we'd have any objection to box 1313. The bank was having a hard time renting it, he said. Jordan wasn't bothered, but the number made me feel uneasy. Before I could say anything, a man called out the news that the first tower in New York had been hit. We never finished our banking that day."

And maybe that same box had still been available years later, assuming Jordan Gilford went back to it.

Having the FBI get a warrant to look into it seemed like a good idea to McGill.

He asked Zara, "Your expressions in the photos on the '18' page, do you think they have any special meaning?"

She said, "I was playing at being surprised, just a game as I recall. Maybe Jordan intended them as three exclamation points."

McGill could see that. It made him feel more hopeful they were on to something.

But now Zara was emotionally drained. She said she needed to lie down.

McGill saw her to her bedroom door and said goodbye.

He checked in with Celsus on his way out.

McGill felt he might have hit a jackpot, but you never knew.

He might just be chasing moonbeams.

# CHAPTER 24

### *McGill's Hideaway — The White House*

The fireplace was alight and McGill and Patti were sipping at the cups of hot cocoa that Blessing had just brought to them. They contented themselves with each other's silent company and the crackling of the flames. When they emptied their cups they put them aside and took each other's hand. For most of the people in Washington — even the government staffers who normally toiled well after dark — the workday was ove

Not so for McGill and Patti. At the president's direction, Byron DeWitt had been detailed to make a quick trip to Boston to check safe-deposit box 1313 in the bank at 18 State Street. The search warrant DeWitt carried allowed him to enter the premises in the wee hours, and the cooperation of the bank president, including a vow of secrecy, had been secured by the attorney general, an old classmate from their undergraduate days at Harvard.

"You figured out your approach to Zara Gilford based on the flowers you swiped from Aggie Wu for me?" Patti asked McGill.

He wasn't surprised Patti had discovered his ruse. Galia had probably snitched him out. Making it look like a slip of the tongue, of course.

He said, "I didn't swipe them. I paid for them. Handsomely."

"Of course. But your sweet gesture still paid off."

"We don't know that yet. But I have a good feeling, up to a point."

"And beyond that point?"

"We might not like what DeWitt finds. Might be embarrassing, politically contentious or both. More headaches, in any case."

"I don't think I have any room for more."

"If it's anything you can tell me, I'll listen," McGill said. "I can always go to the gym and hit something for release."

Patti looked at him and asked, "Do you know how to hit that bag the way boxers do, rat-a-tat-tat?"

"The speed bag? Sure. You want me to teach you? You have the coordination and reflexes to do it. Shouldn't take long at all before you're working it like a champ."

"I love it when you sweet-talk me."

McGill leaned over and kissed his wife.

"The two men who searched Zara Gilford's condo?" Patti said.

"Yeah?"

"Hume Drummond didn't recognize them, but running their images through a DOD database found matches. Their names are Mark Henry Colton and Warren Newland. They work for the Defense Intelligence Agency. Neither of them went to work today, and the FBI didn't find them at home either."

"People are looking for them, I trust," McGill said.

"Here and abroad."

"Abroad would be my guess. There's more of it."

"Celsus did well to upload the video of Colton and Newland to the Secret Service server."

"He's adjusting to private life better than I'd ever have guessed," McGill said. "If I'm not careful, I might wind up liking the guy."

Patti grinned and said, "Moving on, Secretary of State Kalman has been in touch with the government of Uganda. The bank there, the one we suspect of being the clearing house for funds stolen from the DOD, has experienced a power failure. No one's quite certain how long it will last, but no business will be transacted for some time."

McGill said, "Now that is going to scare the bad guys."

"We hope it will crimp their cash flow and mobility, too, as well as provide the kind of evidence that will be damning in court."

"Speaking of being damned, how much of this mess is going to blow back on you?"

Patti said, "I don't know. It started under the previous administration, but it's my baby now. The only thing I can see to do is try to wrap it up as fast as I can, catch as many of the perpetrators as possible, try them and lock them away for the rest of their miserable lives. See if I can't come out of this looking like a tough law-and-order president."

"You know there's almost certainly a political dimension to all this, people in the House and/or Senate grabbing cash with both hands."

"Yes, I know. That's going to be the ugliest part. That and the battle of how to bring substantive reform to the Department of Defense so this kind of thing never happens again."

"How about we stop being the world's cop?" McGill asked.

"That would simplify things, but there is this military-industrial complex, you see. Its lobbyists like things the way they are and want the money involved to become even bigger."

"And then there's the battle with the domestic gun lobby."

Patti sighed. "Yes, there is."

The phone rang and though it was McGill's Hideaway, Patti answered.

She listened for the better part of a minute and said, "Thank you. Yes, first thing. Eight o'clock this morning." Clicking off, she told McGill, "We'd better get to bed."

McGill stood and extended a hand to Patti. "They found something in box 1313."

Getting to her feet, she replied, "Yes, and it is going to be very ugly."

Patti didn't give any details and McGill didn't ask for them.

## Consolidated Forensic Laboratory — Washington, DC

According to its mission statement, the Office of the Chief Medical Examiner of Washington, DC is obligated to investigate all deaths that occur as the result of violence. Abel Mays, inconveniently, had expired during a brief interregnum, the old CME having departed shortly before her replacement's arrival. As a result, Mays' corpse chilled a bit longer that it might have otherwise.

It was also discovered that Mays had not died as the result of the two gunshots fired into his head from close range.

Hearing that tidbit, the new CME, Dr. Marlon Donaldson, took a step back as if he'd been shoved and said, "I beg your pardon."

Donaldson had been called out of his suite at the the Willard and arrived at the lab shortly before midnight. He was not in the mood for a prank. Especially since his tenure didn't officially begin for another thirteen minutes.

Dr. Lenore Nuñez, the board certified pathologist who had performed the autopsy on Mays, told him, "No joke. A guy gets plugged twice in the head, he's dead, you think you've got a clear cause of death, but guess again."

"I don't want to guess," Donaldson replied, growing more peeved.

"And you really shouldn't have to, a man of your eminent position."

Nuñez's tone suggested the-powers-that-be might have done better to promote from within.

And she might be considering a gender discrimination suit against the OCME, too.

Donaldson, a veteran of medical bureaucracies, caught both points. "You're saying the man was dead before he got shot."

"Very good." Nuñez had to restrain herself from giving her new boss a treat.

Donaldson elaborated, "An underlying medical condition manifested shortly before the shooting. Given the damage that must have been done to the man's brain by the shooting, it would be far easier to see … he had a myocardial infarction?"

Nuñez nodded. "Guy's heart had all the structural integrity of a rotten tomato. One that had been hit with a hammer. Shame was he didn't die of his bad ticker a day earlier. Spare all those people he killed."

Donaldson agreed. "Damn bad timing." Then his thoughts turned back to himself. "But why did you call me in? You're authorized to sign off on this."

"Authorized, yeah," Nuñez said. "But how would it look? An underling having the final say on such an important death. You're the man with the big job and the big bucks." She handed Donaldson her report. "You sign off on it and carry the political weight that's going to come with this finding."

What political weight, Donaldson wondered.

Nuñez turned her back on him and started to walk away.

"Wait a minute," Donaldson said, "you can't do this."

"You don't like it, fire me."

She didn't even look back.

Donaldson was tempted to oblige, but if Nuñez was planning to sue, firing her would only make things look worse. Now, he'd have to do his own examination of the body to make sure he wasn't being sandbagged into signing something that wasn't true. Goddamnit.

Before Dr. Nuñez was lost to sight, she called out, "Welcome to Washington."

### Midtown Manhattan — New York City

Hugh Collier, chief executive officer and largest shareholder of WWN, walked up Sixth Avenue and passed Rockefeller Center at 11:59 p.m. He was headed home to his townhouse on Central Park West. The night was cold and raw. A relentless wind from the north pressed against his every step and turned the walk into something of an ordeal.

He might have called for his car if the heat of his anger hadn't moderated the wind chill.

That goddamn Ellie Booker was driving him mad. If anyone else who worked for him had spoken to him the way she had ... Well, if a man had said it, he'd have been both sacked and beaten bloody. Any other woman would have been dismissed and had her reputation shredded.

Ellie had asked, "What's wrong, Hugh? You leave your balls in the last pansy you buggered?"

Had she been in his office, not in Washington, he might well have taken a hand to her.

Woman or not.

Of course, Ellie had once waved a knife under his nose not far from where he was at the moment. That and told him to go drown himself in the East River. So getting physical with Ms. Booker would have been no small task.

Even making the decision to terminate their professional agreement, something either of them could do at will, had been beyond him for the moment. Ellie Booker had a nose for big stories unlike anyone he'd ever known. And now she had seemed to cultivate a special relationship with James J. McGill. Once that fact became apparent to WWN's competitors, they'd start throwing bags of cash at the woman.

For just a second, Hugh wondered if Ellie was having it off with McGill. A gay man, he didn't have the best fix on what kind of woman a straight bloke was more likely to fancy. Patricia Grant was certainly more beautiful. But Ellie was younger, and he could imagine the ferocious energy she might bring to the bedroom. Which quality might McGill prefer?

Or was he the kind of man who might think he could have both women?

Not from what Hugh knew of him. He was too smart for that. The fact that McGill so famously got along with his ex-wife, Carolyn Enquist, said he wasn't the sort to publicly embarrass a woman who was important to him. Stepping out on the president of the United States ... well, McGill was the first man ever to have that opportunity.

But Hugh just didn't see it.

So sex wasn't the reason McGill was passing scoops along to Ellie.

Good God, could he actually like her? If that was the case, she'd have the inside track on every big story to come out of the White House for the next three years. He couldn't afford to let any other media company have that kind of asset.

And yet he'd all but dismissed Ellie that very day.

She'd come to him with the story of the Winstead School putting up one of those new gun death counters on their playing field. Ellie had wanted him to run it on WWN's evening national news broadcast. He said he'd let the local station in Washington carry it, as a favor to her.

She said, "Bullshit. You've had your first chance. I'm taking it elsewhere."

"Nobody will buy it," he'd told her, hoping he was right.

The whole idea just seemed so depressing to him.

"Somebody will, and if they won't, I'll give it to PBS. They'll run it."

"Well, if you're happy with that boutique audience."

"You're ridiculing PBS's viewership?"

Then she'd asked him where he'd left his balls.

And reeled him in a second later by saying, "It's too bad, your going all chickenshit on this piece, what with it featuring Hal Walker giving a tearjerker speech."

Hugh Collier had been a top-flight Australian rules football player back home.

The game was all but invisible in the U.S., but going with the cultural flow in America, he cultivated an interest in gridiron football. He even came to enjoy it. He knew who Hal Walker was, not just a future pro footballer but someone who would become a celebrity off the field as well. Someone who might even be brought into the WWN sports broadcasting family.

Crikey, he was starting to think like Uncle Edbert.

The late Sir Edbert Bickford, founder of WWN.

Whom Hugh had drowned, assuring his rise to the top of the company.

"Why didn't you say so right off?" he'd barked at Ellie. "Of course, we'll put your video on the national broadcast."

More than anything else, he was furious at the way he'd let Ellie play him.

"Hey, hey you!" a male voice called out. "You're Hugh Collier, right?"

The man's voice had an accent Hugh couldn't place. Maybe somewhere in the middle of America. He still hadn't learned all the inflections; it was a big country. The man standing in front of him looked both angry and nervous.

For the first time since he'd stepped out of his office building that night, Hugh noticed how empty the sidewalks around him were. Manhattan, truly, was the part of New York City that never slept. There was still plenty of automotive traffic rushing past, but the cold wind had scoured the walkways clear, except for him and —

"Yeah, you're him all right, Hugh Collier."

The idiot sounded as displeased with him as Ellie had been.

Not acknowledging his identity, Hugh asked, "What do you want?"

The man's face turned even redder than the wind had made it.

"I'll tell you what I want, you goddamn faggot, I want my old WWN back, the way it was when your uncle ran the place. Not the swish-city liberal sissy outfit that supports the faggot-pride parade."

Supporting the annual Gay Pride parades in New York and other cities had been one of the more definitive signs not only of Hugh's personal sexuality but also of WWN's new editorial point of view.

Hugh pressed his steepled hands to his chin and smiled, as if a prayer had been answered.

Here at last was someone he could bash into a quivering mass.

All he had to do was let the dolt make the first move.

"And if you don't get it back?" Hugh asked softly.

"Then you'll get this."

The cretin didn't rush him. Didn't throw a punch. He reached into a jacket pocket.

In that chilling moment, Hugh was reminded he wasn't back home in Oz.

He was in the U.S.A. where every state allowed the concealed carrying of firearms.

Hugh threw himself forward, landed a straight right hand that flattened the fool's nose.

Knocked the wanker unconscious before he crumpled to the ground.

But Hugh got shot in the leg anyway.

# CHAPTER 25

*Mindanao Sea — 5.85°N, 123.14°E —*
*Wednesday, March 12, 2014*

The *Shining Dawn* lay motionless beneath a clear starlit sky. A waxing, nearly full moon added to the brightness of the night at 3:30 a.m. Philippine Time Zone. The calm sea reflected the celestial lights like a mirror. In water too deep to use an anchor, a captain would keep his vessel's bow head on to the wind to maintain position with what was known as a sea anchor. With no wind that night, the maneuver was unnecessary.

Tyler Busby stood at the stern of the mega-yacht and looked at the ovoid boat connected to the mother ship by a nylon line. The smaller craft was almost thirty feet long. It was called a Fassmer SEL-RT 8.5. It functioned as the *Shining Dawn*'s tender or lifeboat. It could hold up to forty people.

Depending on their average avoirdupois, Busby supposed.

In any case, the lifeboat offered more than enough elbow room for its sole occupant, Ah-lam, former dragon lady of the *Shining Star.*

Ah-lam had given herself away when she'd told Busby he could sleep with her only once. The implication of a black widow's sexual cannibalism might have been regarded more subtly in Asian cultures, but it was clear to him. Bed Ah-lam and it was goodbye,

Charlie.

The fact that she would always be nearby and sexually available, though, even when he might become depressed and give in to a temptation to end it all in bed with Ah-lam — there were many far worse ways to go — told him something else that was important.

While he had secured a five-year lease for the *Shining Dawn*, the deal would become far more profitable and politically less risky to the yacht's Chinese owner if Busby cashed in his chips early. Indeed, Ah-lam might already have been reprimanded by her lord and master for not bringing the deal and Busby's life to a swift end.

He had to hand it to Ah-lam for bringing her sisters aboard to serve as his concubines. The two stunning young women, whom Busby had nicknamed Toots and Bubbles, did resemble Ah-lam closely. And the psychology of the ploy was brilliant. After having the two princesses, Busby would feel compelled to bed the queen.

Instead, he decided to do what gave him even greater pleasure.

Outwit a competitor. He came up with a plan that pleased him no end.

Busby had quickly seen that both Toots and Bubbles chafed under their older sister's authority. So he used them to launch a hostile takeover. In this case, it wasn't a company he would seize but the *Shining Dawn*. His weapons were subversion and money. Everyone on board got a million-dollar signing bonus; the captain and first mate got five and three million respectively. Once the captain confirmed that his booty had been wired to an account in Singapore held in his wife's name, everyone else came aboard.

And Ah-lam was cast adrift.

Once she managed to untie her hands she'd be able start the engine of the Fassmer SEL-RT 8.5. She had more than enough fuel aboard to reach the island of Mindanao. True, it was a dicey place what with the Abu Sayyaf guerrillas and other troublemakers running around kidnapping people and whatnot, but Ah-lam was a resourceful young woman.

Busby was counting on that.

The yacht's captain, Busby's new best friend, appeared at his shoulder.

"Sir, there are three vessels approaching. They may be pirates."

"You told me they're small-timers in this area."

"Yes, sir. Mostly they extort poor local fishermen. But seeing a vessel like ours or even the lifeboat sitting dead in the water, they'll want to sniff around."

Busby didn't think some riffraff could pose a threat to the yacht; it was too well armed. But giving Ah-lam safe passage was critical to his plan.

"Discourage the pirates, Captain. Send them on their way."

"Yes, sir." He motioned to two crewmen, each of whom had overheard Busby and carried a SMAW II, a shoulder-launched multipurpose assault weapon — the updated model of the rocket launcher used by the U.S. military. The captain told his crewmen, "Fire a warning round. If they change course, let them be. If they continue coming at us ..."

He looked to Busby for a decision.

"Destroy them."

One of the crewmen fired a rocket at the lead boat. It looked to Busby as if it were going to hit its target squarely. But it splashed into the water and exploded just short of the vessel. Close enough to douse everyone in the small craft and apparently scare the hell out of them.

All three boats veered away. Busby waited five minutes to make sure they didn't circle back. When he was satisfied the pirates weren't going to return, he told the captain, "Let's get under way."

"Yes, sir, and the destination?"

"Montevideo. We can make it that far, can't we?"

"Of course, though we will have to refuel. And it would be prudent to purchase a new lifeboat."

"Yes, of course," Busby said. "Let's get the new lifeboat as soon as possible and then be on our way."

"Yes, sir."

The man was about to return to his helm when Busby stopped him.

"Cut the line to this lifeboat. We don't want to tow Ah-lam all the way to South America."

The captain blushed and delegated the chore to one of the crewman.

Busby watched until Ah-lam's boat was lost to sight.

Stay safe, my dear, he thought.

### Q Street — Georgetown

Sweetie felt a hand gently rouse her from sleep. As her eyes fluttered open, she remembered she wasn't at home. It wasn't Putnam waking her.

A voice with a charming Spanish accent told her, "I took a vow of celibacy many years ago, but if you are the angel you appear to be perhaps we might enjoy a spiritual union."

Sweetie laughed and raised herself on one elbow.

"I took a wedding vow, and I'm as far from being an angel as I am from heaven. *Buenos dias*, Father. I hope you don't mind my borrowing your bed."

Sweetie swung her feet off the narrow cot, necessitating a retreat by Inigo de Loyola from the tiny space beneath the staircase of Dikki Missirian's second commercial property in Georgetown. Keeping her head down, Sweetie also stepped out of the tiny chamber the priest called home.

"You had nowhere else to go last night, my child?" de Loyola asked.

"I share a very nice townhouse with my husband and the young girl we're going to adopt, Father. But I was out looking for you last night. I hoped you'd return here. Dikki let me stay in your space; he said you wouldn't mind."

"Of course, I don't. I am his guest as well. And though I have never seen an actual angel, sinner that I am, I hope they look just as you did a moment ago."

"Come on, Father. If I wasn't a tough old copper, you might make me blush."

"I'm sure that would only add to your beauty. But now that you've found me, how may I serve you?"

"I'm told that you pray for the president, Father."

"I do. Daily. I pray that she may be safe, wise in her actions and lead this great land with a compassion for all those less fortunate than herself."

"As someone who knows her, I can tell you she does her best to do just that. What I'd like to know now is whether you'd be willing to lend both her and me a hand. Help us with a job I think you'd be exactly the man to do."

"What might that be?"

"Take a trip to Costa Rica. See what a certain American politician has been doing down there. Discreetly look into his relationship with a certain American woman who might have visited him in Costa Rica."

The priest's face took on a pensive look, as if he were silently asking himself several questions. He came to a conclusion and bobbed his head. "I think I can do this. Costa Rica is perhaps the only country in Central America where I am not a wanted man, that I know of."

That gave Sweetie pause. "Father, I can't ask you to put yourself in danger."

"No, no. It will be all right." He stroked his lush beard. "I will have to shave, of course. Perhaps cut and dye my hair as well. But this I do not mind."

"You're starting to worry me, Father."

De Loyola gave Sweetie a smile that was almost saintly.

Spoiled by just a hint of mischief, maybe even devilry.

"I will be happy to help you, Ms. Sweeney. Your request reminds me that I have a task or two left undone for myself in that part of the world. I assume my expenses will be paid."

"Of course, and you'll be compensated for your time, too. But, Father, I have to ask you to take care of my concerns first."

"Without doubt. Now, may I know the specifics of what you need?"

Hoping she wasn't making a mistake, Sweetie told him.

### United States Capitol — Washington, DC

Auric Ludwig sat on a park bench facing the West Front of the Capitol, looking glum and maybe even dangerous. Two Capitol Hill cops — Congress had its own police department — had stopped their foot patrol a minute earlier and asked what business he had in the area. He didn't look like a tourist, and there were precious few of them about anyway. The weather, ever since the shooting at the Winstead School, had remained persistently overcast and bone-chilling.

If that was a sign of divine disapproval, Ludwig thought, God would have to do worse before he worried about it. A plague of locusts maybe. Or True South becoming the peace and love party.

"I'm here to visit two House members, officers," he'd told the cops. "I'm a little early and I thought I'd rather look at the Capitol than the Rayburn House Office Building."

All of which was true, but the cops asked to see his ID anyway.

The resulting, red-faced grimace should have identified Ludwig immediately.

Caricatures of that visage had appeared on every news magazine in the country.

To his disgust, and just a bit of concern, he went unrecognized and had to show his Virginia driver's license and his House lobbyist's ID number. They checked the veracity of both forms of identification, and ignored his business card.

CEO of FirePower America? They didn't give a damn.

Ludwig didn't have any Capitol Hill cops on his payroll.

But once he checked out, they did offer him a perfunctory, "Have a nice day, sir."

"Do my best," he replied.

What he really wanted to do was … no, not shoot anyone.

More like kick some ass.

Starting with the city's goddamn new medical examiner.

Ludwig already had enough to worry about. His new lawyer, who was supposed to be a tough SOB, had called that morning and told Ludwig that angling for a plea deal might be their best course after all. Then this new sonofabitch, Dr. Marlon Donaldson, does a TV interview. And what had he said?

He said goddamn Abel Mays died of a fucking heart attack.

That made Ludwig's good guy with a gun look like a prize putz. Dumbass shot a guy who was already dead? Some hero he is.

Ludwig had responded the only way he could. He'd called every hard-right radio host he had on speed-dial. He claimed Dr. Donaldson was a shill for the Grant administration. He said the fix was in because James J. McGill was trying to fleece Jordan Gilford's widow for all she was worth. On every show, he was asked how he could prove his case if the real shooter, the guy who did kill Abel Mays, didn't come forward?

As a response to every talk-show host, he said the same thing, "I'm now doubling my offer to anyone who finds my good guy with a gun, $2 million. And somebody should look into that new medical examiner's connections to McGill and the president."

Ludwig's increased offer quickly made its way up the media foodchain.

It went viral on the Internet. People all over the country were looking to cash in.

Shortly after making his round of the radio shows, news reached Ludwig that the man who had shot the death counter billboard outside his office — his hero of the day — was going to be turned over to the federal courts and would wind up serving his sentence in Alaska.

Ludwig absolutely would not stand for that, but he wasn't sure how to stop it. The new governor of Virginia and the state's new attorney general, both elected only a few months ago, said that Kenton Platt, a convicted felon, would be tried in federal court. Starting to feel more than a little desperate, Ludwig had made an appointment with the two senior Republican members of the House of Representatives from Virginia to plan a political counterattack. They agreed to see him, of course. But not immediately.

Truth was, Ludwig hadn't arrived early for his appointment.

He was cooling his heels, outdoors.

The fact that Ludwig had a substantial criminal charge hanging over his head had made the normally servile politicians skittish. He wondered what else might go wrong.

His dismal reverie was interrupted by a cheerful voice.

"Hey, Auric Ludwig, what are you doing out here in the cold?"

The gun lobbyist looked up and saw Representative Philip Brock.

Ludwig knew all five hundred and thirty-five members of Congress at a glance. Brock was a Democrat. Not exactly a member of Ludwig's hallelujah chorus. Still, Brock had said publicly that even if he didn't own a gun or like to go hunting or target shooting, he didn't mind if other folks raised all the gunsmoke they wanted.

Enablers were every bit as good as toadies in Ludwig's book.

"Just waiting my turn to visit with some of your colleagues, Congressman."

The fact that Ludwig had to wait for anyone and admitted it registered with Brock.

The universe was out of balance. Something momentous might be in the wind.

Maybe he could stir the pot a bit, cause a little trouble.

"Come on, Mr. Ludwig. You can wait in my office where it's warm. I'll buy you a cup of coffee and we'll talk. See if we might be of help to one another."

Brock's gesture of respect warmed Ludwig's heart.

Made him feel strong and important again.

It never occurred to him Brock might be playing him somehow.

### St. Luke's-Roosevelt Hospital — Midtown Manhattan

Ellie Booker pushed the wheelchair with Hugh Collier in it toward the exit where his town car was waiting to take him either home, as his doctor recommended, or to his office, as was his inclination. Ellie had flown to New York in the dead of the night after Hugh had called her from the hospital. He wanted her to produce a big story for WWN.

Network CEO Shot in New York City.

The subhead being: Hugh Collier Subdues and Disarms Gunman.

Ellie had called in the senior anchor of the network's nightly news broadcast, Jack Clooney, to do a bedside interview with Hugh. Five minutes would run on the news that evening, and two teaser clips of thirty seconds each would rotate on the network throughout the day. Dozens of other media outlets were also clamoring for the opportunity to talk with Hugh.

Reporters of all stripes were both titillated and terrified by the story.

One of the big bosses in their business had been shot: That was news.

The prospect that anyone in the media might be targeted: That was damn scary.

Christ, was the U.S. becoming as dangerous for journalists as war zones?

Ellie had directed several large security people, all of them former cops, to keep reporters from other networks and the newspapers at bay. This was her story. Calling on her to work it was Hugh's way of apologizing for being a jerk yesterday about not wanting to do the story of the gun death counter going up at the Winstead School.

Hugh's first-person experience with gun violence had changed his mind about not broadcasting gun death totals on the network news. He had a newfound empathy for shooting victims and the people who loved them. Not that he and Ellie loved each other, not even platonically, but they felt a deep mutual respect as two ruthless news professionals.

And maybe some visceral sense of challenge, too.

An urge to arm-wrestle, if nothing more.

They spoke privately in Hugh's hospital room before Clooney and his crew came in.

"I thought I got to the bastard in time, Ellie. Landed my punch before ... well, you know."

"Should've used both hands," Ellie told him.

"Beg pardon?"

"You just thought of clocking the shithead, right?"

"Putting my fist through his face, yes."

"You should have slapped his gun aside at the same time you threw your punch. That's why God gave you two hands."

Hugh smiled. "Oh, is that why?"

"Well, also so you can diddle yourself and answer the phone at the same time."

That made Hugh laugh, which caused him to wince.

He'd been shot in more than the leg. Ellie had stolen a glance at Hugh's medical report when a nurse was looking the other way. The slug fired at Hugh had indeed grazed the soft tissue of the inside of his left thigh. That would leave an interesting physical scar. What would certainly linger in his mind, though, was the fact that the projectile had also sliced open the outer left side of Hugh's scrotum.

The description of his effort at self-defense as balls out was literally half-true.

He'd had to be repacked and stitched up.

There was no indication of lasting physical damage, but the leg wound wasn't why the doctor had prescribed bed rest at home. Ellie decided not to let Hugh know what she'd found out. She'd also have to be a little more careful from now on about suggesting where he might have left his balls.

She even humored him to the extent of bending over and letting him kiss her cheek after he got seated in his car. "I've said it before," he told her, "but there really are times when you almost make me wish I was straight."

"Yeah, I get that from all the guys."

A minute later, Hugh's car was out of sight; smart man, he was on his way home.

The media posse took up pursuit.

Alone on the sidewalk, in terms of newsies anyway, Ellie made a call to a rival.

Didi DiMarco at MSNBC answered, listened to what Ellie had to tell her and asked, "Why are you giving this to me?"

"Because you had the class not to try for a bedside interview with a guy you can't stand."

"Maybe I'm just too busy working on something else," Didi said.

"But you have the time to talk with me?" Ellie laughed.

"Okay, so I know the reason you called. You're trying to use me."

"Right, but in a nice way."

"And if I put a national gun death counter on my show, Hugh Collier will have a much harder time either not putting one on WWN or yanking it soon after he does."

"Yeah," Ellie said. "So you gonna do it? Not wait and be a me-too?"

"Tune in and find out," Didi told her.

### The Oval Office — The White House

Byron DeWitt looked so tired when he met with Patricia Grant and Galia Mindel that morning that the president insisted he have a cup of coffee.

"If it's all right with you, ma'am, I'd prefer a cup of tea," DeWitt said.

"Darjeeling?"

"Oolong. Any variety will do."

A Navy culinary specialist brought a tea service within minutes. Galia took hers with honey. The president and DeWitt had theirs without a sweetener.

"What did you find in Boston, Mr. Deputy Director?" the president asked.

"The names of two members of the House of Representatives and estimates of how long the looting of the Pentagon has been going on and how much money has been stolen so far."

"And the details?" Galia asked.

"The House members are Wesley Tilden, Republican, South Carolina and Tanner Rutledge, True South, Texas. The plan went into operation in the sixth year of your predecessor's presidency. The take from the scam thus far exceeds $10 billion."

"My god," Galia whispered in awe.

"These are just Jordan Gilford's preliminary estimates. His notes say there have to be several more people involved and the money stolen might be twice his initial estimate." DeWitt shook his head and took another sip of tea. "When I first read Mr. Gilford's report, it made me think that Willie Sutton's reasoning is way out of date."

"Saying he robbed banks because that's where the money is?" the president said.

"Yes, ma'am. These days, the real money is in the federal budget, and nowhere do you find more of it than at the Pentagon. Mr. Gilford speculated that the plan was initially intended to last only until your predecessor left office. But when the perpetrators saw how well the Tabulation Team worked without any suspicions being raised, they saw no reason to stop."

Galia's eyes momentarily lost focus as her mind went in another direction.

The president and DeWitt waited quietly for her to seize whatever thought was passing through her mind. A minute later, she had it. "That name, the Tabulation Team, it's a perfect fit for Wesley Tilden. Before coming to Congress, he was an accountant, and his brother, James, went to prison for fraud in the DataCom scandal back in 2001."

DeWitt nodded. "Mr. Gilford noted that, too. James Tilden was a senior partner in DataCom. The company supposedly audited the books of a number of mid-size banks and found every penny accounted for when in fact the banks were about to collapse from bad investments and outright theft of funds by and for bank officers. The taxpayers wound up on the hook for billions of dollars."

"And James Tilden committed suicide the night before his trial was supposed to begin," the president said.

"A point that counsels urgency, Madam President," DeWitt said. "Representative Tilden certainly knows about the death of Jordan Gilford; he has to be getting very frightened. With a family history of suicide, he might decide that's the easy way out."

Galia added, "And if his co-conspirators see Tilden as a weak link, they might do him in. Possibly making his death look like a suicide."

The president asked, "If you were to bring Representative Tilden in for questioning, Mr. Deputy Director, do you think he'd break down and confess? Tell us everything he knows for some measure of leniency?"

"He very well might, ma'am, but I can't make any guarantee."

A ruthless smile appeared on Galia's face.

"Ma'am?" DeWitt asked her.

"It's an old police ploy to make one bad guy look like he's snitching out his accomplices, isn't it? Then make the sap think if he doesn't cooperate and is released, he's certain to be killed by his own people."

"That tool has been used before, yes, on both the local and federal levels," DeWitt said.

"If it is used here," the president said, "I'd want FBI agents watching Representative Tilden quite closely, ready to step in and prevent his murder. If Tilden were to see an actual threat to his life, I'd think he might be more forthcoming."

"Most likely, ma'am."

"Catching a would-be killer in the act should make that person open up, too, wouldn't it?" Galia asked.

"Possibly," DeWitt said, "but if the assassin weren't a part of the larger plan, simply a contract killer, he might not have much information to share."

Galia looked a bit humbled. "I should've thought of that."

"I'm relieved that you don't have a complete understanding

of the criminal mind, Galia," the president said. To DeWitt, she added, "Please bring Tilden in for questioning, discreetly but at the first opportunity. We don't want to lose him to his own hand or anyone else's. But, Byron."

DeWitt blinked at the president's use of his first name.

"Yes, ma'am?"

"Delegate this job to someone else. You're clearly exhausted. Would Special Agent Benjamin be a good choice for this job?"

"Yes, ma'am, she would."

"All right then. Brief the special agent and then get some sleep."

"There is one more matter to discuss, ma'am, as long as I have this opportunity to speak with you."

"And what's that?" the president asked.

"Congressman Philip Brock, ma'am."

DeWitt told the president and Galia of the conversations Brock had with Senator Howard Hurlbert shortly before the senator's murder. He also told them how Hasna Kalil, a suspected terrorist sympathizer, had informed him that her late brother, Dr. Bahir Ben Kalil, had Brock as a friend before he disappeared and was recently found dead.

"And then, of course, Brock visited Inspiration Hall before its official opening with Tyler Busby, whose whereabouts still remain unknown. Representative Brock bears close scrutiny, ma'am. I've shared this information with Director Haskins, but I thought you should know my opinion, too."

"Thank you," the president said. "Galia, do you have anything to add?"

"I assume the FBI is using its considerable resources to find Busby. Doing so and getting him to tell us how Representative Brock fits into all this would be a great help."

"The FBI and several other agencies have hundreds of people looking for Mr. Busby. I recently received a suggestion from Mr. Putnam Shady that I'm acting on. He said we might look at recent purchases of, well, what amounts to palaces around the world. Mr. Shady suggested that Mr. Busby's ego would demand that he find the biggest, most opulent hiding place possible."

Once again, Galia was struck by an idea.

This time she didn't have to wait to articulate it.

"A palace, an estate, a mansion, however you want to characterize it, has a fixed location. If it's a big fancy place, it will also have a high profile, physically and in terms of public awareness. You're bound to find it eventually. But isn't Busby a yachtsman?"

"Yes, ma'am. He was anyway. He had three yachts, but we haven't been able to find any of them."

"Yachts can be reconfigured, repainted and renamed," the president said, getting into the flow of Galia's idea. "And looking at things through Mr. Shady's lens of Busby dealing only in superlatives, he might have wanted something grander than any of the vessels he already had."

Galia suggested, "Maybe Busby traded up."

DeWitt liked the idea. He wrote it down so he wouldn't forget it.

The president said to Galia, "Let's have Attorney General Jaworsky get warrants to listen in on both Congressmen's phone calls. If they're getting antsy, they might let something slip."

Then she repeated her instruction to DeWitt to get some rest and he left.

The president told Galia, "Please contact Special Agent Benjamin. As soon as the warrants are issued and the taps are in place, have her bring Congressman Tilden in for questioning. Give her all the background information she needs to be effective."

"Yes, ma'am. I assume you want the taps for both residential and mobile phones."

"Office phones, too. We can't worry about propriety or politics, if these characters are robbing the government blind."

Galia knew Patricia Grant would never face another election, but she still had almost three years left in office, and there was her legacy to consider. Bugging Congressional offices would cause a monumental uproar. But the look on the president's face told Galia she didn't want to hear about any of those things. So Galia took the easy road.

"Yes, ma'am. It's a shame we can't nab Brock now, too."

"All in good time," the president said.

### Metro Police Headquarters — Washington, DC

Captain Rockelle Bullard met McGill and Sweetie at the main entrance security station. She told the cop on duty, "These people are with me."

She led her guests to a conference room with a uniformed officer guarding the door. He saluted the captain and opened the door for her and the two civilians. Sitting on the far side of the table, facing the door, was a man wearing a navy blue sweatshirt. He had dark hair, a two-day growth of beard and looked to be in his early thirties. He grimaced upon seeing Rockelle, revealing that he wasn't big on dental hygiene.

Rockelle sat directly opposite the man.

McGill sat to her right, Sweetie to her left.

Rockelle told her guests, "This is Officer Leonard Garry. He's eight years on the job and after reading his personnel file I'm kinda surprised it took him this long to get in trouble."

Garry said, "I'm not saying a —"

"Shut up," Rockelle told him. "Nobody asked you to talk." Glancing at McGill and Sweetie, she added, "He's pretty stupid, too."

Sweetie asked Rockelle, "With all that time on the job, didn't he ever take a test for promotion?"

Rockelle shook her head. "Probably didn't want to embarrass himself. But now he's screwed up big time. We have a phone record for Officer Garry's personal mobile phone. He made a call to the office of Auric Ludwig at FirePower America during the time he was on duty at the scene of Abel Mays' death. Two other officers saw him talking on his phone there. Then he called Mr. Ludwig's office again later that day."

McGill asked, "How do Officer Garry's calls line up with Auric

Ludwig going public about Abel Mays being shot?"

Rockelle said, "His first call was made shortly after he arrived at the crime scene. Detectives Meeker and Beemer located other officers who saw Officer Garry looking right at Abel Mays' body. They said he couldn't have missed seeing the man's head wounds. The second call from Officer Garry's phone to FirePower America was made just a minute before Mr. Ludwig made his announcement that Abel Mays had been killed by a good guy with a gun."

Sweetie nodded. "I can see why the officer doesn't have anything to say; he's talked too much already."

"Yeah, and guess what?" Rockelle said. "Officer Garry, he's a member of FirePower America."

"This poor guy has dug himself a deep hole," McGill said.

Garry began to grind his grubby teeth.

"Metro PD has to have regulations against compromising an investigation," Sweetie said.

"Oh, yeah," Rockelle agreed. "And if you do it for money or other material gain, then it's not just regulations you've got to worry about. Then you've broken the law."

McGill shook his head. "Never easy for a cop to do time."

"He's going to make his union lawyer work hard, that's for sure," Sweetie added.

Rockelle smiled. "Now, that's the real interesting part. He didn't ask for an FOP lawyer. Guess who he called for help."

McGill looked at Garry with disbelief. "Don't tell me it was FirePower America."

Rockelle said, "Okay, I won't tell you, but it was."

Sweetie looked at Garry now, too. "You are one dumb bunny."

"Sad thing is, there have to be other cops just as stupid," McGill said. "There always are when someone is handing out money."

Rockelle nodded. "That's what I told him."

"But he's too tough to turn them in and save his own backside, right?" Sweetie asked.

"A stand-up guy," McGill agreed. "But, hey, you know what?"

"What?" Rockelle asked.

"If it turns out that Mays' death is connected to the death of Jordan Gilford on the National Mall, Officer Garry might have compromised a federal investigation, too. If that's the case, he might serve his time at that new prison up in Alaska."

Rockelle said, "'Specially if that FirePower lawyer doesn't ever show up. It's been going on two hours now since Officer Garry made that call."

Garry developed a tic at the corner of his right eye.

The three conversationalists got up and left.

Garry called for Rockelle five minutes later and started talking.

### En route to McGill Investigations, Inc — Washington, DC

McGill and Sweetie rode in the back of his Chevy. Leo maneuvered through traffic as if every other vehicle was standing still. Deke observed the shifting threat horizon moving his eyes from the windshield to the mirrors and dashboard monitors that gave him a 360° view.

A separate radar display watched for threats from above.

But monitoring that and taking evasive action was Leo's responsibility.

Sweetie told McGill, "I'm having second thoughts, Jim, about sending Father de Loyola to Costa Rica. I didn't know he was wanted anywhere, much less everywhere in Central America except Costa Rica."

She added the priest's comments about altering his appearance.

McGill said, "Maybe he just wants to look like the photo on his passport."

Sweetie considered that. "I might find that reassuring if it didn't also mean he changed his appearance from that likeness when he came to this country."

"Ask yourself this, Margaret: Do you have any doubts about Father de Loyola's character?"

Sweetie said, "No."

"How about his chances of doing the job?"

"No."

"You think he's going to overthrow the government in San José?"

That one gave her pause. "I don't know. Does it need overthrowing?"

"It's the most stable democracy south of the Rio Grande."

"Then no."

"How far has he traveled so far?"

Sweetie glanced at the dashboard clock. "If his first flight is on time, he should just be about to land in Miami. From there, it's on to San José."

"You want me to call him in Miami?" McGill asked.

Sweetie sighed. "No, I'll try to have a little faith."

McGill looked at his longtime friend. "It's not like you to get nervous, Margaret. You're usually the rock on which everyone leans. Even me on occasion."

"I know. It's just … I worry about Maxi. Being in school, you know. I think I should be with her all the time. Only I know that's no way for a kid to grow up, in the shadow of a bodyguard. I'm starting to make progress with Maxi, and I don't want to blow that."

"Have a little faith in yourself, too."

"You think Patti is going to advocate for that idea Putnam and I came up with? The one to make schools safer for kids with responsible parents."

McGill said, "I haven't heard of a definite decision, but Patti told me if she were in your position, she'd want to do it. So I think there's a pretty good chance she will."

Sweetie nodded, and let some of the tension she felt drain away.

"You hear about Hugh Collier getting shot last night?" she asked.

McGill nodded and was about to say something when his phone's ring tone sounded. He saw it was Carolyn calling and it was his turn to feel anxious. Had anything bad happened to any of his children?

His ex-wife said, "Hello, Jim. I hope I'm not interrupting anything important."

"The kids are okay? You and Lars, too?"

"Everybody's fine."

McGill's shoulders sagged in relief.

"But all three of our children are causing some big ripples."

"How's that?"

"We all saw your interview on WWN. Kenny was inspired by your spinoff of Six Degrees of Kevin Bacon."

"In what way?" McGill asked. "You mean, how most people would need only —"

"Four degrees of knowing someone who has gotten shot. He thought that was a brilliant idea for making people realize just how bad gun violence is in our country. So he and some friends from school who are good at math, computers and animation created an app for mobile phones."

McGill was stunned. "They're calling it what, four degrees of getting shot?"

"Exactly. One of the friends' mom is an attorney. She filed for a copyright on the name."

"Oh, God. Tell me, please, Carolyn, that nobody's trying to make money off this."

"Actually, yes, they are, but not for themselves. Every penny will go to either aid gunshot victims and their families or to help groups advocating for more responsible gun ownership."

McGill felt his heart swell with paternal pride. God bless Kenny and his friends.

"Well, then, let's hope they bring in some big money."

"They're already starting to. That's where Abbie and Caitie come in. Abbie's publicizing the app through college social media. Word is spreading fast. And Caitie —"

"Is talking to her movie friends?"

"Right again. She's gotten an overwhelming response. In fact, she's going to do a segment on Showbiz Tonight this evening."

McGill's thoughts moved beyond good feelings for his children.

"Jim, are you still there?"

"Yes. Carolyn, why didn't any of the kids call me about this?"

"They were unsure how you'd feel. I got elected. You're okay with it, aren't you?"

"More than that. I'm at a loss for words, but awe in its original sense comes to mind."

"But?" Carolyn always knew when the other shoe was about to drop.

"But they are all raising their public profiles. They'll need extra security. For a while anyway."

"Damn, I hadn't thought of that."

"You and Lars, too, just to be safe."

"Goddamnit, none of that is right."

"No, it isn't."

"But you'll arrange it?"

"I will. Tell the kids I love them and I think they're great. You and Lars, too."

"I will, and thanks for the compliment. Give our love to Patti."

McGill clicked off. They'd arrived at Dikki's P Street building. The others were waiting for him to exit the Chevy. Before McGill could do that, he had another call.

Ellie Booker.

She said, "Hugh Collier changed his mind. WWN is going to start broadcasting gun deaths on the evening national news, daily."

McGill replied by telling Ellie about the four degrees of getting shot.

The discussion about guns, at least, was about to change.

### Four Seasons Hotel — Washington, DC

Maxi took a look around the hotel lobby, turned to look up at Putnam and asked, "Are you and Margaret rich?"

Maxi's bookbag was slung over Putnam's shoulder. He'd put it there when he'd picked her up from school. He could have left it in his car; he trusted that the hotel staff wouldn't filch it, but he liked carrying it, the weight of it. An anchor that held him fast to being a dad.

He sometimes still had trouble believing he'd become one, a father.

Both Margaret and Maxi gave him a sense of fulfillment he'd never known.

The old Putnam wouldn't recognize the new model.

He told Maxi, "Rich is a word that keeps changing."

Putnam pressed the button to call an elevator car.

"What do you mean?"

"Well, a hundred years ago a hundred dollars was big money."

"That's still big money to me," Maxi said.

"You're right, and that's a good point. What was big money a long time ago is still big money to some people, but it's not so big to other people."

"Because if you have a lot of money one little bit isn't so much, but if the little bit is all you have, then it's important."

Putnam beamed. "I couldn't have put it better myself."

The elevator came and they stepped inside. Maxi looked back out at the lobby.

"You and Margaret have more than a little bit," she said.

"Yes, we do, but not nearly as much as some people, and there's one more thing for you to remember."

"What?"

"Whatever Margaret and I have is yours, too. Not all of it and not right away, but maybe by the time you have your own children or even grandchildren, then it will be all yours."

"If you mean when you and Margaret die, I want you to live forever."

"The way you and Margaret make me feel, I think that's a fine idea."

The two of them got off the elevator and saw the door to one of the hotel's Capital Suites was open and Jerry Nerón was waiting to greet them. Putnam anyway. He looked surprised to see Maxi.

He recovered nicely, bending from the waist and extending his hand to Maxi.

She looked at Putnam and receiving a nod took Jerry's hand. "I'm Maxi Shady," she said.

"And I am Jeronimo Nerón, but my friends call me Jerry."

Maxi grinned and told him, "I like Jeronimo."

She trilled the "r" in his first name.

"And you never need call me anything else." He gave Putnam a wink and and extended an arm to Maxi. The little girl took his arm without checking for approval. Putnam followed them inside and closed the door behind him.

Jerry was far from feeling courtly earlier that day. He'd caught the news report on TV that Abel Mays had died of a heart attack before he'd shot the *cabrón*. That made Jerry an *imbécil*. Mays hadn't pulled to the curb behind his car to take a nap after the strain of his murderous labors. He'd probably felt chest pains and thought it best for his own safety to stop driving.

He'd managed that and then he died.

No wonder he hadn't so much as looked up when Jerry had opened the door to his SUV. And Jerry hadn't noticed his intended victim had already stopped breathing. Some assassin he was. It was a damn good thing he was retiring. Well, had only one target left at any rate.

Jerry's Google Alert on Auric Ludwig advised him that the man was being interviewed on a talk radio show. He seethed when he heard that sonofabitch had raised the bounty on him to $2 million. This was intolerable. There was a handful of men in Little Havana who knew he'd killed Galtero Blanco, and some of them had hinted to him from time to time that they suspected Jerry of using the lethal skills he'd been taught to dispose of other objectionable *pendejos*.

Jerry had always laughed off such suggestions.

But $2 million was a lot of money and some of the old ones only just got by.

Their loyalty to him might be overcome by greed.

They had no way of knowing for sure that he'd killed either

Abel Mays or Jordan Gilford, but some of them did know he'd been in Washington when Mays was killed. His name might be suggested to Ludwig purely as a matter of chance, like buying a lottery ticket. In this case, they wouldn't even have to pay a dollar for an opportunity to win.

Jerry was getting very anxious, an unfamiliar and unwelcome feeling.

He had to move quickly. When Jerry met with a tailoring client, he offered him the choice of having his measurements taken either at a place of the client's choosing, the client's office or home, or at the hotel suite where Jerry was staying. Now, Jerry had to get together with Ludwig, just the two of them, ideally at Ludwig's office, with the man's home or Jerry's suite as fallback locations.

If Jerry could manage that, and he'd damn well better, he would slit Ludwig's throat as he'd done with Galtero Blanco. If he had the luck to visit Ludwig's office or home, he'd leave the body there. If he had to kill the man in his hotel suite, he'd have to be careful to leave no blood behind and find a way to move the body elsewhere.

As to how he could arrange the meeting in the first place, Ludwig's own troubles provided that opening. The man was in deep trouble with the police; his arrest had been shown on television. Jerry would call him at his office. Say friends of Ludwig's who chose to remain anonymous had hired him to make new suits for Ludwig's court appearances. All expenses had been paid for.

Jerry felt optimistic that playing on the man's vanity in a time of need would work.

If not, he'd have to do something desperate. Just what, he didn't yet know.

In the meantime, he needed to complete his cover obligation, the reason he would give for returning to Washington, should anyone ask.

Asking was just what Putnam Shady did.

"So what was the reason you wanted to look at my new suit?"

Putnam was wearing the first of three suits he'd ordered from Jerry.

Maxi was sipping on a ginger ale Jerry had provided and doing homework on her iPad at the suite's wet bar.

"I was working in my shop after delivering your suit," Jerry said, "and my vision got blurry. I couldn't even clearly read a trade publication. I thought I might be ill or at least that my eyesight might be changing. I went to my doctor, and asked whether I should go to an ophthalmologist. My doctor said I was simply working too hard, get a good night's rest, take a day off and make sure I had adequate lighting in my workspace."

Putnam nodded, following along with the story.

Jerry shrugged. "I did as I was told. My vision cleared and I resolved to ease up on my workload."

"You check your lighting, too?" Putnam asked.

"Yes, of course. I was greatly relieved, but one thing bothered me. Did I make your suit properly? Were my measurements, cutting and sewing all as precise as I demand of myself?"

"You might have called. I love this new suit."

Jerry placed a hand on his chest. "You warm my heart. I feel better already. And it does look good on you. You have become very fit and the suit compliments that."

Putnam knew he was being flattered. Still, he felt he'd earned it.

"What I'd like to see," Jerry continued, "is whether the stitching is up to my standards. Examining the coat will be enough, if you would be so kind."

Putnam obliged, after removing his cell phone.

Jerry took the garment to a window. The sun had finally broken through the overcast and provided more than adequate light. As the tailor studied his work, Putnam observed him. For all his moral reclamation, Putnam was still the son of two con artists.

He also continued to work in the politics of Washington.

He knew when someone was trying to put one over on him. He also knew not to let on when he caught wise to someone else's play. He didn't know what Jerry's game was, but he was sure there was one. He didn't think it had anything to do with money. Jerry had a long list of prominent clients and his suits were not cheap.

The tailor had to have another reason to come back to DC and —

Jerry stepped away from the window and held the suit coat out to Putnam, slipping it on his client with practiced ease.

"I'm happy to say my work is exquisite as always," Jerry said. "I apologize for taking up your time, but I am so happy to have met Maxi."

Hearing her name, Maxi slid off the barstool with her iPad.

"Are we going?" she asked Putnam.

He looked at Jerry. "We're done?"

"Yes, thank you."

The two men exchanged a handshake.

Maxi shook Jerry's hand, too. "Thank you for the ginger ale."

"My pleasure. If you ever come to Miami with Mr. Shady, I will have to take you both to lunch."

"And Margaret, too?"

"Yes, of course, anyone you like."

Jerry ushered them out of the suite and said goodbye at the elevator bank.

After the doors closed, Maxi said, "I like Jeronimo. He was nice."

"Yes, he was."

Polite to a fault, Putnam thought. Everything the tailor had told him had been plausible. Or at least beyond disproof. Nevertheless, Putnam was absolutely certain he'd just been used.

Now, he just had to figure out for what purpose.

In the suite adjacent to Jerry Nerón's, Arturo Gonzales, the pilot who had flown Jerry to Washington and would take him home, lounged on a sofa with a drink in hand. The weather outside was too cold for him and the sun, after it finally appeared, was too pale, a poor substitute for the warmth and brightness it radiated in Miami.

A Spanish-language edition of People Magazine lay on Arturo's lap. His attention, though, was on the radio broadcast coming from the suite's audio system. As with many Cuban-Americans of his generation, Arturo's political views were staunchly conservative. He liked listening to right-wing talk radio. These were his kind of people.

The ones who would free his homeland someday.

By the grace of God while he was still alive.

Today, clips of an interview with Auric Ludwig were being replayed constantly. Ludwig was offering $2 million to anyone who could tell him the name of the man who shot Abel Mays. The first time Arturo had heard the offer he'd smiled and thought to himself, "I know someone who could have done it."

Arturo could still remember helping to carry off the staggering dead weight of Galtero Blanco. *Bastardo gordo.*

Given the frequent repetition of the reward offer, Arturo came to wonder, "Did Jerry kill this Abel Mays?" There had been whispers on Calle Ocho that Blanco had been only the first man Jerry Nerón had killed. Following Blanco, there had been many others.

Of course, that was the kind of thing it was best not to examine too closely.

At least, Arturo had never done so — before now.

He looked closely at the furnishings of his suite. Whatever the defects of Washington's climate, this hotel was far nicer than his humble home. He was a man who flew a Gulfstream jet but not a man who owned one. Arturo began to think it would be nice to have more money in his remaining years. Two million dollars would make life so much sweeter.

If Jerry really was the man Auric Ludwig wanted.

Well, that would be for Ludwig to determine, wouldn't it?

What Arturo needed to figure out was how to make an anonymous tip and still get paid.

The answer came quickly. He called the radio station with his suggestion.

# CHAPTER 26

## *Rayburn House Office Building — Washington, DC*

Representative Philip Brock sat in his office, alone with his thoughts. He'd left instructions with his chief of staff he was not to be disturbed — with one exception. If a call came in from Columbus, Ohio, it was to be put through immediately.

While waiting for that hoped for message, he reviewed his meeting with Auric Ludwig and two-thirds of the State of Alaska's Congressional delegation: Senator Tom Hale and Representative Lorna Dalton. It was a rare thing for a sitting Senator to visit a House office building. Something akin to a college student deigning to return to his old high school.

But the two Republicans from Alaska were hopping mad at the president and eager to plot some sort of reprisal. Even at the cost of meeting with a Democrat, albeit a maverick member of the opposition party. The big draw, of course, was Auric Ludwig. Besides getting even with the president and Galia Mindel, Hale and Dalton had to make clear to him that they were not part of this wicked plan the administration had hatched.

Working the other half of the equation, Brock had persuaded Ludwig that if the House members from Virginia with whom he usually worked were proving faint-hearted, he could do worse than to team up with two tough pols from The Last Frontier. Ludwig had liked that characterization, as Brock knew he would.

As neatly as Brock had schemed, though, Hale and Dalton were still suspicious of meeting in a Democrat's office, even if he was a DINO. Democrat in name only. They entertained a natural suspicion that Brock might be working for Galia Mindel, having hatched some underhanded deal with the White House.

Brock had smiled when Hale had gone so far as to voice that possibility.

"Senator, I'm just trying to be helpful here on an otherwise slow day for me. If you think I'm up to no good, Representative Dalton's office is just over in the Cannon Building. If you'd care to stretch your legs a bit more, you can walk over to your office on the Senate side of the Capitol."

That suggestion, of course, pitted one Alaskan against the other as to who might host the meeting. Brock tossed in another consideration. "If it's just the three of you, though, you'll have no one to play the devil's advocate. No one to test the soundness of any plan you might devise."

That was when Ludwig decided the matter. "Let's do it right here, right now."

Whether the gun lobbyist acted out of gratitude to the man who brought him in from the cold or he just didn't want to go for a walk, Brock didn't know. He was glad, though, that he'd have an opening to sow some mischief. If he couldn't mess with these fools' heads, he could hardly think of himself as an anarchist.

Hale and Dalton looked at each other and came to the silent agreement they wouldn't buck Ludwig's choice but would remain wary of any trickery on Brock's part.

Having both seniority and a seat in the upper house of Congress, Senator Hale was the first to address Ludwig, "Auric, I want you to know that Lorna and I had no idea of what the president had in mind for our new prison, turning it into a depository for the nation's scum."

"Can you fight her at least on where the damn thing will be built?" Ludwig asked. "Get it put down on your panhandle near

Juneau where it isn't quite so damn cold all the time?"

The two pols from Alaska looked at each other.

Dalton picked up the baton. "The thing about that is, the federal government is the biggest land owner in the state: 222 million acres."

Pride wouldn't allow Hale to restrain himself from putting that figure into context. "That's an area larger than the entire state of Texas." Seeing Ludwig's sour expression, the senator added, "Just saying."

"With the prison being federally funded, constructed and operated, and the government owning all that land, the Bureau of Prisons could site the new facility north of the Arctic Circle, if the president told them to," Dalton explained.

"That's what has Lorna and me so upset," Hale said. "We let this happen, the rest of the country will start thinking of Alaska as Siberia."

Brock grinned. "Well, that might have a chilling effect on street crime."

Ludwig swiveled his head Brock's way. "You think this is funny?"

"Hey, I'm a law-and-order Democrat. When it comes to criminals, you could flash-freeze the fuckers and it'd be okay by me."

Put that way, no one in the room could argue with Brock. Nonetheless, Ludwig was only too aware that sales to criminals represented a not insubstantial market share for firearms in the United States. If anyone ever figured out a way to get a significant number of bad guys either off the street or to voluntarily disarm, it would affect his clients' bottom lines negatively.

And the threat of locking up drug cartel members, gang-bangers and assorted mafiosi for years north of the goddamn Arctic Circle might be just the thing to turn the trick.

Brock wasn't done having his fun.

"Here's the problem, Senator and Congresswoman. You two set yourselves up for this with your request for a new prison in your state. And you, Senator, even provided the rationale for what the president did: Alaska will take in other states' surplus prison population. Well, you'll be getting that in spades."

"I didn't mean it like that," Hale said with a growl. "I thought we'd lock up our own felons mostly and take some extra from the lower forty-eight."

"But that wasn't the way you wrote your amendment to the Farm Bill. Specificity is usually a good idea when you ask for something."

Now, all three of Brock's guests looked like they were ready to leave.

So he roped them back in.

"There is one way to address the problem. Not that you could ask to return your federal funding. That would be too terrible a precedent for any legislator to set. So what you have to do is take a page from our liberal friends' book."

From appearances, it was clear that Ludwig, Hale and Dalton didn't have any liberal friends. They had no idea of what he meant. So Brock told them.

"As you may have heard, there are those progressive souls in Congress who would like to see convicted felons have their voting rights restored. Some left-leaning states have already done as much. So if that right can be restored —"

Ludwig saw where Brock was going. "Why not restore the right to bear arms, too? That's brilliant. Say some knucklehead goes a year without committing another crime. Bang. He can buy, own and carry a gun again."

Brock said, "You might want to make the waiting period two or three years — and not use bang as an interjection."

Ludwig brushed Brock's suggestion aside with a wave of a hand.

"That's just quibbling about details and vocabulary; it's the idea that's magnificent."

Senator Hale and Congresswoman Dalton seemed less taken by it.

Gun were certainly important to them, but they weren't the only thing. If they backed a restoration of gun rights, they'd be hard put to oppose doing the same for voting rights. Adding former prison inmates to the rolls of voters would not be good for the GOP. The way demographics were already going in the country, the Republican idea was to limit the diversity of the voting public. Pretending the issue was really a way to block voter fraud.

Then there was the Republicans' tough-on-crime image. That would take a really big hit if the party came out for giving ex-jailbirds their guns back. Especially if the rate of violent crimes soared as a result. But looking at Ludwig, they saw him smile like a junkie who'd just had the best fix of his life.

So now the question became: How could they appease Fire-Power America without politically slitting their wrists in the process?

Hale and Dalton turned to Brock with the same thought in mind: You fucker.

Brock kept a straight face and ushered his guests out of his office. Where they'd go to try to resolve the conundrum he'd handed them he didn't care. He had a bigger game to play.

Hours later, the congressman was just about to leave the Rayburn Building when the call he'd been waiting for all day finally came. The speaker of the Pennsylvania House of Representatives, having gone to Columbus, Ohio to confer with his legislative colleagues there, had news.

"We've counted the votes three times over. We've got more than enough. Ohio will vote later tonight to petition Congress to convene a second Constitutional Convention, and it will be held in Philadelphia. We got everything we wanted."

"Call me again after the vote has been taken," Brock said. "Then we'll celebrate."

"I'll do just that. I'll come to Washington and you can buy the drinks."

Brock said nothing would please him more.

He might have felt less self-satisfied had he known Father Inigo de Loyola had landed in San José.

## McLean Gardens — Washington, DC

Byron DeWitt woke up in his apartment and saw it was four o'clock. The volume of light in the sky informed him it was late afternoon not early morning. For a moment, that only confused him. He couldn't remember the last time he slept the better part of the day away. Maybe it had been when he was eight and had been burning up with scarlet fever.

He'd been treated with antibiotics, but across the distance of years all he remembered was an impressionistic haze of heat and fatigue, as if he was being roasted from inside but couldn't muster the energy to care. Even after the fever broke, his torpor remained and his mind was fuzzy for days.

He felt almost as lethargic now, but he was far more disciplined as an adult and he had awakened with an idea he wanted to pursue. He picked up his bedside phone and called Abra Benjamin's mobile number. She answered before the second ring.

"How are you?" she asked.

The note of intimacy in her voice surprised him.

Almost made him long for the days when they'd been lovers.

But having conceived a child and given him up for adoption was caution enough not to go down that road again. Even after hearing what sounded like real concern in Benjamin's voice.

"I'm fine," he said. "Just burning the candle at both ends too long. Had to crash eventually and I did. I'll be fine."

Benjamin said, "Galia Mindel called me, had me bring Congressman Wesley Tilden in for questioning."

That perked up DeWitt. "How did he take it?"

"He wept. Then he clammed up. I really shouldn't say more on a cell phone."

"Cripes. How soon can you get on a secure line?"

"Two seconds."

So she was at work.

"Fine. Call me back."

His phone rang almost immediately.

Benjamin was all business now. All calls made from FBI headquarters were recorded. And not just for quality control. She told DeWitt that the decision was made not to arrest Tilden as he'd declined to self-incriminate. But all of the congressman's phones were now tapped, he was being watched and if he developed a sudden yen to travel abroad he'd be detained on grounds yet to be decided.

DeWitt said, "Well, if Tilden is going to play against type and try to tough it out, maybe we should take care that Congressman Rutledge doesn't go the other way."

Benjamin said, "You think a True South Texan might commit suicide?"

"Only after he takes a couple dozen other people off the stage first."

Adding the thought of murder to suicide made for a far more plausible scenario.

"You're right. I should have thought of that. I'll alert the detail watching Rutledge."

"You might want to double the number of agents, too."

"Okay. You're authorizing that?"

"Yes."

"Anything else?"

"Yes, do you know if the Navy has ships on all the world's oceans?"

"I'd think so. I remember reading somewhere they have almost three hundred ships on active duty. Shouldn't that be enough to do it?"

"Seems like it. Get in touch with the National Reconnaissance Office."

The NRO designed, built, launched, operated and maintained the country's spy satellites.

"Mr. Deputy Director," Benjamin said in a tone she formerly used to call him Byron.

"Yes?"

"I think you've been anticipated."

"I have?"

"Chief of Staff Mindel has already tasked the NRO with finding any yacht on which Tyler Busby might be hiding."

"Oh." DeWitt tried not to sound too disappointed. The world did move forward while people slept. Even him. He asked, "What search criteria are being used?"

"Size and price."

A glimmer of joy burned off some of DeWitt's mental fog.

He still had something to contribute.

"I think I might be able to narrow the parameters a bit."

"How's that?"

"See who insured Busby's phony paintings at Inspiration Hall. Not just the company but the CEO, owner or grand high poobah. See if that esteemed individual just happens to own some vast ocean-going vessel that he might have lent to a friend in need."

"Damn, that's good," Benjamin said.

She was truly impressed or she wouldn't have let even a mild profanity be recorded.

It was, of course, a variation on Putnam Shady's idea, DeWitt clearly remembered. One that he should have gotten around to checking on sooner, if he hadn't been run so ragged. If it turned out to be worth anything, he'd give credit where it was due.

If it was a dud, he'd take responsibility.

"I'll get right on it," Benjamin said. "Oh, one more thing. That hair Captain Yates found in the suspect's car for the Jordan Gilford killing?"

"You pinned somebody?"

"Not directly, but we came up with a family member. A guy named Dario Nerón. Age eighty-eight. Lives in Miami, just barely. He was supposed to take part in the 1961 invasion of the Bay of Pigs, but he got the sniffles or something and stayed in Florida. The link turned up in the CIA's database."

"Nobody did DNA samples back in '61," DeWitt said.

"You're right. They just did blood-typing and issued dog-tags. But as a gesture to the exile community, the Company kept updating the means of identifying any potential fallen heroes. To let the Miami Cubans know their cause hadn't been forgotten. It was an honorary thing. Anyway, Dario Nerón took advantage. He's in hospice care at the moment, but we're looking at his off-spring, legitimate or otherwise."

"Let me know if you find anything."

"ASAP?"

"When I wake up tomorrow morning. No earlier than seven a.m."

"As you wish."

A perfectly proper response, but also a direct steal from *The Princess Bride*.

A way they and a million other couples had once said, "I love you."

What was the woman doing to him, DeWitt wondered.

He hung up his phone, lay back down and drifted off to sleep.

Telling himself he was not going to dream of Benjamin.

### *McGill's Hideaway — The White House*

McGill and Patti sat hip to hip on his leather sofa. Flames danced in the fireplace, but the First Couple's attention was focused on McGill's iPad. Ellie Booker had called to say WWN would be debuting its National Gun Death Counter feature. The broadcast began with a cold opening: no title credits or voice-over announcer.

Just a shot of a blue sky as "Taps" began to play softly.

A sans serif graphic message appeared: Number of Americans Killed by Gunfire Since January 1, 2014. Beneath that message a number appeared: 2,588.

That message faded out to be replaced by: Some of the People We Lost Today.

A horizontal row of eight faces appeared. Men, women and two children.

Their names, ages and hometowns appeared beneath the photos.

As the last note of "Taps" sounded, WWN moved on to its usual opening graphics and musical theme. The lead anchor and managing editor of the broadcast, Ethan Judd, explained the unusual opening.

"What you've just seen is the only part of tonight's broadcast that I was asked to include by the network. My contract with WWN gives me complete control over this broadcast's editorial content. That's not to say people on our staff don't offer suggestions as to what stories we cover and in what depth. They do, frequently at the tops of their voices. But the final decision is mine.

"For the first time since I began working at WWN, this company's CEO, Hugh Collier, came to me with news he thought we should be covering: just how many people are killed in this country every single day by gunfire. Hugh candidly told me this wasn't his idea. He originally opposed it ... and then he got shot. Funny how something like that can change your mind.

"Hugh told me he got the idea from senior contributing producer Ellie Booker. She told me she got it from James J. McGill. Mr. McGill authored a bit of wisdom that is becoming nationally known. He said, 'If a situation stinks and you want to change it, you can't let people to hold their noses.' Brother, does he have that right.

"So from now on, this broadcast will open, close or put smack dab in the middle the number of Americans who have been killed by gunfire. Placement will depend on what other stories each day brings us. Too many of our people find themselves caught in the midst of a raging uncivil war. The victims are young, old, male, female and come in every color God has devised for us. Chances are we will never achieve a complete ceasefire, but we must all work toward the day when a death by gunshot is considered shocking rather than routine.

"And now in other news ..."

McGill and Patti looked at each other.

"I didn't realize what kind of punch that would pack," McGill said.

"It was more than the just the numbers. It was the faces and the music. The sense of horrible waste and irretrievable loss." Patti dabbed at her eyes.

McGill gave her his handkerchief.

"It will be hard for other news organizations to either ignore that feature or top it."

"Let's see how it's rolling out in social media," McGill said.

The father of three tech savvy kids, he'd been instructed in the rudiments of Twitter.

WWN Gun Deaths was already number one in trending topics.

McGill and Patti had sandwiches and soft drinks brought in while they watched the Didi DiMarco Show on MSNBC. Didi's take on the national gun death story didn't use music or have the stark simplicity of WWN's coverage, but it was far more comprehensive, featuring maps, charts and interviews with cops, judges and local pols from around the country.

She wrapped up her show with a two-minute memorial to a woman who had been shot and killed that morning sitting at a bus stop in Topeka, Kansas waiting to go to work. It would have been her first day on a new job, after being unemployed for three months. She left a husband and two children. She sang in her church choir and had donated twenty-eight pints of blood at her local blood bank.

The driver of the bus that would have picked up the woman told police that she'd been shot for no apparent reason by a man driving a car in the oncoming lane. The bus driver was able to give the police a license plate number and a description of the shooter. The police were hopeful they'd be able to make an arrest.

"None of which will do the victim or her family one bit of good," Didi said in conclusion. "And if James J. McGill happens to be watching, I'd like to invite him to come on the show and talk about the horrendous state of gun violence in our country."

McGill powered down his iPad.

He and Patti turned their gaze to the dying blaze in the fireplace, lost in thoughts of sympathy for a woman in Kansas they'd never met. Realizing that the tragedy afflicting her family was repeated in huge numbers every single day in the United States. Knowing they had to do whatever they could to end the scourge of gun homicides.

"Are you going to accept Ms. DiMarco's invitation?" Patti asked.

"I think so. Assuming we get Jordan Gilford's killer sometime soon."

Each of them had a surplus of prior obligations.

Patti nodded. "I'll be speaking at a District public school tomorrow."

"Good. It's important for you to see as many people as possible."

"Comforter in chief, that's me. But I've got to back my words with action."

McGill said, "Speaking of which, I talked to Elspeth about bumping up Abbie's security and to the Evanston PD about doing the same for Kenny and Caitie. You know, after Kenny raised their profiles with his new smart-phone app."

Patti squeezed McGill's hand. "Good. I am so proud of our kids."

By unanimous consent of McGill, Carolyn, Abbie, Kenny and Caitie, both Patti and Lars Enquist were accorded the honor of thinking of themselves as full parents of the McGill children.

Moving on to other matters, Patti told McGill about Congressman Tilden's refusal to talk with the FBI and DeWitt's speculation that Congressman Rutledge might go off the deep end in a homicidal/suicidal fashion.

"Never been one of those among Washington pols, has there?"

"No, and now is definitely not the time to start."

McGill thought the shock value on Capitol Hill might be salutary.

But a price paid with any bloodshed would be too high.

"No, it's not," he said.

"Deputy Director DeWitt came up with a good idea playing off of Galia's good idea for finding Tyler Busby," Patti said. She explained in detail.

"Can even the National Reconnaissance Office find one particular yacht out on the ocean? Doesn't that fly in the face of 'O, God, thy sea is so great and my boat is so small?'"

"I believe that line was written before the launch of spy satellites. The NRO reply is: 'Eyes and ears where no human can reach.'"

"Lacks the poetry of my reference," McGill said, "but it's probably right on the money. Come to that, I wish I'd had the idea linking Busby to his insurance company. That just might pan out."

Patti massaged the back of McGill's neck. "Don't be too hard on yourself; even the original Holmes had Watson to help him out."

"Speaking of which, on the ride home tonight, I got a call from Paris."

"Gabi or Yves?" Patti asked.

"Both. The two of the them and Odo Sacripant have found office space over there. They've all but completed the necessary paperwork to operate a private investigations agency accredited to work throughout the European Union."

"Okay, I heard the 'all but.' What's the hang-up? Something I can help with?"

"No, they're fine politically and financially. Yves' father, Augustin, has provided the seed money. What Gabi and Yves want to know is whether I'll lend my name to their endeavor: McGill Investigations de Paris."

Patti smiled at him. "What did you say?"

"What any good husband would say: I have to talk with my wife first."

Patti laughed. Then she saw McGill, beneath the jest, was serious.

"You're concerned how they'll conduct their business might reflect on both of us?"

"You more than me. Everyone knows I'm a troublemaker."

"Sure, but most people love you anyway. If we were talking about someone you knew only slightly, someone looking to capitalize off your good name, I'd say no. But even though I wasn't with you, I still dream about the story you told me of the fight beneath the Pont d'Iéna. Gabi, Yves and Odo were there. They risked their skins right along with you. I trust them completely. I have no objection to the idea."

"Sort of fits with your notion about my moving up to management when we leave the White House, too, doesn't it?"

"Serendipity. You told me Special Agent Ky would like to take over your office here in Washington. Maybe you could open a few more and become the twenty-first century equivalent of Allan Pinkerton."

McGill said, "Never saw myself as a business mogul, but what the heck? I'll email Gabi and give her the go-ahead."

"Good. There's one more thing you should know."

Patti told him about the DNA family identification of the hair found by Welborn.

"That's great," McGill said, "we're getting closer to this guy."

"And the closer you get, the more I worry. Especially after recalling that night in Paris."

"That was scary," McGill admitted.

"Maybe you should ... no, never mind. You have your client to consider."

"I did promise to be careful, and bring the bad guy back alive."

"That last part is optional."

McGill glanced at his watch. "Too early to go to bed."

"Just as well. I have to polish my speech for tomorrow."

"Maybe I should put a gloss on a thing or two myself."

Patti looked as if she wanted to ask what that might be, but she didn't. Some questions were better left unasked. She'd already told McGill she was on edge about his safety. She didn't need to say anything more. She'd let it go, knowing he'd always come through the tough spots before and would again.

Please God.

"Whoever gets to bed last gives the other a nudge, okay?" Patti asked.

"Deal," McGill told her.

# CHAPTER 27

*State Capitol — Columbus, Ohio*

The Ohio Statehouse was a structure beset by problems from the start. There were arguments about its design, construction and siting. The state government in 1838 held a design competition to determine just what its seat of government should look like. Of the fifty entries that were received, three winners were chosen to design one building. This feat would be achieved by melding elements from each of the finalists. While the wrangling over how to do that proceeded, the legislation that had made Columbus the state capitol was about to expire.

Towns from around Ohio vied for the honor of becoming the new capital.

The excavation for the statehouse's foundation was filled with earth and became grazing land for livestock.

Then a cholera epidemic further delayed construction.

Eventually, though, a modest two-story Greek Revival structure with a humble dome, eight columns and two flagpoles was erected. Far from inspirational, it did manage to suggest that important matters affecting the fortunes of Ohio's residents could reasonably be decided there. Well, sometimes reason would prevail, as was all that could be expected of any government.

On the night of March 12, 2014, as the state's House of

Representatives was about to call the roll for a vote on whether to petition the United States Congress to call a Constitutional Convention, the building suffered another setback. The power went out.

This was not a citywide failure. The diameter of the blackout was one mile with the statehouse at its epicenter. The majority of House members who had intended to vote for the petition did not think the sudden descent of darkness was a matter of happenstance.

They cried, "Sabotage!"

Followed quickly by, "Candles!"

The vote might have been carried out old school, if not for the stench.

A sulfurous stink of rotten eggs filled the statehouse.

Politicians of all stripes ran for the exits, trying to repress their gag reflexes.

In the coming days, as the building was airing out, the finger of blame was pointed at White House Chief of Staff Galia Mindel. She denied the charge vigorously. The accusers persisted. But no one was ever able to prove Galia guilty.

Or anyone else for that matter.

In the end, The Big Black Stink was just another page added to the statehouse's lore.

### White House Gym

SAC Elspeth Kendry was just about to go home when she got word Holmes had left his personal quarters and gone to the gym. The man was going to do a workout now? Why? Dear God, she thought, don't let him be planning some midnight escapade.

She snagged Special Agent Deke Ky before he could go home and dragged him along to see what was happening. They found McGill holding a knife with a wicked-looking black blade. He held it in a reverse grip — tip pointed down, cutting edge out — in his right hand. His left hand rested against his chest. Ready to shield his heart, neck, abdomen or groin.

He balanced himself on the balls of his feet, giving the impression of a cat about to pounce. Instead of taking to the air, though, he glided to his left and right, forward and back, changing direction fluidly and in no particular pattern. As he stepped in one direction or another, his knife dipped and rose, like a hen pecking kernels of corn with her beak.

Someone with an untrained eye might have wondered what the point of such an exercise could be. Both Elspeth and Deke, however, had long exposure to knife-fighting cultures. They could infer the invisible opponent McGill was fighting: someone else with a knife held in a standard grip — tip pointed forward, cutting edge down — was trying to stab him in the gut or groin.

Each time the imaginary foe lunged to strike, peck-peck-peck, McGill's blade came down hard, fast and repeatedly, deflecting his foe's thrust, damaging the opponent's knife hand, probably causing him to drop his weapon. Once disarmed —

McGill stopped pecking. His knife hand flashed upward and to his left and moved through a horizontal figure-eight. Elspeth and Deke understood this maneuver, too. McGill saw his assailant go for his throat. He barricaded the attack with his knife, slashing his opponent's wrist. He turned the first loop of the figure-eight to go for the other man's throat, following through with a return loop to reverse direction and slash his adversary's abdomen.

Then McGill took a quick step back, as if to see the damage he'd wrought.

Apparently, it was sufficient to let him look over his shoulder and see his audience.

He waved them into the room.

Before entering, Elspeth told Deke, "You see anyone approach Holmes with a knife —"

"I'll shoot him."

"Damn right, you will."

Then McGill explained to Elspeth and Deke why life would not be that simple. He informed the Secret Service agents that the president would like to have Jordan Gilford's killer taken alive, if at all possible. The problem with that was doing trick shots, shooting to wound not kill, was not a standard part of Secret Service procedure.

They were all about taking out anyone who threatened their package.

That being the slang for a protected person.

McGill wasn't entirely happy with the situation either.

He said, "I know I'm making things harder for you, but we need this guy alive to help sort out some very big problems. I'm reasonably good with a knife, but there's still a probability any wound I might inflict could hit a major blood vessel and the guy could exsanguinate in a hurry."

Elspeth gave McGill a look. "What about you? You're not worried about bleeding out?"

"I'll do my best not to."

"What if the other guy brings a gun to your knife fight?" Deke asked.

"I'll have my firearm with me. You'll have yours. If Elspeth is around, she'll surely have hers. There's no question: If it's me or him who has to go, let's make it him. Still, the preferred choice would be to bring him in alive without my buying the farm. You know what? Let's say the other guy uses a blade but I fight with something that has superior reach."

McGill opened a cabinet and brought out two six-feet long bamboo poles.

He asked, "Do either of you know anything about fighting with longstaffs?"

To their chagrin, both Elspeth and Deke did; neither looked forward to sparring with McGill. Elspeth asked, "You going to keep a longstaff in your pocket?"

McGill grinned. "Maybe somebody will leave one lying around."

Being a good soldier, Deke volunteered to be McGill's first sparring partner.

But Elspeth took her turn, too.

Their techniques were grounded in classical kung-fu.

McGill's style was pure Dark Alley.

"Whatever works," being the mantra of that martial art.

### Connecticut Avenue NW — Washington, DC

Representative Philip Brock looked at the glass of Pappy Van Winkle bourbon he held in his hand. It contained less than two fingers of the sought-after elixir. The drink was his first and last of the day. A nightcap to ease him into sleep. Despite all that, he wondered if he was coming to like the damn stuff too much.

The taste pleased him so well that as a private joke he'd once partaken by means of an eye-dropper. Savoring each drop that fell onto his tongue while anticipating the next one. He'd done that just the one time, but he could see doing it again. Soon.

Wouldn't it be the most comic and karmic of jokes if Howard Hurlbert's preferred drink ultimately did him in? Would his final sip of the bourbon turn bitter in his mouth? Would he hear the ghost of the senator from Mississippi cackle as he breathed his last?

Nah, bullshit. One of the perks of being an atheist — a personal point of view he'd never shared with his voters — was that you could thumb your nose at all that superstitious crap. God, ghosts, the hereafter. He didn't believe in any of it.

Come to that, even the power of ethics shrank to the vanishing point when you didn't believe in anything greater than yourself. Eggheads might call that sociopathy. He regarded it as focused self-interest and a proper allocation of his time and resources.

Those very traits had earned him a fortune in investment banking.

Alienated his parents, too, but that was an acceptable loss.

These days, he had a hard time remembering what Mom and Dad looked like.

He finished his drink and picked up his iPad for one last glance at what the Washington Post had to report about the world's state of decay. Paired photos of Bahir Ben Kalil and his sister Hasna Kalil caught his eye. Sis was taking her brother's bones home. She urged the American authorities to give her family justice for the death of her brother.

The story went on to mention that the deceased and his sibling were fraternal twins.

To Brock's eye, though, the resemblance was even more striking than that.

If not for the gender difference, they might be considered identical. Would Bahir have shared his and Brock's secret plan to assassinate the president at Inspiration Hall with Sis? Sure, he would, especially if she used her respectable job, a do-gooder doctor, as a cover the way Bahir had done with his. Just looking at the likenesses of the two of them, he couldn't imagine the one of them keeping any secrets from the other.

Hell, the woman might have been the one to recruit Bahir to the jihadi cause.

So the question of the moment was: Did she have the assets in the U.S. to get to Brock? Maybe, maybe not. If she did, she'd at least want to ask him what he knew about her brother's death, and Brock would bet she could be a very persuasive interrogator.

If she didn't have any local muscle available, she could still be a threat. All she'd have to do to cast suspicion on him would be to drop his name to the FBI. If the feebs were on the ball, they'd see that Bahir had disappeared the same night Senator Howard Hurlbert had been killed. Shit. Any number of people at The Constellation Club could put Brock together with Hurlbert in the days before his death.

As another worry, he'd already considered the possibility that Tyler Busby might try to use him for leverage in a plea deal. Then there had been that suspicious visit by Putnam Shady to his office. Brock still didn't know what the hell that had really been all about.

But he was sure it didn't bode well for him.

So an evening that started out mellow and lazy was veering into near panic.

And then his phone rang.

His friend, the speaker of the Pennsylvania House of Representatives, had news for him, but far from what he'd wanted to hear. "The goddam power at the Ohio statehouse went out before the roll could be called on the big vote, and the place filled up with a stink like the devil's asshole, and it'll be days before we can get back on track."

Brock hung up without saying a word.

He filled his glass with bourbon and gulped it.

Then he started packing for a quick and possibly permanent return to Costa Rica.

### *Federal Correctional Institution — Danbury, Connecticut*

Prison was rarely a quiet place, even after the lights dimmed just enough that the inmates didn't have to squeeze their eyelids shut to get some sleep. People could adjust to almost anything, and once a prisoner acclimated to the fact that she wouldn't be sleeping in anything near total darkness, it was possible to get some rest. Snoring from any number of inmates attested to that. But not even those who'd been locked up for decades slept deeply.

You had to watch your ass even when your eyes were closed.

In the interest of not making any unnecessary enemies, among either the general population or the correctional staff, it was a good idea not to raise a ruckus during the night. Ticking people off for any breach of manners could be cause for retaliation. Usually when it was least expected.

So when Erna Godfrey spoke to her new cellmate, Joan Renshaw, shortly before midnight, she spoke softly. "They tell you who I am?"

Joan had been pretending to sleep. She opened her eyes. Looked at Erna.

She was relieved to see the woman didn't have a weapon in hand.

That hadn't always been the case.

Her first jail experience had been at the federal corrections center in downtown Chicago. They'd taken her there after she'd admitted her involvement in the thwarted attempt on Patricia

Grant's life at Inspiration Hall. Every morning she'd awakened since then and seen she was still incarcerated, she'd cursed herself for her stupidity.

Admitting that she'd been in on the plot to kill Patti Goddamn Grant.

Just so she could get a rise out of the woman. Hurt her feelings.

Yeah, shit. She'd shown Patti Grant, and got her own ass locked up. Probably for life.

Not that her life might be all that long. One morning, soon after she'd been locked up in Chicago, she'd awakened to find her cellmate staring at her and holding a toothbrush with a handle that had been carved to a needle-sharp point. For one heart-stopping moment, Joan thought the woman meant to murder her. Seeing and enjoying Joan's fear, the woman had just laughed and used the pointed handle to extract particles of food from between her teeth.

The other woman did have a clean if maniacal smile.

Joan had tried to recant her confession. Said it was just a mean joke. Nobody was buying that story. The public defender who'd represented her in court on that effort told her privately he'd been stuck with the assignment; his boss had given him no choice. Didn't matter. The judge had denied her motion to recant without comment. O.J.'s lawyers couldn't have sprung her.

So she rotted away behind bars, hadn't even gotten to trial yet.

She needed a new public defender because the old one had quit his job. That and all her assets had been seized as funds meant to further a terrorist conspiracy. She had no money to hire her own advocate. Nobody on a public payroll wanted to take the job either. Who the hell would risk his reputation defending a woman accused of working with foreign terrorists to kill the president of the United States? Sure, she had wanted to see Patti Grant dead, but when she'd heard the terrorists had intended to use a truck-bomb to do the job, that had made even her cringe.

The real surprise, something she never would have anticipated, was the reaction she'd gotten from the other prisoners. Many, if not all, had called her a fucking traitor. As if before committing their own crimes they'd all been Daughters of the American Revolution.

Actually, there had been two women who'd said they had voted for Patti Goddamn Grant — and had threatened to kill Joan. She had to be put in protective custody until those bitches could be transferred to another facility. Now, she was the one who'd been sent to a new lockup.

And she had some old broad staring at her in the middle of the night.

Joan told her, "No, nobody told me anything about you."

"Well, here's the first thing you ought to know," Erna said. "I'm here for life. I murdered a man. Blew him to bits, and that's no exaggeration."

Joan saw nothing but truth in the woman's eyes.

She scuttled back on her upper bunk until she hit the wall.

Wishing she had a sharpened toothbrush or some other weapon.

Erna said, "It's all right. I put all that behind me."

Joan didn't feel one bit relieved.

Erna sat on the lower bunk, her back against the wall, too. Her feet dangled over the edge of the narrow mattress. She said, "I've done my best to repent and help other poor women. I've started a ministry. They even let me do podcasts so I can reach out to inmates in other facilities. Just women so far, but I'm hoping they'll let me minister to men, too, before long."

Erna saw Joan lean over her bunk and take a quick peek.

"Really?" she asked, retreating out of sight.

"Yes. I have the background. I graduated Bible school."

That brought a return appearance and Joan asked, "How'd that happen? One or the other. They don't teach homicide in Bible school, do they?"

Erna laughed, and for a brief moment Joan relaxed.

"No, they don't. They make you memorize and think about Scripture. Like, 'Vengeance is mine; I will repay, saith the Lord.' That's Romans 12:19. Meaning don't get your own hands bloody. God will even out all things."

Pulling her head out of sight, Joan asked, "So what happened? You got impatient?"

A note of regret filled Erna's voice. "You hit the nail right on the head. I decided I couldn't wait any longer. Not only did I go against Scripture, I violated Caesar's law, too. Got caught and here I am."

Without putting in an appearance, Joan asked, "How do you feel about that?"

"It's what I deserve; I've come to accept that. The hardest part was losing my husband."

"So you loved him?"

"Loved him and feared every day that I failed him, too. He was part of my crime, part of my sin. From what I've heard, he died without getting right with the Lord. That's my deepest sorrow, that's he's doing time that's far worse than my sentence. With no release even by death."

A moment of silence passed.

Only the sounds of hampered respiration from other cells intruded.

"You mind if I come down and talk some more?" Joan asked.

"Don't mind a bit. Don't be afraid either. I'm not going to hurt you."

Joan slid off her bunk. Erna patted the space next to her.

"Have a seat," she said. "We'll talk as long as you want."

Joan sat on the bunk, close to Erna. She studied the older woman's face.

"You know," she told Erna, "you really are the answer to at least one of my prayers."

"You believe in God?"

"Used to be my faith came and went. Situational, you know. Like the old saw about no atheists in a foxhole. When you need God, you want him to be there for you."

"That's only natural," Erna agreed.

"Right now, though, I'm not scared but I still believe."

"You've taken a step in the right direction."

"For most of my life," Joan said, "I had a great plan, and I was really close to making it work. Then, pardon my language, everything got royally fucked. Went to hell in a handbasket, if you prefer that description."

"Maybe it wasn't what you really needed," Erna said.

"Oh, no. I'm sure it was, and it was so close. You know who ruined it for me?"

"Who?"

"Patricia Darden Grant, the president of the United States."

Joan watched closely for a reaction, but got none.

"You know the president, too, don't you?" Joan asked.

Erna remained silent.

"You do," Joan said. "Looking down at you from my bunk, I realized who you are. Your picture was in all the newspapers and magazines. You're Erna goddamn Godfrey."

"I am," she admitted.

Joan leaned in close to Erna. "Andrew Hudson Grant was the love of my life. Patti Darden stole him from me, but I had a plan to get him back. My life with him could have been fabulous. But you and Reverend Godfrey sure fucked that up, didn't you? I mean, look where I am now."

Erna had no response.

"So you're afraid your husband is in hell, huh?" Joan asked. "Well, I hope he is. I hope he's got a blowtorch up his ass, him and all the other self-righteous hypocrites. I was ecstatic when I heard he died. That left me only one thing to pray for. You know what that is?"

Erna knew exactly, but didn't say so.

She silently prayed for her deliverance.

For her soul, not her physical form.

Joan leaned in still closer and whispered in Erna's ear, "I prayed that someday I'd be able to get my hands on you."

Joan locked her hands around Erna's throat. Squeezed with all her strength.

Erna fought not at all, but produced a strangled cry as the air was forced out of her.

The microphones planted in the cell to catch Joan's confession recorded Erna's last gasp.

Correctional officers came on the run, but they were too late.

By the time they arrived, Erna's windpipe was crushed and her head rested on Joan's lap.

Joan said, "I sure hope this was Patti Grant's idea, putting me in here."

# CHAPTER 28

*McLean Gardens — Washington, DC*
*— Thursday, March 13, 2014*

D eWitt was toweling his hair dry at 6:30 that morning, feeling
hungry but otherwise better than he had for months. Nothing
like thirty hours of sleep to put the spring back into a guy's step, he
thought. For much of that time, he might as well have been coma-
tose. If there had been a fire or a gas leak in the building, he was
sure he would have slept through any din the alarms in his apartment might have made.

That disturbing thought prompted another one.

When was the last time he'd changed the batteries in the smoke
and carbon monoxide detectors? If he'd been badly neglecting his rest
— and he had — he probably wasn't current on his housekeeping
chores either. Damn, he had to talk to Director Haskins. Any
emergency that came down the pipeline could no longer be
automatically delegated to him.

He knew how much Haskins trusted him, and he'd done well
with all the tasks he'd been assigned, but he couldn't allow himself
to be worked to death. Strong as a mule and just as dumb wasn't
the epitaph he wanted on his tombstone. For that matter, he didn't
want any funeral arrangements for quite some time.

Once he got most of the water out of his hair, he brushed it back and let it air dry. He looked at himself in the bathroom mirror, pleased to see his eyes were no longer bloodshot. He gave himself a jolt of mouthwash, swished and spat. Smiled and was happy it looked like he'd been brushing his teeth regularly — but he couldn't remember the last time he'd had a dental checkup.

Maybe that was when he'd last changed the batteries in the smoke detectors.

He'd have to make a dental appointment soon. Get the rest of himself examined, too. Make sure no part of his fatigue was due to anything worse than overwork. He tugged the waistband of his running shorts out. His abdomen was still flat, but the equipment down below looked like it had atrophied from lack of use.

The remedy for that was obvious, but who would want to lend a hand?

Or other point of stimulation.

One name came to mind quickly. Jean Morrissey. The vice president of the United States, just about any time he had occasion to see her, had been directing remarks his way that he read as mildly flirtatious. Then again, maybe his imagination was getting the better of him.

Wouldn't do to make a move on the VP only to discover he'd misinterpreted.

Still, considered purely as a question of his interest in her as a woman, he'd be happy to get back in the game with Ms. Vice President.

Before he could take that notion any further, his doorbell rang.

Not the buzzer from downstairs. The bell at the door to his apartment. DeWitt stepped into his bedroom and picked up his Beretta from the nightstand. The bell rang again, more insistently. Standing well off to one side of the entry door, DeWitt said, "Who's there?"

"Who has a key?" came the reply. "Who has a key to this door, too?"

Benjamin, he thought. Showed how badly he was slipping. He'd never gotten his keys back after she'd stopped spending the night with him. He let his gun hand fall to his side and opened the door for her.

She had a bag from Au Bon Pain in hand. He could smell coffee and pastries. Saliva welled up in his mouth.

"I know I'm early," Benjamin said. "I know I was supposed to call not drop in. But I thought you might be hungry."

She kissed his cheek, stepped past him and gave him a pat on the butt.

"Nice to see you're staying in shape. We'll eat in the kitchen, okay? I'll tell you the big news."

The combination of the aroma of food, the kiss and the hand on his backside reassured DeWitt that his equipment was fine. For the moment, though, that response had to be stifled. As a symbolic gesture, he clicked the Beretta's safety on and followed Benjamin into the kitchen.

She had the cups of coffee set out on the table and had taken a cinnamon scone for herself. That left his coffee, a cinnamon roll, a cherry danish and a bear claw for him. He wanted them all, and she'd better be quick eating that scone, too.

Still, he didn't want to let Benjamin know how susceptible to temptation he was at the moment. Before he so much as sipped his coffee, though, he asked, "What's the big news?"

She reached across the table and squeezed his hand.

"You were right. Tyler Busby is connected to his insurance company."

DeWitt leaned forward, his attention diverted from Benjamin's warm hand.

"We got him?"

"No, not yet. You can put your gun down, you know."

DeWitt hadn't been aware he was still holding it. He put it on the table and pushed it off to one side.

"Here's what happened. Per your suggestion, we looked into the company that issued the insurance policy on Busby's forged paintings, Asian Global Liability, and its CEO, Donald Yang. The company has its headquarters in Hong Kong and Mr. Yang resides there."

"But Wang is wired into Beijing, isn't he?" DeWitt said.

"Hard wired, right up to the top."

"Jesus. Did their government know what was planned at Inspiration Hall, the plot to kill the president?"

"The director wants to know that, too. So will the White House when we tell them. But if you'll recall, you're the Bureau's top China guy. Everyone's waiting for your opinion."

DeWitt decided his faculties would be aided by some sugar and caffeine.

He took a large bite of his cinnamon roll and a slurp of coffee.

After swallowing, he said, "The Chinese probably did know what had been planned, but it's almost certain they had no direct involvement in either the planning or the attempted execution of the plot. They'd just want to position themselves as advantageously as possible. Maybe make a grab for the Diaoyu Islands from Japan while our country was reeling and Jean Morrissey was still getting her bearings."

DeWitt's casual use of the Vice President's name wasn't lost on Benjamin.

For his part, DeWitt thought it might be a bad mistake to develop a lech for a woman who might someday sit in the Oval Office. On the other hand, James J. McGill seemed to be happy.

Sticking to business, Benjamin asked, "Do the Chinese dislike the president enough to just sit by while she's assassinated? How would it look if it ever came out they had advance knowledge of the plot and sat on it?"

"Awful, terrible, end-of-diplomatic-and-trade-relations bad," DeWitt said. "But they must have thought there'd be no chance of that. As for their dislike of the president, I've heard whispers she intends to make a full repayment of our debt to China soon and not allow them to buy any more government bonds. That'd cut China's leverage with us big time."

Benjamin's eyes got big. Not only as to the substance of the president's plan, which was enormous, but also to the fact that

DeWitt knew about it.

Benjamin said, "Maybe that explains it."

"Explains what?"

"We didn't find Busby. But Mr. Yang took the initiative to call the director and told him where to find Busby: on Yang's yacht, the *Shining Dawn*. Damn thing's the largest privately owned motor vessel in the world, like five hundred feet long. Yang says the yacht was leased to an American interest, but he only just found out that it was a shell company. Busby put up the money for the lease and is on board. The light dawned, pardon the pun, when Busby high-jacked the yacht and cast Yang's onboard representative adrift."

It was DeWitt's turn to look stunned. "That sounds like Beijing is trying to avoid looking complicitous, all right. When and where did all this happen?"

"Yesterday, off the Philippine island of Mindanao."

"So Yang's person, the one Busby put off the yacht, he survived and got the word out?"

"She did, yeah."

DeWitt consumed more coffee and finished the cinnamon roll. "Why didn't Busby just kill the woman?"

"Maybe he'd been sleeping with her."

"What, Busby loved her just enough to ditch her but not do her in?"

"Well, we can ask him when we catch him. The NRO has satellites looking for the *Shining Dawn* within a radius of eight hundred miles of Mindanao. That's as far as it can go in a day, making it a lot easier to find than searching the whole world. Once the yacht is located, aircraft and ships from the navy's Pacific Fleet will reel Busby in."

DeWitt thought about that as he started on the cherry danish. "Don't count on getting Busby until the navy has him locked up."

"Stop being a party-pooper," Benjamin told him. "The director said you and I have to get over to the White House to brief the president. Putting the best spin on the situation is a good idea." She looked at her watch. "That's one of the reasons I came over early. To plan our presentation … and we have a little extra time if you'd care to renew acquaintances."

The temptation to do just that was there for DeWitt.

Until he remembered how things ended the last time.

So he said, "Abra, there's something else on my mind. Would you object if I recommend you for a promotion?"

Like asking a cat if it would object to taking a nap.

"What kind of promotion?"

When he told Benjamin, she was torn.

She wanted to use sex to cement the deal.

But she wanted to hear the tiniest details of DeWitt's idea even more.

Once that was done, they had to hurry to get to the White House.

### The Oval Office — The White House

The news that greeted the president and her chief of staff that morning was uplifting on one hand and the cause for despair on the other. The pope, the National Conference of Christians and Jews and the Council on American-Islamic Relations would all come out that day with firm statements calling on Congress to pass laws banning the sales of weapons of war to the general public, and saying it would be immoral of them not to do so.

The pope also said any American parish that wanted to put up a sign tallying gun deaths had his permission to do so and his blessing in their effort to save lives. Funding the erection of the signs by taking up collections of funds from the faithful was to be seen as a worthy effort.

As good as that news was, the word from Danbury, Connecticut that Joan Renshaw had killed Erna Godfrey late last night left Patricia Grant and Galia Mindel momentarily dazed. They hadn't been spared any of the details. Renshaw had strangled Erna, and made a brutally quick job of it. There had been no chance for intervention and no hope of resuscitation.

No bruises or lacerations had been found on Renshaw.

Signifying that Erna had made no effort to defend herself.

She'd simply submitted to her fate.

For her part, Renshaw had offered only two statements to the warden and correctional officers who'd raced to the cell.

"I sure hope this was Patti Grant's idea, putting me in here." And …

"I told Phil Brock not Roger Michaelson."

Then Joan Renshaw suffered what a doctor at the prison described as a psychotic break. There was a good chance she wouldn't be offering a rational explanation for what she'd done for a very long time, if ever. She'd been transferred to a secure hospital ward and placed on suicide watch.

Several minutes of silence passed before the president said, "I know I'm not being lied to, but I'm having a hard time believing that Erna Godfrey is really dead. Now. After I granted her clemency from the death penalty. After … I'd almost found it in my heart to forgive her for killing Andy."

Galia nodded. Not that she'd been thinking of the irony of the situation. She'd been unable to divorce herself from the political and practical realities of what had happened. Roger Michaelson had been exonerated, as Margaret Sweeney had hoped, and Erna Godfrey was dead, as Galia had long thought fitting for what she'd done to Andy Grant and the president.

So one of Galia's long-time nemeses, Michaelson, was redeemed.

The other, Erna, had gone on to whatever judgment awaited everyone.

And she hadn't put up a fight to save her life. Did she know, in some way, dying at that moment was her fate? The violent outcome of her own deadly actions. Had she accepted her death in the hope that if she saw Jesus again, this time he'd be more compassionate?

Maybe a divine figure would be forgiving, but Galia didn't think the president's political enemies would be. Reverend Burke Godfrey had died after he'd refused to submit to arrest and had faced off against the government. Now, Erna had died after the president had sent Joan Renshaw into the same cell with her.

Galia shuddered to think how that would be portrayed on the political right.

As if reading her chief of staff's mind, the president said, "I'll make the announcement of Erna Godfrey's death in the briefing room this morning, and explain the circumstances. Can we get Warden Timkins down here from Connecticut quickly? If the media want a detailed explanation, she can provide it. We're going to be absolutely transparent about all this."

Galia thought that was far from the best idea the president had ever had. She thought there should be an investigation, a report written and — No, that would be worse. Any delay would look like an attempt to create a coverup. It was better to make a clean breast of it.

"Yes, ma'am. I am truly sorry about all this. I never should have let it —"

"The responsibility is mine, Galia. I could have said no, but I didn't. I don't want you to think that Margaret Sweeney is at all responsible either. She acted in good faith, thinking she'd help prove her client's innocence, and it looks like that was what happened."

Galia shook her head. "I'm not so sure about that, Madam President. Even though there are people who heard Renshaw's declaration, the fact that she's suffered a mental collapse might make her words suspect. It's also possible she was just screwing with all of us. Having one last joke."

"By saying enough to make it impossible to convict either Michaelson or Brock?" the president asked.

"Wouldn't that be crazy like a fox? Especially if Renshaw escapes liability for killing Erna because she's judged to be mentally incompetent."

The president shook her head. "No, I don't think it's going to work out like that. Joan Renshaw had no previous record of violence. I don't think she could kill Erna, consciously muddy the waters on who she told about my planned trip to Inspiration Hall and then fake a psychotic break that fooled a trained physician."

Following the president's logic, Galia said, "Well, we know for sure that Erna's dead, and if we assume the mental breakdown is real too —"

"Then Joan really did tell Brock not Michaelson. Brock's involvement with a plot to kill me seems much more credible in light of Byron DeWitt's suspicions that Brock is involved in the killings of both Senator Hurlbert and Dr. Ben Kalil."

"Yes, it does."

"So when I make my statement to the media, I'll reveal that Joan's statement exonerated Michaelson without mentioning her implication of Brock."

Galia nodded. "Brock will hear the news and be waiting for the other shoe to drop. Under that kind of pressure, he might do something foolish, maybe even incriminating."

"Let's have around-the-clock surveillance on Congressman Brock. Get the FBI on that right away."

Just then the intercom buzzed and Edwina said, "Madam President, Deputy Director DeWitt and Special Agent Benjamin of the FBI are here to see you. They say they have important news."

### FirePower America — Falls Church, Virginia

The goddamn roof had fallen in on Auric Ludwig. He hadn't been able to sleep all night, and he'd turned on the sunrise network news programs. Except for SNAM and Fox, every damn one of them now had a National Gun Death Counter on their program and, of course, the damn things kept ticking off a new death every few seconds, or so it seemed to him.

If his freaking stock holdings went up half as fast, he'd be able to chuck his job and retire somewhere ... well, he didn't know just where he'd go. Somewhere warm and remote. Argentina maybe. He thought they still had a lot of open land down there. He probably had enough money right now to buy a pretty good sized rancho out on the ... what'd they call their plains down there? The pampas, that was it.

They were supposed to have great beef in Argentina, too.

He could become a rancher. Have a hacienda of a few thousand acres and run his little kingdom the way he saw fit. He'd have a posse of … what'd they call their cowboys? Gauchos, yeah. See, he was halfway there to fitting in.

All his men would be armed to the teeth, of course.

To protect his property and his cattle.

Do whatever else he told them.

From what he remembered reading about South America, quite a few Germans had immigrated there. He'd fit in on that account, too. Learn to speak passable Spanish and he'd be good. At first glance, he didn't see any holes in his plan.

What made even thinking of such plans necessary was the reaming he'd gotten from his three biggest clients last night. The top dog in the industry, Liberty, Unlimited, was fighting for its financial life against a group of Winstead School parents and their friends. LU couldn't be touched in the gun market; they controlled forty percent of it. But at heart LU was an investment bank, and the Winstead group was fucking with all the other deals they had pending.

The bastards intended to keep it up, too, unless LU sold them its gun manufacturing base.

Of course, every firearm manufacturer and retailer hated the goddamn gun death counters. That and the fucking Four Degrees of Getting Shot app that was spreading like the plague. Word was, goddamn James J. McGill's son had created it. The little prick.

Ludwig had tried to tell his clients he had a great plan to fight back.

The restoration of gun rights for felons.

The damn president wouldn't be able to send them to prison in Alaska once that legislation passed. Over the president's veto, if need be. Ludwig was sure he could get the votes to —

Get cut off in mid-sentence. His clients hated the idea.

It was one thing to give a wink and a nod to straw-purchasers for criminals, but to be seen siding with thugs was a non-starter. Thinking of lobbying for legislation to benefit lawbreakers never should have entered his mind, Ludwig was told. Had he lost his senses?

Pussies, Ludwig thought.

Now that he'd had the rug pulled out from under him, he was left to fantasize about starting a new life. That didn't help him one bit, though, with what he was going to say to the press conference he'd set up for that morning. Absent the announcement to restore gun rights to felons, he had nothing.

He got dressed and went to his office. That didn't inspire him. Just standing in front of the newsies and ripping the president would make him look weak, especially in light of all the real moves the other side was making. So what could he do except to cancel the press conference?

Only that would make him look really feeble.

He was tempted to pray for a miracle.

Only he didn't believe in either praying or miracles.

Not until his phone rang.

Danny O'Day, uber-conservative radio host, real name Fred Walters, broadcasting out of Arlington, Virginia — home of the Pentagon — was on the line. O'Day always sounded cheerful, asserting that a new day was about to dawn for right-thinking Americans. Patricia Grant had been reelected by one stinking, stolen electoral vote? Didn't matter. Great times were just ahead.

"Got some news for you, Auric, old buddy. Bet it's gonna knock your dick stiff, too."

Something that hadn't happened for a long time, Ludwig thought. Not for any reason.

"What is it, Danny?"

Ludwig wasn't in the mood for any happy horseshit, but he didn't want to tick off anyone who still sympathized with him.

"I got a real interesting call yesterday."

"You get hundreds of calls every day."

"Not like this one. The guy had some sort of Spanish accent.

Not thick like he just swam the Rio Grande. Maybe like he's been in the country a long time, got himself acclimated."

"Is this an immigration story? If it is, you've got —"

"Auric, listen to me." Danny's voice had gone hard, and then it got quiet. "This compadre thinks he might have your shooter for you. Your good guy with a gun."

Ludwig felt his heart race, but he didn't want to get his hopes too high.

"What makes you think he could be legit?"

"Well, the guy said his man was in DC at the time Abel Mays got shot. And here's the good part: The caller knows for a fact his man has already killed one bad dude for sure. The caller helped the guy dispose of the body."

"Jesus, this could be real. But why didn't you call me yesterday, after you got your call?"

"I've been working on it since then. The caller made a good point. Your reward offer didn't provide a way to collect the money anonymously. You know, like the Crime Stoppers program."

Ludwig winced. He should have thought about that. But another thought came to mind. "How do we know this guy's not full of shit, some lousy con man?"

"I asked the same question."

"What'd he say?"

"He said you can pay him after you see that he's delivered the goods."

That idea made the offer seem real, if the informant was that confident.

"Okay, that's good," Ludwig said. "Let's assume he's for real. How does he want the money, a wire transfer to a numbered offshore account?"

O'Day laughed. "That would have been my idea, too, but this guy has another way of doing it. He wants a suitcase filled with cash delivered to a boat in international waters. He wouldn't say exactly where, but it's one more thing that makes me think he's for real."

"That is good. The person making the delivery wouldn't have to know what he was dropping off. The person taking delivery wouldn't have to know either. The guy getting the cash could be watching from another boat or even an aircraft to make sure no one tries to cheat him. He could wind up with all the money and no one would ever know who he is."

"Yeah, sounds like a spy caper, doesn't it? Something the CIA might cook up. Anyway, the guy's going to call me back this afternoon. You want me to tell him you'll come across with the money if he gives you the right guy?"

"Yes. Under the terms we've just discussed, absolutely. Wait. When this guy with the accent called your station, you must have logged his phone number. Did you —"

"Yeah," O'Day said, "we checked. That's part of the reason I didn't call you yesterday. We just found out the guy called from a disposable cell phone, what they call a burner on the cop shows. I thought that was intriguing, too. This guy knows his stuff, and if he doesn't want any money until you're happy, where's the harm?"

"There isn't any that I can see … and that's almost enough to worry me."

"Well, it's up to you. I was just trying to help out," O'Day said.

"And I appreciate it, Danny, I really do. You just might have helped me a lot."

"Anything to advance the cause."

The radio host said goodbye.

Leaving Ludwig with a decision to make. No, there really was no choice. And he already had his press conference scheduled.

The only thing left for him to do was tell the world: He'd just made the arrangements to put his hands on his good guy with a gun. Revealing the man's identity to the world was now just a matter of time.

Then Ludwig's phone rang again. He thought it might be O'Day calling back, having forgotten to mention something. But it was someone else, an unfamiliar voice.

"Hello, have I reached Mr. Auric Ludwig?"

"Yes, what is it?"

"Sir, my name is Jerry Nerón. Some friends of yours have contacted me on your behalf. They've paid me to make three new suits for you. Perhaps you've heard of the custom tailoring I do."

Now, that the man mentioned it, Ludwig did know his name.

Other members of the DC lobbying community wore Jerry Nerón suits.

They were exquisitely made with the finest fabrics.

He'd thought more than once he'd like to have one; he was just too cheap to pay the price.

"Sir?" the voice on the phone said.

"Yes, I'm still here, and I do know your work. You say friends of mine have paid you to make three suits for me? Did they say why?"

"I assume this is a gesture of friendship and respect. Perhaps you have some important events to attend in the near future?"

That was it, Ludwig thought. The suits wouldn't be a gift; they'd be somebody's idea of a cruel joke. He had enemies like any other lobbyist. Hell, he had more people who wanted to see him fall than any other lobbyist. Somebody wanted to see him wear Jerry Nerón suits to court for his obstruction of justice trial, and then he'd get shipped off to prison somewhere and have to wear a jailbird jumpsuit for the rest of his life.

Leaving behind only the cruel memories of what he'd lost.

Like the custom-made suits by Jerry Nerón.

"Sir, if you are not interested, I will let your friends know."

"No, no. I'm definitely interested. I only wish I had one of your suits to wear this morning when I speak to the media."

Nerón chuckled. "I'm sorry, but I don't sew that fast. If you like, however, I can do a fitting for you this afternoon."

"That would be great."

"We can do the fitting either at your office or my hotel suite."

"My office. You know where it is?"

"Yes, sir. Will three o'clock be good."

"Fine. Can you tell me the name of my generous friends, the

ones paying for your services?"

"I am not supposed to say, but I can ask. If I get permission, I'll tell you when I come to your office."

"Fine. See you then."

Ludwig laughed to himself. Some of the SOBs he knew, they'd love to see him laid out in a casket wearing a Jerry Nerón suit. But they didn't know he was on the verge of finding his damn good guy. That was going to turn everything around. He felt sure of it.

He'd expose that bullshit medical examiner's report about Abel Mays suffering a heart attack as a fraud.

He'd ruin James J. McGill's reputation as an investigator, him with his supposed alternative killer to blame for the death of Jordan Gilford.

He'd turn the tables on the national discussion of gun death counters and all that other shit.

And he'd do it all in style, wearing Jerry Nerón suits.

### McGill's Hideaway — The White House

McGill called Ellie Booker. "I wanted to give you a heads-up."

"About what? Something good or bad?"

"You decide. Didi DiMarco invited me to do an interview, and I accepted."

"At the White House?"

"No, if I speak at the White House, it's only in the press room, and everybody's welcome."

"That's fair. So, what? You're just being considerate?"

"My manners are fairly good, but I appreciate what WWN did, taking the lead with the gun death counter, and I'm sure you had at least something to do with that."

"Something, but it was getting shot that put Hugh on board."

"Well, anyway, I wanted to say thanks and let you know."

"And tell me I can't count on a string of exclusives with you," Ellie said.

"That would ruin your credibility and mine," McGill said.

"Yeah. I hate it when there's a good reason for not getting my way."

"Makes us both work all the harder."

"Try not to give Didi anything too good, will you?"

McGill laughed. "You were the one who got her to jump in so fast on the gun death counter, weren't you?"

Ellie was quiet.

"Had to be you, because it wasn't me," McGill said.

"You know what? Sometimes you're a scary guy."

"Why? Because I can do basic arithmetic?"

"You graduated from DePaul magna cum laude, I checked. So don't play humble."

"It's part of my charm," McGill told her.

## MSNBC — *Washington, DC*

Didi DiMarco could see McGill's master's degree and raise him a doctorate.

From Oxford yet.

But McGill felt he could hold his own. He and Didi sat in facing chairs.

"Are you trying to change America's gun laws, Mr. McGill?"

"No, that's not within my power to do."

"You're married to the president of the United States."

"For which I give thanks every day, but it's not within her power to do, either."

"So you're saying it's all up to Congress?"

"In terms of passing legislation, yes."

"Congress hasn't shown any inclination to take on the gun lobby."

"The great thing about the people in Congress, Didi? They can all be replaced."

"Do you think they all should be replaced?"

"I'd be more inclined to pick and choose, if it were up to me, but it's not."

Didi said, "I read your master's thesis: A Cop's-Eye View of the Second Amendment. You say Congress should be made irrelevant until it has no choice but to be responsive. Do you really think that approach could work?"

"I do. Something the president and even private citizens can do is lead the national conversation. As I've mentioned before, from the time our Constitution was written in 1787 until the second half of the twentieth century, virtually no civilian had access to military-style assault weapons, and no one said the Second Amendment was under attack. People got along just fine with their hunting rifles, shotguns and revolvers. You know what else? We didn't have massacres in schools, shopping malls and places of business in those days either.

"The gun manufacturers want to maximize their profits by pitching weapons of war to young men, and some not so young, who have no intention of ever joining the military but fantasize that they can be warriors anyway."

"How do the gun manufacturers do that?" Didi asked.

"They do it through their advertising. They use words like 'assault' and 'combat' to describe the weapons they sell. One manufacturer uses the label ACR to describe a rifle. ACR is short for adaptive combat rifle. One gun company's website has a headline for a firearm that says 'Forces of opposition, bow down.' That kind of corny language would be laughable if it weren't combined with a deadly weapon that's put into the hands of someone who's developmentally immature, emotionally disturbed or mentally ill."

Didi asked, "So what do you hope to do about this situation?"

McGill said, "We have to persuade most Americans that their Second Amendment rights will be every bit as strong as they were before the gun companies started selling weapons of war to civilians. Persuade our fellow Americans that the biggest reason we have these horrible tragedies, like the one at the Winstead School, is to protect gun company profits. Once we make that clear to the voting public, Congress will fall in line. That or we'll have a lot of new faces in Washington."

"So you do want to change the laws."

"I want to change hearts and minds. A majority of the American people will drive any changes in law, not me or any other individual."

"Where would you start changing hearts and minds?"

McGill said, "The best place to start is to track every weapon from its point of origin to its current owner. Each of us has a right to bear arms, but the Constitution does not say we have a right to bear arms secretly. I don't understand why any law-abiding gun owner would oppose this idea. You just say, 'I'm John Smith. I bought my handgun, shotgun or rifle at Wal-Mart or wherever.' What's the big deal? If the police know all the people who have legally purchased their firearms, it will be a lot easier for them to identify the bad guys who came by their weapons illegally."

Didi said, "The other side of the argument is that if the police know who has bought firearms that would make it easier to confiscate those weapons."

"My response to that idea is why and how? Why would the police want to take a law-abiding person's legally purchased property from him or her? Cops are too busy busting criminals to say, 'You know what, let's go grab John Smith's hunting rifle from him.' On the other hand, if you're talking about a general seizure of everybody's firearms, my question is: how? How could that be accomplished?

"You've seen situations in which some deranged person with a gun takes hostages in a home, a store or elsewhere. Any major police department will respond with massive force: patrol officers to establish a security perimeter, negotiators to try to end the incident without bloodshed, SWAT teams standing ready, if it looks like violence is unavoidable. The expense of mounting an operation to disarm one person is staggering. No police department has the budget necessary to take away a neighborhood's guns, much less all the guns in a town or a city. The very idea is ridiculous.

"It's also insulting to our country's police officers to think they would participate in a wholesale violation of a community's constitutional rights. If you're an average citizen and you need help fast, the first thing you think of is to call the police. If you're an average citizen, you spend a lot more time thinking about how to pay your bills than worrying about the cops coming to take your legally purchased firearms."

"How many guns should a person be allowed to own?" Didi asked. "Is there any limit at all?"

McGill said, "That's a very good question. I've pointed out that the Constitution was written before there were any police departments in our country. Now, even the smallest town will have police protection provided by the county sheriff's department. But the police response time for one locale might be a lot longer than in another. Some people live in wilderness areas. It seems reasonable to me for them to keep more weapons in their homes than someone living in the middle of a big city."

"So some limits for urban and suburban areas, but not for people who live in rural areas or on mountains or out in the woods?" Didi asked.

"There are four hundred and thirty-five congressional districts in the United States," McGill said. "Let the voters in each district decide how many firearms a homeowner should be allowed to keep on their premises. Let's say the Constitutional minimum is two, as the Second Amendment cites a right to bear arms. Arms being plural would indicate at least two. So every other year when people go to elect their congressman or congresswoman there could be a question on the ballot: How many firearms shall be allowed to be kept in this district's residences: two-to-five; six-to-ten; unlimited? Let the voters decide, not the gun lobby."

"But why shouldn't everybody be allowed to buy and keep all the guns they want?" Didi asked.

"Because no right is absolute. The Second Amendment says nothing about a right to accumulate and maintain your own arsenal. If you want to take a literal view, maybe the right to bear arms should be construed as the right to own only as many firearms as you can personally hold in your hands and arms at any one time.

No going back for seconds."

Didi smiled. She liked that.

"Do you feel that popular culture, such as movies and video games, has contributed in any way to the epidemic of gun violence these past several years?" she asked.

"I do, at least in part."

"In what way and what part?"

"In the examples I'm thinking of, some movies and games treat marginal characters as nothing more than fodder for violent deaths. Figures who pop up for no other reason than to get gunned down. Implying that such characters have little humanity and no value. If you mow down straw men who have no families, no friends, no standing of any kind in the community, what harm have you done?

"To me, that is hack storytelling done to provoke only the basest of thrills. As awful as the material might be, though, it's still able to influence people who can't or refuse to distinguish fantasy from reality. The way I see it, in the minds of the people who commit these atrocities, they're the stars of the show — and everybody else is an expendable extra."

"You don't think all action movie fans and gamers are potential killers?" Didi asked.

"No, but that's not the point. There are some movies and some video games where the graphic depiction of large numbers of people getting kill by gunfire is the biggest drawing card. How does all that violence get internalized and recycled? If only some of the audience for that stuff gets ticked off at real people and has access to an assault rifle ... well, peaceful conflict resolution probably won't be the first thing that comes to their minds."

McGill and Didi ended the interview there.

It was scheduled to run that night.

# CHAPTER 29

*Playa Pacifica — Costa Rica*

F ather Inigo de Loyola arrived at Representative Philip Brock's property in Costa Rica driving a truck filled with food, clothing and the promise of divine forgiveness. His appearance was considerably different from the one he affected in Washington. Rather than wearing a workingman's clothing, he'd donned a short-sleeved black shirt, black slacks and the Roman collar of a Catholic priest.

His beard had been shaven and his hair dyed as black as his clothes. The effect was to make de Loyola look much younger, harder and far more dangerous than he did in the U.S. His bloodlines and features were clearly those of the conquistador, not someone whose ancestors had intermarried with the indigenous people. Should one such as him ever be shown disrespect or otherwise driven to anger the consequences might well be fatal.

Lending a further air of authority, de Loyola was accompanied by Lieutenant Miguel Poncé who wore the uniform of the *Fuerza Pública*. Public Force. Shortly after leaving San José, de Loyola had pulled to the side of the road and offered to hear Poncé's confession.

"You are truly a priest, not an American spy?" the lieutenant asked.

"I am a priest, a Jesuit. I come both to do God's work and to help an American friend. But he is not with the American government nor am I."

Poncé believed de Loyola and felt a little better, but still had his suspicions.

"Even if you are not a spy, your friend must still be powerful to provide you with this truck, all the goods inside it and my company to ease your way."

Having disposed of its army, Costa Rica relied on the United States for help in the event of an attack by a foreign power. So the government looked kindly on reasonable requests from the giant to the north. Including, apparently, whatever mission brought this new priest to San José.

De Loyola admitted, "He is a man with considerable sway in some circles, but a good man all the same."

"And your presence in Costa Rica, will it help my country?"

"It might spare San José an embarrassing situation."

"And it has nothing to do with illegal drugs?"

De Loyola thought about that. "Not that I know of, and certainly not involving the man who asked me to visit your beautiful country."

"We've heard of you, Father. We know of your battles in Nicaragua and other places."

"I've never shed a drop of blood in Costa Rica nor is that my intent."

"*Bueno.*"

"So you have no wish to confess?"

"I did so with my parish priest only yesterday."

"And you passed last night faultlessly?"

Poncé blushed, laughed, waited for traffic to pass and told de Loyola of his most recent sin.

He was absolved and said his act of contrition as they headed toward the Pacific Coast.

When they arrived at the gate to Brock's property three young men holding rifles rushed the truck, each of them trying to look more fierce than his *compañeros*. The starch went out of all three when they saw the driver was a priest and his passenger was *Fuerza*

*Pública.* Though de Loyola and Poncé perceived no threat, they shared a look.

Each was impressed by the young men's vigilant response and their weapons, if not their spacing — tightly grouped — and the manner in which they held their weapons — muzzles pointed at the sky. Such a combination would get them all killed if they encountered regular military with a hostile intent. De Loyola waved the young men to his side of the truck.

They hurried to comply, relieved to move away from Poncé.

Each of them dropped to one knee, showing their respect for a priest.

"*Buenos dias,*" de Loyola said.

"*Buenos dias, padre,*" they said in unison.

Clearly, they'd had a Catholic education. He gave them his blessing and asked them to stand. They did, rifles held loosely at their sides, butts of the weapons resting on the ground.

De Loyola said, "My friend, the lieutenant, and I are here on a charitable mission. We have brought beans, rice, peppers, onions, chicken and everything else you need to make a wonderful *casado.*"

*Casado* was also known as *comida tipica.* The most commonly enjoyed dish in the country.

"Might the working people at this grand property enjoy a meal courtesy of Mother Church?" de Loyola asked.

Poncé looked at him. He hadn't known the food came from the church. Still, he wasn't about to contest the word of a priest, especially one with a powerful American friend.

The young sentries weren't about to reject such courtesy either.

The oldest looking one stepped forward, "We would be honored, *padre.*"

"Good. I am sure that only the finest people work here, but because we are all imperfect I will be hearing confession in the back of this truck for any who feel the need. Will that be all right?"

The heads of all three young men bobbed. They looked at each other. De Loyola knew immediately they had at least one sin in common to cleanse from their souls.

The oldest got into the cab to show them the way to the work-ers' communal kitchen. The first woman they met there took de Loyola's hand as if to kiss his ring. Only he didn't wear one. He clasped the woman's hand in both of his and offered a blessing. He repeated it for all the women who gathered around him.

They were only too happy to accept the food he'd brought. Children were sent running to every corner of the land to share the word that there would be a great midday feast courtesy of the *padre* and the lieutenant.

As the cooking began, Father de Loyola heard the confessions of men, women and children. None of the deeds he'd learned in the truck would ever pass from his lips. As with any good priest, he held the privacy of the confessional, even one with a diesel engine, as inviolable.

Each penitent was asked if he or she might need a new item of clothing either for themselves or *los niños*. The gifts were accepted with gratitude. His hand was kissed by some of the young girls.

The place of honor at the main table was held open for him.

As de Loyola ate and drank with all his new friends, they shared many stories, as people do over joyful meals. Having already bared their souls privately to the priest, there was little anyone chose to hide about Brock, his property and his plans for a future life in Costa Rica. Dinner conversation, unlike the confession of sins, was free to be repeated without concern.

The priest took photographs out of his wallet to show everyone the people he knew El Norte. One was a portrait of McGill. De Loyola said, "*El marido de la presidenta.*" The husband of the president. Everyone wanted to see that one; even Poncé took a good look.

Almost as an afterthought, de Loyola brought out one last photo: Joan Renshaw.

That was greeted with even more excitement than McGill's picture.

"*Señora Joan,*" several people exclaimed. A boy was sent running into the *casa grande*. He returned with a framed photo:

Joan Renshaw and Philip Brock, arm in arm, smiling for the camera.

De Loyola, with the consent of his new friends, had Poncé take a digital picture of the framed photograph with his cell phone.

### Wisconsin Avenue — Georgetown

Both Sweetie and Putnam had driven Maxi to school that morning.

The kid had told the two adults in her life, "You don't have to worry anymore. Dorothy said our school is as safe as Fort Knox."

Dorothy Kern was the headmistress of the Greenwood School.

She encouraged her students to address her by her given name.

Sweetie asked Maxi, "You know what Fort Knox is?"

The girl nodded. "It's the place where America keeps all its gold. Dorothy told us about it. She says there are lots of soldiers guarding it."

"And how is the Greenwood School like Fort Knox?" Putnam asked.

"Dorothy said us kids are the school's gold."

"Will there be soldiers guarding you?" Sweetie asked.

"Well, not soldiers, but men and women who'll protect us."

Putnam said, "Is this something maybe you were supposed to mention to us?"

Maxi looked embarrassed and reached into her bookbag. "I forgot."

She handed Sweetie a sealed envelope bearing the school's letterhead. Sweetie opened it and read the enclosed letter from Ms. Kern. Greenwood had hired a full-time staff of armed security personnel. They would be dressed in civilian clothing not uniforms so as not to upset the students. Some would appear to be office staff; others would wear custodial staff clothing; still others would seem to be visiting parents.

All parts of the school would be covered at all times.

A master plan would dictate responses by the security force, faculty and students.

The Metro PD would also be called in the event of an emergency, but help would be immediately at hand any time classes or extra-curricular events were in session.

After Maxi had been dropped off, Sweetie reread the letter in full to Putnam as he drove her to McGill Investigations, Inc. Then she asked, "So what do you think?"

"I think there's going to be a big tuition increase."

"Do you mind that?"

"Not one bit. No better way to spend our money."

"Because we have the money to spend," Sweetie said.

"Meaning the less fortunate still have to take their chances."

"Patti's going to advocate our plan today. Segregate all the kids whose parents admit to owning guns but won't let the authorities see that they keep their guns locked up. Jim told me."

Putnam nodded and sighed.

"You're having second thoughts?" Sweetie asked.

That had been their idea, after all.

Putnam said, "No, not really. It's just that given my family history I hate to see kids pay for the sins of Mom and Dad."

Putnam turned onto P Street.

"Life isn't fair," Sweetie said. "Sometimes, it's downright mean."

With no way to dispute either of Sweetie's points, Putnam changed the subject.

"Something strange happened yesterday. I forgot to mention it earlier."

"You have a sealed envelope to show me, too?" Sweetie asked.

Putnam grinned and shook his head.

He told Sweetie of Jerry Nerón's return to town, wanting to take a look at the suit he'd made for Putnam.

"Now, the guy is a great craftsman, and I can buy that he'd go to any length to protect his reputation, but the whole thing seemed like some sort of scam to me. Just didn't feel right. I've been try-ing to figure out what's going on, but I can come up with only one thing."

Intrigued, Sweetie asked, "What's that?"

"Seeing me, looking at the suit he made for me, that was Jerry's legit reason for being in town. Something he can point to and I can corroborate if somebody suspects him of doing something not quite so innocent."

"Like what?" Sweetie asked.

"I don't know; I'm still working on that."

"You ever get the feeling something was wrong about this guy before?"

"No, and that bothers me, if he is up to something. I like to think I'm pretty good at reading people. If I lose that ability, I'm in trouble in this town."

"Maybe it's something objectionable but not illegal. Stepping out on his wife."

"Jerry's single."

"Maybe he's gay. Nerón sounds Latino."

"Cuban-American."

"Okay. Sometimes coming out is harder in some cultures than others."

"I don't think he's gay."

"All right then, you've got a mystery. You want me to take a look at the guy?"

"Let me think about it. We'll talk tonight."

Margaret nodded, was about to say okay.

Only she saw something she'd never expected to see.

Jim McGill was standing outside Dikki's building with Roger Michaelson.

And the two of them were shaking hands.

### Zamboanga City — Philippines

Ah-lam, former dragon lady of the *Shining Dawn*, called the FBI desk at the American embassy in Manila from a bar with a view of a water-filled ditch in which a water buffalo was cooling itself. It took her less than a minute to get through to the special agent in charge. All she had to do was mention the magic words Tyler Busby.

A man with a strong American accent came on the line and said, "John Rosewall, how may I help you?"

"You are FBI? Man in charge?" Ah-lam asked, coarsening her own accent.

"Yes, ma'am. You say you have news of Tyler Busby?"

"Yes, yes. He about to give self up, but —" Ah-lam sobbed, doing a good job of sounding truly distraught, she felt.

"But what, ma'am?"

"He taken by Abu Sayyaf."

"Oh, Christ."

"Yes, yes, very bad. Guerrillas say ransom be very high or they cut off head. Mail it to American president as gift."

"Shit. How long ago was Mr. Busby kidnapped?"

"Just now, maybe one hour."

"And who are you, ma'am?"

"Bar girl. Name don't matter. Mr. Busby hear shooting before taken. Write note and give to me. Say call you. Read message."

"Why didn't the guerrillas take you, too?"

"I hide. Guerrillas don't take bar girl. They stone me, if catch."

The FBI man grunted his understanding. Maybe even a bit of sympathy.

"What does the note say?" he asked.

"Say man your president want is Philip Brock, no Roger Mike … something. Also, other man. Tanner Rutledge, something like that. He go down fighting. Never give up. Mr. Busby say these good faith offering. Please to save him from Abu Sayyaf. That all."

"You're sure there's —"

Ah-lam hung up. A motorized tricycle cab waited for her outside. It took her to the city airport. She paid her fare, gave her burner phone to the driver and made her way to a Gulfstream G650 waiting on the tarmac. Unlike the G150 Arturo Gonzales flew, this was the top of the line model. The gold standard, as Gulfstream referred to it. The aircraft carried a crew of four for long-distance flights and up to seventeen passengers.

That day, there would be but two travelers aboard the plane. The first was already in the private quarters at the rear of the custom passenger compartment. Ah-lam joined him. The plane taxied to its runway, waited little more than two minutes for clearance and took off, banking to the west. The pilot announced that flying time to Colombo, Sri Lanka, 2,900 miles away, would be five hours. The weather looked good all the way.

In their private quarters, Ah-lam and Tyler Busby toasted the beginning of their journey.

Busby's takeover of the *Shining Dawn* had actually begun on the night when he'd called Ah-lam to his stateroom.

She'd asked, "Is this to be our one night together?"

Meaning, have you chosen to end your life by sunrise?

Busby answered with his own question, "How much money will you earn from Donald Yang during the time you'll work for him, and will it buy you both everything you need and everything you want?"

Busby had asked his question while reclining on the room's enormous bed, his head propped up by a pile of pillows. A bottle of champagne chilled in a silver bucket. The lighting was soft. All that was missing was mood music, but Ah-lam had never cared for that. She preferred the sounds of exertion and passion. She wondered if her sisters had told Busby that.

In any case, the man clearly expected to have sex with her.

On his terms not hers.

"Millions," she said in response to his question.

Busby laughed and asked, "That's all?"

Before Ah-lam could get angry at the implied insult, Busby asked another question, "How much money would it take to have what you need and want and avoid having Yang take his revenge on you? Would a hundred million do it? Two hundred million?"

Ah-lam stared at Busby. She knew he was proposing a betrayal for which there would be no forgiveness. Neither from Yang nor the men who were his masters. Money mattered in China, but political power mattered more. She would have to take more than one angry man into account. The rulers of a great and rising nation would consider her an enemy.

So how much money would she need to break faith with them and survive?

Not just survive but live like an empress.

Was there enough money to do that?

Most women would have shied away from even thinking such thoughts. Ah-lam, though, was interested. If there was anyone who could do it, she would be the one. Given a sufficiently huge sum of Busby's money, that was. She poured a glass of champagne for Busby and one for herself. She sat on the edge of the bed looking at him.

"We might have to bargain for hours," she said.

They did. Busby distributed a handful of millions of dollars on the officers and crew of the yacht to show Ah-lam that he both had all the riches he claimed and didn't mind spending it. Then again, he said the millions he spent showing his good faith to Ah-lam amounted to nothing more than pocket change.

So they came up with their plan. Ah-lam allowed herself to be put off the yacht when Busby and the treacherous crew seized it. In that way, she'd merely failed Mr. Yang and his masters; she hadn't betrayed them. Yang had ordered her to come home, of course, after she'd reported the hijacking, and she had disobeyed that command.

That was understandable. She feared punishment, and would run only as far as the pittance she carried with her allowed. She would forfeit her accounts and assets in Hong Kong. Even if she evaded Yang's vengeance, she would impose a sentence of poverty and misery upon herself. Become a toothless back-alley whore addicted to heroin, her former beauty a vanished memory.

When the *Shining Dawn* put into port on Mindanao to buy a replacement life boat, at the captain's suggestion, Busby had declared he wanted to take a walk, be alone with his thoughts and work out a plan for the future. Or so he told the captain.

Then as ill fortune would have it, Busby let himself be spotted by Abu Sayyaf guerrillas and was kidnapped, but not before leaving a message with a bar girl. The reasons for this were many. Misdirection was only the beginning. By letting the president know she should be looking at Philip Brock and Tanner Rutledge, Busby was giving the feds two primary actors in two huge crimes: the would-be attempt on the president's life at Inspiration Hall and the looting of the budget of the Defense Department.

That Busby knew of the crimes clearly implicated him as a participant in both of them. But, hey, ratting out your accomplices was what bad guys did when bargaining down their punishment. Not that Busby ever expected to live freely in the U.S. again. He was merely trying to have the government understand he'd like to live quietly — and quite well — abroad without having to look over his shoulder all the time.

If he ever escaped his imaginary kidnappers, that was.

Maybe Washington would exhaust its interest in finding him after a couple futile years of combing through the Philippine jungles. That would also be acceptable.

So Busby and Ah-lam jetted to Sri Lanka, the jewel of the Indian Ocean.

The two best funded fugitives in the world.

After enjoying each other's carnal company for an eighth time — Busby was keeping count — they relaxed next to one another, thinking their own thoughts.

Busby asked Ah-lam, "Do you regret what will happen to your sisters when Yang gets his hands on the *Shining Dawn* again?"

Ah-lam looked at him and said, "They were willing to betray me, and we never really got along anyway."

# CHAPTER 30

## *The Oval Office — The White House*

Special Agent Benjamin told the president and her chief of staff of the business connection between Tyler Busby and Donald Yang, and how Yang now claimed that Busby had leased his yacht using a front company and then had commandeered it.

"Deputy Director DeWitt thought to look for the connection," Benjamin said.

"Actually, I got the idea from Putnam Shady and I put it together with Ms. Mindel's suggestion that Busby might be aboard another yacht," DeWitt said. "Special Agent Benjamin took the initiative to involve the NRO and the navy."

"Nice synergy," the president said. "There's credit enough to go around."

Edwina buzzed the president. "I'm sorry to interrupt, Madam President, but Director Haskins is here and he says the matter is urgent."

The president looked at the two FBI officials already present.

They gestured their ignorance.

"Please send the director in, Edwina."

Haskins gave his two subordinates a brief glance and said, "Madam President, Madam Chief of Staff. If you don't mind, I'd like to ask the deputy director stay and have the special agent step out before I speak."

The president looked at DeWitt. He cut his eyes briefly toward Benjamin. The president interpreted the glance correctly.

"Jeremiah," the president said to the director, "I've just heard of some very good work the special agent has done, and I may want to speak with her some more. So why don't we just let her stay?"

Haskins knew he'd just been overruled, but he didn't let any displeasure show.

"Very well, Madam President."

The director told all present of a call from a self-described bar-girl in Zamboanga City alleging that Tyler Busby had been kidnapped by Abu Sayyaf guerillas. He added, "The motor vessel Shining Dawn was found in port in Zamboanga City. The Philippine military has taken custody of the vessel and everyone aboard."

"Galia?" the president asked, not needing to finish the question.

The chief of staff filled in the blank. "The DOD has a Special Joint Operations Task Force on Mindanao and the CIA has paramilitary officers from its Special Activities Division on the island."

Before a rescue effort could start to be organized, Haskins dropped the other shoe.

"The bar-girl said Brock is the man you want not Michaelson — and Tanner Rutledge will never let himself be taken alive; he'll fight to the end."

"That bastard Busby is trying to set up a plea bargain," Galia said. "He has to be part of the Inspiration Hall conspiracy and the looting of the Pentagon."

"Or he wants us to think he is," the president said.

Benjamin had the nerve to chime in. "Busby might also be scamming us with this bar-girl, Madam President. A fugitive couldn't ask for a much better dodge than to say he'd been kidnapped by jihadi guerrillas with their very own jungle to hide in."

"A very good point, Special Agent. Mr. Deputy Director, do you have any ideas?"

DeWitt said, "Busby's use of an unknown surrogate, the bar-girl, is classic Sun Tzu: 'Spread lies amongst your enemies ... sow confusion in their ranks through deception and sabotage.' This so-called bar-girl has told us something we have no way of knowing is true, at least right now. We should interrogate the people on the *Shining Dawn*. Find out if Busby, in fact, did get off the yacht in Zamboanga City. If it looks like he did, we need to find out what other boats or aircraft left Mindanao at or about the same time. These are things we can pin down factually."

Benjamin said, "And ask the locals if anyone saw men resembling Abu Sayyaf elements kidnapping a Western man. Have the CIA work its assets on the island before the military starts beating the bushes."

"Mr. Director?" the president asked.

Haskins said, "I concur with both those ideas. The only criticism I have is that playing it cagey might cost a man his head. Then again, so might going in gung-ho with the military."

The president showed the room as ruthless a smile as anyone in it had ever seen.

"It might cost Tyler Busby his head, and I can live with that."

Giving the go-ahead for DeWitt's and Benjamin's suggestions, the president turned to the next items on her agenda.

Bringing in Philip Brock in for questioning by the FBI.

Mere surveillance was no longer enough.

Bringing in Tanner Rutledge for questioning, too.

Taking care he didn't get his hands on any assault weapons or explosives.

## McGill Investigations, Inc. — Georgetown

In all their years together, McGill had seen Sweetie cry twice. Both times were when she'd felt she came up short helping another cop, resulting in those officers being wounded by gunfire. For the other two men in the office, Putnam and Michaelson, that day was the first time they ever saw Margaret Sweeney weep. Putnam gathered his wife in his arms to comfort her.

Michaelson, also on his feet, looked like he wanted to add his touch, but wisely held back.

McGill, sitting behind his desk, had just shared the news that Joan Renshaw had killed Erna Godfrey. Deke, who'd already heard, stood guard in the outer office.

McGill had received word of what had happened in Connecticut less than an hour ago from Patti. It had been a jolt to him. More than once he had wished Erna was dead. When Patti had decided to commute her death sentence to life in prison, he'd gone along with it. But on more than one night before he fell asleep, remembering how he had failed to keep Andy Grant alive, he second-guessed Patti's act of mercy, even if he hadn't shared his misgivings with her.

Michaelson had arrived earlier that morning to see Sweetie and ask how the investigation was going. McGill had told him of Renshaw's statement exonerating him and implicating Brock. The former senator had heaved a sigh of relief, and then he had the decency to express concern about how Erna's death was going to affect Sweetie.

More astounding, he'd seen how the homicide in a prison cell would reflect on Patti.

"Jesus," Michaelson said, "the Republicans and True South will try to crucify the president for this. They'll say she's the one who approved Renshaw's transfer into Godfrey's cell."

"That's right. She did," McGill told him.

Michaelson had hung his head and covered his face with both hands.

When he looked at McGill he said, "Please tell the president how sorry I am. All the antagonism between us, it's on me. My wounded ego and juvenile temper have led to so much stupid shit over so many years." Michaelson's face tightened. "Anybody goes after the president politically, they'll have to come through me. Anything I can do to help her, I will."

McGill had decades of experience listening to people lie.

Whether they were cons or pols, he'd been able to see through them.

Every so often, though, he heard a heartfelt truth, and Michaelson's promise rang true. That surprised him more than a little. Reminded him that William Cowper had got it right when he wrote about God moving in mysterious ways his wonders to perform.

Letting a minute or so pass, McGill said, "Margaret, no one had any idea that Joan Renshaw was capable of what she did. What were the odds that one woman could kill another with her bare hands? How could anybody have guessed that Erna wouldn't fight back long enough for help to arrive? It was a horrible miscalculation we all made, not just you."

Sweetie looked up from the shoulder of Putnam's suit, now wet with her tears.

"It was my idea," she said. "I thought I was so smart. Get a jailhouse confession. What could be easier? Save myself the effort of digging up evidence."

Putnam leaned back and looked at his wife. "You're questioning your work ethic, Margaret? Come on now. You've made a whole new man out of me."

"You've always made me a better man," McGill said.

Michaelson added, "You've helped me to remain a free man."

Sweetie looked at each of them, finishing with Putnam, and wept all the more.

"Maybe a visit to your confessor would help," McGill suggested.

Sweetie's head popped up and she nodded. "Yes, right away."

The idea of both absolution and penance held great appeal.

"I'll take you," Putnam said, "but give me just a minute with Jim, will you? Senator, will you please escort my wife down to my car? It's right out front."

Michaelson nodded. Sweetie kissed Putnam, gave McGill a smile and took the arm Michaelson offered. McGill and Putnam heard Deke tell her, "Stay strong."

Putnam closed the door.

"What's up?" McGill asked.

Putnam put a hand on the shoulder of his suit Margaret had

used as a crying towel.

"Wet all the way through," he told McGill. "That reminded me of something. Margaret and I were going to work on it. But now ... I thought I'd better tell you before I forget."

He told McGill of going to see Jerry Nerón and how he'd felt something was wrong.

McGill's eyes went wide, he held tight to the arms of his chair.

Putnam asked, "You see an apparition or something?"

McGill blinked and looked at Putnam. "More like a revelation. You did say Nerón, right?"

"Yeah, first name Jerry, short for Jeronimo."

"Was this guy's father involved in the Bay of Pigs invasion?"

"Not his father, his grandfather: Dario Nerón. How'd you know that?"

McGill told Putnam of the FBI identification of a particular strand of hair.

"You're saying my tailor is a killer?" Putnam asked.

"Unless it's his father," McGill replied.

"I can't see it being either of them, but something was up with Jerry. Shit. I had Maxi with me when I went to see him."

That thought rattled Putnam.

"Do you know who else this guy might be seeing in town?" McGill asked.

Putnam shook his head.

"Where did you meet with him?" McGill asked.

"He has a suite at the Four Seasons. He'll do measurements and fittings either at a hotel or the client's office or home." Another thought jarred Putnam. "You think Jerry is after one of his other clients?"

McGill said, "I don't know. I'll go to the Four Seasons and see what I can find out. Take things from there. You go help Margaret. Don't keep her waiting."

"I won't. Hey, give me a call when when you can. All right?"

"Sure thing," McGill said.

### *Rayburn House Office Building — Washington, DC*

DeWitt and Benjamin, minding their manners, had called ahead to the Capitol Hill Police and had four of their officers with them when they entered the building where Representative Philip Brock had his office suite. The House of Representatives wasn't in session that afternoon, but the FBI pair had done their due diligence and had gone to the House chamber to make sure Brock wasn't doing a solo performance, giving a speech for the benefit of the C-SPAN camera. He wasn't. The next step was to check for him in his office.

If he wasn't there, DeWitt and Benjamin would look for Brock at his DC residence.

They stopped hallway passersby in their tracks as they marched in formation to Brock's suite. DeWitt and Benjamin had their FBI badges on display; the Capitol Hill cops were in uniform. They looked exactly like what they were: a half-dozen hard-asses out to make an arrest. People stared at them as they passed.

More than a few wondered: Do they have anything on me?

And prayed that they didn't.

A few congressmen poked their heads out of their suites. Tried to muster a show of indignation at the idea that any of their colleagues might be treated as roughly as a common criminal. Their disapproval, however, was limited to scowls and grimaces. No one said a word.

Benjamin picked up her step and opened the door to Brock's suite for the others. DeWitt stopped in front of a goggle-eyed receptionist and said in a measured tone, "We're here for Congressman Brock. Is he in? Please don't say he isn't, if he is. We'll check the entire suite, if need be."

The young woman looked to be in her early twenties and couldn't find her voice. Had no idea of what to say. Seemed as if she might burst into tears.

DeWitt was just about to ask the Capitol Hill cops to look for Brock when a mature woman, who'd clearly bumped up against more of life than the receptionist had, stepped out of an office and asked DeWitt, "Is there something I can do for you people?"

Her tone suggested people was a synonym for morons.

"We're here for the congressman," DeWitt said. "Is he in?"

"He's not." Understanding the feds and cops were not about to take her word for it, she added, "See for yourselves, if you like."

Benjamin and the cops did just that.

"You're the congressman's chief of staff?" DeWitt asked the woman.

"I am. Janet Wagner."

"Ms. Wagner, do you know where Congressman Brock is right now?"

"I do not."

"Are you aware if he's made any recent travel plans?"

"No, I'm not."

"To your knowledge, is the congressman ill or has he suffered an accident?"

"Not to my knowledge, no."

"You answer questions as if you've been to law school, Ms. Wagner. Is that right?"

"It is."

That being the case, DeWitt knew the woman would cooperate while being of little to no use whatsoever. Benjamin returned with the cops. She said, "He's not here."

DeWitt looked as if he might address the half-dozen curious staffers watching the drama that was unfolding before their eyes, but Ms. Wagner held up a hand and beat him to the punch.

"This gentleman is from the FBI. I advise you to cooperate with him, but only after each of you has had the benefit of conferring with your own lawyer. That way, we'll all be protected."

The woman was good, DeWitt thought.

She was messing with him, but in a way that left him no leverage over her.

At the very least, she'd just bought Philip Brock time to run, if that was what he was doing.

There was only one thing left for DeWitt to do. Four of the junior staffers were women. Neither as young as the receptionist nor as old as the chief of staff. DeWitt looked their way. He ran a hand through his longish surfer blonde hair. He directed a winning smile their way.

"She's right, Ms. Wagner is. Everyone has a right to legal counsel. But lawyers are expensive, and calling on one, well, that makes it look like you have something to hide."

"Hey!" Wagner said.

Benjamin backed her off before she could say more.

DeWitt continued, "I'm not saying there is anything wrong with talking to a lawyer. Just that how things look matters in this town. Politics, you know. Conservative voters like Congressman Brock's constituents, they believe in law and order. They don't expect their elected representatives and their staff to stonewall the FBI."

"Wait a goddamn minute!" Wagner said, her voice louder this time.

Benjamin walked her out into the hallway.

DeWitt smiled again, all charm and good will. "All I'm asking for now is a show of hands. How many of you would like to talk your lawyer before you talk to me, and how many would like to save yourselves the time and expense?"

One hand after another went up, followed by the declaration: "Lawyer."

Until the young receptionist said, "I want to report a theft."

Bemused, DeWitt looked at her and said, "I beg your pardon."

She said, "I don't know where Congressman Brock is. What I do know is somebody stole a tube of sunscreen from my desk. I put some on every time before I go out. So my skin won't get old and wrinkly. Everyone here knows I do it. They know I keep my sunscreen in my desk. That's all I have to say. Except that my sunscreen was gone when I came in this morning."

DeWitt looked at the other staffers. "Anyone here steal this young lady's sunscreen?"

They all shook their heads.

"Well then. Thank you all for your time."

DeWitt thanked the Capitol Hill cops for their time, too.

Leaving the building, he told Benjamin, "Brock grabbed a tube of sunscreen. He went somewhere sunny and warm."

"You didn't ask Ms. Wagner if she stole the sunscreen."

"I got a good look at her," DeWitt said. "Too late to stave off wrinkles."

## CHAPTER 31

*M Street NW — Washington, DC*

McGill was headed to the Four Seasons Hotel in his Chevy with Leo and Deke when the call from Father Inigo de Loyola reached him.

"All's well, Father?" McGill asked.

"I am tempted to remain in San José."

"Not at the insistence of the government, I hope."

The priest laughed. "No, amigo, I have not been arrested. As I have shown to my compadre, Lieutenant Poncé, my visit here is largely pastoral and entirely peaceful."

De Loyola told McGill of the fiesta he threw on Brock's property.

"I made many new friends, and they introduced me to many details of their lives."

"Learn anything that might interest me?" McGill asked.

"Señor Brock has a fine property along the Pacific coast of this lovely country. He has the land and the resources to build both a runway and a helipad on his land. He plans to do just that. Depending on his choice of aircraft, he might fly to Panama, Venezuela or even Bolivia. By no coincidence, he has met in recent months with gentlemen from all three of those countries."

"You know what I'm thinking, Father?"

"If you are thinking of drugs, you are mistaken. Our friends in Costa Rica are all too familiar with that problem. They are doing their best to eliminate it. Lieutenant Poncé assures me his government has investigated all of Brock's new friends. No drug connections among them."

"Then there's the next most obvious thing," McGill said.

"Looking for a second safe haven? Yes, that is much more likely."

McGill said, "Depending on how high the heat gets turned up under Brock, he'll need a country that won't comply with an extradition request."

De Loyola offered geopolitical opinions. "Panama might cooperate with the U.S. Venezuela will not, but that country is in turmoil. A new government might prove friendlier to Washington. Bolivia is more of a certainty. Dislike of *los estados unidos* is an article of faith in La Paz. President Morales might take Señor Brock in just to have the pleasure of thumbing his nose at Washington when it asks to have him back."

McGill asked, "What's the level of creature comforts in Bolivia, Father?"

"As an American would think of it, there is not a lot of nightlife."

McGill laughed. "Is there an expatriate community in which Brock might come to be an important figure?"

"There are some Europeans. They range from Spaniards to Russians. There are also some people from the Middle East."

"Arabs?" McGill asked.

"Yes."

"Huh." McGill wouldn't have thought of that. Turning to a more immediate concern, he asked, "Did any of the people at the fiesta say when Brock might return to Costa Rica?"

"He is here already. Lieutenant Poncé told me of this only an hour ago."

The SOB was on the run, McGill thought.

"One last question, Father. Why might you stay in San José?"

"To warm my bones until summer comes to Washington."

Understandable, McGill thought.

"I have something for you, my friend," de Loyola said.

"What's that?"

"A photograph taken by Lieutenant Poncé with his phone. He will send it to your phone momentarily. Do we not live in a world of wonders?"

McGill agreed that they did.

He thanked de Loyola and said goodbye.

As promised, the emailed photo arrived in seconds.

Philip Brock and Joan Renshaw, looking all chummy, smiling broadly. It wasn't conclusive, evidence but the image lent credence to the idea that Brock, not Michaelson, had been Renshaw's co-conspirator in the attempt to kill Patti. He'd wait to see how well Sweetie had rebounded before showing it to her.

A moment later, Leo said, "We're here, boss."

Deke asked, "How do you want to do this?"

Meaning was it going to be just the three of them confronting Jerry Nerón.

Not bothering about calling in the cops or the FBI.

"We'll play it as it lays," McGill said.

Meaning it would be just the three of them.

At least to start with.

McGill got out of the Chevy before the hotel doorman could open the door for him. Deke was almost as touchy about outsiders getting a glimpse of how heavily armored the car was as his colleagues were about letting civilians see what beasts the presidential limos were.

The doorman stepped back. He recognized the president's husband and knew a Secret Service agent when he saw one. He touched the bill of his hat and gave McGill a smile.

The doorman said, "If you'll ask your driver to pull up about ten feet, sir, I'll see to it that no one asks to have your car moved while you're visiting the hotel."

Courteous guy, McGill thought. Sharp, too, the way he grasped things so quickly.

That prompted McGill to say, "I understand the hotel's need for discretion, but have you met a guest by the name of Jerry Nerón?"

Just asking put the guy in a bind. He wanted to help. But he wanted to keep his job, too.

Deke showed the guy his badge and stepped forward to whisper into his ear.

The doorman nodded and Deke stepped back.

"Yes, sir. I've come to recognize Mr. Nerón. He's a regular guest."

"Do you know if he's in the hotel at the moment?"

"He isn't, sir. I got a taxi for him not ten minutes ago."

"Did you hear where he wanted to go?"

"Falls Church, Virginia."

"The address?"

The doorman sighed and gave that up, too.

McGill told Deke, "Please double whatever tip it was you offered this gentleman."

Deke gave McGill a look but dug out his wallet.

Starting out for Falls Church, McGill told Leo, "Fast as you can, use the siren and lights."

Leo grinned and did as he was told. Revving up his old racing skills was always a moment to be treasured. Technically, the only time McGill was supposed to have his Chevy run hot was in case of a true emergency, e.g. he was bleeding profusely or the president had declared a national emergency.

Sometimes, though, a henchman had to go with his gut.

McGill had recognized the Falls Church address the doorman had given him. It was opposite the location of the second gun death counter site: the office tower where FirePower America had its headquarters. Auric Ludwig had been begging for the good guy with a gun — whom he'd thought had killed Abel Mays — to come see him. Well, Jerry Nerón was on the way, making it a clear case of needing to be careful what you wished for.

If McGill was right, and he felt sure he was, Jerry had killed both Mays and Jordan Gilford.

Having Ludwig trying to ferret him out would be the last thing

Jerry wanted.

With Ludwig showing no sign of giving up his quest, he had to go. So Jerry was on his way to take care of that. McGill was not far behind, and the way Leo was driving the margin was closing quickly.

Deke said, "I didn't offer that doorman a tip."

"No?" McGill asked. "What did you tell him?"

"That you'd send him a personal letter of thanks on White House stationery and stand up for him if anyone at the hotel gave him grief."

McGill nodded. "Quick thinking. I'll do both those things. So how much money did you give him?"

"Since you told me to be generous, a hundred bucks."

McGill opened his wallet and repaid Deke. "Fair is fair."

Somewhat mollified, Deke asked, "So are we going to call for backup?"

"After you and I go in, Leo is going to call the FBI."

McGill had promised Patti to try to take the killer alive.

No way he could do that if he passed the baton to anyone else.

Of course, Patti wanted him to come home in one piece, too.

Women were so demanding.

### Cowboy Café — Arlington, Virginia

Changing their tactics, DeWitt and Benjamin dispensed with the Capitol Hill cops when they went to the Cannon House Office Building in the hope of picking up Congressman Tanner Rutledge — the guy would rather die fighting than surrender. Or so it was said. The two feds kept their FBI eagle-and-shield badges in their pockets. Benjamin entered Rutledge's suite alone. DeWitt stayed outside listening for yells of help, which he thought might come from anyone except Benjamin.

In fact, there was no outcry at all. Benjamin returned within a minute.

"No problem?" DeWitt asked.

"The congressman is dining at the Cowboy Café in Arlington, his preferred destination for chicken-fried steak."

"I thought that was a breakfast dish," DeWitt said, "not that I have personal knowledge."

"Me either, but I did ask. The congressman, being a Texan and a good tipper, can order it anytime he likes."

"His staff bought your story?"

"What's not to buy? The application of a kid the congressman nominated for a slot at West Point got routed to the FBI when something disturbing popped up. We just want to keep Rutledge from winding up with egg on his face."

DeWitt had decided to dip into Sun Tzu's tactic of spreading falsehoods.

He and Benjamin found Rutledge right where his staff said they would, the Cowboy Café. They decided the decent thing to do would be to let him finish his meal. It also gave them the opportunity to see if they thought he might be carrying a gun. Weapons were not allowed in the Capitol, but when a member of the Texas delegation to Congress stepped out to lunch, who knew if he'd feel the need to arm himself?

Neither DeWitt nor Benjamin saw a giveaway bulge. They contented themselves with burgers and soft drinks, and grabbed Rutledge without resistance in the parking lot when he went to retrieve his car. Contrary to the warnings DeWitt and Benjamin had received, he offered no resistance. He simply invoked his right to summon his lawyer and otherwise remain silent the way any perp might.

"You're not under arrest yet, Congressman," DeWitt said, "but you might be if you refuse to talk to the attorney general."

"There's room to deal?" Rutledge asked.

DeWitt and Benjamin kept smiles off their faces.

"That would be up to Attorney General Jaworsky," DeWitt said.

Just as they put Rutledge into the back seat of their car DeWitt's phone sounded.

Leo Levy was calling.

"Mr. Deputy Director, the boss asked me to call. He'd like you and your ten best men to get over here to Falls Church right quick."

Leo gave DeWitt the address.

The deputy director asked Benjamin to drop him off on the way to taking Rutledge in.

Benjamin gave him a curt nod, unhappy about not being in on whatever McGill was doing.

She also wasn't pleased with Leo's choice of words.

"Bring your ten best men?" Benjamin said. "That guy's a chauvinist."

### FirePower America — Falls Church, Virginia

The entrance to Auric Ludwig's office suite fell under the scrutiny of a surveillance camera. Jerry Nerón had thought the building might have such a security measure and wore a fedora for the occasion. The brim shadowed the upper half of his face, and the hat matched his suit perfectly. Over his shoulder hung a soft black Italian leather attaché case that carried the tools of his trade and completed his ensemble.

The security guard in the lobby had let him sign in — F. Castro — and proceed to the elevator bank without a moment's hesitation. The man clearly knew a great suit when he saw one. Felt well-dressed people were to be trusted.

Jerry tapped the button next to the door of FirePower America's suite with a knuckle, heard a buzz from inside.

"Yeah?" a deep male voice responded.

Pitching his voice higher than normal and affecting an effeminate tone, Jerry said, "I'm Mr. Ludwig's three o'clock."

For a brief moment there was no reply. Then the door to the suite produced a click and Jerry pushed it open. He stepped inside and saw a raw-boned man of about forty. His hair looked as if it had been cut with a hedge trimmer and his suit was clearly off the bargain rack. The bulge under the left side of his coat clearly suggested that was where he carried his gun.

He had to be Ludwig's bodyguard.

Jerry wasn't disturbed to see him; he was relieved.

He thought Ludwig might have a secretary. The idea of having to kill a woman, something he'd never done before, was the only trepidation he'd felt about coming to Ludwig's office. Dealing with this *cabrón* —

"Open the bag," the bodyguard told him.

Jerry complied. He put the bag down on the desk in the anteroom. Two framed photos also resided there: a smiling fortyish couple in one, two cherubic girls under five in the other. So there was a secretary who worked for Ludwig. Maybe she was out for the day or possibly just doing an errand for the boss and would return shortly.

Jerry wouldn't have time to dally.

"Empty the bag," the bodyguard said.

Jerry did as he was told. He took out his measuring tape, the folded length of white paper stock on which he'd normally do the blueprint for a suit, a small square of what looked to be tailor's chalk and a pair of sheathed shears. It was only the last item that drew the bodyguard's attention.

"What's with the scissors?" the man asked.

Jerry extended the index and middle fingers of his right hand. Opened and closed them, mimicking the motion of cutting something.

"They are the tools of my trade. I take measurements with the tape, draw them on the paper, cut it just so and make the suit from that. Cutting the cloth, too, you see?"

The bodyguard nodded, as if he understood.

"You do the sewing, too?"

The guy's tone implied, "You really that much of a pussy?"

Jerry was only too happy to have him think that.

"Yes, of course."

"Where are your needles and thread then?"

Jerry smiled. "I do that part in my shop."

The answer seemed to satisfy the bodyguard. He was growing

bored.

"Okay. One last thing. Take the cover off the scissors so I can get a better look."

Jerry removed the plastic sheath. Stepped closer to offer a better view. Turned the shears this way and that. The overhead light gleamed off the polished metal. The bodyguard smiled, as if he could appreciate the craftsmanship that went into making the shears. It was only at the very last moment that he realized how close Jerry had come to him.

Now, he got a good look at Jerry's eyes, too.

This guy was no sissy, he thought. He was —

A killer, as proved by the powerful thrust of the shears into the bodyguard's body. Slicing through the upper abdominal muscles and piercing the heart. A tailor, after all, had to know human anatomy. And having learned from slicing Galtero Blanco's throat, all those years ago, this method was far less likely to splatter blood on him.

A single grunt was the bodyguard's response. Jerry shoved him into the secretary's chair. Wiped his shears on the man's cheap suit coat. Saw the bodyguard's handgun. Wondered for just a second if he should use that on Ludwig. Decided, no, look what happened when he used Abel Mays' weapon.

Jerry opened the door to the CEO's office.

He said, "Mr. Ludwig? I'm the man you've been dying to meet."

The same security guard who had admitted Jerry Nerón to the tower where FirePower America had its offices without any fuss stopped McGill and Deke. Well, delayed them a moment anyway. Deke flashed both his badge and his Uzi.

Told the security guy, "One of your tenants, Auric Ludwig, is about to be murdered. You can come with us if you want, but we're going up."

McGill had gone to check the building directory and rolled his eyes.

"Suite 1776," he said. "Let's go."

The guard said, "I'll stay here, call the cops."

"You do that," Deke replied. "Tell them the FBI is on the way, too."

McGill was already on the elevator when Deke caught up with him.

He hit the button for the seventeenth floor and the car rose quickly.

Deke told McGill, "You get in trouble, I'm blowing this guy up."

"Right, but only if I'm in trouble."

"I don't care what Holly G. says afterward. You're not dying while I'm here."

"Absolutely. Don't let him shoot you either."

"Don't worry about me, damnit."

"Never do. But if there's room for me to work, let me have it."

"Sonofabitch."

Deke might have said more but the doors opened and McGill was first out.

A violation of protocol right from the start.


"Jerry Nerón?" Ludwig asked. He got up and stepped to one side of his desk. Looked around Jerry. "Isn't Marvin out there? He's supposed to show you in."

"Marvin's resting."

"What? I thought I heard his voice just now."

"He has nothing more to say."

Ludwig got the uneasy feeling something wasn't quite right.

He yelled, "Marvin. Get your ass in here."

Jerry let the lack of response speak for itself.

Ludwig started to sidle back behind his desk, until Jerry shook his head.

"No, no, no," Jerry said. "You invited me here. I expect to be treated with courtesy."

"I don't want any of your damn suits. Keep them and get out."

Ludwig was scared, but he was also getting pissed off.

He couldn't help himself; that was just who he was.

Jerry remained unruffled. "All right. We'll forget the suits. I'll just take the two million dollar reward you've offered to meet me."

Ludwig blinked furiously, as if his eyes were sending semaphore messages to his brain.

"You?" he asked.

Jerry halved the distance between them. "Me. You've caused me a great deal of bother, Mr. Ludwig. I like to do my work and disappear, but you keep offering people money to find me. That has to stop, and now it will."

Jerry set his attaché case down on Ludwig's desk and unsheathed his shears. He saw there were still traces of Marvin's blood on the blades. Damn cheap suits with their synthetic fabrics. They didn't even qualify as decent swabbing cloth. Ludwig noticed the blood, too. His eyes went wide and stayed that way.

"You killed Marvin with those things?" Ludwig asked.

His tone was both incredulous and indignant.

What kind of American didn't use a gun to do his dirty work?

Jerry laughed at him, interpreting his pique accurately.

"Oh, these shears will get the job done. They're sharper than Damascus steel. Just ask Marvin. No, I'm sorry. He really can't speak anymore. But allow me to demonstrate."

Ludwig wanted to scream, only his constricted throat wouldn't allow it.

He couldn't squeeze out a peep, and that pleased Jerry.

He was less than happy, though, when he saw Ludwig's face sag in relief.

A voice behind Jerry told him, "Far enough. We've already heard what we need to."

Judging Ludwig to be no threat, Jerry turned to see two men had entered the office behind him. One he knew immediately. His face was nationally known. James J. McGill, the president's husband. The other man was a stranger, but with an Uzi pointed at Jerry he was compelling nonetheless.

"Would you care to make things easy?" McGill asked.

"To hell with that," Ludwig growled. "He killed Marvin and he was going to kill me."

If only they'd arrived a minute or two later, McGill thought.

Well, that and sparing the life of the guy in the outer office.

McGill kept his sentiments to himself.

Saying only, "But now he can't kill you. So he gets a chance to surrender."

McGill distracted both Jerry and Deke by plucking the Virginia flag on his right from its stand. He rotated the pole until the banner was furled around it. Giving himself a longstaff. Testing the weight and balance of his new weapon, McGill asked, "What's it going to be, Mr. Nerón?"

"You're really going to do this?" Deke asked McGill.

Keeping his eyes on Jerry, McGill replied, "You can see what Mr. Nerón is thinking, right?"

"Shit, yeah, I see it. Suicide by cop. Thing is, I don't mind obliging him."

McGill started to say, "Under other circum —"

Jerry sprang forward, lunging with his shears pointed at McGill, hoping to draw Deke's fire. He really didn't want to be taken alive. McGill had been waiting for the move, though, and was ready to parry the attack.

He brought up the butt end of the flagpole and drove it forward. His weapon had by far the greater reach. He delivered a sharp blow to Jerry's gut, and took a quick step back bringing the pole with him.

Jerry tried to grab it, but missed. The fact that he wasn't doubled over and landed flat on his ass told McGill that Jerry was one tough SOB. Jerry took a step back, too, rubbing his bruised middle with his free hand. Trying to work out what he'd do next.

Out of the corner of one eye, McGill saw Ludwig taking something off the wall behind his desk. The distraction was enough for McGill to miss seeing Jerry sticking his free hand in one of his coat pockets, but he saw it come back out. Problem was, he couldn't tell what Jerry was holding. It was too small, mostly obscured by his fingers and thumb.

Jerry made a feint in McGill's direction, maybe hoping to get McGill to commit with a swing of the pole and open himself to being stabbed in the back. McGill didn't buy the fake. When he held his position, Jerry whirled and slashed at Ludwig who was trying to creep up from behind, holding an museum-piece musket he'd taken off the wall.

Damn thing looked like it might still be functional.

And Ludwig was enough of a loon to leave it loaded.

McGill brought the flag pole around in a sweeping arc and cut Jerry's legs out from under him at the ankle. The tailor crashed to the floor with a bang, leaving McGill staring down the barrel of Ludwig's musket. Biggest caliber weapon weapon he'd ever seen. The damn thing made a .357 Magnum look like a pea-shooter.

He swept the barrel of the weapon aside with a swing of the flagpole and then drove the butt end into Ludwig's gut. The lobbyist went down exactly the way McGill had hoped Jerry would. He landed on his ass, curled into a ball and began mewing in pain.

A sharper cry came from behind McGill. He pivoted to see Deke stepping on Jerry's hand, the one he'd stuck in his pocket. A glance showed McGill the shears were already out of the tailor's reach. Deke rolled Jerry over and put a knee down on the small of his back. He secured the tailor's wrists with plastic handcuffs.

Then Deke picked up a small square object.

Held it up on the palm of his hand.

"Look at this," Deke said. "He was going for it."

"Looks like tailor's chalk," McGill said.

"Yeah? Feel it." He dropped the object in McGill's hand.

"Metal." Lightly thumbing the edge, he added. "Damn sharp metal."

Deke said, "He couldn't get me to kill him, so ..."

"Yeah. Given no other choice, he was going to open one of his own veins. Someone's going to have fun questioning this guy. Glad it won't be me."

"Does that mean I have to?"

McGill and Deke turned to see that DeWitt had arrived.

With a passel of feds and local cops in tow.

McGill said. "You or somebody else. I just make deliveries."

DeWitt decided to delegate the interrogation to Benjamin. She could question this guy after she got Congressman Rutledge's confession. Earn her promotion. The deputy director felt much better about his new approach to his work.

He rode back to Washington in the Chevy with McGill to get the story of what he'd missed. Leo started things off by asking McGill, "Good guys win another round, boss?"

"More or less."

It had occurred to McGill by then that the antique rifle Ludwig had pointed at him was probably non-functional. In the heat of the moment, though … ah, to hell with it, he couldn't worry about that prick. He and Deke had saved Ludwig's life and —

Deke told McGill, "So you were right. Somebody left a long-staff, or the next best thing, lying around. But what if they hadn't?"

McGill took his switchblade out of a pocket, clicked it open.

"Would've been a knife fight," he said.

"No," Deke told him, "I would have shot that asshole first."

McGill put the knife away and turned to DeWitt.

"You have trouble with your people, too?" he asked.

# CHAPTER 32

### *Kalorama Circle — Washington, DC*

A fter dropping DeWitt at the Hoover Building to take charge of his minions, McGill had Leo drive him to Zara Gilford's house. Celsus Crogher opened the front door for him. He looked like he hadn't gotten ten hours of sleep all week long.

"You holding up okay?" McGill asked.

Indulging a moment of pique, he'd left Deke in the car with Leo.

Saying he and Celsus, together, could fend off the Mongol hordes.

"I'm fine," Celsus said. He saw Deke had been left behind, but didn't say anything about it. That was no longer his worry. "I'll just plug in for a few hours tonight."

McGill smiled as Celsus closed the door behind him.

"So ... everything good?" Celsus asked.

"Far from everything, but there's been some resolution."

Zara came downstairs from the second floor. "I thought I heard voices. Do you have news, Mr. McGill?" Off his nod, she suggested they have coffee in the kitchen. At her insistence, Celsus stayed to hear the story.

McGill told them what had happened at FirePower America, playing down his part and sparing Zara the detail of how Marvin the bodyguard had died.

"Special Agent Ky and I didn't overhear Jerry Nerón admit to killing Mr. Gilford, but I'd bet the farm that the hair follicle found in the car that was parked next to Abel Mays' SUV will be a DNA match for Nerón."

"So this man will spend the rest of his life in prison?" Zara asked.

McGill would have liked to say yes without equivocation.

Only he knew that prosecutors at both the federal and state levels had let killers go with a slap on the wrist if they provided evidence to convict bigger fish.

That was what McGill told her, adding, "I will talk with the president and raise holy hell with anyone else in the government who tries to offer Jerry Nerón a deal for anything less than life without parole. But this kind of case could carry over into the next administration. None of us knows who that president will be, but it's certain I'll have less influence then. My suggestion is you get a good lawyer and a great public relations firm to make sure it becomes politically impossible for anyone to cut your husband's killer a break."

Tears welled in Zara's eyes as she nodded. "I'll do just that, Mr. McGill. Fortunately, Jordan left me all the money I need to see that he gets justice." She gave McGill's hand a gentle squeeze. "Thank you so much."

Before things got too sappy, Celsus nudged Zara and told her, "Tell him your idea."

She brightened immediately. "Oh, yes! I'd like to speak with your son, Kenneth, if that would be all right with you."

"Speak with Kenny? About what?"

"Well, Celsus and I have done quite a bit of talking. I said I was so terribly sad about losing Jordan, and my heart ached all the more for the families at the Winstead School and all the people around the country who have lost loved ones to shootings. I said there had to be something we could do. Then one night, almost as if I could hear Jordan speaking to me, I got this idea: Start a whistle-blower program."

She looked at Celsus, handing off the narrative.

"The program would be called Save Our Schools," he said.

McGill saw where that was heading: "SOS."

"Right," Celsus said. "The program would be based on a cell-phone app. Send an anonymous text to a central database if you hear someone at your school is planning to do something dangerous: bring a weapon to school, attack someone before or after school, anything that could hurt or kill one or more members of a school community. The program will then inform the local cops."

Celsus gestured for Zara to pick up the thread.

She said, "As with federal whistle-blowers, there will be monetary rewards. Not to individuals. But if a tip proves valid and harm is prevented, the school will receive a $5,000 grant to be used for the student body at large or it may be divided equally among five faculty or staff members, as decided by a vote of the student body."

McGill played devil's advocate. "Okay, but a lot of kids from middle-school on up can be really mean. Text in false accusations just to pick on some poor kid or get even with a rival."

"Celsus thought of that," Zara said.

"We're going to use me as a spokesman for the program," Celsus told McGill.

"You?" McGill asked.

"Yeah, I'm a scary-looking guy, right?"

"Absolutely."

"So I go on YouTube, tell everyone I used to protect the president of the United States, and now I want to protect them. I tell the kiddies any legitimate message they send in will be held as absolutely anonymous. But if they try to prank us we'll hunt them down like dogs. Or words to that effect. And when we expose them they'll look like —"

"Assholes in front of all their friends," Zara said with a smile.

"If they're in high school, it'll screw up their college applications, too," Celsus said. "We'll still get some wiseguys who think they can outsmart us or just don't give a damn, but overall we think this idea could be helpful."

Zara said, "I'm going to invest $5 million to get it rolling, Mr. McGill. The reason I'd like to speak with your son is to ask whether he and his friends would like to develop the app. I'd pay them for their time, of course."

McGill took his phone out of his pocket. "Let's give him a call right now."

### Edgar Hoover Building — Washington, DC

When DeWitt got back to his office his secretary handed him a message slip.

Please call VP at your convenience.

DeWitt asked his secretary, "Any VP in particular?"

"The one who's a heartbeat away from the Oval Office."

"Oh, that one. Did she say what she wants?"

"To take you to the prom."

"I beg your pardon."

"There's a state dinner coming up at the White House."

"There is?"

"The vice president is a single woman."

"She doesn't want to go stag?"

"You'll have to ask her, but I don't think so."

"Is my tuxedo clean?"

"Not my job to know," his secretary said.

DeWitt was saved from having to make an immediate call to the vice president by the arrival of Benjamin, who didn't look to be in the mood for light banter. The two of them stepped into his office. DeWitt closed the door behind them.

Once they were both seated, he asked, "Did Rutledge lawyer up?"

Benjamin shook her head. "No. He's a singing cowboy. He's confessing right, left and up the middle. He's given up six members of the House Armed Services Committee already. He's writing a preliminary statement as we speak."

DeWitt could feel another shoe was about to drop.

"What else?" he asked.

"Rutledge said there's a corresponding group of senators making the thievery work on their side of Capitol Hill."

"There have to be defense contractors involved, too," DeWitt said.

Benjamin nodded. "Them and their lobbyists. This is shaping up as the biggest scandal ever to hit the country. But that's not all."

DeWitt asked, "What else could there be?"

"All the bad guys in the House? They're GOP or True South. Rutledge doesn't know if it's the same in the Senate, but he suspects it is. How will it look for a Democratic president to go after a bunch of bad guys from the other side of the aisle? How will that play with the public?"

"It won't be good. And there's one more thing."

"What?"

"Somewhere in this cabal is the SOB who hired Jerry Nerón to kill Jordan Gilford."

"Better and better," Benjamin said.

"Actually, it might be."

"How's that?"

DeWitt said, "We find the guy who arranged a murder for hire, that gives us an apolitical start to the investigation, reduces any public pressure on what follows by at least half and maybe more."

Benjamin nodded. "That's good, but how do we do that?"

"You remember who confirmed for us that Rutledge was part of this mess?"

"The so-called bar-girl in Zamboanga City."

"She called the FBI at the behest of?" DeWitt asked.

"Tyler Busby."

"Right. The spider who seems to be at the center of any number of webs. He might know who hired Nerón even if Nerón doesn't. Catching Busby should be our first priority."

The two of them took that notion to FBI Director Jeremiah Haskins.

## *Metro PD Headquarters — Washington, DC*

McGill stopped in to visit Captain Rockelle Bullard as a courtesy call. To let her know about the arrest of Jerry Nerón in Falls Church. It never hurt to maintain good relations with the local cops, even if you lived at the White House. Rockelle had Detectives Meeker and Beemer sit in with her.

Meeker said, "Now wait just a minute. This Cuban dude from Miami, he killed one guy with a pair of scissors and was going to do in Auric Ludwig the same way? And you took him down with a flagpole?"

"Right at FirePower America," Beemer added, "and nobody fires a shot?"

McGill said, "Ironic, I know, but that's the way it worked out."

"Your Secret Service man had to be armed," Rockelle said.

"He was, but the president asked me to bring Nerón in alive," McGill explained.

"Glad my wife don't get involved in my work," Beemer said.

"Glad I'm single," Meeker added.

"That's enough," Rockelle told them. She said to McGill, "Sometimes I think these two are going to drive me into early retirement."

Both detectives knew better than to smirk.

Rockelle continued, "Why do I think, Mr. McGill, that there's more than good manners that brings you by to see us?"

"Well, that was my first impulse, but on the way over here I had an idea."

"Man's a thinker," Meeker said.

Rockelle gave him a look, guaranteeing a moment of silence from the peanut gallery.

"What's your idea, Mr. McGill?"

"Just that all of us were wondering how Nerón got away last time. We never did figure out how he did that, and now he's back. We thought he was traveling alone before. My idea now is maybe he had help. Nerón was staying at the Four Seasons; maybe his accomplice, if he has one, checked in with him. If some sharp Metro detectives were to scoot over there quickly, they might actually find another bad guy. Somebody who hasn't had time to think something's gone wrong."

Meeker and Beemer lit up with smiles.

"You musta been good police back there in Chicago," Beemer said.

"I had my moments," McGill admitted.

"Boss?" Meeker asked Rockelle.

She gave the two detectives a nod and they took off.

McGill told Rockelle, "I've got a few things to take care of, too."

The captain stood and extended her hand to him.

She knew McGill didn't have to cut her people in on the case.

Shaking his hand, she said, "You aren't careful, Mr. McGill, you might give private investigators a good name around here."

### Wyman Consulting, LLP — Washington, DC

Former Vice President Mather Wyman, now a political consultant helping mostly public interest groups find their way along the paths of power in Washington, agreed to see McGill when he dropped in without an appointment. With McGill's consent, Wyman had his niece and partner, Kira Fahey Yates, sit in on the meeting.

McGill told them of Tyler Busby implicating Representative Philip Brock in the conspiracy to assassinate the president at Inspiration Hall. He also mentioned that Brock had left Washington to travel to Costa Rica and might be planning to move on to one of three countries farther south. Quite possibly on a permanent basis.

Wyman and Kira shared a look.

They understood why McGill had brought this news to them.

The former VP said, "You know, Jim, if word of all this were to reach the Ohio legislature, they might not want to petition Congress to call a constitutional convention."

McGill nodded. "Yes, and Pennsylvania and other states might want to withdraw their petitions, too. Avoid the taint of being connected in any way with Brock. You don't win any votes being associated with a possible assassin, do you?"

Kira said, "It'll be interesting to see if anyone backs Brock."

"Oh, there will be some on the fringe," Wyman said. "There always are. But I think a wholesale rewrite of the Constitution will be pushed back for the foreseeable future."

"May I offer a suggestion?" McGill asked Wyman.

"Of course."

"Only if you need some last-ditch help, you know who you might turn to?"

Both Wyman and Kira laughed, knowing just where McGill was going.

"The gun lobby," Kira said.

Wyman nodded. "Right. They think they've got the Second Amendment interpreted just the way they want. They'd hate to take any chance with a rewrite."

Playing the contrarian, Kira said, "Of course, if your new ideas start gaining traction, they might want to revisit that idea."

McGill said, "We'll pay the toll on that bridge when we come to it."

### Florida Avenue — Washington, DC

McGill found Putnam Shady sitting on the front steps of his townhouse reading a book titled Becoming the Dad You Always Wanted. McGill sat next to him. Told him everything that happened.

Then he asked, "How's Margaret?"

"Turning the corner. Going to confession really helped. Thanks for the suggestion."

"She'd have thought of it soon enough."

"Yeah, but you knew enough to speed things up."

"Tell her not to worry about coming back to work until she's ready."

"Will do. I'll let her know as soon as she wakes up."

McGill gave Putnam a look. "Kind of early to turn in, isn't it?"

"We picked up Maxi from school. The two of them are napping

together."

"God bless our children."

"Amen," Putnam said.


## *The Oval Office — The White House*

McGill was on his way to the White House when he got a call from Edwina Byington.

"Mr. McGill, the president would like to see you at soon as possible."

Edwina's voice was appropriate to a simple business message.

Nonetheless, a chill passed through McGill.

He felt sure that something bad had happened.

"Is everyone all right, Edwina?"

"Family and friends are well. Politically … I don't have specific information, sir, but I think things are anything but right."

Leo hit the lights and siren again and made short work of getting to the White House.

McGill was equally quick getting to the Oval Office. Patti sat behind her desk looking pale. Jean Morrissey and Galia were the other two present. Their expressions were grim. McGill closed the door behind him.

He looked at Patti and asked, "What is it?"

She told him, "FBI Director Haskins and Deputy Director DeWitt have informed me of Congressman Rutledge's confession to looting various Pentagon projects for several years now. He has implicated colleagues in the House and says there more accomplices in the Senate. The FBI has advised me the first step should be to step up the hunt for Tyler Busby, as he has shown to have knowledge of and is likely involved in this series of crimes."

"But?" McGill asked.

"But we've just received word from the police in South Carolina that Congressman Wesley Tilden, one of Congressman Rutledge's alleged partners in crime, was found shot to death outside his home."

McGill said, "That's probably why Rutledge is cooperating. He thinks it's his best chance to save his skin. The other members of the House that Rutledge fingered —"

"They're safe, too," the president said. "The attorney general has decided that Rutledge's confession constitutes sufficient grounds for them to be arrested, and the FBI has taken them into custody."

"Well, at least they're out of physical danger," McGill said. "That's good."

"Their incarceration was not universally appreciated," the president said. "Galia has told me that a majority of the House has already expressed its disapproval of me."

"With what? A resolution?"

The president shook her head. "No."

McGill waited a beat and then asked, "What else did Galia tell you?"

The president said, "That I'm going to be impeached.

# ABOUT THE AUTHOR

Joseph Flynn has been published both traditionally — Signet Books, Bantam Books and Variance Publishing — and through his own imprint, Stray Dog Press, Inc. Both major media reviews and reader reviews have praised his work. Booklist said, "Flynn is an excellent storyteller." The Chicago Tribune said, "Flynn [is] a master of high-octane plotting." The most repeated reader comment is: Write faster, we want more.

Contact Joe at Hey Joe on his website: *www.josephflynn.com.* You can also read excerpts of all of Joe's books on his website.

All of Joseph Flynn's novels may be purchased online at *amazon.com.*

**The Jim McGill Series**
The President's Henchman, A Jim McGill Novel [#1]
The Hangman's Companion, A JimMcGill Novel [#2]
The K Street Killer A JimMcGill Novel [#3]
Part 1: The Last Ballot Cast, A JimMcGill Novel [#4 Part 1]
Part 2: The Last Ballot Cast, A JimMcGill Novel [#4 Part 2]
The Devil on the Doorstep, A Jim McGill Novel [#5]
The Good Guy with a Gun, A Jim McGill Novel [#6]
The Echo of the Whip, A Jim McGill Novel [#7]
McGill's Short Cases 1-3

*Continued on next page*

**The Ron Ketchum Mystery Series**
Nailed, A Ron Ketchum Mystery [#1]
Defiled, A Ron Ketchum Mystery Featuring John Tall Wolf [#2]
Impaled, A Ron Ketchum Mystery [#3]

**The John Tall Wolf Series**
Tall Man in Ray-Bans, A John Tall Wolf Novel [#1]
War Party, A John Tall Wolf Novel [#2]
Super Chief, A John Tall Wolf Novel [#3]

**The Zeke Edison Series**
Kill Me Twice, A Zeke Edison Novel [#1]

**Stand Alone Novels**
The Concrete Inquisition
Digger
The Next President
Hot Type
Farewell Performance
Gasoline, Texas
Round Robin, A Love Story of Epic Proportions
One False Step
Blood Street Punx
Still Coming
Still Coming Expanded Edition
Hangman — A Western Novella
Pointy Teeth, Twelve Bite-Size Stories